...secrets of her past leads Janet
to the highlands of Scotland and a future she never dreamed of in...

THE
JOURNAL

GEORGINA SINCLAIR CAPONERA

Discovering the secrets of her past leads Janet
to the highlands of Scotland and a future she never dreamed of in...

THE
JOURNAL

GEORGINA SINCLAIR CAPONERA

Published by Tate Publishing & Enterprises, LLC
127 E. Trade Center Terrace | Mustang, Oklahoma 73064 USA
1.888.361.9473 | www.tatepublishing.com

Tate Publishing is committed to excellence in the publishing industry. The company reflects the philosophy established by the founders, based on Psalms 68:11,
    "The Lord gave the word and great was the company of those who published it."

Book design copyright © 2007 by Tate Publishing, LLC. All rights reserved.
Cover design by Taylor Rauschcolb
Interior design by Sarah Leis

Published in the United States of America

ISBN: 978-1-60247-526-7
1. Christian Fiction   2. Romance, Mystery
05.24.07

Dedicated in memory of my own Scottish mother,

E LIZABETH K IRKBRIDE S INCLAIR

who brought fun and laughter into our lives. My sister and I are still try-ing to figure out to this day what some of her expressions meant. We still laugh at them. She worked hard her whole life to supplement our dad's salary to make sure that her family's needs were always met.

Alice Stevens' character was loosely based on my mother, especially all the funny sayings and superstitions, and her generous giving heart.

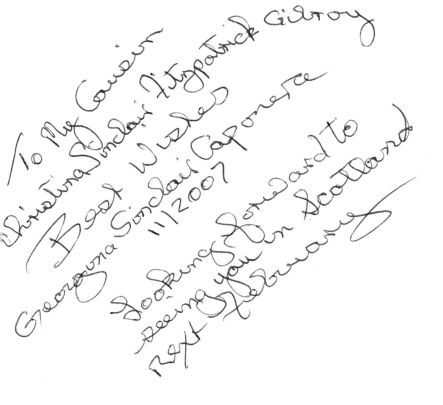

CHAPTER ONE

Happy is the bride that the sun shines on; happy is the corpse that the rain falls on. Yes, thought Janet Stevens, mom would be happy with the rain today. It actually was pouring, or as my mom would say, "It's stoting pennies from heaven," Janet thought, trying not to laugh. "What are you smiling at," her sister Maggie whispered. "We're burying mom; what's so funny about that?"

"I'm just remembering mom and all her funny little sayings. She'd be happy with the pouring rain on the day of her funeral."

"You're right," Maggie said smiling through the tears, as she was also remembering how she and Janet would look at each other, shrug their shoulders and screw their faces up wondering what the heck their mom was talking about. Alice had made many friends through work, church and social activities. She had been a very outgoing person, which was acknowledged by the huge number of people that showed up to say their final goodbyes. She was only fifty-one years old when she had a heart attack and died. The Presbyterian Church that she had attended was packed with all those friends who came to pay their last respects. The pews were so full that the doors to the sanctuary were left open, so that the people standing out in the foyer could be part of the service. The rain from the many umbrellas made puddles on the foyer carpet, but no one seemed to pay attention, they were so stunned and grief-stricken from the sudden death of a very dear friend. Alice Stevens had emigrated from Scotland when she was only almost eighteen years old to live with her older, married sister Moira in San Francisco.

Thirty-two year old Janet had never been married. She was five feet six inches tall with thick shoulder length reddish-brown hair, like her mother's, and hazel eyes. She wasn't sure who she got the color of her eyes from. Her dad's were blue. She was the oldest of four children. The other three siblings, twenty-nine-year-old Tom, twenty-seven-year-old Maggie, and twenty-five-year-old Ian, lived in other states but they came to California for their mom's funeral. Maggie and her daughters, six-year-old Andrea and four-year-old Marie, were staying at their mother's house until the day after the funeral. Janet was happy she had made those arrangements as it gave her time alone with her brothers. Both of the brothers stayed with Janet in her small home. Tom stayed in the guest room while Ian slept on the couch. Her third bedroom was used as an office. It was bittersweet to say goodbye to them all the day after the funeral. She was happy to have them with her at this time but she was exhausted from making all the arrangements for the funeral alone. Janet loved her sister, but Maggie was always asking why there was no special man in her life and Janet was just too tired to be going through the same old hassle. "Maggie, I have had relationships with men but they just haven't worked out for me," Janet said a little annoyed. "It isn't unusual to still be single in this day and age."

"I know, Janet, but now that mom's gone I hate for you to be alone."

"I'm not alone. Really Maggie, I do have friends and some of them are even men."

"Janet, you're so pretty but so darned independent. You probably scare men off. But I'm sure there's someone out there looking for you. Just make yourself accessible." Yes, as much as she had loved spending time with them, she was quite happy to see them go home.

"Have a nice drive home and girls don't give your mother grief on the drive back to Oregon. Goodbye Tom." Maggie and her brother had driven down together. They both lived in Eugene, Oregon.

"Goodbye, Aunt Janet," both girls yelled as they waved out the window all the way until they were out of sight.

She decided to wait until the following weekend to start clearing out her mother's house. Alice had a lot of furniture and had collected a lot of stuff. She even still had her late husband's clothes and tools and he had died four years previous. Jim Stevens' car had been hit head on by a drunk driver who had come across into Jim's lane. He was killed instantly. She had loved her dad and had had many wonderful times with him, but she had always been much closer to her mom. They just seemed to have more in common. Her death would be harder for her to get over.

Today she would rest and clean up her own apartment. After having had her two rather messy brothers staying with her she would have enough to do there. In spite of the mess, she had to admit to herself that she enjoyed having them with her, especially without her sister, who usually dominated the conversation. It was one of those very rare times when she got to sit and talk to them one on one. Janet was so busy with her pottery business that she didn't phone her brothers very often, especially Tom. Since he also lived in Oregon, she knew Maggie kept him up-to-date on her affairs. She and Maggie talked on the phone at least once a week. Ian had a busy life working for a sports company in Colorado. Any time off from work would most likely find him climbing a mountain or hiking up some steep trail. He was definitely an outdoorsman. Janet would call him maybe twice a month to check on him to make sure he was not in the hospital with broken bones. He also loved to fly fish, which was a much tamer sport and she wished he would do more of that than his more dangerous past-times.

Janet was happy with her choice of career. She loved creating beautiful things. Her moods would control the product. This past week her mood had been sad and lonely due to the death of her mother. She decided to rest from her work one more week.

She made a run up to San Francisco on Friday of the following week to make some deliveries to the gallery that displayed her art. She was doing so well that she was outgrowing her little shed in the back yard. She had been thinking of leasing a building to do her work. She didn't like the idea of having to work outside her home, but it looked like she had no other option. She mentioned her problem to Keith, the curator of the gallery.

"Why don't you think about moving your residence to somewhere else, like Mendocino? Maybe you could find a bigger piece of land and buy a shed," Keith suggested.

"You've talked to me quite a bit about Mendocino. It must have a special place in your heart," she said smiling.

"It has a special place in the heart of many artists. That's why a lot of them live there. It's a very artsy town, yet quite small."

"I hadn't thought of it, Keith. It's an idea. I may be able to get something cheaper with more property than I could get in Redwood City. At least I could look around and see what's available. There's nothing keeping me in the Bay area anymore."

"I'm sure you could find a bigger piece of property for around the same price as what you could get for your house in Redwood City. Real estate is more expensive in the Bay area."

"I'll have to try and schedule a trip up there; meanwhile, I have to take care of cleaning out my mom's house so we can sell it. Wow! I would have some money from that also."

Janet was not quite ready to tackle her mother's house. Besides being a lot of work, she still felt sad about her mother's death and she knew it was going to be very emotional for her to go through her mom's personal things; but she knew she had to do it. She had decided that an auction house would handle the tools and furniture and the like. She just didn't have the time to take care of it all. Her siblings had agreed with her decision, realizing that they had to leave their sister to do all the work; it was the least they could do. She arose early in the morning so she could get started. As she approached her mother's home, Janet already felt her absence. It brought a lump to her throat looking at the well taken care of lawns and her mom's special touches with the flower gardens. Inside, she felt her mom's absence even more. The house was so quiet without her there. Janet was so used to her bustling about. *Mom always enjoyed having me visit. She treated me like a special guest,* Janet thought. She looked into the kitchen where her mom usually was making tea and fixing her daughter something to eat. She often sang as she went about these chores, which always made Janet smile because she knew her mom was happy with her there. Her heart felt as empty as the house.

She boxed her father's clothes in a couple of boxes and a couple of cardboard wardrobes and her mother's in separate boxes and wardrobes and marked them "men's clothes" and "women's clothes".

As she went through her mom's clothes she remembered dresses that she had bought for special occasions. The sage colored suit she wore at Tom's wedding. She remembered how lovely her mother looked in it. When she hung up the champagne colored, "mother of the bride dress," she remembered how emotional her mom had been watching Maggie walk down the aisle. It made Janet realize that her mom would not be there for her wedding or to see her children. "My children will never know what a wonderful grandmother they would've had," she said out loud to herself. Each piece brought memories that brought smiles and tears to her eyes. She carried them out to the garage to take to the Goodwill. She boxed up pictures and personal items and documents. The last place to clean out was her mom's office. She took all of the computer supplies and put them in her car. She intended to take them home. She also dismantled the computer and put it in the car. She could use the supplies but she had arranged for her computer-savvy friend, Linda, to go through the computer and sweep it clean with some program. Janet wasn't too computer literate but if she was going to sell or give the computer away, she wanted to make sure no personal information was on it. As she opened up the bottom drawer of the two-drawer file cabinet, she noticed a journal. She opened it up. Personal information looked back at her in her mother's handwriting. She closed it faster than she had opened it. She felt strange. It was almost like her mother was right there with her. She sat for a few moments not sure whether to open it or not. She felt like she would be spying. *Maybe it's just about things I already know, like when each of her children was born,* she thought. *That's probably it. Well I'll just put it in the car and read it another time.*

After she thought she had done enough for the day, she headed back home. She picked up some Chinese take-out so that she wouldn't have to cook. She was exhausted. After dinner, she called her sister Maggie. "Hi! I've pretty much cleaned out the house. The auction company is coming the weekend after next," Janet told her.

"Thanks Janet. You've been a big help."

"I just wish one of the guys could be here for the auction. It's a lot of work, Maggie, and I'm running behind on my own work," Janet complained.

"I'll call Tom and see if he can go down. I think someone else should be there with you."

"Thanks! He might want to look at dad's tools and see if there is anything he wants before the auction company goes in," Janet suggested.

"I'll make sure and mention that to him. Will it be on the Saturday of that weekend?"

"Yes. If they don't sell everything on Saturday, they will go back on Sunday. It starts very early in the morning to give people an opportunity to look over everything and decide what they want to bid on. I threw out all the little miscellaneous things and other things I put in a box for the Goodwill."

"Janet, I'm sorry we had to leave you with all that work. The girls are in school and I can't take them out. Well, Marie could miss nursery school, but Andrea would have a hard time trying to catch up. They already missed a couple of days for mom's funeral."

"That's okay! The auction people will take care of the big stuff. Just see if you can get Tom to come down the weekend after next." She hung up the phone. It was only nine o'clock and she was already tired. "What a way to spend a Saturday night," she said aloud. "Maybe Maggie's right. I need to find a nice young man. Okay Maggie, where do I start; the Yellow Pages?" She decided to soak in a nice long bath and then go to bed.

The next morning she got up and made some coffee then walked over to her shed to check out some work. *It's rather warm and sunny for February,* she thought. "This is a day for going somewhere," she said aloud. Just as she said that, her cell phone rang. She pulled it out of her pocket and answered, "Hello?" she said questioningly since it was only eight o'clock on a Sunday morning.

"Janet, Keith here. How would you like to take a drive up to Mendocino, just for the fun of it?"

"Gee Keith, I can't think this early on a Sunday morning," she joked.

"I know it's early but we need to get an early start. It's about a three hour drive from my house."

"My mom won't be happy with me for missing church, but actually, Keith, it sounds like a great plan to me. Ever since you put the idea of moving up there into my head, I've been anxious to go look around. Even if we don't have much time, it will give me a feel for the town."

"We can pick up some of those little freebie real estate papers and maybe be lucky and find an open house or two. How about you driving up to my place, then I will drive us up there."

"I should pick you up. After all we're going up there for me, aren't we?"

"Yeah…sort of," he said and then more excitedly, "I bought a new car. I can't wait to really try it out. San Francisco's not the place to try out this baby. You can't move around here."

"What kind did you buy?"

"You'll see it when you get here."

"Okay!" she said laughing. "Then at least I owe you lunch. Give me an hour. I have to change my clothes." Redwood City was about half an hour south of San Francisco.

Janet pulled into Keith's driveway and walked to the front door. The door opened before she could even knock.

"Were you sitting at the window waiting for me to come up the street?" She asked laughing.

"Something like that. Okay, to the garage," he said leading her through the door.

"Oh Keith, it is beautiful," she said eyeing a brand new, shiny black mustang.

"Thanks!" he said proudly. "I've been wanting one for a long time. I just didn't think my old car suited my lifestyle."

"Which is?" she said jokingly.

"Okay, okay! So I don't have any girlfriends right now, but this will help," he said nodding at the car and winking at her. Keith was a handsome young man of twenty-eight. He was very excitable and seemed like a man that loved life, except for the time about three years ago when he lost his girlfriend in a car accident. It took him about a year to get over it.

"Well, show me what this thing can do," she said getting into the car.

Going through San Francisco was pretty slow. Once they got across the Golden Gate Bridge, the traffic seemed to taper off a little, but the freeway was no place to try out the new car. Most of the time was spent on highway 101. They passed the turn offs to

San Rafael, Petaluma and Healdsburg and continued north. They turned west onto highway 128 and drove through the Anderson Valley. There were occasional cars but plenty of room for him to see what his car was capable of doing. He was able to drive a little faster and show off his car's performance. "How about it?" he said.

"I don't know much about cars but this is real comfortable and very fast."

"It goes zero to sixty in five seconds," he said stopping, then accelerated very fast to show her.

"Whoa! Too fast for me. I believe you. Zero to sixty in five seconds. I believe!" Janet was yelling and laughing.

They drove quietly for a while. Janet was admiring the scenery all around her.

"This place is beautiful. This has to be the most beautiful valley in the world," she said almost breathlessly. The rolling green hills were dotted with grazing white sheep and stately old oak trees and on this unusually warm February day, the sky was bright blue with a few wispy white clouds. Janet felt so peaceful and happy. "Keith thanks for asking me to come along. This is the happiest I've felt since mom died."

"I admit I wanted to try out my car but I really thought it would be good for you to get away." At the town of Boonville, Janet asked if Keith could pull off. He pulled into the town and looked for a real estate office. "Do you want to look here before looking in the town of Mendocino?" he asked.

"I love the look of this area and I'm afraid by the time we get through with Mendocino, the realtors here will be closed. The floor person may not stay all day since it's Sunday."

"Okay! Let's go in here."

The floor person's name was Margaret and she was only too happy to let them see what listings their office had. It had been a very quiet day for Margaret Dunbar so Janet and Keith were a welcoming sight. They sat at her desk as she brought out the books with pictures and descriptions of their listings. There were some listings in the various towns in the Anderson Valley, including Boonville and Philo and much more on the Mendocino coast.

"The coast seems to be a little more expensive," she said looking over the listings.

"It is more expensive mostly due to ocean views and being closer to the town of Mendocino. We have a beautiful listing right here in Boonville. It's in the hills and has five acres, lots of windows and decks, beautiful views and a three-car garage. It has been on the market a couple of months. Here's a picture of it," she said turning the book to face them.

"Oh my gosh! It's a great house and you're right, the scenery and landscaping are beautiful. I have to admit to you though, Margaret, that I've just started to think about this. If I decide to make the move, I will have to get my house ready for sale."

"Where is your house located?" Margaret asked Janet.

"It's in Redwood City. I've only had it five years so I don't know how much equity I have in it. However, my mother just passed on and my three siblings and I will be selling her home which is mortgage-free."

"This house is listed at $750, 000," she said looking at Janet questioningly.

"I'll have to put everything together before I can give you an answer. I've absolutely no idea what real estate is doing now.

"Real estate is very high right now, especially in the Bay Area. It's quite a move from Redwood City all the way up here. May I ask what you do for a living?"

"I'm an artist and I work out of my home. Keith is the curator of the gallery in San Francisco that displays my work."

"There are a lot of artists that live around here. There are galleries in Mendocino that might also enjoy displaying your work."

"Perhaps!" Then changing the subject back to the house, she said, "Would it be possible for us to drive up to the house and look at the outside?"

"Sure, that would be okay. The owners are out of town this weekend. Here are the directions to it," Margaret said handing her a piece of paper. "If I wasn't on floor duty, I would take you up and show you the inside."

"I don't want to take your time right now, Margaret, until I know for sure. Can I also have one of your cards? I'm really seriously thinking about the move and whether I decide to move to Boonville or one of the other surrounding areas, I'll be sure to contact you."

"I'd appreciate that very much, Janet. If you want to keep me abreast of what you're doing and what's happening, my e-mail address is also on my card."

"Okay, Margaret, I'll do that. I really am quite excited about this area. I hope it works out." She shook Margaret's hand and said goodbye.

They drove up to the house which was the last house up a hilly road, and Janet fell in love with the property. "Keith, I feel so peaceful up here. I think I could create some beautiful pottery in this place." They walked around the grounds and were inspired by the views that overlooked the valley and the tall oak trees. She looked at the gardens down the hill and said, "I wonder what these gardens will look like in the spring when the flowers and plants are in bloom?"

"I'm sure it will be beautiful all around here in the spring," Keith answered. The house appealed to her very much, at least from the outside. Like Margaret had said, it had lots of windows and was situated on five acres with lots of trees, giving it a feeling of complete privacy. They looked at the outside of the garage and peeked through the windows on each door. "This garage is so big I could park my car in it and have a good size workshop too."

"You sound like you're moving in," Keith said smiling at her. He was feeling good because he had turned her on to the idea.

"To be honest, Keith, I would love to. I have a very good feeling about this place."

"To be honest, Janet, I would love it too. Then I could drive up and visit you."

"You could spend the weekend and we could go and check out the vineyards and the wineries," she said excitedly. Janet checked her watch. "It's noon, let's grab something to eat. Maybe we can get something fast, like some clam chowder. I don't want to spend too much time sitting in a restaurant."

"I agree," Keith said "There is a good restaurant I know of on the coast where we can go to for dinner later before we head on back to San Francisco," Keith said.

"Remember, I'm buying," Janet reminded him.

They drove down the hill and continued west on highway 128, alongside a river that Keith informed her was the Navarro River.

There was so much to look at. There were acres of beautiful vineyards, the Navarro River and the most magnificent trees.

"These Redwood trees are so majestic. How tall do you think they are and how old?" she questioned Keith.

"Redwood trees can be as tall as 300 feet or more and they can be over 4,000 years old. I am not sure about these particular trees, I think maybe the coastal redwoods only have a life span of about 2,500 years," he answered.

"Do you come here often? You seem to know a lot about the area."

"I grew up in San Francisco and have always loved Northern California. My dad used to take me camping a lot here and we would always go and listen to the ranger explain the area to the people." They continued alongside the river.

"The river seems to be getting wider," she noted.

"It is. Pretty soon we will come to Highway 1 and the river really widens as it joins the sea."

As they reached the coastal highway, she marveled at the almost emerald green river as it joined the sea just as Keith had said. "This is Navarro Beach," he said of the wide sandy beach at the mouth of the river. As they turned on to the Pacific Coast highway, Keith suggested, "If we have time, after looking at some real estate, we should go to Headland National Park. You are in for another treat there."

"I almost wish I didn't have to look at houses. I would rather take in all of the sights around here," she said "but I also want to get a good idea of the cost of real estate so that I can go back home and try to put my finances together. That home is over $700,000," she said making a face indicating she could hardly believe it could be so much.

"Well, you'll probably be surprised when you find out how much your house will list for. Your mom's will probably be way up over a million. I've been there. It's not only a beautiful house but it's in a very exclusive area."

"No! It couldn't be worth that much," Janet said in an unbelieving tone.

They went to three different agencies and looked through their books and picked up some material. They didn't go to see any of the houses. None of them leaped out at her like the one in Boonville. She would keep her mind open though. They drove around the town for quite a while, getting out of the car to admire the work of the many artists including potters. *Why haven't I come up here before, she thought?* She knew Keith had mentioned it a few times but she was quite involved with her life and her mom in Redwood City and the gallery in San Francisco.

"Keith, did you purposely bring me here at this time; I mean now that I'm alone in Redwood City?"

He looked at her for a few seconds then admitted, "I knew how you would feel about this area. It's just right for you but I didn't want to suggest anything because I knew you felt you needed to be close to your mom." By the time they finished looking around, it was getting a little too late to go to Headlands Park.

"We can go there next time we come back," Keith said.

"You're such a good friend, Keith. Thank you for helping me go through this big decision-making period."

"Remember, I have my own interests in mind," he teased her.

"If I move up here, I would hope that you would come often to see me."

CHAPTER TWO

Like every Friday, Janet always quit work early, usually around three o'clock, but today she stopped at noon because Tom would be arriving around mid-afternoon and her friend Kathy was coming to dinner and she wanted to tidy up a bit. Kathy was a real estate agent and Janet had asked her help in figuring out what she might get for her home. Through the help of her parents, she had bought the house five years ago. Margaret had told her that real estate had gone through the roof in the last few years, so she was hopeful that she would have enough equity to make the move. Tom arrived close to two-thirty. "Thanks for coming, Tom. I really appreciate it."

"I should have suggested it myself, Janet. I'm sorry to have left everything up to you."

At six o'clock the doorbell rang. *Kathy is always prompt,* thought Janet. She liked that about her, especially since she was going to hire her as her agent. "Hi Kathy! Come on in."

"Hey Tom! It's good to see you again," Kathy said.

"It's good to see you too, Kathy," said Tom giving her a hug.

"I brought the comps, you know, homes that have sold recently that are comparable to yours. I brought them for both your house and your mother's."

"Great!" Janet said handing her a drink. "Let's get caught up first. I haven't seen you in quite a few weeks. Of course I saw you at the funeral but I didn't have time to talk to you then."

"I think I talked to Tom more than I did to you. You were busy so I didn't want to bother you at that time. I was surprised to hear that you're looking to sell your home."

"Only if I can buy a house up in the Mendocino area. Keith said he thought I would enjoy living up there, so he took me up on Sunday and I loved it."

"I haven't been up there in years. When I go to the wine country I usually end up in Napa or Sonoma. The last time I was in Mendocino it was still a very artsy little village. Has it been 'Carmelized' yet?"

"What in the world does that mean?" Janet said laughing.

"Well at one time Carmel was an artsy little village. I think during the Bohemian age, when an influx of artists like Jack London and Sinclair Lewis moved there, I believe that was right after the San Francisco earthquake of 1906, and many others left the devastated city and moved south to Carmel. In fact the first theater in the area was built, I believe, in 1907. Since then of course it has been built up and the sleepy little artsy village is now a lot more commercial. Some of the other small artsy places like Mendocino and Half-Moon Bay don't want to be developed as much as Carmel has. Personally, I love Carmel and Monterey."

"Wow! I didn't know that," said Janet. "Where did you get all that information?"

"I was looking at some property for my parents and got involved in the history and found it quite fascinating."

"Very interesting," said Janet and then changing the subject, "I'm going to put the food on the table." She set out the pasta in a big bowl. It was tossed with pesto, sun-dried tomatoes, Parmesan cheese and a little olive oil. She then brought out a green salad and some garlic bread. "Okay, I think we are ready to eat."

"This looks and smells great, Janet."

After dinner they looked over the comps. First they looked at the ones for Janet's home.

"This is the most recent one that sold, that is actually very close to the same design as yours," she said showing the listing from the Multiple Listing Service. Janet's mouth fell open.

"You're joking, Kathy. Nobody in their right mind would pay that kind of money for this little thing. I've been told that real estate in this area has been going crazy but surely not that crazy."

"That crazy, Janet. This one is the same size as yours, 1600 square feet, three bedrooms, two baths, but you have a really big back yard for such a small house. Also your home is in much better shape than this one. Actually, your home is in great shape. I would just maybe suggest that you get a new roof since it is older than twenty-five years of age and the buyer's lender would require it. Also, perhaps get the exterior painted. That would give it much better curb appeal. Very important! The front of your house is the first thing a potential buyer sees."

"Six hundred and fifty thousand dollars. I thought I paid too much when I bought it five years ago for three hundred thousand. This scares me."

"It also helps that you live on the west side of the city."

"I'm afraid to ask what my mom's house would list at. Her home is almost twice the size of mine and in a very exclusive area. She also has a huge lot which is beautifully landscaped back and front," Janet said still in shock.

"Your mom's house is in excellent shape. You're right; it is more than twice the size of yours. It is 3,500 square feet, 5 bedrooms, 3 baths and her lot size is 20,000 square feet. Are you ready?"

"I'm not sure. I'm afraid there will be nobody to buy these homes," she said taking the paper from Kathy. "Oh merciful me!" she said acting like she was going to faint. "My mom and dad bought this home twenty-five years ago and I believe they paid around two hundred and fifty thousand dollars and now you're saying it could go on the market for two million four hundred and fifty thousand dollars?"

"You're kidding," said Tom astonished. "We grew up in that house. Almost two and a half million dollars? Wow!" was all he could say.

"Yes! Like you said Janet, her home is in an exclusive area of Redwood City. Here are some of the homes that have sold recently up around Farmhill Boulevard," Kathy said showing her some comps.

"What do I have to do to get her home ready to go on the market?" Janet asked.

"Nothing! You could put it on the market right now. Like I said, it's in excellent shape. If you are serious about all of this, Janet, I would suggest you put hers on ASAP. I don't know how long we will be in a seller's market and her home is the one you want to get going."

"I'm having an auction company come in tomorrow and Sunday to auction off all the furniture and dad's tools. I took clothes and some trinket items to the Goodwill and I brought some personal things that I wanted or felt my sister might want here to my house. Tom took some of dad's tools."

"Well, why don't we do this; you guys talk it over with Maggie and Ian, and call me Monday. By that time the auction company will be through and I'll be happy to help you with any cleaning up that has to be done," Kathy volunteered.

"Thanks Kathy. The whole thing is very frightening. I mean the prices really are unreasonable. Where in the world do all the assembly workers in Silicon Valley live?"

"Many of them commute from the central valley, and some of the young adults are still living at home with their parents." After finishing with business, Janet shared her experience in Mendocino and the house in Boonville. Around ten o'clock Kathy decided she should go and let Janet get a good night sleep to prepare her for a busy weekend.

Actually, she had a hard time falling asleep. The prices had been so overwhelming to her. She had heard that real estate was going through the roof but in her line of work she never paid much attention to that. She was too busy creating beautiful art to care about the real estate world. She hadn't even thought of moving until her mom died and Keith brought the idea up. There really was no reason for her to live in the Bay Area except for her friends. After taking the trip up north she could see where she could probably accomplish so much more there. It would be quieter and there was so much more beauty to inspire her. She was not sure at what time she fell asleep but six o'clock in the morning came too soon. The auctioneers were coming at seven o'clock to set things up. The furniture would stay inside and the tools would be auctioned off from the garage but things such as books, cookware, sewing machine, lamps, and the like would be set up on the long tables that the auction company would bring. The people could come as early as eight o'clock to look over things to see what they would want to bid on and how much. She took a quick shower and pulled on a pair of jeans and a sweater and drove over to her mother's house. Tom was still asleep so she let him sleep on. She was not sure what her part in all of it would be. If she needed Tom, she could call him. The auction company was pulling up in the driveway right in front of her. *Luckily mom's house has a large circular driveway that could park quite a number of cars,* she thought. She was happy that the house was not on a cul-de-sac, which would accommodate very few cars. The auction was to begin around ten o'clock. She was hoping most of the stuff would sell today.

"Good morning," she said to the auctioneers. "Is there anything I have to do?"

"No! You just go and enjoy the day. You won't want to hang around here. It's too personal for the owners," they informed her.

"If I leave you the key, will you lock up and open up tomorrow morning by yourselves?"

"Yes, that's the best way. Hopefully we'll get most of it sold today. It's all good quality stuff."

"That's what I'm hoping. Okay, I'll go and let you get started."

She was glad that she didn't have to be there. She understood what they meant by being too personal. She had been at auctions before and people try to get things as cheap as possible. She couldn't bear to watch that happen to the things that were so dear to her parents. When she got home, Tom had just gotten out of the shower.

"Good morning. Did you sleep well?" she asked Tom.

"I slept real well. I heard you leave. I was hoping to go with you in case you needed me."

"No! We're not needed. In fact they said it's best we're not there because of personal ties to the stuff being auctioned off."

"Good. I was not looking forward to it." She made some coffee then called her sister.

"You're pulling my leg!" Maggie almost screamed into the phone, not being able to believe her ears when Janet told her what Kathy had said their mom's home was worth. "I know mom and dad had a beautiful home but you couldn't call it a mansion," she went on.

"Listen, I couldn't believe it either and I live here."

"So the auction is happening today and tomorrow. When are we putting it on the market?" Maggie asked.

"Well, that's why I'm calling you. I think you just agreed with me to do it as soon as possible."

"Of course. You never know about real estate. The bottom could fall out any day."

"That's what Kathy said. She also said that the house is in such great shape we don't have to do any fixing up. She and I are going to vacuum and tidy up any mess that might be left by all the people going through it this weekend. I will hire someone, probably mom's old gardener, to do any yard work that might be needed."

"Janet, thank you for all the hard work you're doing. Just make sure and keep records of whatever money you pay out to have the place looking good. We will put the expenses in escrow and we'll all share the costs," Maggie reminded her.

"Okay, Maggie. I'm going to hang up now and call Ian. By the way, we will all have to sign the contract and all the documents involved." Maggie understood. She then called Ian and was surprised to find him at home. Of course it was only nine-thirty in the morning. She got the same shocked response from Ian as she got from Maggie. "List it as soon as possible," he said.

"Okay! We're all in agreement. Tom picked out some of dad's tools but we didn't think you were interested. Do you want to talk to Tom?" she said then handed the phone to her brother. Tom and Ian talked for a while then Tom hung up the phone.

"He wasn't interested in any of the tools. He's quite excited about selling the house."

"It's exciting but also sad. We grew up in that house and I visited mom often before she died. It's hard to think of another family living in it."

"I know. We just weren't ready to lose mom. I don't suppose anyone ever is, but it was so sudden and she was still a young woman." This was the first time she was able to share with her brother the affect that the death of her mother had on her.

"When I was cleaning her house out, I felt so sad that she wasn't in the kitchen fussing around getting me tea and some 'biscuits' as she always called cookies. I miss her so much."

"I do too, Janet, but I know it's harder on you because you were with her almost every day." They talked for a long time, sharing the times growing up together and memories of their mom. They laughed and sometimes they just sat quietly for a while. It made Janet feel good to share with her brother Tom. "I wish all four of us would have taken the time to share our memories with each other while we were together for the funeral," she said.

"I do too," he said. Then glancing at his watch he said, "It's almost noon. Why don't I take you out to lunch."

"Sounds like a good idea." Janet took him to a Mexican restaurant that was a favorite of hers and their mother. "What did you and mom like to eat here?"

"We would share a large fajita but I'm not sure if that would be enough for you," she replied.

"Maybe we'll do that and I'll have an enchilada on the side. If I don't need it, I'll take it back to the house and eat it later."

"Mom and I came here every Saturday for lunch after we got through shopping."

"I'm glad you brought me here then. It makes me feel a little closer to her. I didn't even know she liked Mexican food."

"She loved it. Fajitas and chimichangas were her favorites. Also she loved the salsa in this place. Did you know she made great salsa herself?"

"No, Janet. I'm just realizing how much I didn't know and now I wish that I would've come down and visited her more often. Eugene is not that far away."

"Don't beat yourself up, Tom. We didn't drive up to Oregon very often either or go to Colorado to see Ian."

"We have to try and change that. We've all got to draw closer."

"I agree, Tom. Maybe you and I can be the drivers of that idea."

After enjoying a wonderful lunch they decided to go to the San Mateo County History Museum. The museum displayed San Francisco history through photographs, artifacts, records and hands on displays. It showed photos of the lumber from the Redwood Trees that was sent up to San Francisco by the way of a deep port that was formed by the Redwood Creek. "It says Redwood City got its name from these great trees that grew up in Woodside," said Janet. Woodside is a town west of Redwood City. The museum was small so it didn't take too long to go through it. Tom asked if Janet would drive down to the marina. He was very fond of boating and wanted to walk around and enjoy watching the recreational boaters.

The auctioneer called early in the evening to say that everything went well. They had gotten a pretty good price on everything and there were only a few trinkets that didn't sell, so they would not be going back. Janet shared the information with Tom.

"I'm glad things didn't go dirt cheap," said Janet.

"Me too, because everything they had was first class," Tom agreed.

Since there was nothing left for him to do, Tom decided to drive back home the next day, Sunday. "Goodbye, Janet, and thanks for everything and all that you're doing."

"You're welcome. Thanks for coming down, Tom. I'm afraid it was a long drive for nothing."

"It wasn't for nothing, Janet. I enjoyed talking with you."

"Me too, I really enjoyed sharing our memories of mom and dad. It did me a lot of good," she said giving him a hug.

"I was thinking that I'd call Ian when I get home and just talk to him and tell him of our time together. Maybe he will open up and share some things. I don't see him very often and right now I just feel that maybe he might need to do that."

"That'd be great, Tom. I'll call you more often instead of letting Maggie pass on information to you."

"I'll call you too. Goodbye Janet," he said getting into his car. She was already missing him when she went back into the house.

She decided that she would wait before listing her own house. She didn't have the money at the moment to put on a new roof or pay someone to come and paint it. She intended to give all her attention to her mother's house, then when she got her share of the sale she would work on her own home. She decided to e-mail Margaret in Boonville.

Dear Margaret:

It has been a week since I walked into your office. I loved the house in Boonville, at least what I could see from the outside. I would like to come up and see the inside soon. The auctioneers were at my parents' house yesterday and sold their furniture and tools, etc. My girlfriend, who is a real estate agent here in the Bay Area, brought me some comps on my mother's home. I almost dropped my teeth when she showed them to me. Like I told you, her house is mortgage-free. My friend is going to list it for $2,450,000. She will probably list it on Monday. Her name is Kathy Nelson, in case you want to check the MLS for the listing. Actually I will have Kathy give you the MLS number when she gets it.

Janet Stevens

On Monday Janet met with Kathy at her mom's home. She brought her vacuum and cleaning materials. It definitely needed some cleaning. She vacuumed while Kathy cleaned counters and any smudges on cabinets and appliances. She had told the auctioneers to leave the refrigerator and washer and dryer in case a buyer might want them included. If they didn't, she could use them herself. After she finished vacuuming the whole house she asked Kathy to look through the house with her to see what else needed to be done. "Do you think I should have someone clean the carpets?" she asked Kathy.

"They don't really need it but anything to make it look better helps, especially at this price. If you don't have a carpet cleaner in mind, I have a great person I use for all my listings when needed," Kathy said.

"I think it's a good idea. Like you said, at this price the buyer would be expecting a gem. I think I'll call John, mom's gardener, and ask him to come out and clean up the yard. In fact I'll have him come over once a week until the house has sold."

"Perfect! I have a feeling though, that it will sell pretty fast. It's a beautiful home and lovely area. I would love to live here myself but I couldn't afford it," Kathy said looking around admiring the house.

John came out and mowed the lawn and trimmed the bushes on Wednesday of the same week and Kathy's carpet cleaner came out on Thursday. The house was already on the market and that weekend, only two weeks after Janet's visit to Mendocino, Kathy was going to be holding an open house.

She was anxious to look inside the house in Boonville so she called Margaret.

"Margaret, Janet Stevens here. How are you?"

"I'm fine, Janet. How are things going?"

"So far everything is going well. I'm still nervous about the high listing price on my mom's house."

"Don't worry. I'm sure your friend Kathy knows her market. She did give me the MLS number and I looked it up. I must say, Janet, the house sounds wonderful and the neighborhood, by what your friend wrote on the listing, is very exclusive."

"Thank you. I was wondering if I could arrange to come up this Saturday and see the inside of the house?"

"Sure! How about eleven o'clock?" Margaret suggested.

"Great! I'll see you then. Goodbye Margaret."

She called her friend Linda, the computer whiz, and asked if she would like to go with her to Mendocino and spend Saturday night there.

"I'd love to. Sounds like a lot of fun. I haven't been up there for years."

"I'll drive and pay for the room," Janet told Linda.

"Well I'll pay for dinner Saturday night," offered Linda.

"No! We'll go Dutch for meals," Janet said definitively. "If I was to go by myself I would have to drive and pay for the room anyway. This way I have a friend to have fun with."

"What about Kathy? Do you think she would like to go?"

"She would love to go, I'm sure, but she is holding an open house at my mom's place and I know that selling the house is a bigger priority for her. I'll pick you up at eight o'clock Saturday morning."

"Great! I'm looking forward to it."

She then called Keith to let him know she and Linda were going back up to Mendocino to look at the inside of the house. "I wanted to spend the night and right now I can't afford two rooms," she said almost apologetically. "Linda and I will be sharing a room."

"Don't even think about it, Janet," Keith said. "I don't have to go. You and Linda have fun. If you buy the house, I'll have plenty of time to spend with you up there."

"Keith, I think it's a very good probability. My mom's house is on the market for almost two million five hundred thousand dollars and there is no mortgage to pay off. I'm not sure what I'll get from my house but it has gone up in value a lot since I bought it so I will have cash from that also. My heart is beating so fast right now just thinking about moving in to that house."

"Good luck, sweetheart. I will keep you in my prayers. I want you to have the house even if it is for selfish reasons... only kidding. I want it for you."

When Janet picked up Linda they were both so excited. They threw Linda's duffle bag in the trunk and climbed into the car. "I haven't done anything this exciting for ever. I wish we could just fly over the entire 101 and get to that other highway you were telling me about. I'm sure I've traveled on it, but like I said it has been at least ten or fifteen years since I've been up in Mendocino."

"It's amazing that a place I love so much has taken me all these years to find," Janet said.

"So close, yet so far." Linda added. "We get so bogged down with our lives in the city that we forget about the beauty of our neighboring areas."

"Keith told me about the time he and Rita, his girlfriend—"

"What happened to her," Linda interrupted.

"I can't talk about it right now. It's still very real to me and it was a terrible experience. They had been on holiday and spent a week traveling through the wine country and picnicking. He said it was the best time of his life. That was two months before Rita was..." she hesitated then said, "killed. It devastated him. It took a long time for him to heal."

"What a sad story," Linda said.

"Keith wants us to have a whopping good time, so let's not think of anything bad right now," Janet suggested.

When they got to the Anderson Valley, Linda was as mesmerized as Janet had been when she came through the area with Keith.

She pulled off at the Boonville exit and drove right to the real estate office. Margaret was at her desk working on printing out some new listings in the area. The receptionist called her extension and informed her that Janet was here to see her.

"Hello Janet," Margaret said reaching out her hand to her. "It's good to see you again."

"Hello Margaret, this is my friend Linda."

"Hi, Linda," Margaret said then turning to Janet, "Your mom's listing sounds great. Here are the only few new listings in the

Anderson Valley. They're both in Philo and here are a few new ones in the town of Mendocino." Janet looked over them and showed them to Linda.

"I like these two," Linda said handing them back to Janet.

"They are nice, but I would like to go back to the house here in Boonville to see the inside first, then I would like to see these two in Philo." She hadn't said too much to Linda about the house, as she wanted to get her own opinion on it. "Okay, sounds good. Let me make appointments for the two in Philo," said Margaret as she picked up the phone.

"This is beautiful up here," said Linda looking out at the views. "It is so peaceful. I think this is truly an artist's environment."

"I'm glad you like it," said Janet then turning to Margaret, "I'm dying to see the inside."

"Let's go then," Margaret said walking to the door.

"I love all this decking," Linda said. Two tall plants stood on either side of the double door entryway. Margaret opened the door and invited them inside. The downstairs consisted of a large living room with a brick fireplace, a family room that had been converted into a library with another fireplace that had a rectangular window on each side of it. The windows reached almost from the ceiling to the floor. Outside of both windows was a garden of green plants like ferns, bushes, tall ornamental grasses and small trees that surrounded a horseshoe shaped patio giving it a feel of privacy, not that it was needed. The wall opposite the fireplace had bookshelves from floor to about two feet from the ceiling. It was full of books and magazines. Both rooms had vaulted ceilings. Also downstairs was a very well laid out kitchen. It wasn't huge but it had lots of cupboard and counter space as well as a nice pantry and small kitchen cart. The cabinets were oak with an indigo finish which Janet thought gave it a real country look. Off of the kitchen was the dining room, which although not real big, looked big enough to seat about a dozen people comfortably. A half bathroom was situated near the door going out to the garage. There was one bedroom downstairs which was a pretty good size, with a full bath. *Probably the master,* Janet thought. There were three more bedrooms and two bathrooms upstairs and a loft. Janet loved the house. She felt that it fitted her lifestyle to a tee but she tried not to say too much. She wanted to hear Linda's comments. Linda looked around one more time then turned to Janet.

"This house is you, Janet, from the country kitchen to the library," she said. She turned to Margaret and said, "I don't know of anyone who reads more than she does," then turning back to Janet, "and those windows with all the plants outside," she said with her hand over her heart acting like she was breathless. "I can just see you snuggling up in a big chair on a rainy day reading a book with the fire burning bright."

"I was hoping you'd like it," Janet admitted.

"I do. I've never seen a house that says 'Janet's house' more than this one."

"Take your time. Look around some more," Margaret suggested. "The other two homes are not too far away so we have plenty of time."

Janet and Linda made one more tour around the whole house then went out and looked at the garage. Janet was mentally putting her pottery wheel, kiln and worktable in place. She decided they would go on the side of the garage that was closest to the door into the house so that it would be convenient for her to go in and out. Her car would go at the farthest end.

The trip out to the other homes proved a waste of time. Not that they were not lovely homes, but they didn't have the pull the one in Boonville had. It appealed so much to her that she didn't think there was another house that could take the place of it in her heart. "None of them hit you, did they?" Margaret asked.

"No!" Janet answered.

"I'll keep looking and let you know what I find."

"Margaret, what is the status on the house? I mean, do the owners have another home they are waiting to move into?"

"Yes they do. In fact they are moving next week."

"Are they in a hurry to sell it? I'm not sure how long my mom's house will take to sell. My friend's holding an open house as we speak."

"Do you know approximately how much you'll have to put down on this house? I'm assuming you are interested in making an offer?" Margaret said questioningly.

"Yes, I would like to. If mom's home sells for full price I would get at least $500,000 after closing costs. Kathy said there shouldn't be any repairs needed because my mom kept her house in excellent shape. She got a new roof not too long ago. There's also $45,000 from the auction, after sharing with my siblings. Then of course there is my own house which Kathy is going to list at $650,000."

"No doubt you would qualify for this house. Do you want me to talk to the owners and see if we can make a deal?" Margaret asked feeling a little excited about possibly getting a sale, especially since she would not only be the selling agent but she was also the listing agent. She, of course, would make sure to include the form with the contract indicating that she was a dual agent.

"Yes. I don't think I could stand it if I lost that home. I don't want to wait. Just pray my mom's house will sell soon. Get back to me as soon as you can, Margaret. We will be here until tomorrow. Here's my cell phone number."

They had some fish and chips at a local restaurant. By the time they were finished with lunch it was about two o'clock. "I'm ready to tour the area," Linda said.

"Check in time at the hotel is four to six o'clock. Let's see if we can find a tour map. We should have asked Margaret if they have any in their office."

"Well let's go ask her," Linda said. They went back to the real estate office where an excited Margaret informed Janet that she had gotten hold of the owners on their cell phone and they were very interested in talking to her regarding Janet's interest, especially after hearing about the house she had on the market. "I have an appointment with them Monday morning. I really am hoping you get the house, Janet. I saw how much it meant to you, and besides we would almost be neighbors." Margaret Dunbar had taken an immediate liking to Janet Stevens and she was never usually wrong about her first impression of people.

"I think it's going to work, Margaret. I just have a feeling."

"I'll talk to you Monday after I have the meeting with the owners."

Linda and Janet had a wonderful time touring around the wineries and seeing the process of wine making, aging and how the champagne bottles have to keep getting turned. They also walked around looking at the vineyards.

"It's absolutely beautiful up here, Janet. You're so lucky," Linda said.

"Well, it hasn't happened yet," Janet reminded her.

"I'm positive it will. Look at all the money you'll be getting from the sale of the two homes. You'll be able to pay cash for this one, if you want to. What are you going to do with all the money?"

"Throw a party, hopefully, at my new house, for all my friends. Also, I'm going to put some away and when I have the time, I'm going to Scotland to visit my aunt Betty and cousin Alice. I want to see where my mom grew up."

"That's a great idea."

She was tired when she got back home on Sunday night at ten o'clock, but it was a good tired. She had such a wonderful time. She was being drawn more and more to the area and to that house. The answering machine had a blinking light. At first Janet thought she would wait until tomorrow to check it. She was not ready to get involved with idle conversation right now. She was tired and she couldn't stop thinking about the house in Boonville. She knew she wanted it so bad and that was all she could think about at the moment. She unloaded her luggage. She started to put some of her clothes in the laundry basket when a lightning bolt thought hit her, *that call could be from Kathy*. She ran back to the phone and pushed the button. "Hi Janet, please call me when you get home." It was Kathy but she didn't sound too enthusiastic. She dialed.

"Hi Janet, how was your time up in Boonville? I hope you had fun. How did you like the inside of the house?" Kathy inquired not too enthusiastically.

"We had a great time and I loved the house. I am ready to move into it, but it doesn't sound like it's time yet. Tell me about the interest in mom's house. I'm ready to reduce the price. My siblings have given me the go ahead to do what I think is best."

"That's great, Janet. I'm glad they're willing to trust you with this. Can I come over for a few minutes? I know it's late but I want to talk with you."

"Of course, Kathy, come on over."

Janet felt a little depressed. Kathy's attitude indicated that things had not gone well. "If we have to reduce the price that is okay," Janet said out loud. "None of us expected this much money anyway. I would be happy to reduce it down to one million dollars. Even then I still feel it's too much." Just then the doorbell rang. Janet opened it to Kathy. She walked inside. Janet knew how much the commission on this house meant to her. When she saw Kathy's sad expression she felt bad for her. "I'm sorry, Kathy, but it is just the first weekend. I'm sure other realtors will be bringing their clients through the house."

"I suppose they will," she said with the same sad face. She hesitated a while, then looked at Janet and said, "Janet, I have news for you." Every muscle in Janet's body constricted. *I can't have anything come in the way of me having that house in Boonville, please dear Lord,* she thought.

Kathy continued. "I had a couple come through the house and they fell in love with it," she said as her voice kept getting louder and more excited, "and they have put in a full price offer," and with a scream, "and they have been pre-qualified for the loan."

Janet was stunned and stood still for a while, staring at Kathy scream and jump up and down. She was waiting for words of doom. She was not prepared for the news Kathy had given her. She looked into Kathy's eyes. She was smiling and nodding "yes".

She walked over to Kathy and put her arms around her. She didn't understand her emotions at this time. She was excited but also in shock. Too many good things were coming together for her so fast. She didn't know how to handle them. She pulled back and looked once again into Kathy's eyes wanting to make sure there was no misunderstanding. There was not. "Oh Kathy, that's fantastic. My agent in Boonville is going to meet with her people tomorrow. I could be moving into that dream house in a month or two."

"I'm so happy for you. For me too!"

"Yes, of course. Congratulations Kathy."

"I owe you and the family big time. I have to figure out what I can do for you all. Of course I'm dropping my commission to five percent instead of six."

"Kathy, I don't want you to drop your commission. Just because you're my friend doesn't mean that you owe that to me. Our family is going to get way more than we had expected and I want you to share in the benefits."

"But I didn't expect to be the buyer's agent as well as yours."

"I don't care. If another agent had brought that client in, we would have to pay that person three percent and you would only get two. I would rather give you the whole six percent and, of course, you have to pay your broker his share. I'm extremely happy for you," she said hugging her again. "Margaret also is the listing agent in the house up north and my agent."

"Make sure she doesn't forget to have you sign the dual agency form," Kathy informed her.

"She said something about that but I didn't pay much attention. My focus was completely on the house."

It was about eleven-thirty when Kathy left. Janet waited until the next morning to call her siblings, since she knew they would be asleep and she was just too exhausted between her trip and the excitement of the sale of her mom's house. The phone ringing awakened her. She looked at the clock. "My word, ten o'clock?" It was Maggie inquiring about the open house. She had wanted to play act like Kathy had with her, but she was too excited. "Maggie, it went very well. So well in fact that it sold."

As usual Maggie was screaming into the phone. "Does it look like it's a done deal, Janet? I mean. . . I hope it won't fall through."

"The buyers offered full price and they are pre-qualified by the bank. They gave Kathy a copy of a letter from the person at the bank who pre-qualified them. She is going to call the bank this morning and confirm. She'll call me later. I'll only call you back if it's a false letter, but I doubt it. Kathy said they looked like a well to do couple of middle age and drove a new Mercedes."

"Oh Janet, I can't believe this. I could cry."

"Maggie, if you don't mind, I would like to share the news with Tom and Ian."

"Of course, dear. I'm glad you didn't call me last night. I couldn't have gone back to sleep."

Janet then called Tom.

"That's fantastic Janet. It's like a miracle. I bet mom is smiling down at us."

"I know she's happy."

She then called Ian.

"It sold so fast. Do you think we didn't ask enough?"

"Ian, almost two and a half million dollars. I was having a hard enough time with the price we were asking," she told him.

The home closed within a month. All inspection reports came in clear and since the terra cotta tile roof was only five years old there was no problem with it. It went through escrow without a glitch. Janet met again with Kathy to get ideas of what she would have to do to put her own house on the market. Since she got enough money from the sale of her mother's home and the auction she decided to go ahead with the purchase of the home in Boonville. Since the family already had moved out she was allowed to move up some of her things from her Redwood City home. That way she was able to clean it up real easy and prepare it to put on the market.

"Getting a lot of your stuff, like your books and supplies for your pottery out of the house, will make it look even neater," Kathy encouraged her. "It will be so much easier to make it look welcoming. Some people can't see beyond clutter."

"Everything is working out so well that I'm nervous something will go wrong."

"Now you're sounding like your mother," Kathy teased.

Thanks for all your help, Kathy."

"Don't thank me. I just did my job. With the commission from the listing and sale of your mom's home, you just made me sales person of the month and a lot richer."

Janet was in Margaret's office going over the Residential Contract of Purchase. Janet was signing all the places where Margaret had put her yellow "sign here" stickers when the phone rang. Margaret picked it up. "Hello! Oh hello Mrs. Cooper. I'm here with Janet right now signing the contract. I should be at your house like I said at one o'clock this afternoon with it." Janet of course could only hear Margaret's side of the conversation. "What was the agent's name?" she asked then waited while she got the name. "Mrs. Cooper if he, or any other agent, call you direct, tell them that they must talk with your agent and not to bother you or your husband." Janet sat staring at Margaret. *Now what? Everything has been going too good so I hope this isn't the bad news I was afraid of,* she thought. She was anxious for Margaret to get off the phone. She finally did and turned to her. "Don't worry, Janet. I know what this is about. Hold on." She started dialing again. It seemed like it must have rung for a while but someone finally picked it up. Actually it didn't take that long. Janet was just nervous about possibly losing the house. "Jack Butler, please," Margaret said into the phone. A few moments later she said, "Jack, Margaret Dunbar here. I would appreciate it if you would not contact my clients directly. You know that is not ethical, Jack. You told Mrs. Cooper you had a contract for substantially more than the asking price. If that is true, then you set an appointment with me to meet at the Coopers home and I will present it to them in your presence along with mine. I'm presenting mine this afternoon, so I would suggest you clear your calendar and bring your contract to the Coopers home at fifteen after one." Janet was surprised at the firmness of this usually lovely, calm woman. She sat there just listening, trying to figure out what was going on. *Sounds like someone has a better offer than mine,* she was thinking. *Well I'll fight this Jack Butler. He won't have my home.* Margaret listened for a few moments and said, "If you can't make it, Jack, you will just have to suffer the consequences. When can you bring the contract around?" Again Margaret listened into the phone then said, "I'm not sure that you have a contract, Jack. If I find out that you called my clients because you know my listing will be running out in two weeks and you were trying to get them to re-list with you, then I will report you to the Real Estate Board and if you ever call my clients again, any of my clients, I will report you. Is that clear?" Janet assumed it was clear when Margaret hung up the phone.

"Does he have a better contract because I'm willing to raise my offer?" she said without taking a breath.

"Don't worry, Janet, he's one of the unethical agents who try to steal other agents' listings when they are about to expire."

"So if your listing was to expire, would you lose it?"

"I'm sure the Coopers would stick with me and give me another three month listing."

"I'm a little worried about the offer."

"Since you're willing to raise the amount then I'll have that in my pocket. I'll take this contract and if they feel they can do better, then I'll negotiate with them. I have to be fair to both of you because I am a dual agent. However, you are offering the full amount that they agreed to sell the home for, but they do have the right to accept a higher offer."

37

"Okay, I have every confidence in you, Margaret," she said then started to laugh. "I loved the way you handled Jack Butler. That was great. I would've liked to have seen his face."

"Well, it's noon, so why don't I take you out to lunch then I'll go on up to the Coopers and present the contract."

After lunch, Janet went back to the hotel to wait for Margaret's call. What seemed like an eternity was really only about forty minutes. "Janet, they accepted your contract and were very happy with it. It helped that you had a big down payment and could qualify."

"Wonderful, Margaret. Did they mention the other agent's contract?"

"I told them that I had invited him to meet with us and I would present it at the same time but that he said he had other things to do. When I told them that, they laughed, knowing that he probably didn't even have one."

"I'm so excited, Margaret. What do I do now?"

"You don't do anything. I'll open escrow this afternoon then it all starts going from there."

Another month went by and the house in Boonville closed escrow and her house in Redwood City was due to close in another two weeks or so. Janet didn't wait for it to close. She moved all her belongings up to Boonville and left her home in the Bay Area in the hands of Kathy.

She had gone up to her new home a couple of different times before moving there. She measured her furniture and bought some blue tape that she had seen on a Martha Stewart show, and outlined where each piece of furniture would go and drew a sketch of where the furniture would be placed, so that when the movers carried each piece in, she knew exactly where to tell them to put it so the only thing she had to do was empty out boxes and put things in their place. While the men were moving in the furniture, a delivery van pulled up and the driver brought a beautiful silk floral arrangement to her. She tipped the driver and looked at the card. It was from Margaret, her real estate agent. Janet knew exactly where she was going to put it. She had bought dining room furniture since she didn't have any. She had thought about keeping her mother's but it was too formal for her country house. She put the arrangement in the center of the table. It looked lovely there with the sun shining directly on it through the window. She immediately called Margaret to thank her. As Janet was putting things away, she came across her mom's journal. With all the past excitement she had forgotten about it. She laid it on top of her desk in the library with intentions of getting to it soon. She moved on a Friday afternoon and by the end of the weekend she had everything in place, even her pottery shop was set up in the garage. Janet knew she was home. The following weekend, she invited Kathy, Linda and Keith up for a couple of days. With Margaret's help she had hired a catering company to bring the food for her housewarming party in her new home for her friends. The food was absolutely delicious. For appetizers there were spreads of hummus and red roasted peppers, an antipasto dish and fresh shrimp and dip. After that there was a selection of salads from roasted salmon with marinated cucumber salad to albacore tuna salad to Brazilian steak salad and deserts of little fruit tarts and chocolate truffles. It was a wonderful breaking in of Janet's house. Janet had even made a piece of pottery for her front door. The background was a vineyard and the writing said, "Welcome to Janet's House". Linda was especially pleased, as she was the one that told her this house says "Janet's House". Everyone loved it and Margaret, who was very interested in Janet's work, asked her if she could do something like it for her front door.

"Janet, I can see why you were so excited about buying this home. It's perfect for you and that workshop is fantastic," Kathy said. Margaret and Kathy spent a bit of time talking about the sale of the houses and how happy they were to be part of Janet's move. Of course, Keith had to remind everyone that it was his idea. The party was a big success and a great way to break in her dream house.

CHAPTER THREE

It was raining pretty hard on Monday, the day after her friends left to go back to the Bay Area. Janet lit the fire in the library and with her cup of coffee she curled up in front of the fireplace in the big overstuffed chair that she had bought just for that space. She remembered Linda saying, "I can just see you on a rainy day, curled up in a big chair with the fire burning bright." *Maybe it was Linda that put the notion into my head to buy this big chair,* she thought. She sat looking out through the big rectangular windows at the rain and all the greenery outside happily soaking it up. She missed her friends but enjoyed the opportunity to sit and meditate on the past previous months. She had been so busy that she didn't have much time to think about her mom. She decided to take this time to reminisce about her. Janet remembered how her mother would never turn away anyone in need. She would somehow find a way to help them even if it was only in a small way. She missed her mother's outgoing personality, her silly little sayings and her superstitions. She remembered how she would yell at Janet if she put newly bought shoes on the table, because it was bad luck; you never cross knives in the sink or anywhere else, because that meant there was going to be a fight; and when you drop a knife, it meant a stranger was coming to visit and the direction the knife was pointing would tell which direction the stranger was coming from. She would also refuse to turn back to the house if she had forgotten something. She would stand outside and honk the horn of her car for Janet to come out then she would have Janet get what she needed. "Do you think you're going to turn into a pillar of salt, ma?" Janet would tease, referring to the story of Lot's wife in the Book of Genesis. She missed her very, very much. She had indeed been her best friend. They loved going shopping on a Saturday morning and then have lunch out. Her mom always paid. She always worried that her daughter was not making enough money to take care of herself. Janet felt herself wishing that she had questioned her mother more about her years growing up in Scotland and of her family. That last thought reminded her of the journal. She got up and walked over to her desk and picked it up. She walked into the kitchen and poured another cup of coffee then went back into the library and curled up on the chair. She sat for a few moments feeling guilty for what she was about to do. *Mom left it behind. If she didn't want me to see it you would think she would have gotten rid of it,* she thought to herself. *Then of course she didn't expect to have a heart attack and die suddenly.* She held on to it for another few moments then looking outside at the rain she said aloud, "This day reminds me of the day we buried mom." Then looking down at the journal she opened it.

This journal begins when I was seventeen years old, although I am thirty years old at this time of starting to write in it. I was born and grew up in Glasgow, Scotland. My parents, John and Elizabeth Douglas, like everyone else around us, were what I would call blue collar class. They didn't have a lot of money but we lived in a nice, though small, tenement flat. We always had good healthy meals and just enough clothes that we didn't have to wear the same clothes two days in a row, although my mother washed clothes every Saturday. We did wear a uniform to school sometimes so it wasn't too much of a hardship on my mother. We didn't lack for anything. It seemed to me that people in our neighborhood judged each other by their cleanliness. Maybe that was because our dignity was about all we had so we could at least keep whatever we did have clean and be proud of it. My mother made sure that her family, her flat, her windows and curtains, and the washing that hung out in the backyard, which was shared by six families, were all clean. Each of the six families had one day a week to hang out their clothes. They had to keep the same day every week unless something came up and one of the other families could exchange with them. Nobody was to hang his or her washing out on Sundays. Although my mother was not a gossip, I remember her gasping as she looked out the window at someone else's wash. "That's a disgrace," she said. "How can she show her face?" My friends and I used to go to the local theater during the week to see a movie that had been around a while but on the Saturday nights that we didn't go dancing, we would go to one of the downtown theaters to see a just released movie. When we went to one of the downtown theaters, we would wait in line for it to open. Usually we would go early, like most people did, because we wanted to get a good seat. While waiting in line, singers, some with an instrument like a guitar or an accordion, would walk up and down the line entertaining us and we would throw coins into their buckets or whatever receptacle they had. They were called buskers.

Janet read on for a while longer until the phone rang. It was Margaret from the real estate office.

"Janet, I would like to take you to lunch this coming Friday to my favorite restaurant in Mendocino. Can you make it?"

"Margaret, you already gave me a beautiful flower arrangement." She knew Margaret was still showing her gratitude for the sale.

"I know, but I really want to do this."

"Okay! What time?" Janet didn't want to resist too much. She knew that Margaret had gotten a pretty hefty commission from the purchase and sale of this home and was very appreciative. It was a pretty easy contract. The sellers were not desperate for the money from the sale and Janet had enough money that Margaret didn't have to worry about her qualifying for a loan.

"Why don't you meet me at my office around 11:30. I will make the reservations for noon. I will make them now as it's a busy restaurant, especially on Fridays."

It was a beautiful restaurant with an eclectic menu of Italian, American, and Thai and Janet knew it was probably very expensive. Margaret made a few suggestions that she had tried from the menu that were her favorites. Janet chose a spicy Thai dish of seafood, noodles and vegetables. It was delicious. After lunch Margaret insisted that they have Crepes Suzette with their coffee.

"What kind of artist are you, Janet?"

"I'm a potter. I fashion my pots after nature."

"I'm a bit of a nature lover myself. I paint and take pictures of nature. I'd love to see your work some day."

"Well now that I'm settled in, are you busy tomorrow?"

"Only in the morning. I'm going out to take a listing and then get it prepared to open escrow first thing Monday morning and put it on the Multiple Listing. After that I'm free."

"If you're through by lunch, maybe you can join me."

"It shouldn't take me long but I wouldn't want to hold up your lunch. You never know how many questions people are going to ask. My appointment is with them at 10:00 o'clock so I'll just let them know I have a luncheon appointment at noon."

"Okay! It's a deal. Please bring some of the photographs you have taken."

Janet and Margaret became fast best friends. Although they had different business interests, they had art and the love of nature in common. Margaret loved Janet's work and bought a couple of pieces.

"You're not just buying these because of the commission are you? Because you don't have to."

"Janet, I absolutely love these vases that I bought from you. I'm happy about the commission because it allowed me to buy them. Not that they're terribly expensive but us sales people can go for months without a commission, depending on the market." She showed Janet some of her paintings and photography. Janet was especially interested in the photography since they were all about nature and she tried to incorporate some form of nature into every piece of her pottery. Even the name of her business was Hands and Nature indicating that the work was of her Hands and the inspiration was Nature. Sometimes she would paint flowers, butterflies, birds or other forms of nature onto her pottery and other times she made her work in the shape of some form of nature, like a mush-room vase she had once made. She was quite busy with her work and traveling to the studio in San Francisco. The drive from Boon-ville to the gallery was a little more than three hours longer round trip than the drive from Redwood City to San Francisco was, but she was happy to accept this burden for the happiness she had at her new home. She actually was getting more work done at her new studio because she felt more inspired and there were no distractions. After a while she didn't have to travel to San Francisco as often so that made up for the long drive.

After a few weeks she got back to reading her mother's jour-nal. It had been fun reading about her mom at a young age and all the antics she and her friends got into and their likes and dis-likes. For instance, they liked the music of the Beatles, Jerry and the Pacemakers and the American groups like Crosby, Stills and Nash and Creedence Clearwater Revival. They went to a certain dance hall because the disc jockey played the music of their favorite groups and they loved to dance to it. Dancing had been a big part of their young lives. Janet was approximately halfway through the journal. There were two chapters and Janet had put it down after she finished the first part, which was mostly about her family and friends. Her father was a truck driver for a furniture company and her mother worked in a bakery. She had an older sister Moira, and a younger sister Betty. Moira, who was six years older, married and moved to San Francisco with her new husband when Alice was sixteen years old.

Janet was surprised to find out that the second chapter had her mother still in Scotland going to the dancing with her friends. She was sure this chapter would have moved on to her immigrating to America.

One Saturday in the spring of 1968, the same year this journal begins, my friends and I went dancing. On this particular night there was a group of boys who had come down from the highlands for the weekend. They came over to us and started to talk. One of them was particularly attractive to me. His name was Robert MacLean. He was over six feet tall with dark sort of ruffled hair, which I thought was adorable. It sort of gave him a little boyish look. When he asked me to dance, I almost fell to pieces. I know I was blushing so bad I could hardly look at him. He flashed me a mischievous grin, which had me blushing even more. The whole time we were dancing I was sure he could feel me shaking. I had never been attracted to anyone like that before. When the evening ended he asked me if I came to this particular dance hall every Saturday night. I told him that we didn't go dancing every Saturday. He asked me to come back the following Saturday as he would like to see me again. He came down to Glasgow every weekend and I went dancing every Saturday with my friends. After a while, my friends reverted back to every other Saturday but I went every week because I would meet Robert.

My mother started to question me about going dancing every Saturday; especially when she found out my friends weren't going every week. I confessed to her that I had a boyfriend. Then came the twenty questions; who was he, where was he from, how long had I known him, etc. etc. etc. She asked if I was seeing him the following weekend and when I said I was, she decided he should come calling on me instead of me meeting him.

He knew he was going to be given the white glove inspection by my parents, but he came dutifully. He answered all their questions to their approval. They really liked him. He was well mannered and my mom said she could tell he was brought up in a very good family. He was not very generous with information about his family. He only said that they lived in a small town near Elgin. My parents didn't feel that it was proper to ask too many questions about them; after all, it was Robert they were inspecting, not his family.

Janet found it amusing to read about her mother's obviously first love. She was having a hard time picturing her mother blushing and being flustered when he asked her to dance. *I wonder if this man is still alive and still living in Scotland,* she thought. Then looking at the clock on the mantelpiece, she jumped up.

"I better put this down for now. I have to drive into the city this morning," she said aloud. She showered and got dressed then went out to her workshop to pack the new pieces she had finished for a few customers of Keith's.

"Hey Janet! How're things going?" Keith asked giving her his customary huge hug and kiss.

"Great! As much as I complain about this long drive, I wouldn't change anything for the world," she said. "Actually it's only the freeway and the city that makes the drive hard, but unfortunately that accounts for most of the trip."

"I know you've been busy with your work, but what else have you been up to up in Boonville?"

"Not much. I see quite a bit of Margaret. I really like her and she seems to feel the same way about me. I don't think she had a really close friend and now I seem to be it. We try to get together and take a nature hike every Saturday. Oh," she said as though just remembering, "I've started reading my mother's journal."

"Oh yeah, you told me about finding that when you cleaned out her house. Is it interesting or is it kind of creepy reading about your mom's private life?" he asked.

"It's been a lot of fun," she said removing her pottery pieces from the packing box. "Where do you want these?"

"Just sit them down here for now," he said patting his hand on a table. "I think I'll put them in the window until Mrs. Tyler picks them up. She won't be in for a few days. She's down in Los Angeles."

"Is she down there filming?"

"No, but she's meeting with some director who is interested in her for a part. She's sort of content to only do little parts. I think she just likes to stay around San Francisco and her house in Carmel."

"I just finished reading about my mom's meeting of her, I believe, first boyfriend. It was so cute. I had to put the book down just after he was summoned to come and meet her parents."

"And what did your grandparents think of him?" Keith asked grinning.

"They liked him very much. They thought he was very well mannered." *I wonder why they never got married?* Janet thought.

"Well keep me updated. Say, when are you going to invite me back up to Boonville?" he asked.

"Keith, you can come up whenever you want to. I might not always be able to entertain you but you always have a place to stay and food to eat. Please feel welcome."

"I'll take you up on that but I'll give you a call. I've been pretty busy these last couple of weekends also."

"Oh? Is there someone special in your life?" she asked teasingly.

"Yes," he replied giving her a smug look. "Her name's Brenda. I've been seeing her for three weeks now." Janet went over to him and gave him a hug.

"I may have been teasing, but I'm happy for you. I'll have to arrange for you and Brenda to come at a time when I can entertain you. I would love to meet her. How about next weekend? I'll invite Margaret over for dinner Saturday night and see if Linda and Kathy can come up."

"That sounds great."

On Saturday Janet and Margaret went on a hike. It was a lovely warm spring day. The spectacular views still took Janet's breath away.

"Look Margaret, the vines are starting to blossom," she said pointing to the vineyard they were walking by. Most of the wineries had picnic tables so they sat down at one of them and took out their lunch.

"There are a lot of wonderful things to experience up here, Janet. In fact, if you don't have anything planned for next weekend, I'd like to take you to the Mendocino Botanical Gardens," Margaret said.

"Ooh, that sounds nice," Janet answered.

"Not just nice. They're fantastic. I'm a member."

"What does that allow you? Do you get in for free?" Janet asked.

"Yes. Right now in bloom are Rhododendrons, Heritage Roses, Lilies, Cactus and more. It's the only public garden that fronts the ocean in this country. While you're looking at all the beautiful plants and flowers, you get to listen to the waves crash on the rocks."

"Wow! It does sound fantastic. I'm looking forward to it," she said bringing out the chicken she had baked the night before and Margaret brought out the salad that she had prepared for them. "We had quite a bit of snow this March, which was unusual and I got a picture of the vineyards and fences all white with snow. It turned out beautiful."

"Do you get snow up here every year?" Janet asked while putting her trash in her backpack.

"No, actually we get a dusting up in the higher elevations but not here."

"I'd love to see your picture. Are you ready to head back?"

"Sure! Oh, I almost forgot," Margaret said reaching into her backpack. "I got this for you. Now that you're officially a Boonville resident, it's time to learn Boontling," she said handing Janet a book.

"What's that?"

"The language invented by Boonville residents in the nineteenth century to keep their conversation private from outsiders."

"You're kidding," said Janet laughing. "A Slib of Lorey," she said reading the title, "by Edna L. Sanders."

"It means A Little Bit of Folklore," Margaret informed her.

"I'll have fun sharing this with Keith and Brenda tonight."

Keith and Brenda arrived at four o'clock. After Keith introduced Brenda to Janet and Margaret, they went inside. Kathy and Linda were unable to come up. Brenda handed Janet an apple pie that she had baked.

"Wow! This is the biggest apple pie I've ever seen. How many apples are in it," Janet asked.

"Enough," Keith answered. "I thought the top crust was going to blow off."

"You know, we have the Mendocino Apple Festival right here in Boonville," Margaret informed them. "Talking about festivals, the Mendocino Music Festival is coming up in July. I believe it's July 11 to July 22. They have Chamber music, Blues, Jazz, all kinds of music. It might be too late to get tickets for the tent seating but we can walk around the headlands and still hear the music."

"Is it a big deal," Keith asked.

"Some of the best artists entertain at this festival. It's big and lasts for two weeks."

"Margaret is taking me to the Mendocino Botanical Gardens next week. It sounds like a magical place. I can't wait to go."

"Besides all the beautiful plants and the Pacific Ocean, there are about one hundred species of birds that come through the gardens. I forgot to tell you, Janet, they also have a four-season photo contest. I'm going to enter this fall."

"Are you going to enter the picture you took in March with the vineyards in the snow?"

"I'm not sure. I'll be taking new ones then when it comes time to pick which one, I'll let you help me."

"That's great, Margaret. Maybe we could work up something where I could buy pictures from you that I could incorporate into my art."

"You don't have to buy them, Janet. It would be a compliment if you used my photographs in your beautiful pottery."

"Okay. I think your photography is so good that you should try and do something with your photos. Why don't you have a display in one of the galleries?"

"You think they're that good."

"I do. Give it a thought," Janet said. Then turning to Keith said, "How did you both meet?"

"Brenda is the new post master at our post office. I don't usually go to the post office, but I'm glad I did that day, a little more than a month ago."

"He doesn't usually come in and I'm not usually out in front with the customers, but on that particular day, the lady that usually works the front desk took ill and I had to take care of everything, otherwise we probably wouldn't have met."

"I felt sorry for her so I asked her out to dinner after she was through," Keith added.

"I don't think you were feeling sorry for her. I think you just wanted her to go out with you," Janet teased.

"The reason that we were late in getting here is because I work half-a-day on Saturdays."

They had dinner around six o'clock; Margaret had come over

early to help with the meal. Janet had baked chicken in a curry sauce, with rice, asparagus and a salad. After dinner Janet made some coffee and they had some of Brenda's delicious apple pie.

"Listen, Margaret gave me this book on Boontling. It's a local language and it's hysterical. Let me just read you the origin of Boontling. The book is called, A Slib of Lorey by Edna L. Sanders. The translation of the title is A Bit of Folklore.

"Origin of Boontling," Janet read the heading then went on to read the verse.

"Boontling originated in Bell Valley in the early 1880's by some young men and women. It was picked up by children and girlfriends. Since it was very entertaining it grew because a harper (talker) would try to shark (to stump) his listeners on a new word and was very happy when he succeeded. Also it was a game to harp in front of bright lighters (city folks,) who were very amazed at this "strange language" those ridgy kimmies (country people) spoke. The vowels are basically English." She turned to a different page in the book. "The book says there was a club formed in 1961 to perpetuate the language for it's historical value and because it was a fun language that could be used today."

They decided to play a game where someone would read a verse from the book and they would guess what the word or sentence meant. Janet gave each of them several pages that she copied of the Glossary in the back of the book to help them.

By midnight, after loads of laughter everyone decided to go to bed. Margaret had gone home at eleven o'clock, as she had to show some houses the next day.

"I think you have your name on that door," Janet said smiling at Keith then turning to Brenda she said, "This is the same room he slept in last time he was here."

"The other one is fine with me. I just appreciate you inviting me up here. I love it. I wish I could move here but a three to four hour commute round trip is way too long," Brenda replied.

The next morning Janet made coffee and brought out some bagels and donuts.

"Brenda and I are going to drive into Mendocino for lunch and some sightseeing then we will head on back to the city," Keith said almost apologetically. "You're welcome to join us," he told Janet.

"No, no. I can go in anytime. Besides Margaret and I have some things to do in there next week. You two go and have a great time. I'm going to sit out in the little patio garden and read some more of mom's journal."

As they were leaving Janet reminded them of the Music Festival.

"We're going to try and come up at least one day," Keith said.

The sun felt nice and warm as she sat out in her patio. She was anxious to know how things went with her mom and Robert MacLean and to find out what happened to him. *I will e-mail Aunt Betty in Glasgow and see if she knows anything about him,* she thought. Opening the journal at her bookmark she read:

>After Robert and I had been going together for three months, he asked me to elope with him. I told him I thought that was a little bizarre. For one thing, my parents would be really upset if I did that to them and also I had never met his parents. He was quiet for a while then told me that he really loved me and wanted to spend the rest of his life with me. The problem was his parents. They were a wealthy highland family with a lot of land, and a very old mansion that had been passed down through generations. His grandfather had been an earl. He tried to say it as delicately as possible, because Robert was a very tender young man, but the fact of the matter was, I didn't fit into their class. He knew they would not let a marriage between us happen. He insisted, though, that he wanted me regardless of whether or not his family would approve and even if they cut him off, he still wanted to marry me. I felt sick to my stomach. I loved Robert but didn't think I could live with the thought that his family would disown him and that the home and land would go to someone else. I wanted to tell my mother but knew how she would feel about it. She was a proud woman and to think that anyone would call her daughter unsuitable would make her angry. After another month had passed and Robert's constant pleading with me to marry him kept

up, I finally gave in and agreed to marry him but only if he would agree we would let my parents know right after the marriage. In Scotland, it is legal to marry at sixteen years of age without parents consent. We made the arrangements with a Justice of the Peace and got married.

Janet couldn't go on. Her mother had been married before. *She had never told any of us,* she thought. *I wonder if daddy knew. What happened to the marriage? It probably got annulled.* She couldn't continue. There were too many thoughts and questions racing through her mind. She thought she knew her mother right to the core.

"I can't even talk to Maggie about this. Not yet. I'm sure it will hit her just as hard. I never thought my mom had secrets from us," she babbled. It was only three o'clock in the afternoon. She had intended spending the whole afternoon reading the journal and perhaps finishing it, but she just couldn't go on. She couldn't spend any time at her work. "I would create a disaster in this frame of mind." She couldn't think of anything to do. Her mind was stuck on the fact that her mother kept a secret from the family. She didn't want to talk to anyone at this time. "Maybe I'll go for a walk and use up some energy." She walked for a very long time not noticing the flowers that she loved, like the Purdis Iris with its creamy white blossoms with brownish purple veins. She loved this flower with its petals spreading out in a horizontal direction. She didn't pay attention to the lupines, the clover or the California poppies. The oak trees and redwoods, the sheep grazing in the hills, the things she had hoped would distract her were totally neglected by her. She couldn't get her mind off of the fact that her mother had kept a secret from the family.

"How could you take this secret to the grave, mom," she said aloud and the tears started to roll down her cheeks. "It isn't the fact that you were married before, but the fact that you made it sound like daddy was the only man in your life. You were not truthful with us." She came to one of the picnic tables and sat down. She put her arms on the table and laid her head on them and cried. She was glad there was no one around. "I'm probably making too much of this, but I was so close to mom and never had an inkling. I almost feel betrayed," she told herself. By the time she got home it was five o'clock. She took out the leftover chicken from the night before and made a salad. She made herself eat even though she wasn't very hungry. She hadn't eaten since the bagel she had with her coffee that morning. She felt a lot calmer than she did earlier but still not calm enough to go back to the journal to find out what happened. She decided not to tell Maggie, at least not until she could go back and read what happened to the marriage and how her mom ended up in America. Aunt Moira, who was now living in Charlottes-ville, Virginia, would probably know everything. Janet had put the money from the sale of her own home into a savings account at her bank. She was planning, when she found the time, to take a trip to Scotland and visit her aunt Betty and cousin Alice, named after her own mom. *Maybe I will make a stop in Virginia,* she thought.

The day Margaret took her to the Mendocino Botanical Gardens was healing for her. At least, temporarily, she could forget about the journal.

Janet was awestruck. "Margaret, I feel like I died and went to heaven. This is beyond beautiful. The Garden of Eden could not have been more beautiful than this. God had to have created this place. Nobody else could create such perfection." Margaret laughed but knew exactly what she was feeling. "Look at the vast array of colors of the flowers and the birds flying around. I feel so heady, like I'm going to pass out from sheer ecstasy." The sound of the blue Pacific waves crashing on the rocks was like music to her ears.

"I knew you would feel that way about this place. I came by myself the first time and I was just about to burst. I wanted to bab-ble on, the way you just did, but they would have come at me with a straight jacket."

"Did I sound that insane?"

"No, but just picture you going through those antics and you were by yourself."

"You're right," Janet said laughing. "I don't know what I would have done if I was alone. I just can't stop marveling at the colors, the different shapes of the blossoms. Some look like angel wings and others look like a bridal veil. I can't even describe them accurately. I don't have the words," Janet said. "The irises are gorgeous." There were beautiful formal gardens, fern covered canyons, desert gardens with all kinds of cacti and a coastal pine forest. "I know I will come back here often, even though it is a little ways away," Janet said.

"I think it's only between ten and fifteen miles," Margaret replied.

"Well it's one of the best places I've been to."

It was a couple of more weeks before she could bring herself to continue on with the journal.

I had left a note for my mother telling her what I was about to do. I didn't want her to worry when I didn't come home. We stayed at a nice hotel downtown the night of our wedding. The next morning, I called my mom to tell her everything was okay. She said, "Everything is not okay, lady, and I want you to get back home as soon as possible." She always called me lady when she was angry with me. My mother yelled at us both telling us that we had done a stupid thing. Robert apologized and explained to her that he loved me and was afraid his parents would not approve the marriage. She may have been yelling but she was the only one that made sense. I should have talked it over with her and got her advice instead of following Robert's silly scheme. He felt that once we were married no one could do anything about it and eventually everyone would get used to it and be fine with it. My mother convinced him to go home and discuss with his parents what he had done and then maybe they could all get together and talk. A week passed and I never heard from Robert. One day shortly thereafter a solicitor came to our door and said he represented the MacLean family. He informed my parents that the MacLean family had the marriage annulled and offered them some money for the inconvenience. My mother flat out refused the money but my father took it saying that indeed we had been inconvenienced and we might need it for something, like maybe me taking a trip for a while to London or somewhere. He reminded my mom and me that Robert was from an influential family and the whole story would probably get into the news. He said I might not want to stay around and face the disgrace. I didn't sleep that night. I was devastated and cried all night long. The next day I received a letter from Robert. He said that his parents annulled the marriage but that they had agreed that they would get to know me and perhaps it would all work out and we could have a proper marriage. I got my hopes back but my father called the solicitor and was told that it definitely was not going to happen. The money that was given to them was to close the deal. It was final. All hope was gone. I loved Robert and was married to him for only one night and now he was gone.

"Poor mom! What a jerk Robert MacLean was. How could he love her so much to want to marry her and then not stand up for his decision? He must have known she would be heartbroken," she said to herself. Then she remembered how hurt she was because her mother had not told her about the marriage. *She probably didn't even think of it as a marriage. After all, it was only one night,* she thought. "I should be ashamed of myself for the way I felt," she said aloud. "I was so busy thinking of my own self and here my poor dear mother had been hurt in a terrible way." She was glad she hadn't shared the marriage with anyone and especially not the way she felt about it. She went on reading.

The media did run wild with the story. "The Son of a Wealthy Highland Landowner Marries a Nobody," one headline read. "The Powerful MacLean Family's Son Marries an Unknown Glasgow Girl," another read. Both went on to say that of course the MacLeans had this foolish wedding annulled. My mom and dad spent the next couple of days discussing what would be the best thing for me. Mother asked if I would like to go visit my sister Moira for several months since they had the money from the MacLeans. I had always wanted to go visit

Moira in San Francisco but we couldn't afford it. Mom contacted Moira and she and her husband Mark were delighted that I could come and spend time with them. It didn't take too long to get my passport and tickets and off I was to San Francisco. I was a little nervous about flying over the Atlantic, but excited at the same time.

Our Port of Entry was New York. Because of a delay in Scotland, we arrived in New York after dark and had to stay over at a hotel that the airlines arranged for us. The most beautiful sight I had ever seen was flying over New York City at night. There must have been a billion lights down below. They call Paris the City of Lights but I can't imagine it could have been more lit up than New York City that night. The next morning we took the hotel shuttle to the airport. The city was bustling with people, yellow taxicabs and horns honking. It was a city that was alive with excitement.

My sister was waiting at the airport in San Francisco. It had only been a little more than a year since I had seen her but it felt like a lot longer when she put her arms around me. In the car, on the way to her home, she told me that she was so sorry about what happened to me. She started to be critical of Robert but I told her not to be, because I was sure his parents had tricked him. I believe they told him that they would arrange to have me up there and we could all get together and have that proper marriage. I told her that probably even now he still thinks that it will all work out. Two weeks after I arrived in San Francisco, I got a letter from my mom. She told me that Robert had come down to talk to me. He was terribly disappointed that I had left for the States. She said he apologized profusely for what his family had done, but mom never told him about the money. He told mom that he really did love me and wanted me for his wife. I was ecstatic. I still didn't think the MacLeans would have any of it but to know that Robert still loved me and really had nothing to do with his parent's scheme made me feel so much better. The letter was a great birthday gift. I had just turned eighteen.

Mark had a partner, Jim Stevens. They had a fledgling real estate brokerage. Both men were brokers. Besides Mark and Jim there were four agents and a receptionist. They were doing quite well and the agents that they had were top sales people who knew San Francisco like the back of their hands. Jim would come over and we would play board games or sometimes we would all go out to dinner. I liked Jim. He was a nice looking man of twenty-four with a very nice personality. He wasn't as handsome as Robert, but he was fun to be with. I still kept thinking what would happen with Robert and me when I got back home.

After I had been with my sister almost two months, I started to feel a little ill. I had been worried because I hadn't menstruated in over a month but I thought it was because of all the stress and the travel. My sister took me to the doctor who informed us both that I was pregnant.

"What?" Janet yelled out. "What happened to the baby? Was it taken away from you? Did you have an abortion? Was it still-born? I can't read this anymore," she said slamming the book shut. She couldn't go on any longer. She was getting all caught up with the emotion of what her poor mother had gone through. It was as though she was reliving her mom's tragedy. First her husband of one night is pulled away from her and now she's in a foreign country pregnant with his child. She decided to take a walk. She had gotten over the marriage thing. Her mother was, after all, only seventeen almost a baby herself but now the pregnancy. She walked for a while just trying to take in the scenery, which always inspired her but once again, nature was unable to capture her attention. She got to the same picnic table she had sat at when she found out about her mom's first marriage. *If this baby is alive and living with someone else, I will find it. After all, this baby is my half-brother or half-sister,* she thought. She sat for a little while and decided to go back.

It was getting close to dinnertime. Maybe she would call Margaret and see if she wanted to eat out. She accepted.

"I really appreciated you taking me to the Botanical Gardens the other week. It was a beautiful experience. I'm going to become a member."

"I'm glad. That way you can go as often as you like," Margaret said. "In fact, I got some really fantastic photos when we were there. I want you to see them."

"I'd love to," Janet said then her expression changed. "Margaret, you know I've been reading my mom's journal?"

"Is there something bothering you?" Margaret asked.

"Well first I found out that she married secretly as a teenager, which upset me so much because I thought my mom and I were so close that she would never keep such an important part of her life from me. Then I found out that she was only married one night and his family annulled the marriage."

"Oh how awful. Your poor mother. Then what happened?"

"She flew to San Francisco to spend some time with her older sister. She was there only two months when she felt ill. Her sister took her to the doctor only to find out she was pregnant. One night and she got pregnant."

"What happened to the baby?" Margaret asked.

"That's what I want to know."

"Well you're the one reading the journal. Didn't she explain?"

"I couldn't read on. I slammed the book shut. I can't stand the thought that she may have aborted it or gave it away. The marriage was hard enough for me to take but the baby thing," she hesitated then said, "I'll have to wait until I feel I'm ready to find out. If she gave it away, then I have another brother or sister somewhere and I have to decide if I am going to try and find him or her," she said flustered.

"Take your time, Janet. I can tell you're really getting emotionally involved. Give yourself time," Margaret suggested.

"I will. I need to pour myself into my work. I'm a little behind."

Janet did exactly what she said she would do. She worked hard and got caught up with her orders. She went to the Botanical Gardens a few times, when she felt upset about her mother's young life, to get inspiration. She was glad she told Margaret about the marriage and the baby. She needed to talk with someone and Margaret had a good head on her shoulders. There was something very mature about her. Janet felt she could share anything with her and it would stay with her. She was not ready to share with her family yet. She thought of her Aunt Moira and Aunt Betty and how they too had kept this secret. She wondered if her cousin Alice knew. *I don't like finding skeletons in the closet. Our family has always been so normal. Now all of a sudden there are secrets,* the thoughts plagued her. Finally she made up her mind to finish reading the journal then make decisions as to what to do with the information. She had to find out if she had a brother or sister out there that may not know anything of his or her real family, before deciding what to do about it.

> Obviously my sister had contacted my mother and informed her of my pregnancy, the journal went on, which of course worried my mom. My mom and dad had thought it out and decided I should stay in San Francisco until the baby was born then come home and they would figure out some story. Jim Stevens, who had become very fond of me, asked me to marry him and he would take responsibility for the child. I liked Jim and thought it would be the best thing for the baby and me. I married Jim and have had a wonderful life with him. He was successful and was able to provide amply for my family and me and we were all very happy. The baby was born about six and a half months later. It was a little girl and we named her Janet.

Janet Stevens closed the book and sat in her chair in shock then she started to sob. She didn't know how long she sat there crying but the phone had rung a couple of different times but she couldn't get up to answer. She couldn't talk to anyone right now. Her thoughts were on her dad or who she thought was her dad. *He had been so wonderful to me. How lucky mom had been and me, too, to have him come in and rescue us. I couldn't have asked for a better upbringing.* She thought of her childhood with Jim as her dad. He was always so tender with her. He would read her stories until she was able to read herself; he would play board games with her and her siblings; he would carefully explain things that she didn't understand and was so patient when he was helping with her homework, always explaining how he came to the conclusion of a math problem so that she would be able to solve the others that came after. He was just the most patient, kind dad a child could possibly want. But he wasn't hers. At least not biologically. That caused her mind to think on the father who was really hers. *I wonder if he is still alive and if he is, is he married and have children.*

Margaret picked up the phone, "Hello!"

"Hello Margaret..."

"Janet, I called you three times. I thought you were staying home today. Is everything okay? You sound like you have a cold."

"No, I've been crying. I found out about the baby."

"What happened to it? Did your mom give it away?"

"No, she kept it and raised it."

Margaret was quiet for a moment then said, "Oh honey, the baby was you wasn't it?"

"Yes!"

"Janet, do you want me to come over? It's only eight o'clock. We can chat over a cup of coffee."

"Yes Margaret. I'd appreciate that very much. You're the only one who knows about this and I feel like sharing my feelings, if you don't mind."

"No, honey my shoulder is available any time for you. I'll be there in a few minutes."

By the time Margaret arrived Janet had washed up and made a pot of coffee. Janet read to Margaret some of the parts in the journal that had upset her.

"I'm glad it all worked out for her, but what an unfair thing to happen," Margaret said. "What do you think you'll do with the information?" she asked.

"I'm going to drive up to Oregon next weekend for a couple of days and talk to my sister and brother. Then in the next month or so, I'm flying to Virginia to visit Aunt Moira and from there I'll fly to Glasgow to stay with my Aunt Betty and I'll probably try and contact Mr. Robert MacLean. Of course I'll confirm things with my aunts to make sure everything will be okay with them."

"Are you feeling alright? I mean you had been crying for a while. You seem to be more calm now than when I talked with you on the phone."

"After I cried for a while I read on and she concluded by talking to me in the present tense," Janet said. "She told me that she knew I would be the one to find this journal and she wished she could've had the conversation with me when she was alive but found it very difficult. She also told me that whatever decision I made she was behind me."

First of all, she read to Margaret, *you were born to Jim and Alice Stevens. You were our first child. Your dad was wonderful with you. By the time you were old enough to understand, your brother Tom was born. It just got more and more difficult. I never wanted you to feel that you were an outsider. Please forgive me, Janet; I didn't know how to tell you. Perhaps we will have this conversation one day and you won't have to read about it in this journal. I made a foolish mistake as a young girl and I didn't want you to suffer for it. I hope you can get over it and know that you were loved as much as, if not more than, your siblings. You were the first-born and Jim Stevens doted over you. Nobody could tell him you weren't his. I suppose I was in denial, pretending you were his biological child. We were such a happy family.*

"She gets more personal and wished me a happy, healthy life. It'll take a little while for me to feel normal, but I will. I did have wonderful parents and a wonderful childhood."

Chapter Four

Charlestown, a Small Village in the highlands of Scotland

Catherine MacLean had invited her friend Stewart Grant out for a day of fishing on the River Spey, one of the country's premiere salmon fishing rivers. Her friend Joan MacDonald had begged Catherine to invite her along as well as Stewart's older brother Jonathan. Joan had a secret wish to be Jonathan's wife and lady of Highland Mist Estate. Catherine was not aware of this. She invited Jonathan along and he agreed. He didn't know that Joan was also going to be there. If he had known, he might have opted for another time without Joan, but he had already accepted and had no excuse not to go. For some reason he felt uncomfortable around Joan Mac-Donald. She seemed to like everything that he liked but when he questioned her on a few things, like about American football, she floundered for answers, and then admitted she didn't know a lot about it but she enjoyed watching it. Catherine hooked her boat up to Stewart's jeep. Jonathan had said that he would drive his own car as he had a stop to make. He didn't have to make the stop, but not wanting to lie and not wanting to travel with Joan, he decided to make it.

Although Catherine's grandma was constantly trying to push her and Jonathan together, Jonathan could see the relationship between his younger brother and Catherine was developing from good friends in their childhood to special friends in their teens and now in their mid twenties, it was a special relationship. Catherine was a beautiful young woman. She had thick dark brown hair and hazel eyes that seemed to sparkle. She was about five feet eight inches tall and had a slim but shapely figure. There was something about her that was so tender and gentle but on the other hand she was sort of tomboyish. He had seen her eyes sparkle with anger one evening when her grandma invited Jonathan over to dinner and not Stewart. At the time Jonathan didn't know what was going on but Catherine had taken him outside and told him. From that time on, he refused her grandma's invitations unless his brother was invited also. He had told Mrs. MacLean that it made him feel bad that Stewart was excluded, "After all, he and Catherine are very good friends," he had said.

They met at the river and Joan came over to him and gave him a big hug. "Jonathan, it's lovely to see you. It's been a while. I'm looking forward to going fishing. I just love it," she gushed. *Yes, Joan, we'll see how much you love it,* he thought. Not very much as it turned out. She couldn't cast, which embarrassed her, so when Catherine did it for her and turned the rod back over to her, she just left the line out in the water most of the day. The rest of them had quite a good day pulling in salmon and trout. Joan kept bragging about the wonderful recipes she had made with salmon and trout. "We should do this more often," she said. Jonathan had to work at keeping back from laughing. Stewart looked at him and knew he was thinking the same thing and the two of them started giggling. "Share the joke with us," Joan said, which made them laugh even more. "It's just them being boys," Catherine said trying to cover for them because she knew what they were laughing at. As they passed Aviemore, a beautiful tourist and ski resort Joan asked, "Do you like to ski, Jonathan?"

"Yes, I do," he said then waited for the inevitable.

"I do too," Joan said.

Catherine swung around and looked at her knowing she had lied. "I go skiing at Aviemore every winter, Joan, and you've never come with me." Joan gave her an angry look and Catherine realized that she had called Joan's bluff.

"Well you always go with Stewart. I'd feel like a third wheel." Again Jonathan wanted to laugh but this time he held back.

"Thanks for inviting me along, Catherine. It was great! I can't wait to take this fish home for mom to cook up," said Jonathan. "She really knows what to do with fish." He wished he wouldn't have said that because it seemed that after Joan bragged about her recipes with fish, he was saying his mother could really show her up.

"She loves when we bring fresh fish home. In fact, why don't I call her and ask if she'd like to do that," Stewart said. Jonathan tried to get his brother's attention. He really didn't want Joan at their house. Stewart didn't catch his brother's pleading glance. He punched the numbers in his cell phone and called her. "Hey mom! We caught some salmon and trout. Do you want to cook them for dinner? We have Catherine and Joan with us."

"Of course, darling. I'd love to do that. When are you heading back?"

"By the time we get the boat out and hooked up, it will be close to five o'clock by the time we get home."

"Okay, sweetheart, I'll go pick some fresh vegetables. We'll see you all then."

"Oh, that was so wonderful, Mrs. Grant," Joan said. "There's nothing like fresh salmon caught right out of the river and cooked right away and the vegetables were delicious."

"I'm glad you all had such a successful catch. I put the rest in the freezer as soon as you gave them to me. Did you catch some, Catherine?"

"Oh yes, she was better than all of us. We stopped by her house and dropped them off," said Stewart proud of how well Catherine had done. He loved it that she had such a passion for fishing. That was why her father had bought her the boat. Joan wished that she could fish as good as Catherine. It was obvious that these Grant boys were proud of her. She would have to learn to fish and to ski. She had to work harder to impress Jonathan. Little did she know that Jonathan was totally on to her and had no interest in her, at least not as a love interest and definitely not as a wife. He knew her interest in him was definitely all about his title and money.

"I noticed how beautiful the gardens were. Your gardener does a wonderful job of taking care of them," Joan said complimenting Mrs. Grant once more.

"Actually mom takes care of the flowers herself," Jonathan said.

"Oh really! Could you take me outside to look at them, Jonathan?" she asked. Jonathan wished he had kept his mouth shut.

"Of course," was his polite reply.

Catherine was rather surprised by Joan's request. She did a quick turn of her head toward Joan and then to Stewart. She could swear Joan was coming on to Jonathan. When she mentioned it to Stewart later, he told her that Jonathan had a feeling that's exactly what Joan had been doing for quite some time. Catherine couldn't believe that she didn't see it before. Joan's brother, Kenneth MacDonald, had tried to get Catherine to like him. His interest was also the money. When his sister became friends with Catherine, he took it as an opportunity to try and win her over. As hard as he tried, she would have nothing to do with him. *She was always hanging around the Grant boy,* Kenneth had noticed, but he kept trying. Finally, after he had asked her out for the fifth time, she told him she liked being with Stewart and, at this point, he would be the only one she would go out with. Kenneth took it as a class thing and turned against her but he didn't show it for his sister's sake because he knew she was trying to impress Jonathan Grant. He would just be happy to have someone in the family come into money.

CHAPTER FIVE

Janet made the trip to Oregon and visited with Tom and Maggie. They naturally were astounded when she told them about her findings.

"I really don't feel so bad. I think I was just shocked at first and hurt because I would rather have heard it from mom's mouth."

"I can imagine," Maggie said. "I'm in shock right now. I'm having a hard time believing it. We were such a happy family."

"We still are," Tom chimed in. "You'll never be anything but our sister, Janet."

"I know that, Tom. Nothing will change the fact that we grew up in a normal, happy home and I will never wish it were any different than what it was."

She told them that she planned to go see Aunt Moira in Charlottesville and then travel to Glasgow to see Aunt Betty. She also told them that she might even try and see Robert MacLean. "I loved daddy, but I would like to find out more about who I am."

"I totally understand, Janet," Tom said. "I'd do the exact same thing."

"You know what I just realized?" she said.

"What?" Maggie asked.

"My background is one hundred percent Scottish. That's kind of unique in this country, unless you are an immigrant."

She only stayed the weekend but felt better about everything after spending the time talking it over with Tom and Maggie. She told Maggie that she wanted to take the journal with her to Scot-

66

land but she would let her have it when she got back. She asked them both not to mention anything to Ian, as she wanted to tell him herself at a later time.

Aunt Moira was looking forward to seeing her niece. Other than the short time at the funeral, the last time she had seen Janet was when she flew out to California to attend her graduation from college. *That would be about ten years ago,* Moira thought as she drove to the Charlottesville airport. She had been in Europe on a business trip with her husband when she got the news that Alice died. She got a flight out of London earlier than planned and flew straight to San Francisco leaving her husband in London to complete his business. By the time Moira had checked into the hotel in San Francisco, she had no time to go visit Janet and the next day was the funeral then the following day she had to fly back to Virginia. She and Janet had only a few brief moments together but she promised her niece that they would get together soon. Moira didn't realize it would be *this* soon.

The plane was due in half an hour. The traffic on Highway 29 had been worse than usual this day. There had been an accident at the intersection of 29 and Hydraulic Road due to a car trying to turn left onto 29 on a red light. By the time she pulled into the airport parking lot, the plane was landing. She knew it had to be Janet's flight because the airport was very small and only had one landing strip.

They hugged and looked one another over telling each other how good they looked. After picking up the luggage they drove back to Aunt Moira's home, which was an old farmhouse, built circa 1850 in the town of Ivy just outside of Charlottesville. Janet was fascinated with the home. It was a two story with a full basement. There was a large porch leading to the front door. The porch had a swing on it. She smiled, seems very Southern. After showing Janet to her room, Aunt Moira gave her a tour of the house. Five acres surrounded the home. Two acres were woods with mostly hardwood trees, some dogwoods and some pine. The woods practically surrounded the house giving it privacy. The other three acres had a meticulously manicured lawn which flowed from the front of the house to the back of the house, surrounded by beautiful flowering trees and bushes, although not flowering at this time, like Dogwoods, American Rosebud, Boxwood, Rhododendrons, Azaleas and many more. In the back of the house was a very welcoming swimming pool, especially on this warm day, even though it was only the middle of June. The humidity was higher than Janet was used to. She enjoyed walking around the garden looking at the landscape and trying to get ideas for her own place.

"Did you have this landscaped or was it like this when you bought the house?" she asked.

"No, this was my project. I love landscaping. It took me a while. I researched native plants to the area which many of these are. I will show you some pictures that I took while the plants were in bloom."

"You did a fantastic job. I would like to do something with my place."

"I'd love to go out and visit your new home, Janet. The way you described it in your letter sounds like a place I would be interested in seeing."

"When I get back from Scotland and get caught up with my work, we can talk about it. I would love to have you visit me."

"Great! Wow," she said looking at the clock on the kitchen wall. "Uncle Mark will be coming home soon so I'm going to get dinner started."

"I'll go upstairs and clean up a bit then I'll come down and help you," Janet volunteered.

After putting her clothes in the closet and drawers, Janet washed up and went downstairs to help her aunt. Aunt Moira gave her some potatoes to peel while she prepared the chicken. They were having a casual conversation about her aunt's own grown up and gone children when Janet suddenly changed the subject. "Aunt Moira, my mom left a journal."

"Oh!" She was hoping her sister hadn't talked about why she left Scotland. "What did she write about? Raising three rowdy kids," she said grinning and trying to keep the conversation casual. Janet was having a hard time bringing this up to her so she blurted out, "No, she talked about Robert MacLean." Aunt Moira was silent for a few moments then she said, "He was a young man she knew in Scotland. I remember his name coming up."

"He was the young man she married in Scotland." Aunt Moira

turned and looked at Janet, her eyes wide with shock. She didn't feel very good that her sister had left this information for Janet to find. *After all, if Alice wanted to keep Janet's birth a secret,* Moira thought, *that was up to her but I didn't expect to be the one confronted about it.*

"What did she say about him, Janet?"

"That he is my real father," Janet answered showing some emotion.

"I'm sorry, honey. I told your mom she should tell you but she was afraid that somehow it would hurt you emotionally or you would feel that you were not a part of the family," Moira said looking straight into Janet's eyes. "Shortly after you were born, about four or five years, Uncle Mark and I moved out here. I told her maybe there was some professional that could help her as to when and how to tell you." She was silent once more. "How are you feeling about it now?"

"I still have a hard time with it. It was a total shock. I mean you grow up with a dad that turns out not to be your own."

"What are you going to do about it?"

"I'm thinking of trying to contact him, if he is still alive."

"He's still alive."

"How do you know that?" Janet asked.

"Your aunt Betty told me. I talk to her weekly on the phone. She called me and said she had seen him in the newspaper signing some business deal. I would contact him if I were you. After all, he is your blood."

"Thanks aunt Moira. I was hoping you would say that. It is a family matter and I don't want to offend anyone. My siblings also agreed that I should contact him. I just wanted to get the okay from you and Aunt Betty. I will talk to her when I get there so I would appreciate if you wouldn't say anything to her on your next phone conversation."

"I promise, honey. I'm just sorry you had to find out the way you did, but I'm glad that it's all out in the open. No more secrets, I promise," she said putting her arms around her.

Janet stayed with her aunt for a week. They spent two days in Washington, D.C. and visited the White House, the Library of Congress, the Supreme Court and all the other important buildings including some of the Smithsonian buildings. Tour busses left from Arlington Cemetery and traveled through the city allowing tourists to get off and on wherever they wanted, as long as they had a pass. There was so much to see, it would take more than two days to cover such a small city. They visited Appomattox Courthouse National Historic Park where General Robert E. Lee, commander of the Northern Virginian army, surrendered his men at the McLean home, to General Ulysses S. Grant on April 9, 1865. She also visited the homes of Presidents Jefferson, Madison and Monroe, which are all close to Charlottesville. She wanted to see the Hollywood Cemetery in Richmond where Confederate President Jefferson Davis was buried and also President James Madison and President John Tyler, but there was not enough time. "Eighteen thousand confederate dead are also buried there," Aunt Moira shared with her.

"Why is it called Hollywood Cemetery? It sure is a far cry from Hollywood on the West Coast," Janet inquired curiously.

"It was given the name because of the holly bushes that grow in the ground there."

"You know, Aunt Moira, I don't know why, but I have a mild obsession with graveyards. Isn't that a bit creepy?"

"No dear. I'm the same way. I think it's an interest in history. Even of regular cemeteries. The people buried there are part of our history. They walked this earth, some of them hundreds of years before us and some day we'll be history."

"I suppose you're right. Well there is so much more for me to see and learn here. I'll have to plan on coming back soon. This area fascinates me."

"I'd love to have you come back, Janet. Besides the Hollywood Cemetery, perhaps we could put Washington's Mount Vernon on the list of things to see and of course Historic Williamsburg."

CHAPTER SIX

It was a chilly morning when Janet arrived at the Glasgow Airport. She was looking forward to seeing Aunt Betty. She had only been in Scotland one time when she was a toddler and Tom was a baby, and would only be able to recognize her aunt from recent photographs that she sent Janet. She looked quite a bit like her mother so she knew she would spot her immediately. It took a while to get her luggage and go through customs. Finally she got out to where the welcoming committees were waiting for their loved ones. Aunt Betty was in front of the crowd. Her aunt was especially anxious to see her since she was the daughter of her dear sister who had just recently passed away.

"Janet, I'm so glad you were able to come. I'm sorry I couldn't get away for your mom's funeral," she said hugging Janet. "It happened so fast."

"I know, Aunt Betty. It shocked us all. I didn't even know that mom was having any heart problems."

"Daddy had heart problems. In fact, he died of a heart attack also," her aunt informed her.

On the car ride home they caught one another up on what was going on in their lives. Aunt Betty told Janet that the reason cousin Alice wasn't with her was because she was ready to have a baby any day. Janet told her aunt about her new home and all about the area where she had moved to. When they got to her aunt's home Alice was there waiting for them with tea and sandwiches. She was so big Janet thought she might be having twins. Alice was two years younger than Janet and had been married two years.

"Janet, it's so good to meet you," said Alice hugging her cousin. "I was just a baby when you were here with your mom."

"I barely remember the visit. I was about four years old and Tom had just learned to walk. I don't know why mom and I didn't come back later, especially after my dad died."

"About five years after your mom and dad got married, Moira and Mark moved from California to Virginia and your dad struggled for a little while trying to build the business back up, but he made it," Betty told her. "He thought it would be good for her to go back home and leave him to get everything straightened out. A little more than a year after that Maggie was born and two years after that she had Ian. Four small children can take up a lot of time and money."

"And when dad died I was working hard to get clientele for my pottery business. I can appreciate what dad did in getting his business going. It's very hard in the beginning."

"How's your business doing now, Janet?" Alice asked.

"It's doing real well. I have several upper class clients that buy for themselves and for gifts. I was just telling your mom in the car that I moved a couple of hundred miles north to near Mendocino and I have an area on my property where I was able to set up a shop, I'm only a short while away from the coast. It's a beautiful area." After a couple of hours of chatting over tea, Alice's husband, George, came to pick her up. After introductions and some conversation, they went home leaving Janet and her aunt alone. Janet knew this wasn't the time to talk about the journal. She was too tired after her journey and she knew she would have lots of time alone with Aunt Betty.

The next day they decided to rest as they had plans to drive up to Oban and spend a few days there. They did a little shopping in downtown Glasgow. As they were walking around Frasers Department store, Janet couldn't help taking in the magnificent interior of the place. "I have never been in a store quite so elegant as this. Just look at this grand staircase and the balconies."

"Oh yes! Frasers is a Glasgow institution. It's almost sixty-five years old," replied Aunt Betty. They spent quite a long time in the store. Janet took everything in from the leading European designer clothes to the local products such as tweeds, tartans, glass and ceramics. Before leaving the shop Janet made sure she got pictures of the staircase that rose up to other floors and balconies.

They had lunch in one of Aunt Betty's favorite restaurants. Janet enjoyed her lunch of wild Scottish salmon, which sat on a bed of spinach with a wonderful vinaigrette and little Ayrshire potatoes, creamed and mashed with fresh herbs. Her aunt opted for a very tender Black Angus steak. They had taken the bus to avoid trying to find a parking place. Janet was feeling a little fatigued, as she had not caught up with the time change, so they decided to go back home. After putting the shopping away Betty put on some tea and they sat down and relaxed.

"I'm looking forward to going to Oban tomorrow," Janet remarked.

"It's a wonderful place. It's referred to as the Gateway to the Western Isles. Beyond Oban lie the Inner Hebrides and the Outer Hebrides. We will take the ferry and go to as many of the islands that we can. I just hope the weather will be perfectly clear," Aunt Betty said. Then laughing she added, "My mother used to say that you can get the four seasons in one day in Scotland."

"My mom must have gotten that from her. She used to tell me the same thing about her home country," Janet said then asked, "will we see the Isle of Skye? My mom used to tell me how much she loved it there. She said she had only been there once."

"Yes I remember that," Aunt Betty said reminiscing with a smile. "We had a wonderful time," then as though coming back to the present she said, "of course we can go there. I had already thought of it."

"My mom used to sing 'Over the Sea to Skye' to me when I was little. I've always thought that I'd love to see the place."

"You'll be impressed. Especially with those wonderful memories," Aunt Betty said pouring them another cup of tea. Once she sat back down, Janet thought it a good time to tell her about the journal.

"Aunt Betty, mom kept a journal. I never knew she did until I cleaned out her house after she died."

"She never mentioned to me that she was keeping a journal. What was she writing about?"

Janet hesitated for a moment. She was trying to figure out how to tell her without jumping straight to the punch but she couldn't find a way. "She talked about being married to someone other than my dad," she blurted out. Her aunt just sat looking at her with a somewhat blank look. She had never thought that she was going to be the one to tell her niece the heartbreaking story of her mother's first love.

"I also found out that he is my real father."

"Both Moira and I asked her to tell you. Did you talk to Aunt Moira about the journal?"

"Yes. My mom actually told me about him in the journal. I believe she left it for me to find."

"Besides coming to visit with Alice and me, do you have another purpose for visiting Scotland, Janet?"

"From what I read in the journal they both loved one another very much and he was as devastated about the breakup as mom was. I want him to know that they had a child together," Janet said watching her aunt for signs of encouragement or not.

"Have you given it a lot of thought, Janet?"

"Yes I have. Aunt Moira said that you told her he's still alive."

"He's still alive. I saw an article about him in the paper. He was in Glasgow signing some deal a couple of weeks ago."

"That's what Aunt Moira said. Do you think I shouldn't do it, Aunt Betty?"

"I think you should do what is right for you. What did my sister say?"

"She thinks I should do it. At least try and meet with him and see how things go."

"Okay, well I'm behind you too."

They got up early the next morning to drive up to Oban, which was about a three-hour drive. It was a nice clear day and Janet enjoyed watching the scenery. It seemed like such a short time before they were in the country and then up in the hills of the low highlands. They made a stop in Inveraray and visited the castle. It was the home of the Campbell Clan and the present Duke of Argyll was Torquhil Ian, who inherited the title on the death of his father in 2001. The guide told them that the architecture of the castle was Baroque, Palladian and Gothic. It had French influenced conical spires mounted on top of four towers at each of the four sides of the castle. Janet was trying to take notes but the tour guide told her there were plenty of brochures in the Castle Shop, if she were interested. The guide went on to tell them about the construction of the castle.

"Construction began with a design by Sir John Vanbrugh who died six years later. Roger Morris developed the design in 1746. He worked with William Adams, then the most distinguished architect in Scotland. Both Morris and Adams died in 1748 and it was Adams' sons Jon and Robert that saw the completion in 1789 for the 5th Duke of Argyll." It was so interesting to Janet to see portraits of people who lived so many centuries ago and to hear stories about them. After the tour of the castle they bought some sandwiches and cold drinks and sat on the banks of Loch Fyne and ate lunch. Somewhere in the distance a lone piper was playing "Over the Sea to Skye." Janet thought of her mother and her eyes started to mist. It was such a spiritual experience for Janet sitting on the grounds of this ancient country with so much violent history of a people fighting for their freedom. She thought of the Scottish heroes like William Wallace, Robert the Bruce, The Black Douglas and Bonnie Prince Charlie. It was the first time she had ever felt Scottish pride. She never thought much about her heritage before. The piper played on and pretty soon Janet found herself joining in. "Speed bonnie boat like a bird on the wing, onward the sailor's cry. Carry the lad that's born to be king, over the sea to Skye," she sang softly then turned and smiled to her aunt.

"It's such an old and beautiful country. I wonder why mom didn't come back and visit more often," Janet said looking out over the Loch.

"About ten miles south of here is the Crarae Forest Gardens," Betty said looking down the loch. "You would love to see them. They have a variety of rare flowers and sub tropical trees. They are breathtaking." Then turning her gaze on Janet she said, "She was afraid of running into Robert. He does spend a lot of time in Glasgow and she knows that he came to our parent's home asking about her."

"He must have really loved her."

"He did, Janet. It was such a tragedy. They both loved each other so much but his mother wouldn't have her son married to a commoner, so to speak. I mean she did, and probably still does, act as though she was royalty."

"I feel sad for mom. I mean she was happy with dad, but to be torn away from the man that you love and at such an early age, that's sad," Janet said with tears in her eyes. Betty reached over and gave her a hug.

"She did have a happy life with your dad, Janet. When she came back with you and Tom we had a long, long talk. Mostly it was your mom that did the talking. I felt so much better after our talk and I know she made the trip for that reason. I had been dealing with some depression. I was closer to your mom than I was to Moira. She was just a few years older than me. It hurt to see what happened to her and then of course I didn't have her with me. I was left here alone. Both of my sisters were overseas."

"That must have been hard for you, Aunt Betty." They sat quietly for a few moments. Betty looked like she was reflecting on the past.

"Do you think Robert would want to know about me?" Janet said breaking the silence.

"Yes, I do think he would want to know."

They continued on up to Oban. The scenery so inspired her that she would have her aunt stop occasionally so she could take pictures. She was thinking of how she could incorporate them into her pottery. They stopped at Loch Awe. Janet took her pictures then took some time to take it all in. "This Loch is appropriately named."

Oban was a lovely little fishing village. Janet made sure she got lots of pictures of the fishermen mending their boats and all the other activity around the wharf, including the ferries.

"They're taking people to the Islands. They're the Western Isles. Tomorrow we can take one to the Isle of Skye and we'll see how much time we have to see more," Betty said. They visited the Woolen Factory and the Glass Factory; after that they checked into their hotel and rested a little while. After dinner they attended a Ceilidh, which is entertainment with songs and storytelling of Scotland. "How do you pronounce the name?" Janet asked her aunt.

"Don't hold me to this, but I think it is like kaylay." By the time they got back to the hotel they were very tired and decided to go right to bed and get up early to catch the morning ferry. "I hope it's a very clear day tomorrow," Janet said as they both headed for their bed.

Her prayer was answered. It had been a little foggy early on in the morning, which put a little damper on their spirits, but by the time they got to the ferry the fog had lifted leaving a perfectly wonderful day for their trip. They had chosen a three-day-tour which included a trip to Skye. Janet had her aunt make the reservations, but she paid for the trip for both of them. When they reached the Isle of Skye, Janet once again felt a little emotional, thinking about her mother and the fact that she, Aunt Moira and Aunt Betty had spent a wonderful time in this beautiful place as children, long before Robert MacLean entered their lives. One of the places they visited there was Prince Charlie's Cave. It was a rough walk and in order to get right to it, the tide had to be low. They were in luck. This was the cave where Bonnie Prince Charlie was hidden in 1746 whilst on the run after the Battle of Culloden. Janet couldn't help thinking that was before America was a country. It was still under British rule at that time. They didn't get to go to the Isle of Mull where they had been told stood the Duart Castle, the home of the MacLean clan.

The day after they returned home, Janet started looking in the Internet to find out about Robert MacLean. She found out the name of the town in which he lived. It was Charlestown. She tried to get his phone number through the operator but it was unlisted. *Of course it would be. Someone with his notoriety and wealth would not make his personal information public,* she thought. "Maybe Aunt Betty could give me some information that might help," she said aloud to herself. She checked the clock. Aunt Betty had taken Alice for her checkup. She was due any day and had to go in often at this point to see the doctor. She was way too big to drive so her mom had been taking her. Her appointment was at ten o'clock. It was now almost noon. Janet had thought they would be back by now. *Maybe they did a little shopping.* Just as the thought left her mind, the phone rang.

"Janet, I'm up at the hospital. Alice went into labor just as we were leaving the doctor's office."

"Tell me what bus to take and where to get off and I'll come and join you." After writing down the information she grabbed her jacket and purse and headed on a new adventure; riding the bus in Glasgow all by herself. She got a seat near the driver and asked him to tell her when she got to her stop. After asking a few questions at the hospital, she quickly found her aunt.

"How's she doing?" she asked her

"She seems to be doing fine but I tell you watching my daughter go through labor," she said shaking her head and not finishing her sentence.

"I imagine it would be hard. You probably wish you could get up on that bed and have the baby for her," Janet said smiling at her aunt.

"Exactly what I'm thinking. George is in there with her." About six hours later George came out with a big smile on his face.

"It's a boy," he said still smiling.

"Congratulations George," his mother-in-law said giving him a big hug.

"Yes congratulations," Janet said, also hugging him. "What are you going to name him?"

"Alice likes the name Ethan Nathaniel. How do you think that sounds with the last name Dunbar?"

"I like it," Janet said. "It sounds like a strong name. Ethan Nathaniel Dunbar. I think it's the name of a great man." George laughed thinking of his tiny son.

"I agree with Janet. It is a beautiful strong name." Just then a nurse came to them and told them that the baby was being weighed and that they could watch through the window. She pointed them in the direction. Betty had a huge smile on her face and tears in her eyes. "Ethan Nathaniel, you're my first grandchild. Welcome to our world. One thing for sure, you will always be loved." Ethan Nathaniel was eight and a half pounds and twenty-one inches long. "Now, I want to go see how my daughter is feeling." Alice looked tired but happy. *Probably happy to have it all over with,* Janet thought. After giving Alice a hug and congratulating her, her mom gave her the baby's statistics and everyone told her how beautiful he was. A nurse brought the baby in and Grandma Betty took him in her arms and nobody dared to take him away from her. Once again Janet thought of her mother. She wished she could have lived to see her children.

Her mom of course had grandchildren by Maggie and Tom but Janet was sure she would have children some day too and her mom would never see them. Janet and her aunt left George and Alice to have some time alone with their new addition. Aunt Betty couldn't talk about anything but the baby on the drive back home so Janet thought she would wait until later to ask for help locating Robert.

"I don't know about you but I need a cup of tea," said Aunt Betty when they got home. "This has been a lot of excitement for me. First I was in pain watching my daughter in labor then I was elated when I saw my grandson. I feel I went through the whole birth myself."

"You probably did, Aunt Betty. He is a beautiful baby and I love the name they chose for him. My friend Margaret back home has the last name of Dunbar also. Thank you," she said as her aunt handed her tea.

"Is that right? I'll have to remember to tell Alice that. Let me see what I can find for us to eat. That sandwich this afternoon was not enough," she said looking in the refrigerator. "I have the left over fried chicken we picked up when we came home last night and the potato salad," she said looking at Janet to get her opinion.

"That sounds great to me."

"I think I'll wait until tomorrow to call Moira. I'm too tuckered out right now." It was nine o'clock in the evening and Betty had been out since around nine o'clock in the morning.

Janet decided not to bother her aunt with questions about Robert MacLean but Betty turned to her and asked, "What did you find out about Robert?"

"He's not listed in the phone book. I'm not sure where to go from here."

"You could take a train up to the town where he lives and try and find him. It's a small town, more like a village. If you stay at a bed and breakfast, you may be able to get information from the owner."

"I suppose you're right but in a small village it seems like it would be hard for me to keep a low profile. I mean I wouldn't want to tell anyone why I was there. Would I be the only American up there?"

"A lot of American tourists go up to the highlands. I wish I could go with you but I feel I need to be here for Alice."

"I wouldn't want you to leave her. It probably wouldn't take too long to travel up there. I better try and get a room. Do you have any suggestions?"

"I have a friend that has a cottage up near where he lives. It wouldn't be in the same village but close enough. Let me call her and see what she says." Betty suggested.

Janet was feeling like time was slipping away. She had already been in Scotland seven days and only had a little more than a week left. She decided she would see how things went and perhaps extend her stay. After taking her morning shower she sat at her laptop typing a script of things that she might say to him and looking at different scenarios. He may be happy to meet Alice Douglas' daughter or he may not. He may not even remember Alice Douglas. If he did, would he be happy to know she had a child by him. She was trying to cover every possible reaction he would have. She also wondered if *his* mother, the woman that broke *her* mother's heart, was still alive and how she, Janet, would react to her, if she were to meet her. Also, did Robert have other children? There was a lot going through her mind that she felt she had to write these things down. After some thought, she decided to leave the journal with him so that he could find out through Alice's own words. That would be less awkward. Aunt Betty knocked on the door and Janet invited her in. "My friend knows the owner of a bed and breakfast in the village where he lives. He actually lives outside the village in the country. My friend called the woman and apparently she can put you up."

"Thanks Aunt Betty, that's great. I appreciate your help."

"Well to tell you the truth, Janet, I'm feeling a wee bit excited about this. I can't wait to find out what the outcome will be."

"Me too but I am nervous. Did you call Aunt Moira to tell her about the baby?"

"No, last night I was too exhausted and right now it's five o'clock in the morning in Virginia."

"Of course! How dumb of me to forget that." Janet was feeling so excited and nervous about what she was about to do that she didn't consider the difference in time. She made a train reservation for the next day and would return four days later. She hoped that would be enough time to accomplish all that she wanted to. If not she would change the return ticket and let her friend Margaret back in Booneville know if she was going to prolong her trip. That way if Keith or anyone else needed to find out when she would be back home, they knew Margaret would have the information.

Chapter Seven

The train left Glasgow and went through places she remembered either from her mother, movies or news stories. As it went through Stirling, she remembered her mom telling her about the Stirling Castle and Statue of Sir William Wallace; as it went through Dunblane she remembered vividly on the television, the mothers running to the school, some pushing prams with babies in them, when they heard that someone had entered the school and shot and killed some of the children. *You wouldn't think something like that would happen in a small, lovely little town like this,* she thought sadly. The train continued through Perth, *Rob Roy MacGregor country,* she thought. She was so excited as the train moved further north to see Loch Ness. Everyone knew of Loch Ness because of the monster. The countryside mesmerized her as the train paralleled the Firth of Tay then rode up to Dundee. After leaving Dundee it paralleled the North Sea for a while then climbed on up the Grampian Mountains to Aberdeen.

She finally reached Elgin where she got off and got a taxi to Charlestown, the small village where the Highland Inn, the bed and breakfast place, was. Mrs. Graham, the owner, welcomed her. "Ye must be Janet," Mrs. Graham said when she opened the door. "Come on in lass. Let me take ye to yer room so ye can put yer clothes away and freshen up if ye need to."

"Thank you Mrs. Graham."

"Can I make ye a cup of tea?"

"No thank you. I think I'd like to take a little walk around town."

"Well there is Nellie's Tea Room where ye can get a wee cup if ye need it," Mrs. Graham informed her. When Janet came downstairs she gave her some information about the inn and the town. Janet wanted to ask her immediately if there were any big estates in or near the town but she decided that would not be a good thing to do. After walking around town and checking out some of the stores she decided to go into Nellie's Tea Room that Mrs. Graham recommended and savor some tea and little sandwiches. She had become quite used to her daily ritual of tea with her aunt Betty.

"Hello dear, can I get ye something?" a friendly, melodious voice asked. She looked up into the smiling face of an elderly woman. She was probably in her late sixties and had white curly hair and blue, blue eyes and a very friendly smile. Janet knew right away that this was Nellie and she liked her. "I'm not sure. I've never been in a tearoom before," Janet said almost in a whisper so that the other clients wouldn't hear her.

"Yer an American," Nellie said in a quiet voice also. "Is it the first time ye've been up in the highlands?"

"Yes. It's very beautiful up here. My mother was from Scotland."

"Frae the highlands?"

"No, she was from Glasgow," Janet said wondering if this highland woman would look down her nose at the fact her mother was from the city. Instead she handed Janet a menu and said, "Well, my name is Nellie. Most of the sandwiches are light, like the cucumber and cream cheese sandwich, and we also have scones, shortbread and oatcakes and we have the soup of the day, which today is lentil. I'll get ye a cup of tea while yer deciding." A few minutes later Nellie came with a small pot of tea and a cup and saucer. "I think I'll have the cucumber and cream cheese sandwiches and an oatcake."

"Where abouts in America are ye from?" said Nellie bringing her food. The other clients had left so she didn't see the need to be quiet.

"California," Janet replied.

"Oh ye'll be feeling the cold here then," said Nellie giving a fake shiver.

"It isn't bad. We've had some really nice, warm days and a few cold, rainy days."

"Well, that's good and what brings ye up here then?" She asked but her attention was drawn to the door when the little bell rang. She turned towards and said, "Hello, Jonathan," she said in an excited, happy manner. "I haven't seen ye in a while."

"Hello Nellie, it's good to be back."

"Were ye away?"

"Didn't you know I was in America for two weeks?" Catching her attention, Janet turned around to look into the most handsome, strong face she had ever seen. She felt her mouth drop open and she gasped and when he smiled at her she felt her face get hot. He looked right at her when he smiled. It was such a genuine smile. She had never felt that way before about anyone. He literally took her breath away.

"No, I didn't know. I haven't seen any of yer family fer a while now. This young lady," then turning to Janet, Nellie asked, "what was yer name dear?"

"Janet," she said in a squeaky voice. "Janet," she attempted once more and this time it came out normal."

"Janet here is from California. Janet, this is Jonathan," then turning to Jonathan she asked, "where in America were ye?"

"I spent a week in Virginia and a week in North Carolina."

"I was in Virginia a couple of weeks ago," Janet offered. "My aunt lives in Charlottesville."

"That's where I was," he said in an unbelieving tone. He was attracted to this beautiful woman and took the opportunity to find out more about her. "May I join you in a cup of tea?"

"Of course," she said with her voice a little shaky. Her hands felt even shakier.

He sat down and they discussed what dates they were in Virginia and found out they were there at the same time for three of the days. "We may have passed one another on the street or at the Downtown Mall. I went there quite a few times."

I don't think so, Janet was thinking. *I would definitely have remembered.*

"I did a lot of touring. I found it fascinating. All the history and the end of the Civil War taking place in Appomattox Courthouse," she said

"I'm afraid I didn't do much touring. I was by myself."

"It's amazing. When you said you were in Virginia I thought maybe Alexandria or Arlington or even Richmond but not Charlottesville."

She couldn't believe how much she was sharing with this stranger. She told him about her Aunt Moira and Uncle Mark in Charlottesville.

"They live in an old Virginia-style farmhouse with the most beautiful yard and gardens."

From there she talked about her mother and how she was from Glasgow and that she still had an aunt and cousin in Glasgow. She talked about her whole family and the lovely house they eventually moved into in Redwood City. He was taking it all in and showing such a sincere interest, staring into her eyes the whole time. When she became aware of how much she was sharing, she apologized. "I'm sorry! I have been rattling on telling you all these things about my family and me, and you don't even know me. I don't usually do that." That made him feel good that he had caused her to do something that she normally didn't do. *Maybe she was attracted to me too,* he thought. This was the first woman that had ever really interested him and he hardly knew her.

"I feel like I know you a little bit," he said smiling at her. The door opened again and this time two young women came in. Jonathan nodded towards them. "Hello Catherine, Joan."

"Hey, Jonathan. It's good to see you," said Catherine. "How was your trip?"

"It was great! This is Janet, Janet this is Catherine." They exchanged greetings. "We just found out that we were both in the same town in Virginia at the same time."

"Did you see one another there?"

"No, we just found out."

"Oh that's right. That's what you said. Well, it's nice to meet you, Janet, and welcome home, Jonathan."

"It's nice to meet you too, Catherine," Janet returned.

Joan didn't say a word and instead walked over to a table and sat down. Janet wondered who they were but of course she wouldn't ask. *I suppose everyone knows one another in this small town.*

Joan didn't look very happy. "Who do you suppose she is?" she whispered to Catherine.

"Her name is Janet. I've never seen her before. She's very pretty."

"That's in the eye of the beholder," Joan said.

"Well I think the beholder at the table with her thinks so."

"Catherine, we can't let strangers come in and take our men."

"What are you talking about? Jonathan doesn't belong to anyone."

"You must know by now that I've got a thing for Jonathan? You're so blind sometimes, Catherine." Catherine thought back to the fishing trip and how Joan had lied about skiing at Aviemore, trying to impress him, and then at the Grant's house when she asked Jonathan to take her out and look at the gardens. She had been trying to get Jonathan's attention. Catherine was not impressed by her friend's behavior.

Jonathan talked a little about himself. He told her that he bred pure Arab horses and had taken some to clients in Virginia and North Carolina. He had a younger brother, Stewart, who was twenty-six years old who actually did the breeding and care of the horses. Jonathan was more at the business end, Janet had found out, although he did help his brother out when the mares were foaling. "We actually have a mare now that is due any day, and we do hope it is day. Most mares foal during the night. Our vet, though, is willing to come out any time of the day or night for us."

"I never thought of Arab horses in Scotland."

"Oh sure! There's the Arab Horse Society that have shows. In fact I think the first show was in the mid sixties. We have quite a large membership."

Jonathan had a most likeable personality. It was positive, strong and yet sensitive. Janet had never felt so attracted to another person before. *What a pity we live on different sides of the world,* she thought. *I would want to pursue this relationship.* She noticed that Catherine's friend Joan was staring at them with a rather nasty look on her face. *Probably jealous of me because I'm sitting with Jonathan,* she thought. Another thought came to her. *He must be rich if he raises Arabian horses.* Then another thought which disturbed her terribly, *Please, Lord, don't let him be my half-brother. Don't let his last name be MacLean.*

"Can I get either one of ye something else?" Nellie asked.

"No, thank you," Janet said.

"Not for me, Nellie. Thanks. You can give me the bill," Jonathan said. Nellie gave him the bill. "I'll take mine too, Nellie."

"I'll take care of it," Jonathan offered.

"It makes me feel a little uncomfortable since you don't really know me."

"Oh yes I do," he said reaching into his back pocket for his wallet. "Your mother was from Glasgow, you have an aunt and cousin who live in Glasgow, you have an aunt who lives in Virginia and you live in California," he said handing Nellie the bill and money. They stood up and when they did she realized how much taller he was than her. He was six feet two inches; he told her when she asked him. Eight inches taller than she was. When they were outside he offered her a ride. "I'm staying at the Highland Inn Bed and Breakfast which is walking distance from here."

"Well let me walk you there."

"Okay!"

"Can I take you sightseeing while you're here?" he asked hoping she would say yes. This girl interested him very much. He felt very comfortable with her and was very attracted to her.

"I'm up here on a personal mission and I'm not sure how much time I have but perhaps tomorrow we could do it. I appreciate you offering to do that." They arrived at the B & B in a short time. "Okay, Janet! I'll call for you at ten in the morning."

"Okay Jonathan. I'll be ready." For some reason he felt so familiar with her that he had the notion to lean over and kiss her but he controlled himself.

Mrs. Graham was anxious to talk with her new guest and find out some more about her. She was curious as to why this young American was here all by herself. Mrs. Graham and Nellie were good friends and loved to gossip. Being that they both provided services, they got to meet a lot of people. "I didn't expect ye tae be gone so long since there isnae that not much in the village tae see," she said inquiringly.

"I went into Nellie's Tearoom."

"Oh, so ye met Nellie. She's quite the character."

"She was very pleasant and she introduced me to a very nice man named Jonathan."

"Tall good looking young fella wae dark hair?"

"Yes. Do you know him?"

"Everyone knows the Grant brothers." Janet was glad to hear that his name was Grant and not MacLean.

"Single women from John O'Groats to the Borders would love the opportunity to meet these boys but mostly they would love to get their attention romantically, especially Joan MacDonald, she's a friend of Catherine MacLean."

At the name MacLean Janet blurted out, "Who is she?"

"Joan MacDonald?"

"No! Catherine MacLean".

"The MacLeans and the Grants are the two wealthiest families in these parts. Nora MacLean, Catherine's grandmother, would do anything to unite her granddaughter with Jonathan. I think she looks at the uniting of these two families as a merger of two big companies." *So Robert's mother is still alive,* thought Janet. *Interesting!*

"Does he seem interested in her?" Janet asked trying to get as much information as she could.

"Jonathan's a very nice person and would never show disdain for anyone but I don't think he is too interested in marrying her."

"Does Catherine have parents and what do they feel about uniting the two families?"

"Robert MacLean couldn't care less about all that. His mother has always kept control of the family even to whom they marry." *Yes, I certainly know that. I'm a product of her meddling.* "Robert's wife passed away shortly after their daughter was born. She is now twenty-five. She gave her mother a hard time during childbirth and the mother never got strong after it," Janet heard Mrs. Graham say when she tuned back in.

"Jonathan's taking me sight-seeing tomorrow," she said trying not to cause too much of a stir. It seems like she might have gotten herself into something here. Two strong families with Nora MacLean trying to unite them and then along comes the stranger Janet and someone from Nora's past.

"Be prepared for all eyes tae be on ye and for all the women tae be jealous," Mrs. Graham said jovially.

Janet was looking forward to being with Jonathan again, but she was also nervous about Nora MacLean finding out about her being with Jonathan. The woman, who was trying to control the merge of Catherine and Jonathan, was the same woman that caused the breakup of her mother and Robert. It was a small village and everyone who was interested would probably find out about her. Janet stepped outside to wait for Jonathan. While standing there, a young man wearing sunglasses and a cap on his head walked passed her and said, with his head down, "Jonathan Grant is spoken fer. It'd be better fer ye if ye don't get involved." Janet thought it weird since she had just met Jonathan yesterday and only the few people that were in the tearoom saw them together. Janet was alone in a foreign place and didn't know what the social climate was in this part of the world. *Who was that person and why was he threatening me?* she wondered. Jonathan was punctual. Janet liked that in a person. It meant he was considerate of the other person's time and patience. Janet, likewise, was all ready to go.

They drove into Elgin, which according to the brochure Janet picked up, said it was "the administrative and commercial capital of Moray, has a long and fascinating history, still reflected today in the buildings and layout of the town, it grew up on a low ridge between the loops of the River Lossie, and by the thirteenth century, which it was created a Royal Burgh by Alexander II, was a thriving town with its castle atop Lady Hill to the west, and the great Cathedral to the east."

"Let's visit the Cathedral. It sounds so fascinating. I'll pay of course," she said excitedly. Jonathan looked at her and laughed then he realized that she probably doesn't know of his family and wealth. Actually, it had slipped Janet's mind. She felt silly when he laughed at her and her face actually flushed with color.

"That's very kind of you, Janet, but I want to treat you today. Will you please let me do that?" he said trying to make up for causing her to her feel bad. She turned and looked at him, then smiled, "That would be okay! I told Mrs. Graham I had met you and she told me about you and your family. I just forgot."

"That's refreshing. Not what I'm used to," he told her

"What do you mean?" she asked once again being naïve regarding wealth and titles.

"Usually it's all that's on women's minds when I'm with them."

"Jonathan, you're a very handsome and entertaining person. I'm sure the women you date enjoy being with you because you are fun to be with," she said sincerely. He leaned over and patted her hand and smiled at her. This woman was growing on him by leaps and bounds. She was so different from anyone he had dated. She was real and interesting. He hoped she could stay around longer than she had told him. He had to see her more than this one day. He would make sure to ask her for her personal information and definitely keep in touch with her.

They went into the Cathedral. The curator took them on a tour. "It was founded in 1224 as the seat of the Diocese of Moray. In 1390 the son of King Robert II quarreled with Bishop Alexander Bur, who excommunicated him. In revenge he burned the Cathedral. It was rebuilt and continued in use until reformation. On Easter Sunday 1711 the great central tower fell, and by the end of the eighteenth century the once-magnificent Cathedral was being used as a quarry for building stone. In 1825 restoration was assumed and is still going on. The building was made of sandstone. Richly decorated tombs and carved effigies remain in vaulted choir chapels. The octagonal Chapter House with traceried windows and magnificent vaulted ceiling makes this eight-sided spectacle at Elgin Cathedral unique in Scotland."

Jonathan smiled to himself when he watched Janet writing furiously trying to keep up with the curator. She hoped she had everything down right so when she shared with people back home she wouldn't sound dumb. She also had a passion for the history of other places. She would have to ask Jonathan what some of the things the curator said meant.

They walked around the old cobbled market place, which Jonathan told her was now known as the Plainstones and is linked to parallel streets by narrow wynds and pends. "What is a wynd and a pend?" she questioned him.

Again Jonathan laughed. He didn't mean to be laughing at her but once again he was refreshed with the fact that she wasn't afraid to let him know that she lacked knowledge in something. There were no airs about this lady. He put his hand on her shoulder. "I'm not laughing at you, Janet. I like that you question things and are not afraid to own up to ignorance. A wynd is a narrow street, like an alley, and a pend is a covered carriageway." He squeezed her shoulder and she felt good. She really felt that he not only liked her but also in some way was impressed by her.

"Well since I'm showing my ignorance of the language let me ask you some more questions. First, what is a chapter room?"

"It's like a meeting room. A place where a chapter meets to transact business."

"Effigys?" she said looking at her notes.

"They are representations of a person, like a sculpture for example," he said smiling at her as she read her notes. She was writing his answers next to the words in her tablet. "One more! What are traceried windows?" she said with her face lifted and a smug little look on it. She was sure he wouldn't know this one.

"They are windows decorated with architectural ornamental work," he said and then without thinking he bent over and gave her a peck on the cheek. He found her just too adorable to resist. She sat up surprised.

"I'm sorry, Janet. I didn't mean to be so fresh."

"It's okay, Jonathan. It was only a friendly little peck. It just took me by surprise."

"Me too!" then after a moments hesitation he said, "Janet, can't you stay a little while longer? I really like being with you."

Janet couldn't believe what she was hearing. She didn't want to move too fast and seem too needy. After all, this man was from an aristocratic family, was gorgeous and could get any woman he wanted. "I like being with you too, but I did tell you I was up here on a mission and I do have to get it done and get back home to my work."

"I don't even like to hear you talk about going back home. I wish I could keep you here."

"Jonathan, I know you can have any woman you want. Why would you want me? I come from a middle-class American family. You're from a wealthy Scottish family with notoriety. You belong with one of the women from a like family, like Catherine MacLean."

When she said that his green eyes narrowed and he stared at her curiously for a while then asked, "Who told you about Catherine and what was said?"

"Mrs. Graham mentioned her just in passing. She said her grandmother would love to pair you and her off."

Running his fingers through his dark brown hair he looked at her again. "Janet, I don't love Catherine and she doesn't love me. Her grandmother kept putting me in awkward positions, like always inviting me to dinner or something else. As a matter of fact, she and my brother Stewart are very close friends." He looked down at his feet. Nora MacLean made him feel frustrated because he didn't want to be pushed into a marriage because they were of equal wealth and position. He wanted a woman that was equal in passion for life and he was feeling that Janet was just that kind of person. He wanted an opportunity to spend more time with her to find out if they were compatible. He did not want to let this opportunity pass.

"Janet, the only women I meet are from wealthy families and they have been groomed and educated to be a certain way. I want a woman who enjoys life and is free to be who she really is. I want someone with character that has a passion for what she likes to do. I would love the opportunity to know you better, because you're the first woman that has come close to her. I thought I would never meet her. You have the personality of an artist and I love it."

"Jonathan, I came to Scotland to follow through with some serious information that I found out about. I love being with you but I can't have my heart getting confused at this time."

"Maybe, I could be of help to you. We can set aside our emotions for now and work on your situation. Would you let me do that? You're not familiar with the people, I am."

"It's a very sensitive subject and involves a very big person up here. I do need your help and your discretion."

"You have it. Let's go to dinner and we can talk about it." He carefully picked a restaurant with some privacy.

When they went inside the man at the reservation desk looked up and broke into a big smile, "Good evening Mr. Grant. Dinner for two?" he said giving Janet a curious look.

"Yes, Michael, and a table in a quiet location, please." Janet was quite impressed. This was the first time she had ever been with anyone who was treated with such respect. He wasn't even questioned about a reservation, which he didn't have.

Michael asked if she would like him to hang her jacket. "Yes, please," she said trying not to act too overwhelmed by the attention.

He led them to a table in a corner of the room. It was perfect. He handed them their menus and left. Looking hers over, she asked if he could recommend something.

"Seafood, fish and Angus steak are all wonderful. What do you prefer?"

"I think I would like to try the lobster. Is that a good choice?"

"Wonderful choice." They placed their order with the waiter and when he left Jonathan looked over at Janet and said, "Who is the big person we are talking about?"

Janet looked at him still nervous but knew she had to trust him. She didn't know how else she could get together with Robert. "Robert MacLean."

"How do you know him?"

"He was a friend of my mother's."

He didn't show any surprise but took a moment before asking the question. He leaned forward in his seat and said in a low voice, "Is your mother Alice Douglas?"

Janet couldn't believe her ears. She stared at him in disbelieve. It took a while for her to find her voice. "How did you know that?" she said almost demandingly.

He told her that his father was one of the young men who had gone down to Glasgow and went to the dance hall with Robert the night that he met Alice and that Robert had gone back often on his own just so he could be with her. "Robert confided in my dad that he was in love with her but knew that his mother would never allow him to marry her." He went on to share how Robert planned to elope with Alice and once they had consummated their marriage nothing would be done and they could go on to live "happily ever after. It didn't happen that way. . . ."

"I know," she interrupted. "I read all about it in a journal my mother kept and left for me to see after she died.

"I'm sorry. Robert will be too when he hears that your mother's dead. He has been widowed for many years and has often wondered if Alice was still married. He still had hopes of seeing her again. He really loved her."

"I'm glad to hear that. I don't think I can go on," she said apologetically.

"That's fine, Janet. I'll be here for you whenever you need my help. I can get you together with Robert."

"I would love that but without the knowledge of his mother and his daughter."

"I can do that, too. When do you want to meet?"

"Is tomorrow too soon?"

"I can try but it's a little late," he said looking at his watch. "I probably won't be able to talk to him until tomorrow and of course I don't know what his schedule is. I want to tell him face to face about you, not on the phone."

"I would expect that you would. It's a sensitive subject. I'm a bit nervous about meeting him."

"Robert's a very nice person. He'll make you feel comfortable."

"Okay." Then changing her thoughts she said, "While I was standing outside Mrs. Graham's waiting for you, a young man brushed past me and said that I was not to get involved with you because you had been spoken for then he went on his way."

"What did he look like?" said Jonathan concerned.

"He had on one of those caps with a visor which he had pulled down and he had sunglasses on and kept his head down. He was taller than me but not as tall as you. Maybe about five feet ten."

"I don't like that. Did he touch you at all?"

"He just slightly brushed against me."

"I'll keep my eye out for someone like that," he promised. "Of course he probably doesn't usually wear the cap or the sunglasses."

Jonathan rose early the next morning to call Robert. He knew Robert always got up early. "Hello," Robert said into the phone.

Jonathan was glad that he answered the phone and not his mother. She was quite nosy and always wanted to know what was going on. *I guess that's part of her controlling nature,* he thought.

"Robert, Jonathan here. I would like to talk to you about something that's very personal so I would like to come over and talk in private."

"Come right over, Jonathan. I have nothing important planned."

Robert opened the door to Jonathan just as Nora was coming downstairs. When she saw Jonathan a big smile came to her face. "Jonathan it's so nice to see you. Shall I call Catherine?"

"He's here to see me, Mother." Her smile faded and she looked at them both with curiosity. "We'll be in my office and we don't want to be disturbed."

Maybe he's here to ask for Catherine's hand in marriage, she thought hopefully. As soon as they were inside with the door closed, Robert offered him a seat. "Now, what is so personal and why did you come to me?" he asked then immediately said, "Your father's alright isn't he?"

"Yes, thank you. He is. The matter is not personal to me, but to you."

"What do you mean, Jonathan? The last time I checked my family, health and finances were okay, so what personal matter should I be concerned about?"

"It's nothing you have to be concerned about. I met an American girl yesterday..."

"Shouldn't you be talking to your own dad about this," Robert laughed. Jonathan smiled back at him and then his face became more serious. "She knew Alice Douglas."

Robert sat up even straighter in his chair. His big six feet four inch frame became quite rigid. "Alice is alright, isn't she?"

"I'm afraid not, Robert. She died early this year."

Feeling a rush of sadness coming over him Robert raised his eyebrows and opened his eyes wide to try and stop the tears that were threatening to flow out. He took a deep breath and asked, "How did she die? She was a young woman, even younger than me."

"She had a sudden heart attack and didn't recover."

Robert was silent for a moment rubbing his hands over his face. The thought of Alice brought so many memories back. "Who is the American girl that you met?" he said finally finding his voice.

"She's Alice Douglas' daughter, Janet. She knows about you and would like to meet you. She's nervous about meeting you because she's not sure that you would want the past brought up."

"Of course I will meet with her. It would be a pleasure to be caught up on how things went for Alice and maybe she can answer some questions that I have had all these years?"

"Great! She doesn't want your family to know about her at this time. Don't ask me why but that was her request."

"I can understand that. Can we meet at your cottage?"

"Yes. Let me call her from here and find out if she is ready." He dialed the Highland Inn and Mrs. Graham answered. After a few minutes Janet was on the phone.

"Are you ready for me to pick you up, Janet? Mr. MacLean can see you this morning." Jonathan hung up the phone. "She's ready, so give me half an hour to pick her up and take her to my cottage."

"Okay, I'll be at your cottage in approximately half an hour."

Janet had lain awake for a while. She was nervous about meeting Robert face to face, but what Jonathan said of his father's remembrance of Robert's love for Alice gave her a feeling of comfort. She woke up feeling fresh. She had slept well in spite of her nervousness the night before. After she showered and dressed she went out to the dining room. Mrs. Graham had told her that breakfast would be from eight o'clock to nine o'clock. There were ten other guests. Janet was the only one traveling alone. The dining room had one long table that seated twelve people comfortably. Four of the guests were already at the table. Janet took her place next to them.

"Hello I'm Moira," one young woman of about twenty-five said.

"And I'm Linda," her friend of about the same age said smiling. "We're from Glasgow."

"Hello," Janet smiled back "I'm Janet and I'm from California."

"Oh my, you have come a long way," Moira said. "What brings you all the way up here in the highlands?"

"I'm visiting an aunt in Glasgow and thought I would like to see some of the rest of Scotland," she said feeling a little guilty. *It's not really a lie, I do want to see this part of Scotland, after all, my father is from here,* she thought.

"We're saving up to go to Florida next year. Have you been in Florida?" asked Linda.

"No I haven't. Except for Virginia, most of my travels have been on the West Coast like California, Colorado, New Mexico, Oregon, Washington and Nevada."

"Linda and I like to travel. We had been going to Spain for the past couple of years, but there are too many Brits there." Janet laughed. She knew her cousin used to like to travel to Spain and she had said the same thing.

"Well you're not going to get away from them here?" Janet said smiling.

"But we expect to see them here. When you go to a foreign country you don't expect to see so many of them."

"Hello dear, we are Mr. and Mrs. Blake from London," said an attractive woman, probably in her fifties.

"We don't care for the European vacations either. Like the young lady said, too many Brits and too much clubbing and partying. We like the beauty and the peacefulness of the highlands," said Mr. Blake.

Mrs. Graham had served up a wonderful breakfast of Scots porridge oats, Belfast ham and eggs, and potato scones with orange juice and tea. It was such a wonderful experience sitting eating and chatting with these lovely people from different backgrounds. Janet was so used to dining alone. *I need to get out more often,* she thought. She went back to her room to wait for a call from Jonathan. It was already nine-thirty. She wished she could call Maggie and tell her about the fantastic man she had met, but it would only be one-thirty in the morning in Oregon. She had put on one of her new dresses that she had bought for this purpose. She wanted her father to be pleased with the way she looked. She went into the bathroom and made her face up ever so slightly; just enough to give it some color and a little glow. She was pleased with the way she looked and hoped he would be too. There was a knock at her door and she heard Mrs. Graham's voice announcing that she had a call. Janet opened the door immediately and almost ran the landlady over in her enthusiasm. Mrs. Graham knew it was Jonathan on the phone and was quite surprised at the excitement the call caused the young woman. Janet tried to calm herself down so as not to draw any more attention to herself. She picked up the phone and quietly said "hello" into it.

"Janet, are you ready for me to pick you up?"

"Yes I am," she said as quietly as she could and still loud enough for him to hear her.

"Good, I'll be right there."

She grabbed her cardigan, since her dress had no sleeves and went outside. It seemed like an hour before he arrived but it had only been fifteen minutes. When he got out of the car she felt the breath being sucked out of her. *How am I going to live in California without seeing this man? He's gorgeous,* she thought. She was trying to smile at him without looking stupid. He had on a black Arran cashmere sweater and designer blue jeans.

"Hello Janet. You look beautiful."

And so do you, she thought but instead said, "Thank you Jonathan. You look rather handsome yourself. Where are we going?"

"To my place," he said staring at her with a mischievous look awaiting her reaction.

"Am I to meet Robert?" she said with a curious look.

"Of course. I was just with him. He said it would be a pleasure to meet you. He said he has tons of questions for you."

"But why your place. Won't your family be there?"

"Only my brother and he'll be in the stables. One of our mares is getting ready to foal. My parents are out of town visiting my mother's family. I have a cottage on the estate and Robert will come there."

The beautiful wrought iron gate at the entrance to the driveway impressed Janet. He pushed a button in his car and it opened.

"Is that a traceried gate?" she said smiling and feeling a little smug that she remembered the windows at Elgin Cathedral.

He looked up at the ornamental work on the gate and turned and smiled back knowing that she was feeling proud of herself and said, "I suppose you could say that. Have you been studying your notes?"

"No, actually I just remembered." They drove down the tree-lined long driveway, "I have never seen a place so majestic," she said looking like Alice in Wonderland. The lawns were so green they looked like an artists painting and there were flowerbeds everywhere. The driveway curved past the house or rather the manor, which stood so strong and proud overlooking the magnificent lawns.

"It must have been wonderful for you growing up in such a beautiful home."

"It had its good points and its bad points."

"What ever could have been its bad points?" she asked not believing that there possibly could be any.

"When I was a boy, I loved to go out into nature. I loved to hike, fish and swim in the lakes, but everything had to be scheduled with someone looking after me."

"Was that because your family was so rich and they were afraid of something happening to you? I mean, I could certainly understand your parents concern."

"I can too, but it was a drawback. There were many times I would see other boys in a group fishing and jumping in the river and having so much fun. I wanted to join in their fun. Being a kid in a wealthy family can be boring at times. It depends on what kind of personality the kid has, I suppose."

"I suppose." She had been so busy talking she didn't realize that they had pulled up to the cottage. When they got out of the car, two wonderful very lively dogs greeted them. "Who are you?" Janet asked rubbing the bigger dog's neck.

"That is Tweed, he's a boy and this one is Skye, she's a girl."

"You can tell she's a girl. She's quite a bit smaller than the boy. What kind of dogs are they?"

"They're both Border Collies." They played with the dogs for a few minutes then went into the cottage. Janet was impressed with the thatched roof. The house was painted white. In her mind, it certainly looked like a cottage that belonged on a Scottish estate. It was a good size for a cottage. She surmised that it was about twenty-five-hundred-square-feet. The front door opened to a large bright living room that opened up to the kitchen. "This is what we would call a great room in the States. Not that we mean a great-looking room…"

"I know. My friend in Virginia has a great room in his house."

To one side of the living room was a large dining room with a table that could seat twelve people very comfortably. "Do you use the dining room?"

"Occasionally, especially when my friends come up from Edinburgh or Glasgow. Usually I have a group of them up to go fishing and we cook, or we get some take-out food. My mother is always willing, but I'm a big boy. I don't want my mother taking care of me." Off from the other side of the living room were double doors that led into the billiard room. "Do you play?" he asked.

"I do just okay, but yes, I do play. When we were teenagers my brothers used to take me to the bowling alleys that also had a pool room." Down the hall there was a half-bath for day guests to use. Then there was the master bedroom which also seemed to double as an office as it had a desk with a computer and phone. There were two guest bedrooms, each with two single beds and each with their own bath. "This is a beautiful house on its own."

"Thank you. I'm glad to live here instead of the big house. I have more privacy and it's cozier." She was so caught up with his house and the estate, she momentarily forgot about Robert. "When is he coming?" she asked.

Glancing out the window he said, "Right now. His car just pulled up." Janet's heart jumped in her throat and she accidentally grabbed Jonathan's arm. He turned in surprise. "Why are you so nervous? I told you he was looking forward to meeting you." Just then there was a rap on the door and Jonathan opened it.

"Hello Jonathan," Robert said giving the younger man a hug. He was a big man. *He must be about six feet four inches tall,* she thought. He looked over Jonathan's shoulder toward Janet. He stared for a moment then asked, "Is this the young lady that I am meeting with? Forgive me for staring dear, but you look so much like your mother, when I knew her as a young girl." He walked over to her and took her hand to his lips and kissed it. "It's such a pleasure to meet you, my dear."

"It's a pleasure for me too, Mr. MacLean," Janet said with a little bit of a shaky voice. *I may look like my mom, but my eyes are definitely yours,* she thought as she looked up into his hazel eyes. Robert MacLean was tall and very fit looking. He still had a head of thick black hair that was changing to gray. He was very sophisticated looking and charming. His hair was cut short and still had a sort of ruffled look. She remembered how her mom had written that she thought it gave him a boyish look.

He sat down on an armchair across from her. He looked at her for a few minutes. He felt like he was looking at Alice.

"Was your mother happy, Janet? Did she have a comfortable life? Did she... I'm sorry I should give you a chance to answer."

"She was happy. My dad gave her a comfortable life. She was able to stay home and raise all of her four children, which was very important to her and not too many women have that benefit. It was only after my dad died five-and-a-half years ago, that she went to work, and only because she was lonely."

"I wish, after her husband died, Alice and I could have met back up. How did her husband die?"

"He was killed by a drunk driver," she said.

"What a waste of a good life. It makes me feel very comforted that he gave her a good life. I worried about her." Janet took some pictures out of her purse and handed them to Robert.

"I chose some from different times in her life so you can see how she looked as she aged."

Robert took time to study each one. He had a soft smile on his face as he looked at them and at one point Janet could swear he had a tear in his eye.

"She was beautiful in each stage of her life," he said handing them back to her. "You're dad was a lucky man. He got to spend all that time with her."

"Thank you. Would you like to keep these?" she said offering back the pictures.

"I'd love to have them. Thank you." After a few moments of glancing through them again he looked at her. "How did you know about me? Did she tell you?"

Janet felt a little uncomfortable. She wasn't sure how she would bring up the journal. She looked a little awkwardly toward Jonathan.

"If you both don't mind, I'd like to go out and check on Stewart to see if he needs me for anything. Our mare is about to foal," Jonathan said.

"Go ahead, Jonathan. Take care of whatever you have to do. Janet and I will do just fine," said Robert.

Janet gave Jonathan a thankful smile and he smiled back and nodded that he understood. After he left, Robert turned to Janet with the question still on his face. "In a way she did," she answered him.

He continued to look at her but his left eyebrow rose. "What do you mean, Janet? Either she did or she didn't."

Janet went on to tell him that her mother had never really spoken about him, which brought a somewhat disappointed look to his face. "How did you know about me, then?"

"After my mom died I found a journal while cleaning out her house. I brought it with me." She walked over to a table and picked it up and handed it to him. "I would like you to borrow it and read it.

"Are you sure Alice would want me to read this?"

"I know my mom left it where I could find it and I believe she wanted me to do what I felt best with the information I found in it. She knew I would treat it with respect."

"I'm not sure how long it'll take me to read it. I mean if it's emotional, I may have to lay it down occasionally. But one thing you can be sure, I will treat it with great respect also."

"I want you to take your time with it. You can mail it back to me in California. I trust you with it," she said smiling at him. She regarded this man very highly. They talked for a long time about Alice and her life, but Janet did not mention anything about the pregnancy.

"Are you going back to Glasgow soon? I would like to see more of you."

"I was going to leave tomorrow to spend a few days with my Aunt Betty, but I've decided to stay up here a few more days."

"I'm glad. You are a reminder of a very happy time in my life. By the way, how is Betty?"

"She's well. I have to get back to California soon to my business. I have some orders I have to fill for my clients but a few more days shouldn't matter."

"What is your business, Janet," he said.

"I have a pottery business. I love throwing pots," she said laughing. Her laugh and smile reminded him of Alice. "Here is my business card."

"Hands and Nature. That's an interesting name."

"I throw the pots with my hands and most of the inspiration comes from nature."

"I see, well I appreciate this," he said holding up the card with her information on it, "and I appreciate you coming all the way here to meet me. Perhaps one day I can come and visit you in California and meet Alice's other children?"

"I'd love to have you come. I could take you to Redwood City and show you the house my parents owned and that we grew up in. My siblings would love to meet you. Alice raised some nice children."

"I can see that," he said smiling. She was surprised when he reached out and hugged her and said, "Once again, dear, thank you for coming and bringing me the news."

"We'll keep in touch, Mr. MacLean. I'm sure you'll have questions for me."

"We'll definitely keep in touch. I lost Alice. I'm not going to lose her little girl."

And yours also, she thought.

After her dad left, Jonathan came running in and grabbed the phone and dialed. "Jennie, this is Jonathan. Meg's in labor." Janet stared at him wondering who Meg was. Did he have a sister? All kind of thoughts was going through her head. She had forgotten that he had said their mare was about to foal. He grabbed her arm and went back outside. "Have you ever seen a horse give birth?"

"I've never seen anything give birth. I might faint."

He smiled at her and said, "It's the most wonderful experience watching a life begin."

They walked into the barn and Jonathan introduced her to Stewart. He was a very handsome young man very much like his brother except a little shorter. Stewart was a little curious. Jonathan hadn't talked to him of her. He wondered how his brother had met this American woman. Jonathan saw the curious look on his brother's face. "I'll talk to you later about how we met. Meanwhile, how is Meg doing?"

"She seems to be doing well. There doesn't seem to be any complications."

"Gee, this stall is impeccably clean" Janet said looking around.

"Jonathan and I spent a lot of time scrubbing it down and disinfecting it and laying down a new bedding of straw. She's been in here for about a week."

"This is not her usual stall?"

"No," said Stewart who was always ready to talk about his horses and foaling. "This is the foaling stall. It's bigger than the regular stall. About a week before we think the mare is ready to foal, we scrub this one down and set it at a comfortable temperature."

"I didn't know there was so much work involved," she said.

In about fifteen minutes, Jennie the veterinarian arrived. "Hi, Jennie."

"Hi Stewart, Jonathan," then looking at Janet she waited to be introduced.

"This is my friend Janet. She hasn't seen an animal give birth so I thought it would be a great experience," Jonathan said introducing Janet.

They exchanged greetings. "Feeding has been changed?" she asked Stewart.

"Yes. She's been on one pound of oats and two pounds of bran morning and evening for about a week."

"That's to prevent constipation before and after the birth," Jennie said to Janet, who just nodded. The whole thing was amazing to her. Jennie walked over to Meg and picked up a bucket of suds that Stewart had brought into the stall. She started washing Meg's udder and genitalia. Janet didn't have to be told why she was doing that. She understood it was all part of the hygiene. "How long has she been in labor?" Jennie asked.

"It's been about twelve hours, but she started to show signs a little while ago that she was ready."

"Did you sleep here all night, Stewart?" she said grinning.

"Both Jonathan and I slept here all night," Stewart said smiling. "Like two expectant fathers." Just then a car pulled up and the young girl that Janet had seen in Nellie's Tea Room came running up to the barn. "Did I make it in time?" she asked.

"Hi Catherine," Stewart said. "She's not given birth yet." Janet realized that this was Catherine MacLean. Her half-sister. Stewart introduced Janet as Jonathan's friend.

"We met at Nellie's," she told Stewart then turning to Janet, "hello Janet; it's nice to see you again." Janet smiled. She felt strangely emotional. She had just met her father, now her sister. She stepped outside of the barn to compose herself. Jonathan noticed her leave and walked out after her.

"Are you okay?" he asked. "You don't have to watch if it bothers you. You can go back into the cottage."

"No I'm fine, Jonathan. I really want to watch the baby being born. It's about time I knew more about this birthing process." She started to walk in and he put his arm around her shoulders as if to comfort her. She liked that. It showed he had a caring personality.

As they entered Stewart was saying excitedly, "Her outer bag just broke, Jonathan. She should give birth any minute." Janet watched as the front feet came out of the mother. She continued to watch in wonder. The little nose was between the knees. It only took minutes before the foal was outside of its mother. She waited for Jennie to go to the foal but she didn't.

Jennie noticed Janet looking at her questioningly. "We let the foal lie behind the mother for about fifteen minutes." She explained to Janet something about the foal getting the remaining blood from the placenta but Janet was so overwhelmed with the whole experience her mind wasn't functioning too well. After a while Jennie went over and cut the cord and dipped the end of it in something. "It's an antiseptic," Stewart was telling Catherine. Then Jennie dipped the feet into the antiseptic also.

Jonathan took Janet into the big house to look for food and cold drinks. She was in awe of the house. She had never seen anything like it. The kitchen was huge but very country-like with beautiful oak cabinets. All, except Jennie, sat around the outdoor furniture eating. "Okay," Stewart said. "How did you two meet?"

"I went into Nellie's Tea Room and she was talking to Janet and when I came in she introduced me because I told her I had just come back from America and she was happy to introduce me to the young lady she was talking to because she was from America."

"So Janet's responsible for keeping you away all day yesterday."

"I'm sorry," Janet said apologetically.

"He's just teasing Janet. He likes to do that. So you had just met when Joan and I came in?"

"Yes, we'd only known one another about an hour when you came in," Jonathan said. Janet just kept quiet. She was still feeling awkward and emotional. She was the only one in the group that knew her secret.

"I knew it had to be a girl. He came home looking rather happy."

"Hey," Jennie was yelling from the barn, "I think the foal is about ready to get up on its feet." They ran to the barn in time to watch the little foal, quite wobbly, getting up on his feet. They all clapped. Jennie had told them it was a boy.

Janet and Jonathan went outside and walked around the grounds. "I have never seen anything like that. Just before I came up here I was at the hospital when my cousin gave birth to young Ethan Nathaniel."

"That's a beautiful name," he said.

"That day I watched her walk out Aunt Betty's door with her belly way out to here," she said indicating with her hands. "Then a few hours later we were watching the baby being weighed. No longer in his mommy's tummy but lying on the scale crying. It was a miracle."

She spent the next two days in the company of Jonathan Grant. They went to Black Isle, which consists of a lot of Scottish history. They spent the day at Cromarty, an 18th century fishing port and saw some very well preserved old buildings, like Hugh Miller's thatched cottage that was built in 1711, Cromarty Courthouse and a lighthouse that was built by an uncle of Robert Louis Stevenson in 1846. They walked around with headphones listening to a tape giving information of what they were seeing. While driving back Janet seemed to be deep in thought. "There is something quite humble about the Scottish people," she said as though trying to figure out what it was.

"We have national pride. We don't forget who we are and where we came from. It's steeped in our history and our dirges."

"I know. I went to a ceilidh in Oban with my Aunt Betty."

The following evening Jonathan invited Robert out to dinner with them. They went back to the restaurant in Elgin where Jonathan had taken her before.

"Your card says your business is in Redwood City. I looked it up on a map and noticed it was not far from San Francisco," Robert said.

"Actually, my business is now in Boonville but I was raised in Redwood City. It's about thirty minutes south of San Francisco. I mistakenly gave you an old card. Here is my new card with my current address and phone number."

"I have a friend that lives in San Francisco. If only I would have known, I would have had James contact her. I'm sure he could have found her in a phone book."

"That's right. What a shame. The two of you could have kept in touch."

"Well, we'll certainly keep in touch. I'm sure and Jonathan will also," he said smiling at them both. He could tell they liked each other.

The next day Janet left for Glasgow. Jonathan drove her to the train station in Elgin. "Do I have all of your personals? I have your phone number, mail and e-mail addresses. How about your aunt's phone number?"

"It's on the back. Her address is there too."

The train was pulling into the station. "Janet, can I give you a kiss goodbye?"

"Yes, but goodbye sounds so final," she said reaching up to him. He bent over and kissed her on the lips. "I won't let it be final, my dear. I intend to spend more time with you whether it be here or in California. I want to see how far this relationship can go. I'll call you tonight at your aunt Betty's."

"Bye Jonathan Grant," she called waving from the train. "Thank you again for being so gracious to me and for being so helpful." She watched him as the train pulled away, leaving him more and more in the distance. On the way back in the train, her mind was so focused on everything that had happened over the last few days that she hardly took in any of the scenery this time. She thought of Robert and wondered how he would react to finding out that she is really his daughter and Catherine how would she feel when she finds out that she is not Robert MacLean's only child. She liked her biological father very much. He had so many good qualities like sensitivity, kindness, a caring spirit and she could go on and on. He showed such respect for her mother and Janet wondered how much he knew about the fiasco when his mother broke up their relationship. *Did he know that she paid off Alice's parents to keep their daughter away from her son?* She had hoped that nobody would have noticed how much she and Catherine looked quite a bit alike. Perhaps only she, Janet, was the only one that would notice it because she was the only one who knew they were related. She liked Catherine and found herself hoping everyone would accept her into the family.

She thought she and Catherine could become very good friends. *Oh well, I'll just have to wait and see how it all turns out.*

Her mind then turned to Jonathan. At thirty-two years of age, Janet had almost given up hope of finding true love. She had come to a point in her life where she was ready to settle with someone who was compatible and had a good sense of humor. After all, her mom was happy with her dad, even though the love of her life was Robert. Now, though, it seemed it could be possible that it could really happen for her. Jonathan was not only extremely physically attractive to her but he had a strong personality yet was sensitive. He was intelligent yet had an acute sense of humor. She was excited about being with him for the foaling. He and Stewart were so tender and worked so hard to make sure everything in the stall was clean and disinfected for the mother to deliver her baby and how excited they both were when the foal came out and finally stood up. She loved the way he let her take him into her confidence and how he fulfilled his duty while being discreet. She wondered how she could have had the meeting with Robert without Jonathan. He brought it all together without letting anyone know about the meeting. *He told me he wanted to pursue this relationship to see how far it could go. Marriage perhaps?* Her mind was quickly brought back to the reality that he was from an aristocratic Scottish family who would probably want him to marry someone like her half-sister Catherine, not an artist like she was. This disturbed her. *Could Jonathan be strong enough to marry someone like me if he wanted to?*

Chapter Eight

Aunt Betty was there at the train station to pick her up. After getting her luggage in the car they pulled out into the traffic. Since the train station was downtown they had to merge into a lot of traffic. "Let's wait until we get through the worst of this traffic before we talk about your trip," her aunt said.

"Sure, just concentrate on the traffic. In fact let's wait until we get home. I have so much to tell you and I would like us to be all settled in with a cup of tea." Janet loved being with her aunt. It was almost like being with her mother. Her aunt agreed that they should wait until they got home.

After about half an hour they were home and Betty had the kettle on. She poured them tea and settled down and asked, "Was it a good trip?"

"It was a very good trip," she said with a huge smile. "It was the best decision I have made in my life."

"Even more than buying that new house you keep bragging about?"

"Even more. Aunt Betty, the first day I arrived I met the most wonderful man. We struck up a relationship and he is going to keep in touch with me. He even talked about visiting me in California."

"Oh my gosh!" said Aunt Betty with her eyes and mouth wide open. "What's his name?"

"Well that is the big drawback. His name is Jonathan Grant."

"The Jonathan Grant that has a brother Stewart. The brothers every young woman in Scotland wants to grab? You met *that* Jonathan Grant?" she said with her eyes getting even wider, if that were possible.

"Yes! I'm afraid I'm totally out of his league. He said he wants to pursue our relationship. I'm crazy about him Auntie."

"You and every other young woman in the world."

"He's wonderful. The first day I met him we sat in this tearoom and chatted for a couple of hours. Then as we were leaving he asked if he could take me sight-seeing in Elgin the next day."

"Elgin is a lovely town. So you said yes, of course."

"Yes and we had a lovely time. We got on so well. Our humor is very similar and he did indicate that he really was interested in me. I told him I was up there to meet with Robert MacLean and he arranged it the next day at his own house, or at least the cottage he lives in on the estate."

"How did that go? The meeting with Robert, I mean."

"It went well. He's such a handsome, dignified man. I was very impressed with him and we had a wonderful talk. I showed him pictures of mom in different stages of her life. He said she was beautiful. I believe I even saw a tear in his eye."

"How lovely, Janet. How did he react to the news that you're his daughter?"

"I didn't tell him that. I gave him the journal to borrow and told him he could mail it out to California when he was through. I want him to read what mom wrote; what she went through; and what his mother did that caused so much pain for mom. I want him to find out about me through reading her words. I couldn't bring myself to just blurt it out."

"That's a good idea, Janet. Let your mom tell him then he can figure out how he wants to handle it." They chatted for a long time before Janet felt too tired to go on.

She went into her room to get ready for bed. Already she was missing everything, from Mrs. Graham's Bed and Breakfast to the countryside to her father and of course Jonathan. It was bad enough being just a few hours away from him, but how was she going to feel being over three thousand miles away from him. She lay in bed thinking about him. She was excited about this new relationship but scared that it wouldn't work because of their social differences. "I wish I didn't have to rush home, but I have to. I've already taken two extra days. I've got orders to fill and I need to keep my clients happy," she said aloud and then as though to console herself, "besides, I would have to go sometime and now is just as good as any." She hadn't yet called her sister, Maggie, to tell her about Jonathan. "I think I'll wait 'til I get home so that I can have more time to talk to her. I wish I could see her face when I tell her," she said once more talking to herself. She had another two days before going back to California but she felt an obligation to spend it with her aunt and cousin. She was so tired that she fell asleep before Jonathan's call. Her aunt had come and knocked on the door several times but there was no answer. When she woke up in the morning it came to her that she had not received Jonathan's call. Thinking he hadn't fulfilled his promise, she ran downstairs in her pajamas to find out what happened.

"He did call but I couldn't wake you up. He said he would call this morning."

"I don't know if it was the mountain air, the trip or all the excitement over the last few days, but I went out like a light and stayed out until about fifteen minutes ago."

"It was probably a combination of it all. That highland air puts me out every time."

"What time is it?"

"It's quarter after eight. He called around nine o'clock last night. You must have slept about eleven hours."

"I think a lot of the excitement is what wore me out. Of course I'm nervous about how Robert will react when he finds out I'm his daughter and whether things can really work out for Jonathan and me." She was still thinking about this when the phone rang. Aunt Betty motioned her to pick it up.

"Hello," she said hoping to hear his voice return the greeting.

"Hello Janet! How was your trip?"

"Oh hi Alice! It was great but I'll have to wait to see you to tell you about it. Too much to tell," Janet said trying to get Alice off the phone.

"Okay, I'll be over this afternoon. Is mom there?" she asked.

"Yes," said Janet and handed the phone to her aunt.

"Hello Alice! Yes that would be fine. Come before noon. Is that all you wanted to know? Well it's just that Janet is expecting an important phone call and we thought this was it. Okay darling, we'll expect you and my precious baby for lunch."

No longer had she put the phone back when it rang. Betty picked it up. "Hello! Oh yes, just a moment please," she said handing the phone to Janet and nodding her head up and down.

"Hello," Janet said trying not to sound too excited.

"Hey Janet, I didn't mean to wear you out when you were up here. Your aunt said she almost knocked the door down trying to wake you up," Jonathan said jokingly.

"Something wore me out. I slept for about eleven hours last night. I've never slept that long at one time in my life."

"Well, you obviously needed it."

"I guess so. I feel very refreshed now."

"Did you have a nice ride home?"

"Yes! I thought about a lot of things. I was only there a few days and it seems like so much took place."

"Did you think about me?" he said only half-jokingly.

"I did. I had such a good time being with you. I was sorry I had to meet you on such a distant shore."

"I'm already planning my time to make a space of about three weeks to come and visit you. Would that be too much time?"

"No! I think you will love where I live. It's in the beautiful California Wine Country." Aunt Betty had gone out into her garden to do some pruning to give them privacy. An hour later Janet stepped out the door smiling. "I'm sorry to take up so much time. I hope nobody was trying to call you."

"Oh girl, when a man talks for nearly an hour on the phone, all I can say is, it sounds serious."

"He told me he was looking at his business schedule and trying to find a three week slot to come to California. When I talk to him I feel encouraged about our relationship but when I'm by myself all the doubts come up regarding our backgrounds."

"Just because it happened to your mom, doesn't mean it will happen to you. After all, look who Robert's mother is. Jonathan's parents may be different."

"I forgot to tell you. His father was one of the boys who came to Glasgow with Robert when he met mom."

"You're joking! Well that gives you an idea of what his dad is like. Are they still good friends?"

"Oh yes! Robert has a daughter Catherine, whom I met at the birthing of a foal, and Nora the Cobra," she said giggling, "I think that's what I'll call her, has been trying to match her granddaughter up with Jonathan. He speaks respectfully of her but says that he doesn't love her and will not marry her."

"Would you ever have thought you would go through a similar situation as your mother? It's strange."

"Yes, and also involving Nora the cobra."

"What did you mean when you said you met Catherine at the birthing of a foal?"

"Actually I met her in a tearoom, but I got to know her a little more at the birthing. Jonathan and Stewart raise Arab horses and while I was there a mare gave birth and Catherine came over to watch also."

"Of course you wouldn't have said anything to Catherine about being her sister?"

"No, but we look quite alike and I was afraid she would see that."

Alice and one-week-old Ethan Nathaniel arrived in time for lunch. "When we had babies we were not to take them out until they were at least ten days old," said Betty checking her grandson out as if to make sure he was okay.

"It was different then. You didn't have a car. It's not like I'm taking him out in public. It's just from my house to the car and the car to your house."

"Of course, you're right," her mother agreed.

"Can I hold him?" asked Janet. She hadn't held him yet. When they were at the hospital nobody could get him out of the arms of grandma.

"Of course," said Alice handing the baby to her. Janet was thinking of the fact that she was thirty-two and not yet married. She had always wanted children and hoped that she would get married before her biological clock ran out. Almost as though she knew what Janet was thinking, Alice said, "Isn't amazing how many people are having babies in their forties today."

"Yes it is," agreed her mom. "It used to be women had their babies in their twenties and early thirties but usually not after thirty-five."

"Well that makes me feel I may still have a chance."

"Oh Janet, you're only thirty-two. You have lots of time. You'll meet someone, if you haven't already," her aunt said winking at her and smiling.

Alice caught the gesture. "Okay, let me in on the secret. Who was the big important call from this morning?" Alice asked.

They sat down to lunch and Janet talked and talked and Alice's eyes were getting wider and wider. Neither Alice nor Betty interrupted her. When she got to the part about meeting Jonathan Grant, Alice almost choked on her food. "You met who?" she asked as though she didn't hear right.

"You heard right," her mother offered. "She met Jonathan Grant and that's not all, go ahead Janet," she urged.

"It was he that called this morning. He said he really likes me and would like to visit me in California."

"You're joking," said Alice. "But of course you're not joking, just look at you. You're gorgeous." Janet went on to tell about the day they went sightseeing, the dinner and how she shared with him that she wanted to meet Robert and that he set up the meeting.

"How did it go with Robert? Did ye tell him that you were his daughter?"

"No," chimed in Betty again. "She left the journal with him so that he could find out reading about it in her mom's own words, which I agree whole heartedly with you on that decision," she said patting Janet's arm.

"I do too," Alice said. "This is like a soap opera. Beautiful woman comes from America, meets the most sought after bachelor in the whole of Scotland, wins his heart and confronts probably the most powerful man in Scotland with the fact that she is the daughter that he never knew."

"You definitely have to keep us abreast of everything," Betty said laughing at her daughter's description.

"It feels like a soap opera to me too and right now it's a cliff hanger. I have no idea what is going to happen. Will my father accept me? Will Jonathan fall in love with me and stick by his guns to marry the woman he loves?"

"Tune in this fall for the answers to these questions," Alice said laughing referring to the fact that cliff hangers happen in the spring and the answers come when the show returns in the fall.

"I'm going back to California in a few days but I don't know how I'm going to function."

"I hope if he is the right person for you, that everything will move real fast. Otherwise, I think you might go crazy being that far away from him. I hear people say that long distance relationships are difficult but yours is a continent away," said Aunt Betty.

Janet spent the rest of her time in Scotland going places with her aunt and cousin. The night before she left the three of them went out to dinner. Alice's husband took care of little Ethan Nathaniel saying, "The three of you go out and have a good time. Us boys will do just fine." They did have a good time and they were all sad the next day when Janet left to go home.

CHAPTER NINE

As her plane was ascending from the Chicago airport, her one stopover, Robert MacLean was settled in his favorite chair, in his pajamas and robe, with his ex-wife's journal. He opened it and just stared at the writing. It brought a sense of sadness to him. This was the closest he had been to his beloved Alice since the day after their wedding night. It felt like a spiritual moment especially since she had passed on. He held the open page to his heart and the tears rolled down his cheeks. *I never stopped loving you my darling Alice.* It took him a little while to compose himself before he could go on reading. He wiped his face with a handkerchief and laid the book on his lap and started to read. He read the first paragraph, at least four times, where she described her young years growing up in Glasgow. It was as though he was trying to get to know who she was. It was such a different lifestyle from his young years. He wanted to relish everything she was sharing. After reading the paragraph a number of times he sat back and tried to picture her and her family. He was so thankful that Janet had allowed him this pleasure. *What a wonderful, loving daughter she is. Her mother must have been proud of her,* he thought. After some time of envisioning Alice as a little girl he decided to continue on. The second paragraph talked about going to the movies with her friends, especially on the occasional Saturday night when they would go to the downtown theaters to see a newly released movie. He smiled when she described the buskers, the entertainers outside the theater. When he got to the third paragraph his heart skipped a beat. She was writing about the time she met him and what her feelings were for him. *She said she was particularly attracted to me.* He laughed out loud when he read that she liked his ruffled hair. "I remember her blushing. She says I gave her a mischievous grin that made her blush even more," he said out loud still grinning to himself. "I don't remember her shaking when I held her in my arms to dance," he said again out loud. If he had read the first paragraph four times, he had to have read this one eight times. He decided he wasn't going to read any more tonight. He wanted to savor what he had just read. He put the journal on the table by his chair and went to bed. He lay there thinking of Alice and how it might have been if his parents hadn't interfered. The lovely girl he had just met, Alice's daughter, could have been theirs. Little did he know that she was their child. He thought about her husband. Janet had said her mother had been happy and had three other children besides her. *I will go and see them someday. Maybe next year,* he thought as he drifted off to sleep.

Janet arrived in San Francisco around seven o'clock in the evening. By the time she got off the plane, got her luggage and drove home it was almost eleven o'clock. She just got inside the door with her first piece of luggage when the phone rang. "Gee! Which of my nosy friends could be calling already?" They all knew what time her plane was coming in and how long it takes to drive up from San Francisco. "Hello!"

"Hello Janet," said the voice with the familiar accent.

"Jonathan, I just walked in the door."

"Is that you just getting home? How long was the flight?"

"I had a stopover in Chicago, but it was long. What time is it over there?"

"Seven o'clock in the morning. Did you sleep on the plane?"

"Yes, I did. Actually, I slept quite well from Chicago to San Francisco."

"I miss you already. I'm anxiously planning my trip out there to see you."

"Are you really coming to see me, Jonathan?"

"You're the only reason I'm going," he said and Janet thought her heart would jump out of her chest. "I talked with Robert yesterday. He said he was going to start reading your mom's journal but wanted you to know he was going to really take his time with it but will make sure to get it back to you when he's done."

They talked for an hour. By the time she hung up the phone, she decided it was too late to call anyone with all her news. She decided tomorrow morning would be strictly phone calls. She had to check in with Keith, call her sister and let her know what happened and also her friends in Redwood City, Linda and Kathy, and she would try and make a lunch date with Margaret so she could tell her in person about the gorgeous man she had met. She put on her pajamas and washed up for bed. It was after midnight when she hit the sheets and was asleep in no time.

She woke up with the phone ringing. At first she didn't know where she was then she realized she was back home. *Who could be calling so early?* She glanced at the clock and was shocked to see it was already nine-thirty. She picked up the phone.

"Hello?"

"Janet, this is Maggie. Were you still sleeping?"

"Yeh! Maggie let me call you back. I want to get up and splash water on my face." She got up and put on her sweats and made a pot of coffee. After pouring a cup, she curled up on her chair with the phone. First she called Maggie back. She told her that meeting her father was a very nice experience. "He was so nice, Maggie. I can see what mom saw in him. He was polite and so gracious. I gave him the journal to read so he will find out everything for himself."

"That was smart, Janet. Is he going to mail it back to you?"

"Yes. Maggie," she said then hesitated.

"What, what?"

"I met the most wonderful man. I'm not sure how it's going to work out but we like each other and he says he's working on a time he can leave his business to come and see me." She went on to tell Maggie all about Jonathan.

"My gosh! It sounds like your waiting has paid off for you. The son of a laird! And if he is as handsome and wonderful as you say, then I say 'show him to me'."

"I'll have copies made of the pictures we had taken together in Scotland and send you some. If he does come out to see me, I will definitely invite you down to meet him. You'll be in awe of him. Like I said, Maggie, I'm not sure how it's going to work out."

118

After hanging up on Maggie, she called Keith and got caught up on her business then she called her friends Linda and Kathy in Redwood City and shared her news with them. She was about to call Margaret and invite her to lunch when the phone rang. She couldn't think who it could be since she had called almost everyone. Perhaps it was Margaret.

"Hello," she said casually into the phone thinking it was probably her friend.

"Hello, my dear. This is Robert MacLean. I wanted to make sure you got home safe."

"Hello Mr. MacLean. It's so nice of you to show such concern. I had a good trip and I'm happy to be home but I miss Scotland."

"Yes, Scotland has a way of grabbing people's hearts. I'm glad you had a nice trip. I also called to thank you again for leaving your mom's journal with me. I can't explain to you what it has done for me already."

"Have you read it all?" she said feeling a little disappointed that he seemed so placid about their relationship.

"Oh no! I started reading it last night. When I saw Alice's writing it made me feel sad. I read the first paragraph over and over and by the time I got to the third paragraph where she met me, well I have to admit I must have read that one a dozen times. By the time I was through with the third paragraph, I had been reading for about forty five minutes."

"I'm so glad you're enjoying it. There may be some things that will not make you feel so good, but I think you should read it all anyway. She is very open about what happened between the both of you."

"Well I'm looking forward to reading it, Janet, because I have never found out why Alice left for America without giving us a chance."

"You will find out. Thank you for calling and sharing with me." After they hung up she called her sister back and shared everything he had said. The phone rang again and this time it was Margaret. They made a date for dinner. It was too late now for lunch. By the time she was through with her phone calls it was already after noon and she hadn't had a shower or brushed her teeth yet. After she got cleaned up she emptied her suitcases and did some washing.

"It's so good to have you back, Janet. I missed you so much," Margaret said as she sat down at the table with Janet.

"I missed you too. But now I'm back, I miss Scotland."

"So tell me what happened with Robert MacLean."

Janet shared once again about leaving the journal with Robert and how much she liked him and what a gentlemen he was. "He even called me this morning to make sure I got home safely."

"You're kidding. That was exceptionally nice of him."

Janet then started to share about Jonathan. She showed Margaret pictures of him.

"He is absolutely gorgeous," Margaret said staring at the picture. "Does he have a brother?"

"Actually he does. A younger brother Stewart." Janet continued sharing about her time with him and how he called her as soon as she got home. "He said he was coming out here to visit me. I'm not sure when but I hope it's soon."

"Ask him to bring his brother," Margaret said teasingly

"I believe my half-sister Catherine is going with Stewart."

"Actually he's a bit young for me. I like men a little older than me."

Janet was so restless she could hardly work. All she wanted to do was get on a plane and go back to Scotland. She was nervous about her relationship with Jonathan. Even though he called her nearly every night, she still felt that he might meet someone else who would be more on his level socially. Also she wished she knew where Robert was in the journal. Did he reach the page that tells of her mother's pregnancy and the baby named Janet? If he had gotten to that page, he had chosen not to do anything about it. She hadn't heard from him since she returned home almost a week ago.

Robert MacLean returned back from Glasgow after being on a business trip. He had not been able to get back to Alice's journal. He wanted to read it slowly as though he was trying to get back the years he had missed with her. He was having some difficulty with his mother. "By the way, Catherine is getting embarrassed about you trying to push Jonathan and her together. I want you to stop meddling, mother."

"Someone has to look out for her future," his mother said curtly.

"I am quite capable of looking out for my daughter's future. I have spoken to Catherine and she would rather choose her own life partner."

He always believed that his mother was the cause of he and Alice being separated but he had never heard what actually happened. He didn't want her messing up his daughter's life. Besides, Jonathan had given Robert the impression that he had an interest in Janet Stevens and Robert was definitely not going to be a part of coming between them.

"The Grant's gardener told ours that Jonathan was with a young woman and took her to his cottage. He said you pulled up and went in also. What is going on?"

"Nothing that you need to be concerned about, mother."

Nora decided she would try and find out from Jonathan. *It's bad enough that Catherine's friend Joan was trying her hardest to get Jonathan's attention, but now there seems to be someone else,* she thought.

"It doesn't sound very good. The gardener said she was a stranger and you all went into Jonathan's cottage."

"I'm going to my room. I have some reading I want to do." He got into his pajamas and robe and picked up Alice's journal. He read her account of their marriage. *She thought my idea of us getting married was silly.* He remembered having to face her parents and how they thought he should tell his parents what he had done and they could all get together and discuss it. He also thought of how he told his parents and his mother told him they would have the marriage annulled and would have a proper wedding later if they still wanted to be married. "After all, Robert, this is not the way people in our society marry," she had said. *Why did Alice not stay around to see if it could have been worked out?* he thought. He continued reading. "What?" he yelled. He had been reading the part where his parents sent a solicitor to pay off Alice's parents to keep her away from their son. He was livid. *I knew she had something to do with it.* He got even angrier when he read about how Alice suffered such humiliation from the media. Due to the MacLean reputation, they had a field day with the story. So much so that she had to leave her home. *So that was why she went to America. They paid her off to get rid of her. My poor dear Alice.* He closed the journal as well as his eyes. He wanted to cry. He was so angry. His mother would be in bed but he would be sure and talk to her in the morning.

Janet was in her workshop trying to concentrate on a pot she was working on. Her phone rang and she picked it up in the shop thinking it was probably a business call. "Hello!" she said as she was wiping her hands clean with a cloth.

"Janet, it's Robert MacLean. How are you dear?"

"I'm fine. Could you hold a second?"

"Sure!"

"Okay! I had to rinse off my hands. I had been throwing a pot," she said as she settled into her chair.

"You said there may be some things I wouldn't like in your mom's journal," he said. "Well I just came to it." She held her breath. Did he not like the fact that she was his daughter? "I finally found out why she left Scotland. My parents, probably my mother, paid her off to stay away from me," he said then hesitated as he was trying to control his anger. "I'm so angry right now and it's a good thing my mother's in bed. Maybe by the morning I'll have calmed down a little, but I don't think much."

"I know, it made me very angry too when I read that because, obviously she was in love with you and she was sent away because of it."

"But why didn't she come back after a while? Perhaps we could have gotten things settled then."

"You just have to keep reading on. I believe all your questions will be answered."

"Okay dear. I have to put it down for now. I am too riled up to go on. I don't think I could take anything that would make me angrier than I am right now. I'm going to bed now. Goodnight dear. I'll call you when I read some more but I don't think it will be for a little while. I can't tell you how bad I feel right now."

"Goodnight Mr. MacLean." *Goodnight, father,* she thought to herself.

122

CHAPTER TEN

Robert could hardly look at his mother when he came down to the dining room the next morning. His grandmother on his father's side, who was ninety-five years old, was there also. "Good morning Robert," said Isabel MacLean.

"Good morning grandma. How are you feeling today?" Robert inquired.

"Oh just the same old aches and pains. You look a little upset, dear. Is everything alright?"

"I am a bit upset, but nothing for you to worry about."

"Is it about a business deal?" his mother inquired.

"You might call it that. One that happened over thirty years ago," he said without looking up from his plate.

"Thirty years ago you were only twenty-two. What kind of business were you in then?" his mother said.

"The marrying business," he said looking her straight in the eye.

She looked back at him with a questioning look. *Surely he isn't still thinking about that little nobody from Glasgow,* she thought. "What are you talking about?"

"You paid off my wife's parents. You told them she wasn't good enough for me."

"Well she wasn't, Robert. You married much better."

"I loved Alice and I never knew until now why she left. You made me believe that we were going to have a proper marriage," he said his voice getting angrier. "Instead you went behind my back and sent her away."

His grandmother didn't have any idea what they were talking about but she was beginning to understand. She thought she should probably leave them alone but she was curious about this. She knew there had been someone from Glasgow that young Robert was involved with but she never found out what happened to her and certainly didn't know that he had married her.

"She took the money and ran," his mother said. "Just like the little money-grabber I knew she was."

"She left Glasgow because her heart was broken. She thought I was a part of the plan that you and dad had to get rid of her."

"I don't believe your dad had anything to do with it Robert," said Isabel MacLean. "My son, Neil, was not like that." Nora stared at her mother-in-law knowing that she was thinking that it was all her doing. She was not in the same class as Neil but Isabel and Neil's father allowed their son to make his own choice when it came to marriage.

"What do you mean you never knew *until now* why she left?" asked his grandmother.

"Alice went to America. She married over there and had children. I just recently met her daughter, Janet."

Nora's head jerked in his direction. She waited for his explanation but he didn't give any. Then it came to her. *That young girl he and Jonathan were with. The gardener said she was a stranger,* she thought. "She was the girl you were with a while back," his mother finally blurted out. "What was she doing up here and what does she have to do with Jonathan?"

"Looking for me; to tell me that Alice had died."

"How did she know about you both? Why would Alice tell her children about another man other than their father?" Nora said disgustingly.

"That was nice of Janet to let you know of her mother's passing," Isabel said ignoring Nora. "Is she still here in Scotland?"

"No! She's back in the States. I talked to her last night after I found out about all of this."

"You talked to her *after* you found out? If she's not the one giving you the information, then who is?" his mother demanded.

Robert stood up, wiped his mouth with his napkin, folded it very neatly and placed it on his plate. He looked straight at her and said, "Alice," then he walked out of the room.

"What?" his mother said looking after him, confused.

Isabel MacLean had to hold back a giggle. Nora had taken away his true love and he was getting even with her. *Or was it Alice who was getting even,* she thought. Whoever it was, Isabel was enjoying it tremendously. She loved her grandson very much. They had always had a great relationship. She knew something had happened back when he was seeing Alice. He was so happy and then all of a sudden he was miserable. When she had asked him what happened to Alice he just told her she had left the country.

Robert drove over to see his friend Malcolm, Jonathan's father. "Dad's not here, Mr. MacLean. He's in town. He'll be back soon, though," Stewart Grant informed him.

"Is Jonathan here?" Robert asked. Stewart told him that Jonathan was in the cottage.

"Hello, Robert. Come on in." Jonathan was glad to see him. Robert was the only person he could talk to about Janet. "I was just thinking about calling Janet later this afternoon. I told her I was trying to figure out when I could go over and visit her."

"You're becoming quite serious about her, aren't you?" Robert asked.

"I like her very much and I would like to visit her in her own environment. I want to see what things we have in common."

Robert told him what he found out in the journal and the confrontation he had with his mother just a few hours ago.

"That's sad. You lived all those years without her because you thought she just chose to leave you. What would you have done if you would've found all this out back then?"

"I would have made someone in her family tell me where in California she went and I would have gone over there and brought her back here and remarried her."

"I'm sorry, Robert. I feel so bad for you."

"Well there is some consolation in knowing that Alice didn't leave me."

Just then there was a knock on the door. It was Malcolm. Jonathan watched as Robert went out with his dad. *If Janet and I are meant to be together, nobody is going to stop it,* he thought sadly thinking about Robert.

Janet had just gotten out of the shower and dressed when the phone rang. She looked at her watch. Eight o'clock. *A bit early, but not for Jonathan,* she thought desperately hoping it was him. "Hello!"

"Hello, Janet. How are you this morning?"

"I'm fine Jonathan. This is a nice way to start the day. Have you found out when you are coming over?" she asked.

"Yes, I have. I will be over in September. It will take me a few months to get ahead of the game. Is that a nice time of the year?"

"Yes it is. The hot months will be over. I will try and get my business in order so I can spend all my time with you."

"I'd love that." He went on to tell her about what Robert had shared with him.

"I knew he had found out. He called me last night after he read it in the journal. He was so furious with his mother, but she was in bed so he was going to wait until this morning to talk to her. What happened?"

"He'll probably tell you but yes, he did have it out with her. He did it in front of his grandmother too. He said he had a feeling she never knew about the payoff."

"Robert has a grandmother? He has to be in his early fifties. How old is she?"

"Ninety-five. She's a cool old lady. I hope you get to meet her. I felt so sad for him today. All this time, he thought your mom had run out on him. I asked him what he would've done had he known then and he said he would have gone to America and brought her back." Janet got so emotional she was afraid to talk in case he would hear it in her voice. "Janet? Are you there?"

"Yes! It makes me angry that someone could be so heartless as to take away a young couple's dream." They talked for an hour before hanging up the phone.

Janet had some deliveries to make to Keith in San Francisco. She was so happy to be living where she could feel the ocean breezes. Redwood City was always hot in the summer. "Hello Keith, I brought the orders that I promised you."

"Great! Mrs. Jones has been driving me crazy. She's been calling every day since you've been back."

"I'm sorry, Keith. I'm just about caught up with all the orders."

"It's good to see you, Janet," he said giving her a big hug. "This is the first time I've seen you since you got home."

"Well, like I said, I'm almost caught up so I'll be able to have some friends over."

"Have you heard recently from the guy in Scotland?"

"He's coming over in a couple of months. He's already got reservations made at the Boonville Hotel."

"Janet, he sounds like a man in love."

"Do you think so, Keith? I have been so scared to hope too much. I'm absolutely crazy about him. I know that I want to marry him and I'm so afraid I'll lose him."

"I wouldn't fly all the way from Scotland to California, unless I was either dying to visit California or I was dying to visit a lady in California that meant an awful lot to me."

"Of course he has money so cost doesn't mean much to him," she said almost looking for an excuse for him to come for another reason. "Although he said he had to get his business in order before he could leave for the time he's going to spend here, so time is a factor."

"You're just scared and I don't blame you. You obviously love him and not knowing exactly how he feels about you must be hard. But like I said, I wouldn't fly six thousand miles unless she was extremely special."

"Thanks Keith. That gives me a little more confidence."

Because of the location of her house mail was not delivered so on the way back from San Francisco she stopped at the post office to check her box. Her heart almost jumped out of her chest when she saw mail from Jonathan. She decided she could wait until she got home before opening it but the whole way home she kept wondering if it was good or bad news. *I hope he hasn't cancelled his visit,* she thought. *That would be a killer. Of course he would tell me by phone, not by mail.* Everything else was dumped on the kitchen counter. She took the mail to her favorite chair and opened it. There were pictures of the two of them in Elgin. She remembered he had asked several people to take their picture. When she saw the two of them together it brought tears to her eyes. *We really do look happy together.* She missed him so much at that moment. There was a picture of the little foal. "He looks a lot more steady on his legs," she said aloud laughing. She stared at the photographs for at least a half an hour when the phone rang causing her to snap back to reality. As was her habit, she checked her watch. *Three fifteen. Possibly Margaret wanting to make dinner reservations,* she thought.

"Hey, Janet. I know I just called last night but I really miss you. I can't wait to come and see you."

"I'm so glad you called. I just got your mail with the pictures and I was missing you so much too. What do you think is happening, Jonathan? I mean we were only together less than a week."

"I talked to my dad about you. He said he wished he had met you."

"I can understand his concern. After all, he is Laird Grant. I don't blame him for wanting to critique someone his son is involved with."

"I want him to meet you as soon as possible. Janet, I know you're busy, but can you come over here for a few days? I will send your ticket and set you up at Mrs. Graham's B & B," he said almost pleading with her.

"I feel guilty about you paying for my ticket," she said. Even though he had lots of money she still felt funny about having him pay for her plane ticket.

"I'm asking you to come over. I would never ask you to pay. Please come."

"When?"

"As soon as you can."

"I'll get back to you tomorrow."

"Will you have an answer for me at nine o'clock in the morning," he said.

"Yes!"

"I'll call you then."

She had no longer hung up the phone when it rang. "Janet, I got the pictures you took in Scotland. He's the dreamiest guy I have ever seen. I hope it works out for you, sister. He is so good-looking," Maggie went on and on until Janet broke in.

"Maggie, he just called. His dad wants to meet me. He is sending me an airline ticket to fly back to Scotland."

"Oh Janet, I am shaking in my shoes. This is getting serious. I'm going to have Scottish Royalty as my brother-in-law."

"Maggie, don't jump the gun. I don't want to be too hopeful."

"I'll call Tom and let him know," Maggie was happy to offer. She was so excited about Janet, not only having a boyfriend, but a gorgeous Scottish prince.

"Keith, I'll have the rest of the orders to you before the end of the week. After that I'll be in Scotland for about a week, so make sure you take that into consideration when you take any new orders."

"Janet. What's going on?" Keith asked.

"He wants me to meet his family," she said in a rather shaky voice.

"I told you. The man's in love."

She gave the flight information to Jonathan the next morning and he said he would call her back as soon as everything was set up. She called Aunt Betty to let her know she was going to be back in Scotland. She wasn't sure how much she would be able to see her.

"Why are you coming back so soon?" Aunt Betty wanted to know.

"Jonathan wants me to meet his family."

"My goodness. This sounds serious. I have to call Alice immediately."

One week later Janet was in Scotland. Jonathan was to pick her up in Glasgow. She had asked if it would be possible to stop by and say hello to Aunt Betty. "After all, she is my family and since I'm here to meet yours, then it would be nice for you to meet some of mine," she had told him.

"Of course. I think that would be a good thing to do," he had said. She had let Aunt Betty know as she knew she would want to spend time cleaning her house.

When she saw him her heart started pounding. He came up to her and they fell into each other's arms. He kissed her for real for the first time, not the friendly little peck at the train station. Janet knew at that moment, for sure, that Jonathan Grant was in love with her. "I've missed you so much," he told her.

"I haven't been able to concentrate on anything since I got home."

"Let's get your luggage and get on the road."

When they got to her aunt's house, her nosy neighbor, Mrs. Carter, was outside scrubbing her doorstep. She did this every time she saw a stranger or a strange car stop outside Betty's house. Her daughter Alice and her husband George and of course little Ethan Nathaniel were there. Janet noticed that the house was shining like a new pin, as her aunt would say. She just knew that her aunt had probably spent the last few days scrubbing it so it would look as good as possible for the important visitor. Aunt Betty fussed around him making sure he was comfortable and his teacup was full. Alice could only sit and stare at him. *I can't believe Jonathan Grant is sitting in my mom's living room,* she was thinking. They didn't stay too long as they had quite a drive ahead of them.

After they left Alice and her mom talked about how exciting it was to not only meet him, "but to actually have him in my house. I'll be the talk of the neighborhood for sure," Betty had said. George laughed at them and told them they were acting like a couple of schoolgirls.

"Was Mrs. Carter out scrubbing her doorstep?" Alice asked.

"Of course."

Well ye'll be the talk of the neighborhood for sure."

"Don't tell her who it was, if she asks. Just say it was a friend of your cousin."

Jonathan pointed out some places to her like Stirling Castle and the William Wallace statue in Stirling. "We'll wait until another trip to see all the sites. This one is too short."

"That's fine with me. I just want to get the first meeting over with. I'm nervous."

"Don't be. My parents are very easy to get along with. By the way, I enjoyed your aunt Betty. Is she anything like your mother was?"

"She actually is so much like my mother. I will say, though, that mom was the prettiest of the three sisters."

"She must have been something special to catch the eye of Robert MacLean."

I must be something special to catch the eye of Jonathan Grant, she thought.

About five hours later they were pulling up to Mrs. Graham's place. He carried her luggage inside and Mrs. Graham was so happy to welcome her back. It was almost six o'clock. "Do you want to rest awhile before I pick you up for dinner?" he asked her.

"I am tired, but I'm afraid if I lay down now I'll sleep the night through."

"Well let's go get something to eat now," he said.

Mrs. Graham had been almost in shock when Jonathan called to make a reservation for Janet.

"Why she just left here. I thought she went back to America," she remarked inquisitively.

"She did go back and now she's coming back here," was all the information he gave her. Mrs. Graham had told Nellie at the Tearoom about Jonathan making the reservation for Janet to come back.

As soon as Jonathan and Janet left, Mrs. Graham picked up the phone. "Nellie, he just brought her up from Glasgow."

"I told ye I was the one who introduced them. They better invite me to the wedding," she said laughing.

"We don't know that they're planning a wedding, Nellie. They only just met."

"Why else would she be here, and him making the reservations and all, makes me more than a wee bit suspicious," Nellie said.

Nellie had told some of her patrons until it finally got to the ears of Nora MacLean.

"What's going on at the Grants? I hear Jonathan has brought that girl back to Scotland," she confronted Robert. He had not spoken to her much since he found out she had paid off Alice's parents. He hadn't been able to read the journal since then either. It had caused him so much pain, although he was still glad that Janet had given it to him. Maybe he'll finish it and let her take it home with her.

"It's none of our business. Maybe he likes her," was all he answered.

"The Grants would never let their son get involved with someone in her class," she said.

"That's all you can think of Nora." He had started calling her by her first name as though he didn't think of her as his mother any more. "Class, class, class. Well let me tell you, the Grants are not like you. They would rather their son marry the woman of his heart rather than one of his class." At that, he walked out of the room. Actually his friend Malcolm had told him Janet was coming out to meet them.

Nora was furious. This little upstart was causing an awful lot of trouble. *It's like it's all coming back to haunt me,* she thought. *Well I'm not going to allow it.*

After dinner Jonathan took Janet back to Mrs. Graham's. "I'll pick you up at ten o'clock tomorrow," he told her and kissed her goodnight. Mrs. Graham witnessed the kiss.

"How was the trip up here?" Mrs. Graham asked Janet after Jonathan left.

"It was really nice. Especially riding in such a luxury car."

"Oh! Did Jonathan go down tae Glasgow tae pick ye up?" she asked surprised.

"Yes he did," Janet said wondering if she was giving out too much information. She realized in such a small town, that people like the Grants and MacLeans were probably under much scrutiny. For Jonathan's sake she had decided to be as discreet as possible.

"I must say when I said 'come back again, soon' I didn't expect it tae be this soon," she said hoping for information.

Janet just smiled at her and said. "I was homesick for your place and you did invite me back."

"Oh, ye like to joke, dae ye," she said smiling back. She really liked Janet and was secretly hoping something was stirring up with her and Jonathan.

"I'd like to stay up and chat, Mrs. Graham, but I'm exhausted. You know the big flight, the drive up here and the time change. I didn't sleep much on the plane. Maybe tomorrow or one of the other days." She said her goodnights and went to bed.

Before going to bed, Mrs. Graham made sure she let her friend Nellie know that Jonathan had kissed Janet.

The next morning Janet went into the dining room but she had told Mrs. Graham that she would just be having tea and scones. The Grants were planning a luncheon so she wanted to save her appetite. She wasn't sure what to wear. *What do wealthy people wear at luncheons?* She decided on a simple gray silk dress and pumps.

Mrs. Graham remarked at how lovely she looked. "Ye look like yer goin' to a very special occasion," she said, once again trying to get information.

Janet just smiled and thanked her. Janet loved listening to Mrs. Graham and Nellie talk, especially to each other. They had that gossipy tone when they talked to one another. It always made Janet smile.

Jonathan was his usual punctual self. At ten on the dot he was there to pick her up. "You look stunning," he told her as he walked her to the car.

"Thank you! I didn't quite know what to wear."

"You look perfect. It's only going to be my family."

"Still I wanted to look decent," she said.

"You look decent," he smiled at her.

Janet was still quite familiar with the drive up to the Grant estate. Her stomach had butterflies that were fluttering like crazy. When they entered the house everyone was in the living room. "Mom, Dad, this is Janet."

"Hello Janet, welcome to our home," Malcolm Grant said.

"Could I get you something to drink, Janet?" asked Helen.

"No! I'm fine for now, thank you. I'm very pleased to meet you both," she said.

"Well, we are certainly pleased to meet you," Mrs. Grant said smiling.

"Of course you already know Stewart."

She shouldn't have worried so much. The family was very pleasant. Malcolm was a tall well-built man with white hair. He had a fun-loving type of personality. He liked to smile and make people feel comfortable. Helen Grant was an attractive woman of medium height, about five feet six inches tall. She had a shapely figure and had a very sociable personality. She also liked to take care of people and make sure they were comfortable.

The luncheon was scrumptious. Mrs. Grant served up a beautiful piece of Scottish Salmon and a garden salad with fresh greens from their own garden.

"This salmon is wonderful, Mrs. Grant," Janet complimented her. "I don't think I've tasted any better than this."

"This fish came out of the River Lossie this morning," Malcolm informed her.

"The River Lossie is a local river," Stewart said. "Jonathan and I go fishing there for salmon and trout all the time." She looked at Jonathan realizing there was a lot about him that she didn't know.

"I met your mother, Janet," Malcolm offered. "She was a very nice girl and I'm sorry about your loss."

"Thank you."

"We want you to know that we are very sorry that Robert and your mom were never able to be together," Helen said sincerely.

"I can tell you that Robert loved her deeply," Malcolm continued.

"I know that. After meeting Robert I could tell that he loved her. I only wish they could have gotten together after my dad died." They talked about her life in California. She told them about the little town of Boonville and nearby beautiful Mendocino. She explained her pottery business to them and talked about her brothers and sister. After a while Jonathan asked her if she would like to go for a walk around the grounds.

Once outside, he told her that he knew his parents liked her. "They were a lot different from what I expected. I really enjoyed talking with them."

"You were expecting them to act like Robert's mom, weren't you?"

"I suppose I was. I shouldn't have prejudged."

"That's okay."

"I didn't know you were a fishing enthusiast."

"It's hard not to be when you live up here. The River Spey, which is not far from here, is well known in the world for its salmon fishing."

"Salmon fishing is great in the Pacific also, especially when they come to spawn in the Pacific Northwest."

"Yes, I know that."

"What else do you like to do that I don't know of?"

"I think you know almost everything. I love the outdoors and I'm a business man."

"They don't seem to go together. Fishing and business."

"Do you like to fish, Janet?" he asked her.

"I haven't really done much. When we would camp by a river we would get our little poles out and fish, but I haven't done any serious fishing. I would like to try. I love being out in the water."

"What do you like to do as a hobby?"

"Well, my job is also a hobby. I paint and I love to take nature walks and get inspiration for the painting I do on my pottery. My friend Margaret takes beautiful nature pictures on our walks."

"She's the realtor friend, right?"

"Yes she is. I'm looking forward to introducing you to her and my other friends. My sister Maggie and brother Tom will come down while you are visiting so you'll get to meet them also."

"I'm looking forward to that. I think it was good for you to come over and meet my family and for you to get to see me where I live and for me to see you where you live."

"It was a good idea, Jonathan," she agreed. "Especially since things seem to be moving awfully fast."

He showed her the different gardens on the estate. They were beautifully laid out and she took pictures of them.

"This is my mom's hobby. She designed all the gardens herself and loves to come out and weed. We have a gardener of course. She has to beg him to tolerate her once in a while, because he gets a little put out when she does it. He says it makes him feel that she doesn't think he's doing a good enough job," said Jonathan. Janet laughed.

"She and my Aunt Moira in Virginia would get along real well. Aunt Moira designed the gardens at her home also."

"Well hopefully we'll get them together someday soon."

"Jonathan, can I see the little foal?"

"Oh sure, let's go to the barn." The little horse was growing and seemed real healthy. "I almost feel like his aunt, because I was here when he was born."

The next day he took her to the Biblical Gardens in Elgin. "Jonathan, these gardens are so beautiful. What an array of color. I've never seen so many different flowers all together. These are all the flowers and plants flowers in the Bible?"

"Here, I downloaded this from the Internet," he said handing her a page that had the description of the Biblical Garden. She started to read.

The creation of the garden, the first of its kind in Scotland, is particularly appropriate on this site, as Moray has for over fourteen centuries played an important role in the development and changing fortunes of the church, similarly, its close proximity to Elgin's historic cathedral, literally just over the wall make this site the obvious choice.

Whilst using the Bible as its reference point and including all one hundred and ten plants mentioned therein, together with sculptures depicting the parables, it is clearly intended that this garden as well as being of considerable interest to those who study the scriptures, will also encourage anyone who enjoys gardens and gardening, to visit.

Obviously, gardens being living things constantly change, not only throughout the season, but also develop and grow through the years, thus sustaining an attraction which may be different upon every visit and thus should encourage one to return time after time, providing the original project captures the imagination.

Made possible by and reliant upon the generosity and goodwill of the people of Moray and its many visitors, the Biblical Garden provides a haven and we believe an enjoyable visit for everyone.

Some ninety trees and shrubs, donated by school groups throughout Moray, have been planted within the garden. A desert area has been created depicting Mount Sinai and the cave of the resurrection and a marsh area has been included within the garden.

An impressive central walkway, requiring over one thousand textured paving slabs, has been laid in the shape of a Celtic cross. The garden, planted around the central cross with every species of plant mentioned in the Bible, also includes a number of life-size sculptures depicting various parables including the Good Shepherd and the Prodigal Son.

The backdrop to the garden features a striking trellis, which mirrors the design of the nearby cathedral and is covered in yellow, white and red roses. The plants are all cross-referenced to a particular passage in the Bible and an indication of their use in biblical times.

"This makes me want to weep. It's so inspiring. Look that looks like Jesus at the well with the Samaritan woman and over there I think is Samson leaning on the two pillars before he brought the building down." They kept walking around.

"Here is the Prodigal Son and over there is the Good Shepherd." She made sure she got plenty of pictures. "My friend Margaret would love this place. So would Aunt Moira."

Nora MacLean was getting nothing from her son as to why that girl was back in Scotland. *She had just gone back to California a month or so ago and she's back again?* The fact that she was visiting with the Grants made it even worse. "I just have to get Catherine and Jonathan together. They belong together. He didn't belong with that little nobody," she said aloud to herself. She had gone into town and even visited Nellie's Tearoom, which she usually didn't do, to see if she could find out any other information. This American girl had been in town three days now.

"Good afternoon, Mrs. MacLean," said Nellie surprised to see her. "What can I do fer ye?"

"I'll just have a cup of tea, Nellie. I was doing some shopping and realized this is the time I usually have a cup at home."

Pretty soon Nellie came back with a cup and saucer and a little pot of tea, with creamer and sugar bowl. "Here ye are, dear. Enjoy it."

"I haven't been in town for quite a while. Anything going on that I might have missed?" she inquired of Nellie.

"Yer son, Robert, was in here this morning wae the young American girl, Janet."

"Hmm! I haven't met this girl. I don't know what she and Robert could possibly have to say to each other," she said with a questioning look at Nellie.

"Well they were talking rather quietly and were at the far table over there in the corner," she pointed to a table that was farthest away from the counter, "so I didn't hear anything they were saying."

"Did they look serious or were they quite casual?"

"I could only see Sir Robert's face and he was quite casual. They laughed a few times. Although at one point he looked very serious. He almost looked apologetically," Nellie said enjoying the conversation. She was hoping Nora MacLean would give her some information. *He was still moaning over her sending that silly little Glaswegian girl away,* Nora thought. Nora MacLean had no idea how much she had ruined her son's life; not being able to live his life with the woman he truly loved.

"Well I'm not sure who she is?" was all she gave the shop owner.

"She seems tae spend more time wae Jonathan Grant than she does yer son." Nellie withheld the information that Jonathan had picked her up from the Glasgow airport and that Agnes Graham had seen them kissing. She liked Jonathan and Janet.

"I'll pay my bill now, Nellie," she said laying down some money and leaving.

Nora MacLean was not the only one trying to get information on the American girl. Catherine's friend, Joan MacDonald, had also been snooping around trying to find out what she was doing back in Scotland and what the Grants connection with her was. After Catherine got back from fishing with Stewart, Joan stopped by to try and get information. Catherine had met Janet the day that the foal was born. She had liked her. Joan didn't like the fact that the American was spending a lot of time with Jonathan. "She walks into town, a complete stranger to everyone, and immediately she is spending time with Jonathan and your dad," she had told Catherine. "How strange is that?"

"I'm not sure who she is, but I'm certain dad will eventually clue me in on what's going on," Catherine had replied. She wasn't lying because she really didn't know who Janet was, but she certainly knew something was going on between her and Jonathan but she decided not to say anything to her friend. Joan MacDonald was from a well-to-do family. Her father had done well in business but their money was not "old money" that Nora was always concerned about. After her dad retired, her parents moved to Inverness, but Joan and her older brother Kenneth stayed up in Moray.

When Nora got back home Catherine was there alone. Joan had already left. "Hello, Catherine. Did you go shopping?"

"No, I went fishing with Stewart," her granddaughter answered.

It bothered Nora that she spent more time with the younger Grant boy, but he's not the one that will inherit the Highland Mist Estate. It always went to the older son and she wanted Catherine to be the lady of the manor. "You spend more time with him than you do with Jonathan," Nora was fishing for information regarding their relationship.

"Stewart and I have more in common with each other. We are closer to the same age and we have been best friends since our childhood," she reminded her grandmother.

"What has age got to do with anything? Catherine, don't you want to be the lady of Highland Mist Estate?"

"Not if it means marrying someone I don't love."

"You're just like your father."

"What is that suppose to mean, grandma?" Catherine asked. She wasn't sure what her grandmother was talking about.

Robert had come in the door and heard the last part of their conversation. Walking into the living room where they were, he said, "Because that's what's important to your grandma; status and wealth. You're like me because you love with your heart. She destroyed my life but she won't destroy yours. I will see to that."

Catherine looked at her father in shock and confusion.

"What's going on in this family that I don't know about?"

"Robert, you have no right to bring this up in front of your daughter."

"I think he does, Nora." It was a different voice entering the conversation as Isabel walked into the room. "My grandson lost the love of his life because you sent her away. She wasn't good enough for you, Nora, but she was good enough for Robert. You robbed him of that." Isabel had never spoken to Nora in that way before but she was angry that Nora had split up her grandson and the woman he truly loved. That was the most despicable thing Nora had done as far as Isabel was concerned.

"You're all making too much of this," Nora yelled almost hysterically.

"Dad, tell me what happened," Catherine almost demanded. "I'm not a child and refuse to be treated like one. I'm part of this family and something is being kept from me." Robert realized he had kept from Catherine what Alice kept from Janet. Neither girl knew that one of their parents had been married before.

"I'm sorry, Catherine. I never meant to keep secrets from you. As a very young man I fell in love and married a girl. I never knew why she went away to America without giving us a chance, but I found out recently that your grandmother annulled the marriage, paid off the girl's parents and sent her away. I was never able to contact her. I loved your mother, Catherine, but not in the same way."

"You were in lust with her. You couldn't see the bigger picture."

"No, mother you couldn't see because you don't know what it's like to love and be loved. I want Catherine to experience that. It is far better dear," he said turning to his daughter, "than being the lady of a big mansion."

Catherine went over to her dad, put her arms around him and said, "I'm so sorry dad."

At that Nora turned and walked out of the room.

"I'm glad I lived to hear the story come out and I'm glad you told Catherine," Isabel told her grandson. "I'm still interested in where you got the information," she continued with a smile and a raised eyebrow.

"I will tell you soon," he promised her. He still hadn't picked up the journal again. He was still hurting from what he had read last. He wasn't ready to get hit in the face with anything else his mother might have done.

When Janet came back from the Biblical Garden to rest and change clothes before going back to the Grants home for dinner, Mrs. Graham handed her an envelope. "What is it?" she asked the elder lady.

"I don't know, Janet. It was put through my letter box." Janet looked at the envelope. It was simply addressed to "The American"

"You're the only American here so I suppose it's for you."

"Thank you, Mrs. Graham," she said as she headed to her room. Once inside she opened it and tried to read it but ended up asking

Mrs. Graham to do the honors. She read out loud to Janet interpreting where needed:

> Yer not welcome in these parts. It would be best fer ye
> tae pack up and go back tae America where ye belong. Ye
> dinna fit into the social class of Jonathan Grant. Everyone
> here knows that ye are quite the schemer, thinking ye
> can just walk in tae toon and lie and manipulate. If ye
> continue to pursue him, ye could be putting yer life in
> danger. This is a friendly warning.

"I wouldn't say it's very friendly. Even though some of us talk that way, most of us write in proper English. This sounds like an uneducated person."

Janet was disturbed. The only person she could think of who would care that she was with Jonathan was Nora but it sounded childish and uneducated, like Mrs. Graham said. She wasn't sure if she should show it to Jonathan or not. She didn't want to bother him. Whoever put it through Mrs. Graham's letterbox sounded like a little girl with a big crush. She decided it was harmless but maybe she should show it to him anyway. When he picked her up to take her to dinner she showed him the note.

"What in the world? I can't think of anyone who would do this."

"Well I hear every young lady from John O'Groats to the Borders would kill for you," she said smiling.

"I know it's probably nothing, but we have to find out who it is and put a stop to this nonsense."

"Let's not say anything to your family. I don't want to spoil this evening. I don't have much time left and I want it to be happy."

"Okay, but I'm going to hold on to it anyway. There was that other incident when that young man brushed past you and gave you a similar warning."

They did have a wonderful time and when Janet got back to the bed and breakfast, Mrs. Graham was waiting to find out if she'd shown the letter to Jonathan. "Just some silly little girl afraid that I'm going to whisk Jonathan off to California," she said laughing making light of it.

"Jonathan wasn't concerned about it?"

"Well, he didn't like it; nor did he like the time that young man brushed against me outside your place..."

"Ye didnae tell me about that? What'd he look like?"

"Couldn't really tell. He was probably mid to late twenties but he had a hat and sunglasses on."

"To be honest with ye, I thought the letter sounded like a young man also. Its tone was a wee bit violent."

Janet only had two more days before her flight back to America. It was a hard decision but she had told her Aunt Betty that she wouldn't see her until the next visit which she said "might be sooner than she thought."

Her aunt understood that she would want to spend as much time as she could with Jonathan, even though he was going to be with her in California soon. "I have a feeling he will be having you over a lot more than you think," her aunt had said. "Jonathan Grant has never, as far as I know from the press, ever been so involved with a woman like he seems to be with you."

"Really Aunt Betty? From what he has said I don't think he has really been involved with anyone. I think he has only escorted the other women."

She had made time for Robert only twice as the Grants had a lot of things for her to do and places to go. Jonathan apologized to Robert for being so greedy with her.

"Don't feel that way," Robert assured him. "You brought her over here and I was just too happy to have the time I did have with her." He had taken her to lunch once at an upscale restaurant and they had met in the tearoom where he talked about Alice having been sent away from him.

Janet could see that it devastated him to find out that it wasn't her mother that left him; it was his mother that sent her away.

"I know things are happening between you and Jonathan and I hope for both your sakes it will work out. The Grants are wonderful people. I can vouch for that. Good luck dear. I'm sorry I didn't get through the journal like I'd hope to."

"Take your time. I took mine. There were times I had to lay it down and couldn't pick it up for weeks," she had told him.

"That's what happened to me after reading what my mother did."

The next two days went flying by and Janet and Jonathan spent every minute they could get alone together. On her last night, after dinner, they went for a walk in the gardens. "Jonathan, we haven't talked about where all this is going. You brought me back here to meet your family. That is a huge thing."

"I know it is. I never thought it would happen this fast so I've been hesitant to tell you that I love you. I want to be with you all the time. That is why I made the hasty decision to visit you in California. When I told my parents they were shocked."

"I would be too if I were them. After all, they were gone last time I was here so they didn't even know anything about me. Do you love me, Jonathan?"

"Yes I do."

"I love you too. I've been so scared that it couldn't happen for us because I'm not in the same social class as you are."

"Don't say that. You're way up there," he said pulling her towards him and kissing her. "I have to make you understand that we don't have rules like the Royal Family. We're allowed to marry whomever we want." They sat on the garden bench and watched the stars. She put her head on his shoulder as she stared up at the sky.

"This long distance relationship is going to be hard, but marriage is not something to rush into," he said.

"No it isn't. I've waited a long time to make sure I would marry the right man. I can hold off a while longer."

"Are you saying you're not sure that I'm the right man?" he said teasing her.

"I'm sure, but I agree that there's no reason to rush into anything." *Except not being together all the time,* she thought.

"I don't want to let you go tomorrow, but I will see you in California soon. Janet, I know you have friends and family in America, but I would be pleased if you would come back and spend the Christmas holidays here. Would you consider it?"

"Actually, I haven't thought about Christmas. It will be my first without my mom," she said thinking that she would be alone. Her friends all have their own families, although she knew she would be welcome in any of their homes, and Tom and Maggie sometimes go to their in-laws homes. Although she was always welcome there too, but being with Jonathan would be like being with her family and her in-laws... well, sort of. But there was Robert and he was family.

"Then you have to come. My mom makes the home very festive and we have a big party prior to Christmas. We have dinner just with the family on Christmas day."

"It sounds wonderful. Of course I would love to come."

"It'll be so much more fun having you with me instead of being alone or with some hanger-on."

"That doesn't sound like you, Jonathan."

"I know. I'm sorry, it's just I've been looking for you for so long and so tired of girls who want everything that comes with me. You know what I mean?"

"Yes I do. I'm glad I'm the person you've been looking for. As for me, I didn't know that someone like you existed."

"Is there any special place you would like to visit in California?" she asked changing the subject.

"You be my guide. I know there are wonderful places like Yosemite, San Francisco and the wine country where you live."

"There's a lot more to the wine country than where I live. There's Napa and Sonoma and so on. I'll plan something."

"I'm sorry I haven't been able to show you much of Scotland but there will be other times."

The next morning Jonathan called Robert and then handed the phone to Janet.

"I just wanted to say goodbye Mr. MacLean." They talked for a few minutes then she hung up the phone then once again she thought, *goodbye daddy.*

Jonathan was watching and thought he saw a sad, faraway look on her face when she said goodbye to Robert. He had noticed it before when she was with Robert. He also was surprised by the instant affection she had for him. *Well, he was an extremely wonderful man,* he thought, *and maybe because he had been married to her mother at one time, made her feel close to him. After all both of her parents were gone now.*

Robert had told her he would call her the next day. Janet said goodbye to the Grant family then she and Jonathan drove away. It was a different drive this day. On the way up to his home he was talking a lot and pointing out various sites. Today he was quiet. She knew what he was feeling as she was feeling the same thing. There was a sadness between them knowing that once again they were going to be separated for a while.

"It's a beautiful country," she said as though to break the silence.

"Thank you. We Scots are very proud of it."

"Jonathan, I'm going to miss you too," she said.

"I'm sorry, Janet. I have been so busy feeling lousy because you're going away but I have you here now and I've been ignoring you," he said patting her knee.

"When I get back, I'm going to start planning your visit and getting caught up with my orders and before I know it, I will be picking you up at SFO."

"I assume that's the San Francisco Airport. I have a lot to do also, so I'll stop moping right now."

"It will be nice to have a place in Scotland and one in California. We can live in California in the winter," he said smiling at her.

"Are you proposing to me, Jonathan Grant," she said smiling back.

"Well, it's not official. I will let you get to know me better first." Janet wanted to throw her arms around his neck and yell "YES!" but she just said a mild "Okay!"

As he put his arms around her to say goodbye, the flood came. She had been feeling sad but was able to hold back the tears but at that moment the floodgates opened and the tears rolled down her face. He took out a clean handkerchief that he brought just in case this would happen, and wiped the tears on her cheeks. "It won't be long, Janet. We'll be together soon."

"I know. I'll be fine in a little while. It's just this moment that's so hard, knowing any second I'll be going through security and you'll be gone."

When Jonathan arrived back home, there was an envelope on the hallway bureau addressed to him. "It looks like an invitation," he said aloud opening it.

Mr. & Mrs. John MacDonald
request your company at a small dinner party
at their Elgin home (residence of their daughter)
on July 28, 2006 at 7:00 pm.

Jonathan knew that probably Joan was behind this, but he had a lot of respect for Mr. and Mrs. MacDonald and hadn't seen them in about a year. He didn't think he could refuse them unless of course he had a legitimate excuse or maybe he could invite his cousin Anna to come up from Inverness and be his companion. *That would be a cruel joke. It would certainly make Joan furious, but it would also insult her parents which I don't want to do.* Just then Stewart came downstairs. "Hey, did you get an invitation to a dinner party thrown by the MacDonalds?" Jonathan asked his brother.

"Yes, Catherine and I both got one. Don't tell me. You got one also?" Jonathan nodded his head up and down a couple of times. "Well," Stewart said laughing, "now we know what the party's all about. Catherine and I were a little curious. Are you going?"

"I don't want to, knowing that I'll be dealing with Joan all night."

About a week after Janet left, the Glasgow Herald had a story about the mystery woman in Jonathan Grant's life. The story went on to discuss the fierce competitiveness of all the young socialite females, especially between Aberdeen and Elgin and Inverness who were strongly vying for the attention of Jonathan Grant to no avail. Now, apparently a young American woman walks into town and captures more than his attention. "She has been here twice, for about a week each time, and the whole time she was here she was accompanied by the young Grant. Who Is She?" the reporter went on to say.

CHAPTER ELEVEN

Janet was very busy getting caught up with and trying to get ahead of orders. She wanted her time to be totally free when Jonathan came. He called the night she got home and every other night after that. As soon as she got home she called Maggie and let her know how things went. Maggie was ecstatic when Janet informed her that Jonathan had said that he loved her. When she said he actually talked of marriage, she thought her sister was going to come through the phone. She was screaming. Janet planned a dinner party on the Saturday after she got home for all her friends. She wanted to share her news with them face to face, so she invited them over the first Saturday she got home.

"Oh my gosh!" Linda cried out. "I hope the wedding will be soon."

"Where will it take place?" Kathy asked.

"You guys are jumping the gun," Janet answered.

"You said he talked of marriage," Margaret said.

"Well he made a comment about having a house in Scotland and one in California," she said raising her eyebrows and shrugging her shoulders. "When I teased him and asked if he was proposing, his answer was 'well it's not official. I will let you get to know me better first'." Again she raised her eyebrows and shrugged her shoulders.

"It sounds like a proposal to me," Keith said adding his opinion.

"I haven't thought where it might take place, if it does. I suppose in Scotland since his family have that big estate," Janet answered Kathy's question.

"Well we better all start saving up for the big affair. We can book way ahead of time and stay at Mrs. Graham's Bed and Breakfast," said Margaret. They all had such a great time talking about it. Kathy and Linda said they were so excited to be going to such an elegant wedding. Later that night Janet lay in bed thinking how romantic and fun it would be to have the wedding at this beautiful big estate with all her friends and family.

She had been home for three weeks and only had another three weeks to prepare for Jonathan's visit. She had made some plans. He loved the outdoors so besides doing some local trips like visiting the vineyards and wineries in Napa and Sonoma and seeing a lot of Mendocino and taking him to the Redwood Forest up in Humboldt County, she would also take him to Yosemite and Lake Tahoe. Both places had lots of beautiful day hikes. As far as Janet was concerned, Lake Tahoe was as beautiful as any of the Lochs she had seen in Scotland. The lake that sat beneath the famous Sierra Nevada Mountains would impress him very much. The waterfalls in Yosemite were spectacular but more so in the spring when the snow melts from the famous mountains. She just hoped there would still be some water left in them since it would be September. *We did have some bad flooding this spring so possibly they will still be quite spectacular,* she thought. She had already asked him where he would like to stay in Yosemite. "I don't have camping equipment. There is the lodge, which is quite reasonable and I can afford that for myself. Then there is the exquisite old Ahwahnee Hotel, where Queen Elizabeth once stayed, but it is very expensive."

"If it is good enough for Queen Elizabeth then that's where we'll stay."

"You might be able to afford that, but the lodge is my limit."

"Janet, you don't think I would possibly put you up in the lodge and I stay at the Ahwahnee Hotel? Book us both a room and see if you can get them close together." It excited her to think of staying at the beautiful Ahwahnee but when she called to make the reservations she was told that they were booked up for a whole year and the lodge was also. She actually felt relieved that it was totally booked when she found out that a standard room at the Ahwahnee was $300 to $500 a night and a suite was $700 a night. When she called him to tell him they couldn't go to Yosemite, he said, "Book a suite at the Hotel for next year. See if you can get it at the end of spring. I would love to see the waterfalls in all their glory."

She had also invited her family to come down while he was there. Ian already had a vacation planned that he couldn't get out of, but Maggie and Tom were coming down by themselves for a few days. That worked out nicely. She didn't want them to be around too long and she didn't want their children to come down, although she didn't ask them not to bring them. They decided, on their own, that only the two of them needed to meet their sister's new suitor. "I can't wait to meet him, Janet," Maggie had told her.

She's so excited anyone would think he was coming to visit her, Janet thought smiling to herself.

Janet was wrapping some vases to take to Keith when the doorbell rang. She glanced out the window to see if it was perhaps UPS or Fed Ex, but it was a car she was not familiar with. *Who can it be?* she wondered. Sometimes it caused a little fear in her when she didn't think she knew the person at the door, because she lived up the hill by herself. If she were to scream loud enough, she was sure the neighbors down hill would probably hear her. She opened the door cautiously. At first she stared at the gentleman as though she was trying to figure out who he was, then her mouth fell open. She could hardly find her voice.

"Mr. MacLean! What are you doing here?" she finally said. "Forgive me, come on in. I'm sorry! I just couldn't place you outside of Scotland. I mean I never expected you to be standing on my doorstep here in California," she kept babbling.

"It is me who should be apologizing, just barging in on you like this. I should have called and let you know, but it was quite a last minute thing."

"Do you have business in California?"

"No but I thought I would take the opportunity to visit my old friend in San Francisco. He's one of the boys I grew up with and who also went down to Glasgow the night I met your mother."

"Yes, you told me of him. Please sit down. Do you drink coffee?"

"Yes, I do. I would love to have a cup with you," he said politely but also with affection in his voice.

When she brought the coffee and sat down next to him she said, "It's so nice to see you. I'm sorry I didn't get to see much of you when I was over there that last time. I'm afraid the Grants kept me quite busy so I'm happy to see you now, Mr. MacLean."

He looked at her for a long time. She actually was wondering what he was thinking and why he had come. *Had he finished reading the journal?* she wondered. *He hadn't brought it with him.*

"You may call me dad, Janet," he said smiling a little sadly at her "but only if you wish."

"So you did finish it. Did it shock you?"

"No, it deeply saddened me. Not only did Nora take my beloved Alice away from me, but she also took the years of watching my baby grow into a little girl then into the beautiful woman that's sitting next to me right now."

At that moment she burst into tears and he put his arms around her and let his tears flow also. She cried when she first read it in her mother's journal, but now that she was sitting next to her father and he was feeling the same emotion, there was no holding back.

"We'll make up for it, Janet."

"Nora won't accept me. I know that," Janet said still sobbing.

"She won't, but she has no control over this matter anymore."

"Have you told her who I really am? She hates me already because Jonathan and I have gotten very close."

"I haven't talked much to her since I read about her being the cause of your mom leaving. When I read about dear Alice being in a foreign country and pregnant with my child, I was truly heartbroken," he said sincerely. "The only person I wanted to talk to was you and I wanted to do it personally. That's why it was a last minute trip for me. I was so angry I had to get away from Nora."

"I do want to call you dad, but I don't think I would be comfortable saying it around her."

"I'm glad and don't worry about her. She's in the doghouse with everyone. I told Catherine and my grandmother about her breaking up Alice and me. They are both upset with her for that. Wait until they hear this."

"You're going to tell them about me?" she asked surprised.

"Yes! I know grandma will want to meet you and I'm sure Catherine will be glad to find out she has a sister. You know you both have the same eyes."

"We take after you. That was the first thing I noticed about you. I always wondered who I got the color of my eyes from."

"Jonathan will be out in a few weeks. Now that I'm officially your dad, can I ask what his intentions are for you?"

"We're talking marriage, but we're not rushing into it." Something very important struck her. "You know what?" she said excitedly.

"What?" he asked.

"I'm so happy that I have a dad to give me away to Jonathan, when it does happen," she said smiling so broadly at him that it melted his heart.

"I would be so honored to do that. Can you imaging how wide Alice's smile will be when she looks down and sees me walking you down the aisle?"

"Knowing mom, she'll be flat out laughing at the top of her lungs."

"Yes! She'll be laughing all right. Laughing at Nora. It'll be Alice's revenge," he said laughing. They were both having such a good time realizing that in spite of Nora's intentions at the beginning, Robert was going to be walking his and Alice's child down the aisle to marry Jonathan Grant. It was the first good laugh he had had since finding out all the things Nora had done to him.

"Daddy," she said and he smiled. He liked hearing her say that affectionate name for him. "Let's get your luggage and put it in the guest room."

"Oh, I wasn't expecting you to put me up. I can get a room in a hotel, if they have one in this little town."

"I want you to stay with me. I wouldn't send my dad to a hotel. Let's put it away and I want to take you around our little town."

"It's a fairly straight drive from the airport to here," he said as they were driving down the hill. "Just go down that 101 freeway then onto 128 and by the way, that is a beautiful road. At one point I thought I was back home with the little white sheep dotted all over the beautiful green hills."

"It does remind you of Scotland, doesn't it?" she answered. She felt so wonderful and she knew he did too. *He probably wondered*

151

if I would accept him as a dad as much as I wondered if he would accept me as his daughter, she thought as she looked over to him and smiled.

Robert had been nervous about coming to her and telling her that he knew he was her dad. He didn't know how he would approach it but it all turned out well. They pulled outside a real estate office. When she got out he asked if he should stay in the car until she finished her business inside.

"No, I want you to meet a really good friend of mine." She was glad Margaret was inside her office alone. She ushered her dad in and closed the door behind them. Margaret looked surprised, especially when Janet closed the door.

"Hi, Janet," she said with a question mark in her voice then looked at the gentleman with her. She thought perhaps Janet had brought her a client. He was very well dressed so Margaret hoped he would be looking for something upscale.

"Hi Margaret," she said smiling. This smile was as big as the one she had when she told her about Jonathan. "I want you to meet someone very special to me. Margaret, meet my dad."

Margaret was further confused. Her dad had died over five years ago and the other one, her biological one, lived in Scotland and didn't know about an American daughter. Margaret stared a little longer then realized this was he. "Mr. MacLean," she said walking towards him and holding out her hand, "it's such a pleasure to meet you."

He took her hand and looked at Janet then back to Margaret. "Then you know about me?"

Margaret looked at Janet guiltily thinking she had let the cat out of the bag. "Yes, Margaret knows about you. I needed someone to talk to when I was reading mom's journal. She was a real friend to me during that time."

"It's very nice to meet you, Margaret, and I appreciate you being there for my daughter when she needed a friend. I know how much I needed to talk to someone and Janet was there for me.

"I was more than happy to be with her. It's been quite a saga," Margaret said misty-eyed.

"Yes, but it's going to have a happy ending," he said. Then looking at his watch, he said, "It's almost six o'clock. Would you young ladies like to go out and eat?"

"That would be great. That way you can get to know Margaret. I want you to know all my friends and my family."

He wanted to take them somewhere special so Janet chose a very nice restaurant in Mendocino. Robert was happy that Janet had such a nice friend. He found out that Margaret was six years older than Janet and was her walking and running partner. He also found out that she was a photographer so he had asked her if she would take some pictures of him and his daughter so he could take them back home and share them when he explained to Catherine and grandma why he had taken the trip. They talked about Jonathan and Margaret told Robert that she had seen pictures of him and thought him very handsome.

"Oh Jonathan's very handsome and I know he's happy to have met someone who is not superficial, like the women he's used to."

"Margaret, when I do get married, whoever the man is, I have a dad to walk me down the aisle."

"That's right! I'm so happy that both of you are accepting of each other. I was worried about Janet when she went over to Scotland the first time. I thought she was going to tell you and I was afraid you would reject her."

"I appreciate you being worried about her but no, I loved her the moment I knew she was Alice's daughter and when I found out she was mine, although I was very saddened about the whole loss, I loved her even more. Not only was she Alice's daughter, but also it was her child by me and that was very special to me. My darling Alice actually had my child."

"I just realized that I've thought and talked about my mother more since her death six months ago, than I probably have most of my adult life. As a child you always think of your mom, but when you grow up and have a career and friends, you don't think so much about her."

"You probably thought a lot about her, but maybe not as intense. You found out things you never knew about her that gave you a lot of food for thought," her dad said.

She nodded thoughtfully. "You're probably right."

Margaret asked Robert how he thought his mother might feel about Janet as her granddaughter.

"Oh, I'm positive she won't accept her, but as I told Janet, I'm in control, not her." He laughed and went on to tell Margaret about his and Janet's vision of Alice looking down at him walking her daughter down the aisle to marry Jonathan and laughing her head off at getting revenge on Nora.

Margaret thought that was really ironic and laughed along with them at how Nora's plan had backfired. She didn't get rid of Alice Douglas after all.

"She probably had no idea when she was writing the journal that it would turn out like this," Janet said.

"I think she wrote the journal so that you would know the truth and left it to you to do what you wanted with it. I'm not sure she thought you would travel to her homeland and uncover, at least for me, the mystery of the disappearing Alice," Robert said.

"She would have a blast with this. I hope she can see what's happening."

Early the next morning they went to San Francisco. Janet took him to the art gallery where Keith worked and introduced them and showed him some of her work.

"This is beautiful, Janet," he said pointing to a large vase. "Is it okay to take pictures of her vases and pots?" he asked Keith. "I know you have to be careful in some museums with photography."

"No, go ahead," Keith encouraged him.

While he was taking pictures Keith told Janet how happy he was that everything turned out so well for her. "Who would have thought?" he said.

After they left the gallery they toured around for a little bit then Robert asked if he could take her to meet his friend. "Sure I'd love to meet your friend. It would be nice to know someone here that knew both you and mom."

He called his friend to find out if it was convenient for them to come. "You come all the way to San Francisco, you better come and see your old friend. I'm looking forward to seeing you and your daughter."

He gave the phone to Janet so she could get the directions to his home. She wrote them down then handed the directions to Robert.

"You read them to me, while I drive." It didn't take too long before they were in the Pacific Heights district of San Francisco. "Wow! I've never been up here. These are some magnificent homes," she said impressed. "Where do I go from here?" Janet asked.

Robert read off the address and they found themselves parked outside a beautiful mansion. Just as they were getting out of the car, the front door opened and an excited man with his arms open wide came running down the stairs to meet them.

"Rab, Rab, it is so good to see you old pal." Both men gave each other a big hug.

"How've you been James?" Robert asked.

"I'm doing well, Rab. You shocked the heck out of me when you called and said you were in San Francisco. Come on in. And is this lovely young lass Catherine?"

"No James, this is Janet, my other daughter." James looked a little surprised. He shook hands with Janet and insisted they come inside. Once settled, James said to Janet, "When I talked with you on the phone to give you directions, I was sure you were American."

"She is," Robert answered for Janet. "I have my daughter in Scotland. This is my American daughter."

"Now you have me confused, Rab. I know of Catherine but I never knew you had two daughters and especially one that moved to America. How could you have kept that from me all these years, Rab?" Janet finally understood that Rab was James' pet name for Robert.

"I only found out myself," Robert said watching James shake his head in confusion. Janet noticed that her dad was having fun with James. "Do you remember Alice?" he asked James.

"Of course I do. How could we forget what she did to you leaving you so down in the dumps?" James said wondering how she fit into the picture.

"Janet is Alice's and my daughter. Alice came here to San Francisco to escape all the gossip and humiliation. She was only supposed to be here a few months, but while she was here she found out she was pregnant."

"Why didn't she go back and tell you so that you two could raise the child?"

"My mother pretty much threatened her family to keep her away

CAPONERA

from me. She married a very nice man here and had three other children." He went on to tell James about the journal and Alice's death. After about ten minutes of talking James turned to her and said, "I'm so sorry dear about your mother. She was a lovely girl. I'm happy though that you and your father have been able to unite. It was so nice of you to take the journal all the way to Scotland so he could know what really happened."

"When Janet came over to Scotland, she met Malcolm's boy Jonathan and he will be here in a few weeks to visit her."

"Oh! Is there something brewing here?" James asked. Janet noticed that he still had his Scottish brogue. When he said the word "brewing" the last syllable was raised almost like a question. She found herself wishing she could master the singsong dialect of the Scots.

"Could be, James. You might be seeing a lot of Jonathan from now on."

"Well imagine that. I'll be seeing a lot of my two best friends' children. How wonderful. You'll come and see me occasionally when your dad goes home, I hope?"

"I'd love to come and see you, Mr...." Janet realized that she didn't know his last name.

"It's Armstrong, but you can call me James, if you like."

"Okay, James it is. You'll remind me of dad and Jonathan."

He had informed Janet that his wife passed away the year before. Of course Robert knew since they were still in touch with one another. Janet looked around this beautiful big room with its antique and elegant furniture. It was all very expensive she could tell. As she was looking around the room her eyes caught sight of a beautiful vase sitting on a bureau. She got up and walked over to it. *Mrs. Armstrong...died last year...*her mind was racing. She turned to James. "Mr. Armstrong, I mean James, your wife was one of my best customers. This is my work." Both James and Robert turned towards her and looked at the piece she was standing by. They were both dumbstruck. "Your wife was Laura Armstrong. She was a lovely woman. She came to an art show that Keith had where clients could come and meet the artists. I met your wife that night and a few times after."

"That's right. I remember the night she went to the show. She

156

was so excited about meeting you. We have many pieces of your work."

"I know you do. She was such a wonderful woman. I really loved her. We had a great relationship."

"I know that. She talked about you often."

"I knew she had passed away last year and in fact was at the funeral service."

"It's strange we have all these connections and never knew one another. You were the daughter of Robert and his beloved Alice and she lived in Redwood City which is only 30 miles or so south of here. Now you tell me my wife was your client and you were at her funeral."

"It is strange. All these years I missed Alice and here she was, living a short ways away from my friend," said Robert shaking his head in disbelieve. "And your wife was acquainted with the daughter I didn't know. Maybe I didn't try hard enough to find Alice."

They sat for a few moments pondering all this information. Then Janet asked, "Do you think you will stay in San Francisco or go back to Scotland?"

"My thoughts are to sell this big home and buy something smaller in Marine County, maybe Tiburon. I like being by the water and maybe buy another home in the highlands near Robert and Malcolm. I am going back to Scotland for the Christmas holidays."

"Me, too! Wouldn't it be great if we could travel together?" Janet said excitedly.

"You let me know, James, because I will be buying her ticket?"

They visited for three hours. James gave them a tour of his home before they left.

On the drive back to Boonville Janet had told her dad that she liked James very much. "Do you think he's lonely now that his wife is gone? I mean living in a foreign country alone?" she asked.

"He has lots of friends here. He met Laura when she visited the highlands twenty-five years ago. It was love at first sight. She was from a well-to-do family here in San Francisco. It surprised me that he left Scotland because he loved the highlands so much."

"But he obviously loved Laura more."

"Obviously. He was the youngest son in the family, so he wouldn't have inherited their property. I miss him though."

"I would like to see a lot of him. I didn't realize how much I have missed a father figure in my life. Now I'll have James when I don't have you."

"Well, I'm glad that I introduced him to you. He will love having you near him. Laura was never able to conceive."

"I know that. She told me and I think she had already adopted me. Margaret's my best friend but she's also like a mother figure, because she's quite nurturing to me. Especially when I was finding out about you and mom."

"She seemed that type to me. Has she never married or had children?"

"No! She was engaged for a year and it didn't work out. I just don't think she has met that someone special. She's kind of like me. Not very needy and wanting more than just a man in her life."

It was a nice drive back. It seemed like the time flew by, probably because they chatted so much. She was amazed and thrilled at how easy she felt being with him. As they pulled into Boonville she was surprised when he asked if they could stop by Margaret's office and invite her out to dinner. "I'm not sure she'll still be there as it is six o'clock, but if she's not I'll call from her phone." They went into the office. "Is Margaret still here?" she asked one of the other agents.

"Yes, she just had a client leave. I think she's getting ready to go home."

"Thanks!" Janet said.

Margaret was just locking her office when she turned and said in surprise "I wasn't expecting to see you. I thought you were in San Francisco?"

"We just pulled in. Dad wants to take us out to dinner again. Can you go?"

"I'd love to. Thank you very much," she said smiling at Robert. They went to the same restaurant and once again they had a wonderful time." Janet was surprised at how well her dad and Margaret communicated. She almost felt a little left out at times.

"Hello! Somebody else is here," she sang teasingly.

Her dad turned his head looking around, "Oh! Another of your friends?" he asked.

"No, just me," Janet said smiling.

They realized that they had been so immersed in their own conversation. "I'm sorry," they both said at the same time.

"I didn't realize your dad was quite an avid photographer," Margaret said. "I just got quite excited about it. I don't know anyone else that knows very much about it."

"I'm sorry, sweetheart. I didn't mean to be so rude."

"It's okay," she said laughing. "It was interesting listening to you both go on about your experiences with the camera."

"Tell me about your day in San Francisco."

"It's a beautiful city. I had never been there before. Janet took me to the gallery and introduced me to her work."

"She does fantastic work."

"Yes, she does. I was very proud of it."

"Dad took me to visit an old friend of his. I have to take you to meet him sometime. He lives in Pacific Heights."

"Ooh! Very exclusive neighborhood."

She told Margaret of the fact that James' deceased wife had been a very good client and acquaintance of hers. Margaret was obviously amazed.

They left the restaurant around nine o'clock. Robert had announced that he would be leaving in two days to go back home. Janet felt a pang in her heart. She didn't like the idea of him going. She was having too much fun with him. When they got to her house she made coffee and they sat and talked for a while.

"I told my brothers and sister about you. They know that you are my biological father."

"How did they react?"

"They were shocked first of all that mom was married before. Then they were shocked that she had a child by you and once again when I told them the child was me. They didn't feel any different about me, of course. We still all love one another like before. They loved mom very much and when they found out she had been married and what happened, they were sad."

"Do you think they would be willing to meet me someday?"

"Yes, they are and they'll love you. I have told them how much you loved our mom and how saddened you were when you found out the pain your mother had caused her."

"I'm looking forward to meeting Alice's other children, but it will have to be another time."

Nora MacLean was fuming when she found out her son had taken off for California without an explanation to anyone. He had been gone two days and not even a phone call. She decided to go over to the Grant's home to inquire of Jonathan. He was outside washing his car and his two border collies were jumping up trying to catch the water that was coming out of the hose. Jonathan was laughing and having a good time teasing them until Nora MacLean showed up.

"I have no idea where Robert is. I haven't talked to Janet in a couple of days. She hasn't been home the past two nights when I called."

"Will you be calling her tonight, Jonathan?" she asked in a demanding voice.

"Yes! I will be."

"Will you find out what's going on and let me know?"

"With all due respect, Mrs. MacLean, I'm not sure it's my business or yours."

"He's my son," she said angrily.

"He's fifty-three years old and Janet is not my wife," he said almost as angry.

Malcolm Grant heard their voices rising and went out to see what was going on. Nora MacLean was storming towards her car when she turned and said to Jonathan. "I don't know what your parents are thinking allowing you to be with that girl."

Malcolm didn't get to her soon enough to tell her what he thought. She was in her car and driving off by the time he reached his son. "What was that all about?" he asked.

"Apparently Robert took off to California and didn't explain to anyone why he was going. This is the third day that he's been gone and hasn't even called. She asked me to find out from Janet what's going on. I told her I didn't think it was my business or hers. I'm not going to be her spy?"

"No! You stay out of it. I didn't like what she said about Janet," Malcolm said.

"I don't care what she thinks but I don't like her talking about Janet they way she just did," Jonathan said angrily.

"I'm glad Catherine takes after Robert and not her grand-mother," his dad said.

"She's had a big influence on the girl's life though," Jonathan answered. *Maybe I'll call her a little earlier. If Robert's with her they may have been out to dinner when I called,* he thought. He always called her around six o'clock California time because she usually ate dinner at home. He decided to start calling her at four o'clock and keep trying until he got a hold of her. Finally her phone was picked up.

"Hello!" she said into the phone. She had an idea that it would be Jonathan. She hadn't been home for his usual call.

"Hello darling, I've missed talking to you. I tried calling the past two nights."

"I've missed talking to you too, Jonathan. I was out to dinner both nights."

"With Robert?" he asked.

"How did you know he was here?" she asked looking at her dad and shrugging her shoulders but Robert had an idea how Jonathan found out.

"Nora was over here demanding that I call you and find out what was going on then report back to her."

"What did you tell her?" Robert was watching her trying to fig-ure out what the conversation was on the other end.

"I told her that I didn't think it was my business or hers."

"Good!" she looked over at Robert. He was motioning her to give him the phone.

"Jonathan, if you would, please tell my family I will be leaving here tomorrow but it is an overnight flight, so I will be arriving in Glasgow the morning after. I'll talk to you then. Thanks Jonathan." He gave the phone back to Janet.

"I'm not going to ask any questions. I'm sure I'll get the answers when Robert comes back."

"Yes, it's better you don't know so you won't have to deal with her. All you can tell her is that he's with me and let her know when he'll be home." They talked for the usual half an hour. When she hung up she told her dad what Jonathan had told her.

"I figured it out just listening to your side of the conversation and knowing my mother. Poor Jonathan."

"She asked him to find out from me what was going on and to report back to her."

"What a nerve she has. I hope Jonathan told her off."

She told him what Jonathan had said to her. He laughed. "Good for him."

These goodbyes were getting harder and harder for Janet. His plane was leaving at one o'clock in the afternoon with a stop over and arriving in Glasgow at nine o'clock the next morning. She noticed he had the journal and a large envelope.

"Janet, you were very kind to let me read this journal. Now that you are officially a MacLean, I would like to give these to you." She took out papers. She looked at him with a curious look.

"These are copies of some old documents that my ancestors thought were important to keep and pass on down. I thought you might be interested in reading them. They are your ancestors too."

"Wow! Thank you, thank you very much. I will treat them with great care."

"I know you will, but like I said these are copies. The originals are at home."

"Are these for me to keep?" she asked.

"Yes. I do have to go, dear."

"Call me and let me know how everything went."

"I will," he said kissing her cheek.

As she watched him drive off down the hill, Janet cried. She went inside and called Margaret. "What are you doing?"

"Your dad just left, huh?" Margaret knew Janet would be feeling a little down. She had been so excited having her dad with her. "Do you want to go for a walk?"

"I'd love that. Thanks Margaret."

"Maybe we shouldn't walk too far. It's quite hot."

"That's fine. In fact let's walk to our shady picnic table and just talk."

"Okay! Give me half an hour to clean up my desk," Margaret said.

As they sat down Janet said, "My dad left at eight o'clock this morning. His plane leaves at one o'clock but he wanted to give himself plenty of time to drive to the airport and go through check-in and security. He is also meeting James at the airport so that they can have some time together."

"I know, he stopped by the office just after I hung up the phone from your call."

"Did he stop to say goodbye?"

"Yes," Margaret smiled.

"How sweet of him," Janet said.

"I thought so. I like him, Janet. He's a very fine gentleman. Handsome too."

"He is, isn't he? I know he liked you too. I was surprised when he wanted to stop in at your office yesterday and see if you wanted to come to dinner with us."

"I was too. I was so surprised to see the two of you coming in. The girls at the office kept inquiring about him. They all thought he was very sophisticated-looking. By the way, did he give you the journal back?"

"Yes, he did." They sat and talked for about an hour, mostly about Robert's visit. Janet told Margaret about the ancient documents he had given her copies off.

"What are they about?"

"I haven't read through them. He just gave them to me this morning before he left. Some are letters that were written by his ancestors. Mine too actually," she remembered.

"What a treasure. You get to read letters from family of centuries ago."

"Maybe you could come to my house soon and we can read them together."

CHAPTER TWELVE

Robert's flight had been very comfortable. He had never flown anything but first class in his life. He slept well and was quite refreshed when the plane landed in Glasgow. Janet had given him the address and phone number of Alice's sister, Betty. He had called her from the San Francisco Airport and asked if he could stop by for a few minutes and talk with her.

She was nervous about the visit but wanted to see him. She didn't invite any family members. In fact, she told her daughter that he was coming and for her not to come over at all in the morning. She knew it was going to be a very personal visit and he might not be too comfortable with others around. It was about half past ten when he arrived at her door.

"Come in, Robert. Good morning, Mrs. Carter," she greeted her neighbor who was scrubbing her doorstep as usual. "I've made some tea, would you like a cup?"

"That would be nice, Betty. I can only stay a little while. I need to get back home and talk to the family about Janet."

"What do you mean?"

"I finished Alice's journal. I know Janet told you that she had left it with me. I went to California to see if my daughter would accept me, after all that happened to her mom, and she did. In fact we had such a wonderful time together."

"I'm so glad for both your sakes and for Alice also," she said dabbing her eyes.

"I just stopped by to apologize to you for what my family has put yours through."

"It wasn't your fault, Robert. You didn't know."

"I know, but my mother won't apologize and I believe your family needs to hear one, so I'm representing the MacLeans in apologizing to the Douglas family."

"Well then, I accept the apology, Robert, and I'll let my sister Moira know also."

"I never did meet Moira. She had just left for America when I met Alice. I'd be grateful if you would do that, Betty."

"She'll be thrilled also to know how everything worked out for you and Janet."

"Betty, I want you and your family to come up to visit us occasionally. When I get home, I'm going to explain everything to my family. I'm going to let my daughter know she has a half-sister who has family in Glasgow that will be welcome to visit any time."

"That's very kind of you, Robert, but your mother will not like it."

"You're right, Betty, she'll not like it, but things will have to change."

He only stayed for an hour but he felt like he was cleansing his soul. Betty was happy that he came and was touched with his apology and invitation to visit them up in Elgin. When she opened the door to let him out, she gave him a hug. "We are all one big family now." He smiled and nodded his head.

"I'll be talking to you again, Betty," he said as he got into the car. Betty could see why Alice had been so in love with him. He was such a gentleman. Betty noticed a few of the neighbors out in the street chatting, including Mrs. Carter. She smiled to herself; *they'll be wondering what's going on at Betty's house. They might even think that Robert MacLean's my fancy man,* she thought smiling to herself.

The drive seemed to take forever. He couldn't wait to get back and get this all out in the open. Nora was not going to destroy his life anymore. Janet was going to be a part of his family. She would be treated just the same as Catherine. He knew Nora would protest but he would rather disown her than Janet. Janet had done nothing to hurt this family. "She was an innocent child born out of either my silliness for asking Alice to run off with me to get married, or for being too young and ignorant to take my stand against my mother. But I swear, she is not going to hurt my child again," he said aloud as he drove up into the Grampian Mountains.

He felt rather tired as he drove up his driveway, but he was going to take care of the matter. He hoped that everyone would be home.

Nora came to the door and immediately started in on him. She was furious with what was happening. "You had us all worried. That was selfish of you to take off like that and not tell any of us."

He brushed past her into the house without looking at her or answering her. Catherine came downstairs to meet him. "Hello, sweetheart," he said hugging his daughter and kissing her cheek. "Hello, grandma."

"Hello, Robert. You didn't have me worried. I knew you were doing whatever it was you had to do," his grandma Isabel said. She had been having some thoughts of her own as to what was going on.

"Thank you, dear. It's nice to know someone thinks I'm grown up enough to handle my affairs without having to get permission. I'm going to wash up, change my clothes and I'll be back down in the living room in an hour. I would like you all to be there."

Nora knew she wasn't going to like this. She wondered what possibly could have sent him off to California in such a hurry. Maybe he wants to marry that girl. Well good, that would leave Jonathan for Catherine. Her mind was running in all different directions. Grandma Isabel went back to her cottage to rest. She set her alarm in case she fell asleep. Catherine said she had a book she promised to give to Stewart but that she would definitely be back in time. She told Stewart that her dad had just come back from California and had wanted to talk to the whole family in an hour. Stewart had told Jonathan and his folks so the whole Grant family was beside themselves with curiosity. After all, Janet was a special part of their lives and they knew it had something to do with her. It was unlike Robert to take off like he did and not say anything to anyone.

Finally an hour had passed and Robert came downstairs. He went out to his car and brought back a large envelope. Everyone was in the living room. Nora was sitting with her arms crossed in a very closed position.

"You all know I've been getting information about my ex-wife Alice, who passed away earlier this year."

"Yes, we know. You said Alice was giving it to you but it probably was that girl, her daughter," said Nora rather hatefully.

"In a way it was Alice. Besides coming and letting me know that her mom had passed away, Janet gave me a journal that Alice wrote, regarding the time she first met me to what happened after she left Scotland. I don't have the journal. I finished it and took it back to Janet."

"You mean you went all the way to America to give her back her journal?" said Nora.

"I told you how my mother, Nora, had sent her away," he said ignoring her once more. "She was only supposed to be in San Francisco visiting her sister for two or three months. When she was there, however, for almost three months, she found out she was pregnant with my child."

Catherine's face showed confusion and shock. Nora's showed anger. Isabel just smiled. Her thoughts had been correct. Beautiful Janet was her great-granddaughter.

"How do you know it was your child?" said Nora.

"Because Alice was a virgin when I married her and just about three months later she finds out she is with child. Up to that point I was the only man my Alice knew."

"So did she get an abortion?" Nora said hoping it was so.

"No Nora," it was Isabel speaking. "I'm assured that Alice loved Robert so much that she would never abort his child."

"You're right grandma. She married a very nice man, who was her brother-in-law's partner in business and he loved Alice."

"You never knew about it, daddy? I mean about this poor young woman thousands of miles from home and pregnant."

"No! Alice knew your grandmother would never accept her and for my sake, she chose to stay in America, marry a man she very much respected and stay out of my life."

"So what happened to the baby? How old would it be now?" Catherine, who was an avid reader, never thought a story like this could be real in this day and age.

"My daughter is thirty-two years old. Six years older than you are and her name is Janet."

"I knew it," Isabel said excitedly. Both Catherine and Nora looked at her.

"The girl that came over here is my daughter and I went to California to find out if she would accept me as her father."

"Did she dad?" Catherine said hopefully.

"Yes, she did."

"When can we meet her? When can I meet my great-grand-daughter?" Isabel asked.

"Wait a minute! What does this all mean? The girl could have written the journal herself. It's been known before. People trying to weasel into a family that has money."

You should know, Robert thought to himself.

"You're not thinking rationally. How could the girl write about things that you did that even I didn't know about? As far as 'what does it all mean'? It means she is now part of this family, my daughter, Catherine's sister, and grandma's great granddaughter."

"I will not accept her as my granddaughter," Nora said haughtily. She was so angry by this time her face was red.

"That is why I didn't mention her as your granddaughter. I know grandma will accept her and I'm sure Catherine will too."

"Of course I will, daddy. I met her for a short time when I went over to the Grants place to watch the foal being born. She was there with Jonathan. I feel terrible about the whole story."

By this time Nora looked like a mad woman and stormed out of the room shouting, "I will have none of this. I don't want to see that girl in this house."

"Nora," again it was Isabel. "Don't you say anything about this girl's class any more. She is Robert's child and because of that she comes from far better stock than you did. Not that I care about this class thing, after all I allowed my son Neil to marry you, but you do care about it and I'm tired of it. Now that she is part of my family, I will not allow you to speak badly of her in this house."

Nora was furious with Isabel for talking to her the way she did and tried to say something back but she was tongue-tied. The truth of the matter was, Isabel was right and Nora knew it.

After she left, Robert picked up the envelope and brought out the pictures that he had taken while in California and the ones that he asked Margaret to take of him and Janet in the restaurant.

"Look Catherine, she has the same eyes as you."

Catherine took the picture and smiled an emotional smile, trying to hold back the tears. "She looks quite a bit like me. I noticed that when I met her at the Grants. I thought it was strange."

"When can I meet her?" Grandma asked again.

"The Grants have invited her for the Christmas holidays. Grandma, take a look at some of the pottery she has done."

"Robbie, you didn't tell me she was a potter. Did you know I used to do pottery when I was a young girl? Of course, I did it for a hobby. It looks like hers is on display at a gallery."

"It's in a gallery in San Francisco."

"It's beautiful, son, just beautiful."

They continued looking at the pictures. There was even one of James and Robert that Janet had taken.

"Who is this?"

"That's James Armstrong, grandma. Remember? Malcolm, James and I were best buddies. I took Janet to meet him and he told her that he had known her mother. We all met her and her friends at the dancing in Glasgow."

"You're joking? I do remember James well." Robert went on to tell them that when they visited James in San Francisco, Janet saw some of her art in his house and then putting two and two together, she remembered that Laura Armstrong was one of her best clients.

"Can you imagine, James lived only half an hour away from Alice and didn't know it? Then my daughter starts selling her work to James' wife."

"That's amazing, son."

"Did Mr. Grant know Alice as well?" Catherine asked.

"Yes and James is coming back for the Christmas holidays also. He and Janet are going to try and get the same flight. James' wife passed away last year. Janet was at her funeral service, but at the time she had never met James. He lives in this beautiful big mansion in San Francisco, but he says he's going to sell it. It was more for his wife but now that she's gone he feels it's too big for him." He had so much to tell them and the coincidence of Alice and Janet living so close to James fascinated them.

He showed them pictures that he had taken of Janet's house

and of Janet working at her potter's wheel. This brought a smile to Isabel's face. "It reminds me of myself as a young girl."

"I should go over and talk to Jonathan and let him know."

"What is going on with Janet and Jonathan? I mean they brought her back after she had just been home a few weeks," asked Catherine.

"I believe they're in love, Catherine, but I don't feel bad because you said you were not in love with him, even though your grandmother has been trying to push you two together."

"No I'm not. Actually Stewart and I like being with each other but grandmother says because he is the youngest he won't inherit the estate."

"Sweetheart, you'll inherit this estate. Well I'm going over there, do you want to come?"

"Yes. I told Stewart I would come back after we had this discussion."

"Grandma, you're welcome to come also."

"You two go ahead. Robert, can you leave the picture of Janet at the potter's wheel?"

Robert was touched.

"You're kidding me?" was Jonathan Grant's response to the news that Janet was Robert's daughter. "That had never entered my mind and she never gave me a clue."

"You know what? It's funny, but the only one that did have a clue was my 95-year-old grandma. She has great intuition."

"Janet kept it to herself, because she wanted me to get the news from Alice and she wanted me to be the first to know."

"I understand and I extremely respect her for that. It must have been difficult for her to keep it to herself, but she knew it was the best thing to do and didn't you enjoy receiving the information from Alice?"

"Yes, I did and I thought it was a very smart thing for her to do. She wouldn't have been able to tell it to me like Alice did. The way it was written was like a book. Both Janet and I had to read little bits at a time in order to absorb it. Alice took us through a very important part of her life, my life and Janet's life. At times it was very sad but look how it has all turned out."

"It must have been a shock to Janet to find out who she thought was her father, wasn't."

"Yes, it was and she had a difficult time dealing with it, but her friend Margaret helped her through it. Her dad was a good father to her."

"I'm so happy for both of you," Jonathan said smiling. "What was Nora's take on it?" he added.

"She went ballistic but grandma and Catherine are quite taken up with the idea of having her in the family. They are both anxious to meet her."

Malcolm was standing in shock listening to Robert and Jonathan go back and forth.

"How are you with all of this now? First you lost your wife, then your daughter. I mean you have her back, but you lost a lot of years with her."

"I'm happy, Malcolm. It was hard at first. I thought of that and I actually wept over the whole thing and I wasn't sure Janet would accept me but we had a great time together. She even called me daddy," he said a little emotionally, "and I took her over to meet James. They became great friends and they are going to try and catch the same flight to Scotland at Christmas."

"You know I said that she never gave me a clue, but she had a melancholy, faraway look in her eyes when she was saying goodbye to you on the phone the last time she was here. I had seen it once before when she was with you. I caught her looking at you with that look," Jonathan said.

"It must have been really hard for her being with me and not being able to tell me," Robert said. "I know that you've asked her over and have offered to pay her fare. If you don't mind I'd like to bring her over. I won't take any of her time away from you, Jonathan. I just want to do it as her dad."

"Sure!" both Jonathan and Malcolm said in unison.

Malcolm hugged his friend and said, "It's almost like she has been a missing link all this time. A bonus is getting to see old Jimmy." They laughed.

Everyone was happy about Janet and the family expanding and the probability of the Grants and MacLeans uniting. Everyone, that was, except Nora MacLean. She could feel her world falling apart.

She couldn't live in the house with that girl, but it was Robert's house. When Neil died, the estate went to Robert with her right to live there as long as she wished. That was so it would stay in the MacLean family in the event the widow was to remarry. She didn't mind that because she still had had a lot of control over Catherine and Robert. She still ran the house as though she was the lady of the manor. That was then, now Robert was taken complete control of the estate.

Robert called Janet to let her know how everything went. "I'm glad that Catherine is ready to welcome me. She was the one I was concerned about. After all, she has been your only daughter all those years."

"I think maybe she had wished, all those years, that she would have had a sister."

"Of course I'm also dying to meet your grandma."

"*Your* great grandma," he corrected her. "Oh, I've been anxious to tell you that when I showed her the pictures of your pots in the gallery, she got quite excited and told me that when she was young pottery was her hobby. She got a little emotional when she saw the one of you throwing the pot. She asked me for it."

"Oh that's so touching. Now I'm really dying to meet her. We'll have so much to talk about."

"Okay dear, it's about nine o'clock here and I'm starting to feel the effect of the time change and the long flight. I'm going to go upstairs to bed." Nora was listening to his conversation in the other room. He had mentioned Catherine and grandma but not her. She didn't care except it made her feel like she was being cut off.

About an hour later Jonathan called and they talked about her relationship with Robert and of her meeting James. "It must have been hard being with him those times when you couldn't say anything about it."

"Remember when I walked out of the barn and you thought it was because I was squeamish about the birthing of the foal?"

"Yes?"

"I was overcome by the fact that I was with my half-sister and she didn't know it."

"I'm glad it's all out in the open now," he said almost apologetically.

They talked of his upcoming trip to California. He told her that Robert had shown everyone the pictures and how beautiful he thought her work was. She told him of the old letters he had left with her.

"He has shown me those documents. I have read them."

"I'm anxious to read them also."

They talked their usual half-hour then hung up.

Catherine's friend Joan made sure to stop by and find out what went on with Mr. MacLean and why he was at that woman's place in California. She sounded so hateful Catherine didn't know if she wanted to share with her or not that Janet was her sister. "Okay Joan, you have to promise not to say anything at this time. If word of this gets out I will know it was you, because you are the only one outside of the family, other than the Grants that know this," Catherine said then hesitated for a moment. "Janet is my half-sister."

"What? Has she proven it? She could be a fake?"

"No, we have the proof we need. She is my half-sister. My dad was married for a short while to Janet's mother and my grandmother had the marriage annulled. In the meanwhile, she got pregnant."

"I see someone trying to come into these two well-to-do families and scam them."

"You sound like my grandmother. She is legit and I don't want to hear you say anything more about her."

"Catherine, why are you buying into this? You're the sole heir to your father's estate. I always dreamed that you and I would be the ladies of the two big estates in this area."

Catherine said she didn't want to discuss it anymore. She wished she hadn't shared this information with Joan, but she knew it would come out soon anyway. "I haven't heard my parents or anyone else in this area talk about his first wife. You don't keep that information quiet around here."

"She was from Glasgow. They got married by a Justice of the Peace there, but my grandmother annulled the marriage. It was all kept quiet. Look Joan, I don't want to share any more right now."

"I just think you should take your time in accepting this."

"I trust my father and Janet looks a lot like me. We have the same eyes, my father's. Joan, this conversation has ended. I'll talk with you later."

CHAPTER THIRTEEN

Janet had invited Margaret over for the reading of the ancient documents. She was so excited. She had asked her dad if it would be okay for Margaret to participate in this important event and he had said that it would. "This first letter is from a James MacLean to his wife Jenny. It says it's from Stirling," Janet said as she began to read the letter.

> To my darling wife Jenny,
>
> I miss and love you so much. How I would gladly give up my bed of grass to lie beside you in our own comfortable bed. I would love to smell the sweet scent of your skin instead of the smell of dirt and animal dung. I would love to wrap my arms around your soft body instead of this hard rifle but as much passion as I have for you I also have for the cause of keeping Scotland free. I'm proud to stand beside Wallace to defend her even until death. I do pray, though, my sweet Jenny, that it won't come to that. I pray God send me home whole to you. Our marriage is young and I so want to have bairns by you but by God's help may they grow up in a free Scotland with all our traditions and standards in tact. The English are approaching Stirling but we are prepared for them.

> Your loving
> husband forever,
> James

"He must have been talking about William Wallace. Gee! One of your ancestors stood with William Wallace at the Battle of Stirling. That's exciting," Margaret said.

"You can obviously tell how much he loves Jenny, but the fight for freedom for Scotland was so prevalent in him that he's willing to put everything aside for it, even his life."

"It's beautiful. It makes me want to weep, especially since they ended up losing their freedom."

"Here's a letter from Jenny to James," Janet said putting the one down and picking up the other.

> My dearest husband James,
>
> I love you darling. I miss you too as I lay in my lonely bed at night and worry about you. I pray every day for you. You are always in my thoughts. I'm very proud of you for standing for the cause and putting your life on the line so that we may keep our freedom. None of us wants a foreign country to come in and take over our beloved Scotland. They don't know of our traditions, our clan system, our laws and how strong they are, and yet they want to come and take them all away. Why can't they stay in their own country and be content with what they have. Surely our leader, William Wallace, will be empowered by God to keep us free. I pray that he will be.
>
> Love,
> Jenny

"Here is another one from James," Janet said as she opened the letter.

My dear wife Jenny,

I hope this finds you well. I feel joyous today. We caused a great defeat for the English. Thanks to the leadership of William Wallace and Andrew de Mornay. Unfortunately, our dear friend de Mornay was mortally wounded. Although we are feeling victorious we also are broken-hearted because of this loss. He was a wonderful leader alongside of Wallace and we'll miss that along with his friendship. He was so significant in our win over the English. I will be home soon.

Love your husband,
James

"Here is an article or document about a notorious MacLean clan chief. He was married to the Duke of Argyll's (Campbells) sister. He put her on a tidal rock in the Sound of Mull and told the Campbells that she had drowned. However, his announcement to the Campbells regarding her death was premature. Passing fishermen had rescued her, and in 1523 her brother, Campbell of Cawdor, avenged her by stabbing him to death in Edinburgh."

"It's wonderful to have such history on your family, even if some of it's ruthless," Margaret said amazed at the information they were reading that dated back as far as the thirteenth century.

They read that the exploits of soldier and diplomat Fitzroy Hew MacLean, who parachuted into Yugoslavia to assist the resistance to WWII, are said to have been the origins of Ian Fleming's James Bond.

They were sad when they read about the Battle of Culloden. The MacLean chief had been killed. They were amazed how the clans were so divided. Some of them sided with the Jacobites and still other clans sided with the Government Army. Janet read over the clans that were with the Jacobites and noticed the MacLeans were there. Then she read over the clans with the Government Army and was almost disappointed to find the Grant Clan was with them. "My family and the Grants killing one another?" she asked.

"There were a lot of clan wars," Margaret said.

"You're right. There's another article that talks of the clan wars the MacLeans were involved in. They were at war with the Campbells, the McKinnons and even the MacDonalds whom they were somewhat related to. I'm just glad they are over all that stuff."

"Maybe that's why some of the clans fought against those that stood with the Jacobites. It's got me interested in reading Scottish history. I'd like to understand the Battle of Culloden. It seems like a Civil War," Margaret said.

"I wonder if there's a class on Scottish history at one of the schools. If so, maybe we can take one together," Janet suggested.

"We'd have to wait and see. You've got a lot on your plate right now."

"You're right."

CHAPTER FOURTEEN

Jonathan decided to ride to the MacDonalds with Stewart and Catherine, that way he would have an excuse to leave when they did. The MacDonalds were as gracious as usual. Jonathan really liked Mr. and Mrs. MacDonald. They greeted him and introduced him to their oldest son Douglas and his wife Sheilagh, and Mrs. MacDonald's brother and wife, John and Mhairi, and her sister Elizabeth and her husband Donald. Stewart and Catherine had met them all before. Jonathan noticed that Joan was dressed as though she was going to a cocktail party instead of a small dinner party. He also thought that she must have had her makeup and hair done. Catherine and Sheilagh looked so natural next to her. She was a little flirtatious with him. In a way Jonathan felt sorry for her. If she had made up like that for him, she was not helping herself. Douglas and Sheilagh seemed to be a little embarrassed about her flirtation with him. They could tell that she was not the kind of woman that Jonathan Grant was looking for. Trying to take the attention away from her and her behavior, Jonathan asked, "Don't you have another son, Mr. MacDonald?"

"Yes, Kenneth. He unfortunately is our black sheep."

"He's a sociable retard," Joan said with contempt for her brother. "It's hard to believe he even belongs to this family." Her brother looked at her in a disgusting manner and said, "If that's what he wants to be, then leave him alone. He's a grown man and doesn't need us to try and mold him into what we want him to be. He's made his choice."

"Okay," said Mrs. MacDonald. "That's enough about Kenneth," then changing the subject she asked, "and what have you been doing lately, Jonathan? We haven't seen you in so long."

"Oh, just keeping busy with our business. I just got back from America."

"Oh, where were you in America?"

"Virginia and North Carolina. We have some people there that buy our horses."

"He's going back in a few weeks," Stewart piped in. Jonathan had wished his brother had not brought it up because there were likely to be questions as to why he's going, etc.

"Back to Virginia and North Carolina?" she asked.

"No, he's going to California," Stewart offered.

"Do you have customers there also?" Stewart was silent and looked to his brother to answer the question. Jonathan looked at his brother and thought, *thanks a lot Stewart.*

"No, I don't have customers there. I'm just visiting a friend of mine and a friend of my father's," which was not a lie because he did intend to visit James. Jonathan thought Joan was drinking quite a bit of wine at dinner. This worried him because he knew that she would be slobbering all over him.

After dinner everyone was sitting around talking and she managed to get Jonathan to herself by asking him if he could look at her computer. She was having some trouble and Jonathan was quite computer literate. He followed her into her room. She closed the door behind them. "If you don't mind I would rather leave the door open," he said and opened it wide. She walked over to her computer and picked something up.

"I want to save my work on to this," she said holding up a small drive about two inches long and less than an inch wide.

"It's a Data Traveler. Sure I can do that. Do you want me to show you how to store your information on it, or do you just want me to copy it on to the Data Traveler drive?"

"You can just do it." While he was copying the information she surprised him by asking, "Why don't you have a girlfriend, Jonathan? Are none of us Scottish girls good enough for you?"

"Maybe I've been looking for someone who fits in with my type of personality. Some people spend a lot of time looking. I guess I'm one of them."

"I thought you and I got along well together," she said getting a little more flirtatious.

"We get along fine, Joan. Just not in that way."

"Does the American girl fit your type of personality?"

"I'm not going to discuss her with you, Joan."

"What is it about her that has so attracted you, Jonathan?" He finished copying her work and started to walk away. She grabbed his arm and said in a loud voice, "Don't you walk away from me, Jonathan Grant." Everyone in the other room heard her. Kenneth who had come into the house also heard. He walked towards her room and saw her with her hand on Jonathan's arm trying to hold him back from leaving the room.

"Stop acting like a fool, Joan. Let him go."

She glared at Kenneth and said, "Well look what the dog drug in."

"Yer drunk. Dae ye have no respect fer yerself?"

"Talk about respect, listen to your speech. You talk like a proper commoner."

"At least I know who I am. You act like you're the Queen of England."

Jonathan gave Stewart a signal that he was ready to go. Catherine caught the signal also and stood up and said, "Mr. and Mrs. MacDonald, thank you so much for the lovely dinner. It was so nice of you to invite us. Stewart and I are leaving early tomorrow to go fishing on the Spey, so we have to say goodnight."

"Goodnight Catherine. It was so nice to see you again." Then when she leaned over to hug her, Mrs. MacDonald whispered, "I'm sorry about Joan. She had too much wine with dinner." Catherine just smiled at her.

Mr. MacDonald shook hands with Jonathan and Stewart. Joan and Kenneth didn't come out to say goodbye.

In the car Jonathan thanked Catherine. "You did that very gracefully, Catherine. I wasn't sure what to do. One thing for sure, that'll be the last time I'll be with Joan MacDonald."

"What happened?" Catherine was curious.

"She wanted me to copy some work on her computer to her Data

Traveler drive and then she started questioning me about Janet and I told her I wasn't going to discuss Janet with her. Then when I finished I started to walk out and that's when she grabbed my arm and yelled at me. You all heard what she said, I suppose."

"Everyone stopped talking and looked toward her room. Her whole family, even Kenneth I think, was embarrassed," said Stewart.

"I was embarrassed for her too. Then I thought of you and couldn't help feeling sorry for you," Catherine said. "I'm going to start pulling away from her. Ever since I found out she was trying to make a move on you, I decided to do that. I don't know how I could have been so blind."

"She wanted to know if she fit in with my personality. Well if she remembers tomorrow, maybe she'll understand why she doesn't."

CHAPTER FIFTEEN

The next couple of weeks Janet got ahead of herself with her work. She drove to San Francisco to take some work to Keith. She let him know which pieces she had shelved in case he got some orders for them. While she was putting some of her pieces on a table a man walked in and started looking around. He noticed her work and complimented her on it. She recognized his accent and said, "You're Scottish."

"That's right. I'm from Glasgow."

"My mother was born and raised in Glasgow."

"Oh? What was her name?" She was about to tell him when she realized that he had asked the question in the past tense as though he knew her mother was dead. It may not be anything but she wanted to be careful, especially since he was from Scotland and Jonathan had told her that there was an article written in a Glasgow paper about her wondering who the mystery woman that had caught the attention of Jonathan Grant was.

"Glasgow's a big city. I'm sure you wouldn't have known her, especially since you probably were just a kid when she left there."

"I might know some of her relatives," he said.

"I don't think so," she said then turning to Keith, "okay, that will be it and I'll see you soon."

Keith gave her a hug and whispered, "I'll keep my eye on this guy until you drive away. He seems a little suspicious to me."

"Okay," she said. Shortly after Janet left the man left. Keith walked to the door and watched him get into a car about a half a dozen cars down from Janet's. He called her. "Janet, that guy got into a gray medium size rental car. I couldn't get the type but keep your eye open for it."

"Thanks Keith. I will."

She didn't see it until after she had crossed the Golden Gate Bridge. She wasn't sure that it was him, but there was a medium gray car a little ways behind her. A short while after getting on highway 128 she saw it again. She was sure it was him. She decided instead of driving to her house she would stop at Margaret's office. She got out of the car and turned to stare at the gray car to let him know that she was onto him but he turned in the other direction and drove on. She went inside. "Hi Margaret. I hope I'm not interrupting anything."

"No you're not. What's wrong?"

Janet explained everything to her and told her she just wanted to make sure he wouldn't follow her up to her house. "Why don't I follow you a few minutes after you leave and make sure he's not there?"

"I'll just check outside. If he's not there then I'm sure I'll be okay."

They both walked outside and checked all around. They didn't see anything suspicious.

"Janet, I really want to follow you."

"Okay, maybe that would be best."

He had gotten her last name from her artwork at the gallery and looked it up in the Boonville phone book. It was listed under J. Stevens. He had watched the two cars drive away and took in as much as he could of the direction in which they were going without letting them see him. If he lost them at least he had the address. He watched them as they turned onto her street and drove up the hill. He found a place to hide until the other car came back down.

The night before Jonathan arrived she had Margaret over for dinner. "Do you think the house looks okay? Even his cottage is bigger and lovelier than this house. I mean I love this house but..."

"Stop," Margaret interrupted her. "If Jonathan is so critical that he would look down his nose at this wonderful home, then he is not for you."

"He's not like that. I just have butterflies."

"Calm down. What time does his flight come in?"

"About five-thirty."

"By the time you get out of the airport it will be time for dinner. You might as well eat at a restaurant by the airport. You don't want to take the time to try and go into San Francisco."

"That's a good idea; I'll make reservations tomorrow morning."

"Really, Janet, I've never seen the house look so lovely. You've picked fresh flowers and made some beautiful arrangements in your very own vases and pots."

"Thanks. By the time we get here it will be quite late and he will probably be tired, so I'll bring him to meet you the day after tomorrow."

"That's fine," she said looking at her watch. "Time for me to go home."

Janet woke up early. After taking her shower and pouring a cup of coffee, she sat down to plan her day. "Make dinner reservations," she said aloud as she wrote it down. "Pick up from cleaners, put gas in my car, check to make sure plane is on time, leave here about two-thirty to give me time to park the car and walk to the security area and pick up Jonathan," she said that last part with her voice getting louder and higher.

With her chores done, reservations made and one hour of primping to make her look gorgeous, she was on her way to the airport. It was quite an easy drive without any traffic problems. She always took that into consideration as the San Francisco area was always quite congested, no matter what time of the day it was. She arrived at the airport a little after four-thirty. By the time she found a parking space and walked to the terminal it was ten minutes to five. She went into a few shops and looked around. By five-twenty she was at the security area. The plane was on time and by fifteen minutes to six one of the first passengers to get off the plane was Jonathan. First class passengers always get off first. She almost cried when she saw him. He was casually dressed but you could tell he was a man of importance. He had a big smile on his face when he saw her. He kept looking at her as he came through security. Jonathan had the most beautiful smile she had ever seen. He was such a genuine person and when he smiled, it was real. His whole face lit up, especially his twinkling green eyes, which he never took off her.

He walked up to her, dropped his carry-on bags to the floor and threw his arms around her. He picked her up about a foot off the floor, then put her down and kissed her hard. People were looking at them but he didn't care. He didn't see any of them. He only had eyes for her. She thought she was going to swoon. She didn't expect such a greeting. Her mom had always told her that Scottish people were not ones for public displays of affection. Someone forgot to tell this man that. She stood looking at him with her eyes and mouth open. She felt like a star-struck teenager.

"I'm so glad this time finally came. It took an eternity," he said laughing.

"It was that way for me too. I did get a break when Robert, I mean dad, came," she said smiling as they walked towards luggage pickup. "It took the monotony out of the waiting."

"He said the two of you had a great time and he got to meet one of your friends and got to introduce you to Mr. Armstrong."

"James. He told me to call him James. He was a lot of fun. We're going to try and travel together to Scotland for Christmas."

"I know Robert, I mean your dad, told me. I have to say; I haven't seen him look so happy in a long time. Catherine and your great grandma are looking forward with excitement to meet you. Of course Catherine has met you but she didn't know who you were at that time."

"That's right. I almost blew it the time I got emotional in the barn that day when I realized she was my sister."

"Sweetheart, that whole time knowing he was your dad and she was your sister and not being able to talk about it, must have been terribly hard for you."

"It was but now I'm happy she has accepted me as her sister and I can't wait to meet my great grandmother. I can endure Nora's wrath as long as the other two want me to be part of the family."

They picked up his luggage. Janet rented a carrier to wheel the luggage to the car.

"Are you hungry?" she asked.

"I am. We didn't have very much on the plane, although I was able to grab a bite when I was laid over in Chicago, but I'm still hungry."

"Good, I made reservations, so let's put the luggage in my car and walk back to the restaurant."

"Good planning. I like that in a woman. I'm quite hopeless at planning ahead myself," he confessed. "I've never been to the West Coast before. It's quite hot here."

"A bit hotter than Scotland, for sure," she answered smiling.

Dinner was wonderful. She was glad to see Jonathan eating like he was famished.

"This is really the first meal I've had today and you picked a great restaurant for it. This was delicious," he said as he finished his halibut dinner." She reached into her wallet to get out her credit card. "Please! Let me," he said putting his hand across her hand that was trying to pull the credit card out. She didn't want to argue with him because he sounded very definite. "I wanted to treat you to dinner," she said.

"Do you cook?" he asked her with a mischievous grin.

"Yes, I do. I love to cook in fact."

"Then maybe you can cook for me and I will pay for the dining out. That would make me feel so much better."

"Okay. Only because I know it's not going to bankrupt you."

"Oh, I'm looking forward to spoiling you," he said as they walked back to the car.

"Ooh!" she said indicating that she liked the sound of that. He wouldn't even let her pay for the parking. "You were gracious enough to come and pick me up. I'm not going to let it cost you."

"You've started spoiling me already. I'm not used to this."

Highway 101 was very busy. It was about seven-thirty when they got started on the road. "There's an awful lot of traffic here."

"This is the worst part of the journey. Once we get across the Golden Gate Bridge it will get a bit better."

"I'm looking forward to seeing the Golden Gate Bridge. I've seen it in movies and in television travel shows. It always looks beautiful," he said enthusiastically.

"It's quite dark now but you will see it and the Bay Bridge lit up. When we come in to visit James in the daytime you will be able to see it better then."

Jonathan was extremely in awe of the sight of the two bridges all lit up. "This is brilliant!"

"Wait until you see the view in the daytime, it's one of my favorites. We'll leave real early some day and come in and spend the whole day and have dinner at one of the places at Fisherman's Wharf," she said feeling his excitement.

"This is going to be a great trip!"

"Yes it is. By the way I let the hotel know you would be a late arrival."

"Thanks. Thinking ahead again. Like I said, I like that in a woman."

"Don't you worry. I'll take good care of you," she said patting his knee.

"Getting fresh, are you?" he said jokingly. She laughed.

They checked him into the hotel then drove up to her house. She gave him a tour. "I love this place. It's so cozy."

"You mean small. You could put three or four of this house in your big house."

"I don't mean small. I mean cozy," he said when she showed him the family room. "I bet on a rainy day you curl up in this big chair in front of the fire and read a book while watching the rain come down."

"I do. This is my favorite chair. I read my mom's whole journal sitting on that chair."

He could picture her sitting there going through many emotions while reading the facts that had been hidden from her. Facts that were the very core of who she was. *It must have been extremely difficult, but I'm glad things have worked out well for her,* he thought feeling a little sad for her at that moment.

"I love these two windows on either side of the fireplace. Everything is so green outside with a lot color from the flowers. I might steal your favorite spot while I'm here."

"I'll just have to get another chair for you. I'll put on some coffee. Tomorrow we'll just take it easy, maybe just do local things. We can go into Mendocino. There are lots of things to see and do there."

"I thought you lived in Mendocino?"

"Well I told you all Mendocino because I thought more people would know it. This is Boonville," she called out from the kitchen.

Jonathan picked up the book A Slib of Lorey and opened it up. He remembered Robert had said something about it. As Janet came in with their coffee, Jonathan let out a laugh. She saw that he had the book in his hand. "Funny words in there, huh?"

"I'm laughing because your dad was telling my dad and me about some language, he couldn't quite remember what it was, but he told my dad that they were 'codgy kimmies' and when dad asked what that was, he said 'old men'. I just found it in the book. They call the language Boontling?"

"Yes! I saw him looking at the book but I didn't think he was memorizing it. That's funny. I can just here him saying codgy kimmies in his Scottish brogue."

"My dad said 'sounds Scottish to me' and it sort of sounds like something that would come from there. For instance what you call the garbage truck here, they used to call the midgy over there. At least that's what they called it when my dad was little. It got that name because the men on the truck would pick up the cans from the midden. My dad told me that some friends of his from Glasgow talked about getting a hudgy from the midgy when they were wee boys."

"Oh my gosh! The codgy kimmies grabbed a hudgy from the midgy sounds like the same language to me. Okay, I know what midgy is what is hudgy?"

He was laughing hard listening to her trying to get her tongue around the words

"A hudgy is when the boys jump on and stand on the little ledge at the back of the midgy until the midden men would see them and yell at them, then they would jump off."

"Didn't they get hurt jumping off a moving vehicle?"

"No! The midgy ran slow," he said still laughing. "We're a lot more modernized now. We have recycling cans."

"Okay! Getting serious now, tomorrow will be a little bit laid back for us. We'll take a drive around the local vineyards here in the Alexander Valley. You'll meet my friend Margaret..."

"Your dad talked about her," he said interrupting.

"What did he say about her," Janet was curious.

"He said she was the one that was there for you when you were reading the journal. He said she would drop everything to be with you when you needed her."

"Yes, she is a very good friend," Janet said affectionately.

"From now on, I will be here for you too."

"That is so comforting, Jonathan," she said sincerely. "That reminds me, talking of Margaret being there for me. About a week ago when I was at the art gallery with Keith a man started talking to me and I recognized the Scottish accent. He told me he was from Glasgow and I told him my mom was from Glasgow. He said 'what was her name?' I started to tell him but I thought it was strange he referred to her in the past tense. I thought that I might be imagining things but I didn't tell him. After I left, Keith called me and told me that the man left in a gray car right behind me. I told Keith I would keep my eyes open for him. Sure enough, he was following me. When I pulled into Boonville I drove to Margaret's office. The gray car turned in another direction. Margaret followed me home to make sure everything was okay and I never did see him again."

"That's strange. Could have been a reporter. I told you a Glasgow reporter wrote an article about you. When I talked with Nellie and Mrs. Graham they confessed they had given out some information they knew about you. Not maliciously of course."

"No, I know that. They just love to talk."

"And gossip," he smiled. Then looking serious again he said, "I don't like the idea that he would come over here and follow you. I know what paper he writes for so I will watch out for any more articles on you."

When she gave him the tour, she showed him the guest bedroom and told him that her dad had stayed there and that he would be welcome to stay there also. He told her he didn't want to rush into their relationship but wanted it to be a relationship from the heart, not built on lust. "He's your dad and I'm someone who loves you in a different way. It's better that I sleep at the hotel."

She drove him back to the hotel. When she got out of the car to say goodnight, he put his arms around her and just held her very tenderly for quite a while. He was holding her like a baby, very gentle and tender. After holding her like that for what seemed about five minutes, she suddenly felt a stream of energy flow into her. It got stronger and stronger until she thought she couldn't take it any more then she relaxed completely into him. They stayed in each other's arms for a few more minutes then he put his hands on her arms, kissed the top of her head and gently moved her away from him and stared into her eyes. She felt extremely weak and totally submissive. At that moment Jonathan Grant was definitely in command. She would have done anything for him. He smiled kindly at her. "Janet darling, go home."

"Okay," she said in a weak little voice.

He opened the door of the car and said, "I'll stand out here until your car is out of sight."

"Okay," once again in a weak little obedient voice.

She thought about what had just happened as she lay in bed. She didn't think about it too long for she was asleep within minutes.

In spite of the experience she had with Jonathan that seemed to zap all of her strength, she felt refreshed when she got up in the morning. She had slept until eight o'clock though and she still had to shower and get dressed. Jonathan called and invited her to breakfast at the hotel. She told him that she just woke up and might be a few minutes late. "It's okay, Love, take your time. I'll be in the dining room, or would you prefer a table on the patio?"

"The patio sounds nice. It's a warm morning."

"I'll be on the patio then."

This can't be happening to me. He's a dream but I don't want to wake up from it. Why am I so lucky? Why does he want me?

She arrived just a few minutes late. He stood up when she came in and pulled her seat out for her.

"Good morning sweetheart, did you sleep well?"

"I slept like a log."

"I did too." He found her staring at him. "What are you thinking about?"

"Jonathan Grant, you've captured my heart and I'm not sure what you're going to do with it."

"Janet, you don't think I'm going to hurt you, do you?"

"No, but I'm getting a little anxious. It's just that I have never known a man like you. You're so tender and charming and, and so... so perfect," she stuttered.

He laughed. "Maybe I should spend a day telling you of my not so perfect side."

"I don't think you have one," she said.

"Janet, I love you. I just want us to get to know each other to the core. I think you are beautiful, intelligent, talented and have a great personality and sense of humor. I don't want there to be any surprises, that's all. I want us to have a time when we can sit down and talk more intimately about ourselves. I want you to ask me anything you want and I want to know more about you. I think we should discuss past relationships, etc."

"I agree with you. Can we do it tonight? I'll cook us a nice dinner and we can just have an intimate night. I want to move forward and find out how you feel about me after the talk."

"That's great. I didn't want to rush you, but I was definitely going to decide to have the talk early in my visit here. Tonight suits me to a tee."

"Okay, now that I got that all of my chest, my dad wants you to call him."

"Okay!" Jonathan said in a casual way but he wondered why Robert wanted him to call. He knew he wouldn't interrupt his first day with Janet for a casual conversation.

"Before we take off on our tour let me call your dad."

"I'll sit out here and finish my coffee." When he came back she asked if everything was okay and he assured her it was.

"Just something he wants me to take care of when I arrive in Glasgow." She didn't question him anymore about it.

She took him and introduced him to Margaret. She could tell by the expression on her face that she was quite taken with him. Finally she got her tongue and said, "I'm so happy to meet you, Jonathan. Janet has told me a lot about you."

I'm happy to meet you too, Margaret. Janet's dad told me how you were such a good friend to her when she needed you."

"How is Mr. MacLean? I really enjoyed meeting him."

"He's doing well and very happy to have his other daughter as part of the family." They talked for about half an hour then the receptionist came in to tell Margaret that her client was here for their meeting.

"We'll get together later."

"Let's stop by the Boonville General Store and get food for a picnic."

"That's right across the street from the hotel I'm staying at."

They bought cheeses and sandwiches and some fruit. Once

again Jonathan insisted on paying. Janet decided she wasn't going to offer any more.

"You're taking time out of your schedule to show me around, so the least I can do is pay for food," he had told her.

They drove along highway 128, taking in the spectacular views of the Redwood trees, the Navarro River and the green hills dotted with little white sheep. "This area had been a sheep farming area a long time ago. There are still sheep but not like there used to be. The vineyards took over."

As they pulled up to the first vineyard, they noticed the vineyard workers harvesting the grapes quickly to get the grapes in the big bins that were trucked to the winery where they would be crushed. Janet and Jonathan got out to watch them. "This is harvest time. It usually is quite a busy time for visitors to the wine country."

"When is the best time to visit?" he asked.

"I've heard people say spring time, but I'm not sure. If you want we can take a tour of one of them and you can ask all the questions you want."

"That sounds like fun."

"Let's go to the Navarro Vineyards and have our picnic. Margaret says there's an excellent view of the valley from there. We can take a tour there or right next door to it is the Greenwood Ridge Vineyards and a little ways from that one is Lazy Creek Vineyards."

"Wow and that probably is just a few of them. I don't think we'll make it into Mendocino today," Jonathan said

"Well we don't have to go to every one of them. We'll go to these three today and then drive into the town of Mendocino. I'm anxious for you to see it." After having lunch they just sat for a while enjoying the fantastic view of the Alexander Valley. It was a very clear day.

"You live in a beautiful place. Vineyards fascinate me. They seem biblical to me. Maybe because they are mentioned so much in the bible."

"I always feel sort of spiritual when I'm in the vineyards, I guess there's just something about putting a seed in the ground and watching it grow. I heard a preacher say you only have to put in one seed but you reap much fruit."

"That's quite heavy. You only have to give a little to receive a lot."

"I guess you could apply that to many things."

"When I look out at these vineyards, I can see all the Italian, German and French immigrants in the early twentieth century coming here with their little cuttings and starting these vineyards and look at them now," Jonathan said with a sense of wonder.

"Obviously they must have felt that this climate was like theirs back home."

They decided to take a tour of the winery after they finished their lunch. There were quite a number of people on the tour and the winery was bustling because of it being harvest time. They found out that the wine was aged in sixty gallon French or American oak barrels. After months in the barrels the wine was moved into the bottles where it continued to age at the winery. A sixty-gallon barrel yielded three hundred bottles of wine. One man asked how much acreage it would take to have a decent crop.

"One ton of grapes yield about seven hundred bottles of wine. One acre would yield about two to four tons for high quality wine and an acre for less expensive wine could yield ten tons. I'll let you do the math."

"When is the best time to visit the winery," Jonathan finally got to ask his question. A lot of heads turned to look at him, probably because of his Scottish brogue.

"A lot of our repeat customers come in the spring for new releases. Only tiny amounts are produced and the wines are reasonably priced. Bargain priced samplers and case specials are offered until April 30."

"Thank you," Jonathan said and once again heads turned. Janet smiled at Jonathan's politeness. A couple of young girls giggled and whispered to each other. They kept looking at him. It was obvious they were taken up with him. After the tour they stopped by the other two vineyards and looked around then they headed down highway 128 towards Mendocino. "The tour was very interesting."

"That's the first wine tour I've been on," said Janet. As they drove further down the highway Jonathan started to take notice of the Redwood trees. "Those trees are enormous. They must be really old. Do you have any idea how old they are?"

"My friend, Keith, said that Redwoods could get up to 300 feet in height and could be as old as 4,000 years, but he wasn't sure about these coastal Redwood trees. This is the Navarro Redwood Forest. We'll see if we have time when we come back to go in, if not it's just down the road, so we can go another time. When you walk through the forest you can't help but marvel at the trees."

"Let's put that off until another day. I would like us to take our time in there. I don't like to rush through things I'm interested in."

"I'm like that also. I had a boyfriend that drove me crazy. We would get to a place we had been wanting to see and he would run through the place and say 'okay I'm done.'"

"Why bother wasting the time to go look at it if you don't take the time to really see it." He watched the Navarro River as it meandered through the Redwoods.

"Have you ever watched tourists get out of their car at a scenic view with their camera and take a picture and jump back in their car and never look at the view?" Janet asked.

"Yes, I have. It's as though all they want is pictures to show people back home to prove they were there."

"Well that's the way he was. That was one of the reasons I broke up with him. He drove me crazy," she said.

They came to the Pacific Highway where the Navarro River joins up with the sea. "What a beautiful sight. The ocean just sort of hits you." As they drove up the coast, the headlands impressed him. The water would squirt high up in the air. "Whoa!" he said laughing.

"That is caused by blow holes. It has something to do with the way the rocks are shaped and when the water hits, it squirts up in the air."

As they entered the Village of Mendocino he was really impressed. He knew a little about architecture and many of the buildings were New England style architecture. He mentioned it to Janet, who told him, "I've heard the New England architecture was the influence of homesick pioneers who 'came round the horn' in the mid nineteenth century. I think I read that on a website. This area is known as the 'crown jewel of the Northern California Coast'," she added.

"I can see why. It is a jewel."

"You had told me a few months ago that you would like to come out here some time in the spring to see Yosemite. That is a good time to go whale watching here as they migrate north then and have their babies," then she laughed. "I have a hard time thinking of them as babies as they are about fifteen hundred pounds at birth."

"That would be fantastic. I'd love that. We do a lot of dolphin watching."

"I didn't know you had dolphins in Scotland. I'm going to start making a list of spring things to do. There is a Whale Watching Festival in March, so remind me to write that down when we get home." She hadn't realized that she said 'when we get home,' but he did and smiled. It sounded good to his ears. They visited a museum where they found out that a German immigrant, who had been the lone survivor of a shipwreck, founded the village. He looked around and saw the redwood forest and decided that the gold miners, who were piling constantly into San Francisco, were going to need building materials. Today Mendocino is still a lumber town. She picked up some information on the town. After walking around for a while, visiting little shops, museums and galleries, they sat down on a bench. Jonathan could have kept walking, he wanted to see everything, but she was getting worn out. She read from one of the brochures.

> Mendocino is one of the most beautiful places in the world. Historic buildings line the weather-beaten cliffs. The Pacific roars and crashes with such force that spindrift floats up to Main Street. Visitors to Mendocino will find a variety of cultural and educational things to see and do. Founding families can be explored at the Ford and Kelley House Museums. Hikers and bikers will enjoy one-of-a-kind, bluff-top excursions to view the seabirds, the seasonal gray whale migration, and spring wildflowers. Nearby Big River Beach is ideal for family picnics, breezy wanderings, sandcastles and getting your toes wet. The town offers shopping and dining and coastal artists show their work at the Mendocino Art Center and in the many galleries. Performing arts include productions by the Mendocino Theatre Company and the annual music

festival. Mendocino is a magical place; in fact, you may
never want to leave!

"That's how I feel. When Keith brought me up here, after mom
died, I fell in love with it. We immediately went to see Margaret,
that's how I met her, and she sold me my home. I guess it's a haven
for artists and that's what I am."

"I'm looking forward to seeing your work and meeting Keith."
He wondered what Keith really meant to her. She had mentioned
his name a few times.

"I do have some pieces in the house I can show you."

"It's five o'clock and I think you're tired. Let's go back to the
house."

Janet had put a couple of tenderloin steaks in a marinade before
she left in the morning. She thought she would barbeque them and
bake a couple of potatoes and make a salad. She didn't want to take
up a lot of time cooking, as she was quite anxious to get to their discussion. She put the coals on the barbeque. After partially cooking
the potatoes in the microwave, she then wrapped them in foil with
butter. She put the potatoes on top of the barbeque and let them
heat up with the coals. That would take about thirty minutes, she
had told him. By the time she made the salad, the coals were ready.
He was quite impressed watching her. He had never barbequed. She
put the steaks on the fire and checked the potatoes. They were well
on their way to being done. He liked his steaks medium-rare, just
like she did. She was finding they had quite a few things in common. "My steak was cooked perfectly," Jonathan said. He helped
with the dishes, after dinner, which pleased her. She put on a pot of
coffee and they retreated into the living room.

"Dad said that when he told his grandma that I was a potter,
she told him she was too, when she was young, but only as a hobby.
It really interested me because she's the only other person in my
bloodline that I know of who has the same interest."

"I didn't know that. By the way, your dad wants to buy your
plane ticket to Scotland at Christmas."

"He told me. You didn't feel offended, did you?"

"No! Dad and I could see how proud he was to do that as the
first act of being responsible for you. We were happy to let him do

that. He promised not to take my time away from you," he said jokingly.

"Actually his first act of responsibility as my dad was to find out what your intentions towards me were."

"You're kidding," he said laughing. "What did you say?"

"I told him we were talking about marriage, but not in a hurry to run down the aisle." They were quiet for a few moments then he spoke up.

"Okay, as far as past relationships, I've been in a couple, but pretty soon into both of them I knew that none of the girls were right for me. It takes more than a pretty face and that is what they turned out to be. Well-intended friends thought because the girls were beautiful, that I would want to be with them."

"You're not shallow, Jonathan."

"Have you been in any serious relationships?" Jonathan asked.

"Not until now," she said smiling at him. "I must admit, when I first saw you I was very physically attracted to you, which is quite unusual for me, but after getting to know you, it's who you are that I'm really attracted to. I'm not big on dating. I would rather be by myself or with girlfriends, than be uncomfortable with a man I didn't love and didn't know what his expectations were.

"Yes! I know exactly what you're trying to say. We didn't feel it was a man and woman thing, but just new friends sharing from our experiences and being honest. You have a great sense of humor, you're sensitive, you have great values and most of all you have a beautiful spirit. Besides all of that you're a treat to look at," he smiled at her when he said the last thing.

It took her breath away to hear him say all those things. She sat staring at him and when she finally found her voice all she said was "Likewise."

"Likewise, what is that supposed to mean?"

"It means I feel exactly the same way about you. I've never had a man treat me with such respect as you do. You remind me of the Southern gentleman of yesteryear." He smiled then his expression became quite serious then he turned to look directly into her eyes. "What happened last night, I believe, was that all the love, the long-ing and desire that I have for you and have kept under control, was released. It was a very intimate experience that I have never felt before. It took so much energy from me that I could hardly take my clothes off to go to bed, but once my head hit the pillow I was asleep," Jonathan said.

"Me too. I slept sound all night."

"Janet, this long distance relationship is not going to work."

She felt panicked. *What is he saying it won't work? Is he about to break off with me?*

"Please say you'll marry me."

She was stunned. She had to have her mind clear at this moment. "Jonathan, I love you very much but so much is happening right now. Please give me a moment to get my composure."

"Sure, come sit by me and we will just be quiet until you're ready to answer me."

She moved over and sat with him on the couch. It was not long before she said what was on her mind. "Jonathan, I do love you and would not want to be with any other man than you for the rest of my life. There is one thing that I'm afraid of."

"What is that? I'm sure we could rectify it. I can't think of anything that I wouldn't do to have you as my wife."

"I'm thirty-two years old and have never been married. Part of the reason for that is because I have never wanted anyone to redefine me. I like who I am. I'm an artist and I love what I do. I need to continue my art and I need to sell it because it makes me feel good when people buy it. It shows they enjoy and appreciate my work. If you want to marry me, you have to let me continue to be the artist that I am even though I don't make that much money at it. It's not about the money, it's because it makes me feel proud. I don't want you to feel embarrassed having a wife that works. Especially at something as humble as a potter."

"Our marriage wouldn't work if you started to act like your grandma."

"Who?"

"Nora! That's what she did. I don't want you to change and neither would my family. It's you I fell in love with. I would be disappointed if you started to act like somebody you're not. I love your passion for your art. I love that you can express yourself the way you do. I don't know if you've noticed but I like to express who I am too."

"Yes, Jonathan Grant. I'll marry you," she yelled and threw her arms around his neck and kissed him.

"One more thing I want to ask you, Janet."

"Uh oh."

"Let's plan on getting married in early spring. I don't want a long engagement. It almost kills me when I can't have you right beside me. Would it be possible for you to get everything situated here so that you can come over about six weeks before the wedding?"

"That should be okay. Since I'm going to be your wife I won't have to worry about making money," she said laughing.

"Janet, I have a suggestion to make."

"What?"

"It's just a suggestion. The decision is yours."

"Okay, I'll listen."

"You keep up with your art and sell it, but instead of keeping the money donate it to a cause. In fact, you can consider creating a foundation as a memorial to your mother. Perhaps you could call it the Alice Douglas Heart Foundation."

"Jonathan, that's a brilliant idea," she said hugging him and crying. "I'll be giving my creations to the memory of mom."

"You will be the president of the foundation."

They discussed the foundation for a while. Janet was so excited about doing this. She was anxious to let her siblings know. *I'll call them tonight. I can't wait.* Her thoughts were so focused on the idea that Jonathan had to bring her back to the moment.

"I would like us to officially announce the engagement when you come over."

"Oh Jonathan, I'm sorry I got so taken away with thoughts of the foundation. I think Christmas would be the perfect time. I won't tell, dad. It will be a surprise announcement, but can I tell my friends and family here?"

"That's fine! They'll need time to make any arrangements they have to make. We'll announce it at the Christmas party my parents are giving. After we're married, we could come back here and do all the spring things, like Yosemite and whale watching that you promised me. Oh! I didn't even realize but I've been talking like I have already decided we're being married in Scotland. We should discuss that."

"I want to be married in Scotland. I'm not sure my siblings can afford to fly over though. I think Margaret and my other real estate friend in Redwood City, Kathy, would be able to afford it and maybe even Linda."

"Don't you worry about your siblings. Do you think Sir Robert MacLean would give his daughter away in marriage and not have her family with her?"

She waited until the next morning to call everyone to tell them the news about the wedding. Maggie was screaming and crying into the phone. Janet was crying too.

"Maggie, I have other news to share."

"What news could be more important than what you just shared?"

"You know how I love to work; well Jonathan suggested a way for me to continue creating but not to sell for profit."

"What did he suggest? I mean it would sound funny Lady Grant selling pottery for a living."

"He suggested I create a foundation in memory of mom and call it the Alice Douglas Heart Foundation and donate the profits to it."

"Oh Janet that's wonderful," this time she was crying gentle tears, not screaming into the phone. "I can't believe the miracles that have happened because mom kept this journal."

When Maggie hung up the phone, she called her brothers Tom and Ian. They were both ecstatic for her. When she told them about the foundation they were truly touched. She was sure she heard Tom's voice break down at one point.

Margaret was not so surprised about the proposal but she was emotional about Janet donating her work to her mother's memory. "I couldn't think of anything more appropriate. You get to do what you love and donate it to the memory of someone you loved," she said. "As far as Jonathan proposing, well that does not surprise me. I saw the way he looked at you, Janet. There was no doubt in my mind that he was in love with you."

"I wish you could come back to Scotland with me this Christmas. It would be good to have a friend at the party when the announcement is made."

"Janet, if it would be okay with your dad and Jonathan's family, I would love to come."

"I know it would be fine with dad and I will talk to Jonathan this morning when I pick him up. I don't see why not. I'm sure it would be okay with him."

"Okay! What are you doing today?"

"We're going to San Francisco to sight-see and visit James. I'll get back to you on the visit to Scotland."

She called her dad and asked if he would mind if Margaret went with her to Scotland at Christmas.

"I would love for her to come. It will be nice to see her again. Did Jonathan tell you that I want to buy your ticket? It will be my first act as a father to you and I will be happy to buy two tickets. One for you and Margaret."

"Margaret's not expecting you to do that, dad."

"I want to, Janet. Please allow me to do that. It would make me feel good."

"Well, like I tell Jonathan when he insists on paying for everything, 'only because I know it's not going to bankrupt you.'"

Robert laughed. He was happy to do this for her and to bring Margaret would be a bonus. He had really taken a liking to her, but he didn't let Janet know. He was not sure how Margaret would feel being with a man fifteen years her senior. Janet called Margaret back immediately and told her what her dad had said. Margaret was insistent that she pay her own way, but Janet told her that Robert had pleaded to allow him to do the honors.

She picked Jonathan up and they drove down to San Francisco. She turned off the highway just before the Golden Gate Bridge and drove up a hill and parked. "Get out. I want you to see this!"

He got out and looked over the most amazing view. They were on the ocean side of the bridge. "Wow!" he said grabbing his camera. He took a picture of the Pacific Ocean flowing under the Golden Gate into the San Francisco Bay. He took a picture of San Francisco's skyline and another of Alcatraz Prison. He zoomed in on the bay itself and took a picture of the boats, especially the sailboats. "Have you ever sailed out there?" he asked her.

"You know, I actually did once. The guy that I dated, you know,

Mr. snap the picture and run, well he had a sailboat and I went out a few times with him. It was a lot of fun."

"Good! That's something else we have in common. I love to sail and go out as often as time and weather allows me."

"I'll enjoy that very much. We should get going as we have a lot to do and see. I have a feeling James won't let us leave him too soon." Driving across the bridge was breathtaking for him. "I'm so glad I'm going to be spending a lot of my time here."

"Me too! I wish we could just elope and get married now."

"No! We're not going to do what Robert and your mom did. You're coming to Scotland and standing by my side in the church while everyone watches and accepts you."

"Everyone except Nora," she said.

"The most important people do; me, your dad, your sister, your great grandmother and my family."

"It seems that it should be illegal to feel this happy. By the way, Margaret would like to come to Scotland with James and me at Christmas. I called dad and he said he would love for her to come. In fact, he wants to pay for her ticket."

"Whoa! Did something happen while he was here?"

"What do you mean?"

"He would *love* for her to come and he wants to pay for her ticket?"

"He's fifteen years older than her. She's my friend. He's my dad."

"Okay!" he said not so convincingly. "Of course it would be fine with me and my family to have Margaret there. Besides, it will be nice for you to have your best friend there when we announce our engagement."

"That's what I said. I told Margaret that I wouldn't feel so alone. Of course, I'll have you."

"I thought for a moment you were forgetting about me," he said raising his eyebrows.

They visited with James. He and Jonathan were so happy to see each other. James hadn't been back to Scotland for quite some time. "You were still quite the lanky lad last time I saw you, Jonathan. You've filled out quite nicely," he said pinching his bicep. "It's good to see you again, Janet," he said giving her a hug and a peck on the cheek. "I'll have to come up and visit with you sometime."

"I gave you my address and I was hoping you would come."

"I figured since you just had your dad here and preparing for Jonathan, I would wait." They spent an hour with him and promised they would have lots of opportunities to visit with him in the future. He understood. "You two kids go off. There's a whole lot to see in San Francisco."

They did cover a lot of ground. She took him down Lombard Street, known as the most crooked street in America. She didn't tell him where they were going and when she turned into the street, he grabbed the handle above him. "Whoa! What is this? Where are you taking me?"

"Welcome to the crookedest street in America. It's called Lombard Street."

"It certainly is crooked. What beautiful old Victorians," he said noticing the homes. "What district is this? Is it Nob Hill?"

"No this is the Russian Hill district." When they got down to the bottom he was laughing. They went to China Town, Coit Tower then Fisherman's Wharf. They were now standing looking at the Golden Gate Bridge from the bay side. "Being this close to it let's you see how remarkable a bridge it is. I've never seen a more picturesque bridge," he said as he took more pictures. "What did your dad think of this area?"

"You mean the wharf, or do you mean the whole Bay Area?"

"I mean the whole area; Mendocino, San Francisco, Marine County; all of it?"

"He loved it. I even took him to see mom's home before she died. It was the home that I grew up in. He was quite impressed with it. He wanted to see pictures of my dad. He thought he looked like a nice man."

"That must have been quite an experience for him. Seeing Alice's husband and their home where they raised their children." Turning his attention back to his surroundings he said, "The highlands are beautiful and peaceful, but this place is exciting. There's so much action here. It's like a big festival is happening. You've got the boats out in the bay, the seals barking, the musicians playing and singing, the men with their big cauldrons of crab, I love it."

"We can walk to the gallery from here. Let's do that before we eat," she suggested. As they walked into the gallery Keith was quite surprised to see Janet. He wasn't expecting her.

"Hi, Sweetheart," he said walking up to her, giving her a big hug and kiss on the mouth. "I wasn't expecting to see you today. What a great surprise."

Jonathan was taken aback by Keith's reception.

"Keith, this is Jonathan."

"Hi Jonathan, I'm pleased to meet you."

"Pleased to meet you too, Keith," Jonathan said not so convincingly. Once again he was wondering about the relationship between the two of them. He felt some jealousy, something he had never felt before. They talked for a little while and Janet showed some of the pieces she had on display at the gallery. He was very impressed and proud of her. After a while, they said their goodbyes and left.

It was almost six o'clock and they thought it was a good time to eat so that they could be back home by around nine o'clock. "A lot of the restaurants have Italian names, does that mean they only serve Italian food?"

"No! You can get Italian food but they have a lot of seafood and they have steaks also."

They ordered. Janet noticed he was a lot quieter than he had been earlier.

"Is something bothering you, Jonathan?" she asked concernedly.

"Nothing that can't wait until we get to your house."

"Was it the way Keith greeted me? I've a feeling it was. We can talk about it when we get back to my house. Don't worry about it."

Jonathan was still a little quiet when they got to her home. She put on a pot of coffee and puttered around the kitchen until it was done. She poured them both a cup and carried them to the couch then sat down next to him.

"When Keith's girlfriend was killed about three years ago, he just about lost his mind. He became quite depressed. It happened one week before he intended to propose to her." She stopped and tried to compose herself. "You have to excuse me if I have to stop occasionally. It was a very emotional and exhausting time for me."

"Where did it happen?"

"On the Golden Gate Bridge. It was raining and very foggy.

There was a ten-car pileup and she apparently had been hit several times. The door on her side was jammed shut and her car caught on fire."

"How horrible."

"The TV news people kept showing the scene over and over until Keith and his family and friends had to stop watching the news." She hesitated again then looked straight at him, "I want you to know that I have never shared what I'm going to tell you with anyone. So outside of Keith and me, you're the only one that knows this."

"Darling, I don't need to know, really. I'm sorry for being jealous. I know it was something very special between you both."

"I want you to know and I will tell Keith that I told you. He will understand. I'm sure that he will share it with his new girlfriend if the relationship gets serious." Once again she hesitated and took a deep breath. "Right after it happened, some of his friends and family members and I went to his house to try and comfort him. He wasn't comfortable. Everyone was trying to say something to help him, but they were awkward. I could see it wasn't helping him. Somehow I could tell he wanted to be alone but he didn't want to be alone. I could tell that all the voices were about to drive him crazy. Actually, they were driving me crazy. I sat beside him and took his hand and held it between both of mine. I didn't look at him but I could see through the corner of my eye that he had turned his head towards me. I sat silently holding his hand for a few more seconds then turned to look at him." She stopped once more and held up her hand indicating to Jonathan that she didn't want him to interrupt her; she just needed to get her emotions together. He handed her a couple of tissues.

"The look of emptiness and fear in his eyes scared me. I thought I was going to lose him mentally and emotionally. 'Send them away but you stay' he said to me. I went over to his mother and told her of his request. She understood and graciously sent everyone away and then she left. I sat holding his hand again between both of mine until I could feel him shaking. I took his head and placed it on my chest and held him like that for an hour, while he sobbed. I've never heard such grieving. It came from deep within him. The tears ran down my face and neck but I had to let them flow because I couldn't take my arms away from being around him. My shirt was soaked. At one o'clock in the morning I could feel his head getting heavier on my chest and I knew he was falling asleep. I woke him up and told him to go to bed. It was too late for me to travel so I slept on his couch. I was glad I had my sweat pants and tee shirt on so it was not too uncomfortable." Once again she stopped as though thinking of how to word her next sentence.

"He told me I was his rock, and not to sound pious, I believe I was. I was there beside him anytime he needed me. He was a friend who I thought would die if he didn't have someone. He has been grateful to me ever since. There is nothing between us other than being true friends."

"Janet, I love you more and more every time I learn something new about you. You are truly your father's daughter."

"What do you mean?"

"About fifteen years ago, my dad had surgery for prostrate cancer. He lay in bed at home and we weren't sure if he was going to live or die. He was in pretty bad shape. My mother worried so much and it rubbed off on Stewart and me. We were teenagers and watched her reaction so we got worried too. That brought more pain to my dad because he felt somehow that he was letting us down. Your dad would come over every day and sit at his bedside. He would read pages of a book to him by a favorite author of dad's then he would sit and remind dad of their younger days when they did some crazy and sometimes dangerous things. I would hear them laughing and it brought hope to my heart. It wasn't long before dad started to get better and to this day he gives credit to his buddy Robert MacLean for bringing him around. 'Laughter is the best medicine, so says MacLean.' Dad would say with laughter."

"Thank you for sharing that with me, Jonathan. I can see the similarity and perhaps I can appreciate more, the MacLean blood in me."

During his stay, she took him to the Montgomery Woods about half an hour east of Mendocino where they saw the awesome, inspiring redwood trees. "It's both a magnificent coastal redwood grove and a beautiful fern forest," said Janet doing her usual job of reading the brochure. "It was a nine acre donation in 1945 by

Robert Orr and is now one thousand one hundred and forty two acres," she continued.

"You cannot look at one of these trees and not believe in a creator. They are amazing."

They also toured and picnicked in the vineyards of Sonoma and Napa. She took him to Carmel where they toured the historic Carmel Mission and went around some of the trendy shops there. In Monterey they visited the Monterey Bay Aquarium and walked around Cannery Row, made famous by John Steinbeck.

"I love the works of Steinbeck and Cannery Row was one of my favorite books. To walk around here feels like walking on sacred ground for me."

"We have a castle here in California, but we're not going to be able to go there this visit. It's called Hearst Castle."

"I've seen a travel documentary of it. It belonged to a newspaper magnate, right?"

"Yes, William Randolph Hearst. Of course it's not nearly as old as your castles, but it is very impressive."

On the Saturday before he went back to Scotland, Janet had a dinner party and her sister Maggie and brother Tom came down from Oregon. They arrived the night before and stayed at Janet's house. They met Jonathan at that time. After he left for the night, they couldn't stop talking about him.

"He's so handsome. I mean he's rugged, but he's also beautiful. Janet, just think of it, you're going to be a real lady. Will you be called Lady Grant?"

"Slow down, Maggie," Janet said laughing. "I'm not sure that he has a title. He's never mentioned it and I don't think he would use it if he did have one. He likes to be thought of as a regular guy."

"Janet, he's not just a regular guy."

"You only met him for a short time. When you get to know him you will see that he really is a regular guy."

"I can say that I like him very much, Janet. I can tell he's kind, considerate and respectful of you. I like that and I'm very happy for you. The mansion and all the other stuff are just a bonus," her brother Tom said.

"I appreciate hearing that from you, Tom. You look at guys in a different way from us. To hear you say that you think he's a fine, upright man, makes me feel good."

"I bet every young woman in Scotland will be green with envy when they find out," Maggie said getting back to the mansion and his title, etc.

"I think you're right. Mrs. Graham said that every woman from John O'Groats to the Borders want to align themselves with Jonathan Grant," she said. "That's the northern most part of the Scottish mainland to the southern most part."

"I knew about the Borders but not the other place. Janet," Maggie said changing the subject, "I'm exhausted. It's a long drive from Eugene to here." They decided it was time for bed.

"We'll see you in the morning Tom," Janet said and she and Maggie went upstairs, since they were sharing a room so that Kathy and Linda could stay at the house in the other guest room.

The party was a great success. Everyone was impressed with Jonathan and very happy for Janet. Kathy and Linda left early on Sunday, as they wanted to take the opportunity to spend some time in Mendocino.

"As long as you have driven this far, you might as well," Janet had told them. Besides it gave her a little more time with her sister and brother.

"I'm so glad I was able to come down, Janet. Not only was the party a lot of fun, but I also got to see your new home, and by the way I love it. I'm going to try and come down more often. The kids will love being here." Maggie said.

"Me too. I would love to bring my family down. This area is awesome and your house is great. It's quite a bit closer to Oregon than Redwood City, which helps," Tom agreed with Maggie.

"You're all very welcome."

"The best thing, though, was I got to meet my soon to be brother-in-law and I'll be happy to report to my husband and kids that he's the cream of the crop," said Maggie.

At that moment the doorbell rang. It was Jonathan who came to say goodbye to everyone. Keith had given him a ride to the bottom of the hill and he walked up from there. He didn't want Janet to have to leave her guests to come and get him, so Keith was kind enough to offer.

"Sorry, you missed Kathy and Linda but Maggie and Tom are still here."

"Tom, it was great meeting you. I hope you and Maggie have a good trip back to Oregon."

"It was great meeting you too, Jonathan." Hearing her name Maggie came out of the room where she was finishing her packing. "Hello, Jonathan."

"Hello! Maggie's the one I really came to see anyway," he said smiling and giving her a hug.

"I'm so glad I got to meet you, Jonathan."

"Not only am I getting a wife but a sister-in-law too. There are no girls in our family."

"I'm very excited for both of you. I can't tell you how happy I am for Janet."

"Yes, she told me you were afraid she was going to be an old maid. Look at that face, Maggie. It's not the face of an old maid," he said smiling at them both. "I grabbed her fast because I was afraid she wouldn't be available for long. Especially since I wouldn't see her very often. Six thousand miles is quite a distance to try and court someone."

"It was quite fast, but you have a point. I guess if you know, you might as well go for it," Tom said.

"Of course, you are going to be my maid of honor. We've decided to marry in Scotland," Janet said to Maggie.

"I'd love to, Janet, but I have to see if we can afford it and also I'd have to have someone take care of the kids for the time that we're gone."

"Yes, you can, and no, you don't," Jonathan said. Maggie looked confused.

"What do you mean?" she asked.

"Yes, you can afford it. It won't cost you and your family anything and since the kids are coming with you, you don't have to have someone to care of them. We want all of you at the wedding, including Tom and his family and Ian. It will be taken care of."

"I love you, Jonathan Grant," Maggie said running up to him and hugging him. "I can't imagine being in Scotland with my whole family. It will be a blast." She started to cry and Janet laughed.

"Well, you'll have eight months to calm down."

"Thank you so much, Jonathan," said Tom handing out his hand to him.

"Well I can't take all the credit. I know Robert MacLean will want to have his daughter's family at the wedding so I'm sure he's the one you'll be thanking." When they were leaving Maggie gave Jonathan another big hug. "Thank you again. My sister is so lucky."

"You better be good to him," she said to Janet while hugging her.

Monday came too fast and Jonathan was on the airplane flying home to Scotland. He had a job to do in Glasgow before heading up to the highlands. Robert had told him, by way of a phone call, of an article in the Glasgow Herald by reporter, Alan Bell, who had apparently gone to San Francisco and wrote about Janet's work, naming the art gallery, and telling her last name, the name of the town where she lived and describing her home. This of course all being part of the reporter's quest to find out who the mystery woman was. It was ten o'clock in the morning when Jonathan Grant strode into the offices of the Glasgow Herald demanding to talk with Alan Bell. The receptionist recognized him and rang through to the reporter to let him know Jonathan was there and wanted to speak to him. When Bell finally came out he led Jonathan into a small conference room.

"How did you get all the information you wrote in your article about Janet Stevens. I know you were in California because she told me that you followed her from the Art Gallery in San Francisco. She said you had been asking questions about her mother."

"There was plenty of information at the gallery. There were articles, plus her business cards."

"You didn't get the information about her town and home from the articles. You followed her in her car. Her friend at the gallery phoned her and said you had taken off after her. She saw you in her rear mirror. She said you followed her all the way to her hometown." Jonathan raised his camera and took a picture of the reporter. "That's for the police department from San Francisco to Mendocino. I filed a report with them naming you as a stalker of Janet Stevens, an artist in the San Francisco area. If you ever go near her again, be prepared to be arrested." The receptionist was sure that Jonathan Grant was going to beat Alan Bell up. She could tell by his countenance that he was angry and was quite aggressive with the reporter.

CHAPTER SIXTEEN

Once again Janet tried to busy herself. It was terrible being without Jonathan. Even her friends couldn't fill the void she felt. She decided to take a trip up to Oregon to spend time with Maggie. She felt she hadn't had enough time with her when she came down for the dinner party to meet Jonathan. They would discuss the wedding and talk about spending time together in Scotland. She called Maggie and they arranged for her to spend the second week in October with their family in Eugene.

It was the best time in her memory that she had had with her sister. After the years of Maggie constantly worrying about Janet's love life and nagging her about it, she was beside herself that, not only was Janet getting married, but to the most wonderful man. They discussed the time they would all spend together in Scotland. The children were ecstatic that they were going to fly in a plane for the first time. They weren't sure where Scotland was, but when their aunt told them about the castles that were there, they got excited thinking of it like a "fairytale land".

She also got to spend some time with her brother Tom. "I told Ian about Jonathan. I told him how much you both were in love with one another. He was happy and is excited about the wedding and going to Scotland."

"Jonathan's planning on getting a small bus to take us all to some tourist spots. Besides our family here on the West Coast, we have Aunt Moira and Uncle Mark that will be going, Aunt Betty, Cousin Alice, her husband and my friends Linda, Kathy and Margaret. There will be about eighteen of us and of course Jonathan, his brother Stewart, Catherine, dad and Jonathan's parents. That brings the total of twenty-four of us. He will get a bus a little bigger in case some others want to come along."

"That sounds fantastic, Janet. It'll be great to have such an experience with our whole family together. We'll have so much fun. Is he going to hire a driver?"

"No! I think he just wants to rent the bus and he, dad, Stewart and Malcolm will take turns driving. They want to be free to spend as much time as we all want in any given place. It will be local places of course, but there is so much to see. They have even included St. Andrews Golf Course."

"Wow! That's my and Ian's dream. Every time we go out to golf we talk about St. Andrews. I'm about to explode right now. Janet will you let me be the one to share it with Ian? I've talked to him about Jonathan and he said he sounded like a guy he would want to know."

"Thanks Tom, Ian called and was real excited for me. I guess Maggie got on the phone to him as soon as she got home and did a fair share of bragging to him also. He's looking forward so much to going to Scotland. He started surfing the Internet to find out about climbs there. You can share the St. Andrews trip with him.

"Will Jennifer be invited also?" He remembered Jonathan saying something about it but he wanted to make sure.

"Of course, Tom. She's family. We wouldn't invite you and not your wife and children."

"Let's call Ian now while you're here."

"Sure! I'd love to hear what his reaction is," she said smiling excitedly.

"I'll put him on the speaker phone," he said punching in Ian's phone number. "Hello!" said Ian.

"Hey brother! I've got you on the speaker. Janet's here."

"Hi! Janet. I've found some great climbs in Scotland and not far from Elgin. A resort named Aviemore. I'm looking forward to it."

"I know of Aviemore. Jonathan goes skiing there and his brother Stewart, who by the way is your age, goes climbing and is an avid fisherman. Tom has something he wants to share with you."

"Great! I'm looking forward to meeting him. I think we'll get along great together."

"Ian, Janet has just shared with me that Jonathan is going to hire a bus to take us to some of the great places in Scotland. Guess where one of the places is that we are going to?"

"Aviemore?" Ian guessed.

"Better than that. If you were able to go to Scotland where would you want to go?"

"St. Andrews, but you have to know someone who is a member or have a certain handicap or something."

"Little brother, we are going to golf at St. Andrews," Tom said sounding like a host of a game show when someone has won a big gift.

"Whoo" he yelled. "Don't tease me on this. It's too important to me."

"I'm not. Janet told me and she got it from Jonathan. The Grants are members and we have the handicap needed to play on the Old Course."

"Janet, I'm so pumped up about this trip and being that I'm half Scottish has me so curious about the place. This is awesome. Thanks for everything. It can't come fast enough for me. It's all I can think of. My friends at work are so envious. Wait 'til they hear about St. Andrews." They talked for quite a while and finally hung up the phone.

"That was so much fun. He's so stoked," Tom said. They laughed at Ian's response to the St. Andrews event. "It's been a long time since I've heard him that excited."

"It was a lot of fun. We're all going to go crazy until the time comes."

"Have you figured out a definite date yet?"

"We're looking at the middle of April, but I will know for sure pretty soon. I'll get back to you with the details. The touring around would take place prior to the wedding so you should plan to be there a week or so before."

"I'll have Ian come to Eugene and we can all fly out together."

As soon as she got back home Jonathan called. "I missed you," he said.

"I gave you Maggie's number. You could have called me there."

"I didn't want to take time away from your family. I know you don't see each other very often. How was it?"

"It was wonderful, sweetheart. It was the best time Maggie and I ever had together. I had a great time with Tom also. I told him of the bus you were going to hire and when he heard one of the places we were going to was St. Andrews, he called Ian. You should have heard them both. It's been a lifetime dream for them. They were so excited. Ian is also looking forward to climbing with Stewart."

"That's fantastic. Stewart is looking forward to it very much. What a way to start our new life together; uniting our families."

"We are so excited about everything, darling, it's going to be a blast," then changing the subject she said, "I'm a little concerned about the kind of dress I should wear for the party. You know I'm not a fashion freak. Is it real dressy?"

"Yes it is. I want you to look extra special on that night when we announce our engagement. I know you'll want that too, since everyone in the place will have his or her eyes glued on you."

"I would certainly want that too, but I'm not sure what dressy is to rich people. I might buy something that would be very pricey to me but not to the other ladies at the party. You know clothes are not a big issue to me."

"Would you please let me take you shopping in Glasgow? There is a lovely shop called Frasers that I would like to take you to."

"It's a beautiful shop. That's the one with the grand staircase that Aunt Betty took me to. I'd love to do that Jonathan."

"I know the couturiere, Christine. She's great. I will give her your size and have her pick out some dresses and you can do a fashion show for me. How's that?"

"Wonderful! I feel so spoiled," she said sniffling. She just wished her mom was alive to see what was happening to hers and Robert MacLeans' little baby.

"Not as spoiled as you're going to be, my love."

After she hung up she went back to her previous thought about wishing her mother was alive. If her mother were alive, this probably would not be happening unless her mom would have finally spoke up about her biological dad. *It's so ironic. If it hadn't been for the journal, I would never have known about Robert MacLean and would never have met Jonathan Grant,* she thought. "Thank you mom, you have not only changed my life for the better, but the lives of all your children," she said aloud.

She called her dad to share what Jonathan had suggested about the Foundation.

"Darling, that's a wonderful idea. I will certainly make my contributions to it and I'm sure the Grants will too and many of our other friends."

"Wow! I wasn't even considering that. That's very generous of you."

"I wouldn't think about not making that as one of my charities. I am so proud of you and Jonathan for thinking of doing that."

She picked up her mail and there was something from her dad. She opened it and found the two first-class tickets for her and Margaret. She called Margaret and asked her to lunch. "Janet, I haven't seen much of you since Jonathan left. Of course I'll go to lunch. I've been dying to see you." They arranged to meet at their favorite restaurant. Janet called and made reservations for noon. She couldn't wait to show Margaret their tickets.

"First-class! I've never flown first-class," Margaret said reading over the tickets again to make sure. "Janet, I can't tell you how elated I am about the trip."

Janet shared with her that Jonathan wanted to buy her a special dress for the party.

"He said he wanted to make sure I feel special when he announces our engagement."

"I should go to San Francisco to look for a dress. For this occasion, I'm going to spend a few thousand dollars."

"I'll come with you," Janet said. "I feel bad though that you will be there all dressed up and looking beautiful with nobody by your side," she said with a sympathetic look. "Maybe one of Jonathan's friends?"

"Well, actually Janet," she said hesitating, "I do have an escort."

Janet looked at her confused. "Who? Who do you know in Scotland?" Margaret just looked at her with her eyebrows raised. A light went on in Janet's head. "My dad! You're kidding! But why not? After all, he invited you over and in fact paid your way," she said then looking suspiciously at Margaret she said, "is there something going on that I don't know about? When did he ask you? It certainly wasn't when he was visiting here."

"He has called me a couple of different times. After I accepted his offer to buy my ticket, he called and asked if he could escort me to the party. I said I would be very proud to have him as my escort."

"Well I'm glad for both of you. I'm glad my dad will have such a beautiful woman as his companion. I wonder if Nora will come. I hope so. I'd love to see her face when she sees me with Jonathan and you with her son. The engagement will be the topper." They both laughed.

"Are you nervous about meeting her, Janet?"

"No! Are you nervous about being with her son?" Janet asked back.

"No! Not in the least."

Janet decided she wanted to share with Margaret her experience with Jonathan the night he arrived. She had never talked about it, but had never stopped thinking about it.

"When I drove Jonathan down to the hotel the first night he arrived, he put his arms around me and something strange happened. At first it was very tender, almost as though he were holding a baby, and then I felt my body being engulfed by energy so overwhelming that I thought I would pass out. It was a wonderful feeling then it left and I was totally relaxed against him."

"What do you think happened?" Margaret asked.

"Jonathan said it was all the love and desire he had for me, but kept under control, that was totally released at that time."

Margaret sat thoughtfully for a few moments then said, "I think I know what he means."

"What do you think it was? I have my own thoughts," Janet asked.

"I've never had a fulfilling relationship because the men that I was with wanted to be intimate so early in the relationship. I wasn't even sure how I felt about them. I wanted more from them. I wanted to know how much they cared about who I was. I wanted what Jonathan is giving you."

"Which is?"

"Real love. He totally loves you as a person, not as an object. He's building up the love he feels for you and not looking for instant gratification. Many men want instant gratification as soon as they feel an urge, which I think stunts a relationship. Instead of stunting the relationship, Jonathan is building it up. I believe that release he had that night was in place of instant gratification and I bet it was much stronger. Your love life with him is going to be phenomenal because he is a man that knows how to love."

"That's what I believe also."

"I'm happy for you, Janet. Not every woman finds that in a man. Sure many of them can hold back maybe until they're married but some of them continue holding back even afterwards. They can't express their emotions. That emotion he released into you is not a man that holds back."

After lunch, Janet called her dad to let him know she had received the tickets. She also wanted to feel him out about Margaret. She remembered the night in the restaurant when they were both in such deep conversation with each other that they had shut her out. They had been very apologetic about it but Janet had no clue that they had already taken a liking to one another. The phone was ringing on the other end and Janet was hoping her dad would answer but it was Nora.

"Hello!" she said with a rather prudish voice.

"May I speak with Mr. Robert MacLean, please?" She didn't want to say dad to Nora. She would already be annoyed knowing who this American girl was that was calling.

Robert was just outside the front door pruning some roses. Nora hesitated. She didn't want to call Robert in to talk to Janet. Robert had heard the phone and knew his mother had picked up the one in the entryway hall. When he didn't hear her talking he started to go inside to see what was going on. Just as he stepped over the threshold he heard his mother say, "I'm sorry; he is not here at the moment." He could tell by her voice that she didn't like the person on the other end. Since he was the only he in the house, he said, "I'm right here," and reached out and took the phone from her.

"Hello!" he said. When he heard Janet's voice, he lightened up. "Hello dear, how are you doing?" He gave his mother a disapproving look and she walked away. He knew she would be trying to listen so he took the phone into his office. *I'm so glad for these wireless phones,* he thought. He closed the door to his office to keep his mother from listening. He had decided that since Nora had opted to keep Janet out of her life, then he wouldn't allow her to be part of his life with his daughter. He sat at his desk and listened as Janet talked about receiving the tickets.

"I'm glad they arrived safely."

"Margaret was shocked that you bought us first-class tickets," she said.

"That's a long journey, even for first-class. I can imagine how unbearable coach would be."

"I want to thank you for that, dad. We are both so excited. Margaret told me you asked to escort her to the party," she said with an inquiring tone.

"Well, we can't have her going alone. Jonathan and I are the only people she'll know. Besides, I'm tired of going with people that bore me."

"She'll also know James and he won't have a partner."

"Too late! I asked first and she has accepted my invitation."

"Jonathan is going to buy me a dress when I arrive in Glasgow. We're going to Frasers."

"What is Margaret going to do about a dress? I never thought about that."

"She's going to San Francisco. She said she's going to spend a couple of thousand dollars on one. She wants to look as good as everyone else."

"That's a lot of money for her," he said concerned.

"I can tell you, she makes a lot more money than I do. She's one good salesperson."

"I can imagine that she is," he said laughing. He thought he might know more about Margaret Dunbar's character than his daughter, even though they were best friends. They finished the call and Janet didn't get as much information as she wanted to but it was more than Nora MacLean got. She only heard his muffled voice each time she passed his office and put her ear to the door.

A week later Margaret picked up her mail and noticed there was a letter from Robert. She was eager to find out what he had to say. When she opened up the envelope she gasped. There was a cashier's check for three thousand dollars. She read the note.

Please don't be upset with this. Janet told me you were going to spend about this much on a dress and I don't want you to spend your hard-earned money. Please allow me to do this for you. I am looking forward very much to seeing you again and to escorting you to the party.

Sincerely,
Robert MacLean

Margaret immediately drove to Janet's house. "Janet, I can't accept this money. It's way too much. What should I do? I don't want to offend him. He's such a gracious man but I don't want him to think I'm a gold digger."

"Wow! Maybe you should tell me what's going on with you and my dad?" Margaret fidgeted around. She wasn't sure what was going on. She knew the first time she was introduced to him that she was immediately attracted to him. The night that he invited her to dinner with him and Janet they fell into conversation so easily. She'd felt as though she had known him before. She also felt he was attracted to her. Usually a man doesn't offer to pay a woman's plane ticket, especially first-class. Janet was staring.

"Janet, I don't know what to tell you. I'm attracted to your dad and I think he is attracted to me, but I don't know that for sure. I know there's fifteen years difference in our ages, but that doesn't bother me." Janet walked over and gave her a hug.

"You feel bad about taking the money and he feels bad about you spending your own money for a function that he invited you to."

"Well I can't just take it casually. I have to let him know he doesn't have to do this for me."

"Let me call him." She was glad when he answered the phone. "Hi dad! I'm here with Margaret. She feels guilty about all the money you're spending on her. She just got your cashier's check for three thousand dollars."

"Janet, I asked her if I could escort her to the party. Jonathan is buying you a dress and I knew she would feel out of place if she couldn't afford a dress as good as everyone else's. I don't want her spending that much money on a dress she may not wear very often, so I want so much to do this for her. Can you talk her into accepting it?"

"Dad, I'll let you and Margaret talk." She shrugged her shoulders and handed Margaret the phone.

"Hello Robert. I received the cashier's check. I have to tell you it is so generous of you, but this is too much money for me to take from you."

"I didn't mean to offend you dear, but I really don't want you to spend that much of your own money. I don't know how to convince you to take it without sounding like I'm insulting you."

"I'm neither offended nor insulted. I think it's a very sweet gesture, but I don't want you to think that it's easy for me to take this kind of money from someone." After another ten minutes or so, Robert had convinced her to keep it to buy a dress. "Accept it as a gift from me and wear the dress in good health."

"Thank you. I will use it to buy something very special that will make you proud to be with me that night. Goodbye Robert." When she put the phone down Janet looked at her wide-eyed. "You sounded quite intimate. Robert?"

"He didn't want me calling him Mr. MacLean. He asked me to call him Robert. I hope you don't mind, Janet."

"Why should I mind? I think it's wonderful. You're both very special to me."

The following weekend they went into San Francisco and Margaret bought a beautiful black silk dress. Just below the collar bone the neckline went straight across from shoulder to shoulder. It had a full skirt that came to her mid-calf. She bought a pair of satin pumps with a crystal ankle strap and a lambskin clutch. The total cost was just a little over twenty-five hundred dollars. "What shall I do with the rest of the money," she asked Janet.

"Don't send it back. Use it to get your hair done and manicure and pedicure."

"I almost feel reckless spending this much money."

"The dress is fantastic on you. The bodice makes your torso look longer and narrower. It will be good for dad. I don't think he's been this happy since he lost mom. He has his daughter by Alice and a beautiful woman to escort to the biggest Christmas party in Scotland."

When they got back to Boonville, Margaret drove Janet home. "Please come inside and put everything on and let me see how you look, again." When Margaret came out of the bedroom in her black full-skirted silk dress and high heel pumps, Janet was in awe. She had pulled her shoulder length auburn hair up on the top of her head revealing the perfect shape of her face. "You look gorgeous. I can't wait to see you with your makeup and hair done. It's a good thing my dad is tall because with your five feet seven inch height and those heels you must be close to six feet."

"More like five feet ten inches but that's getting up there. I'm glad he's tall also, because I love wearing these shoes."

CHAPTER SEVENTEEN

It was December 19th and they were boarding the plane. Janet and Margaret sat together and James was right behind them, sitting next to a very pleasant woman of about his age. They struck up a conversation and after a while Janet and Margaret didn't feel obligated to constantly turn around to try and keep him in their conversation. In fact they would have been annoying him if they did. It was nine o'clock in the morning when they arrived at the Glasgow airport. Jonathan and Robert were both there with separate cars. After welcoming hugs Robert explained that he would be driving Margaret and James in his car and Jonathan and Janet would go shopping for her dress and shoes. "First I'm going to take all of us to breakfast," he said. He took them to a very fine restaurant in Glasgow. They had a fun time catching up with all that was going on in each other's lives. After about an hour, Robert, Margaret and James were on their way up to the highlands but first they had a stop to make. They stopped at Betty's house and Robert walked to the door to get her. Her neighbor, of course, was scrubbing her doorstep and desperately straining her neck to see who else was in the car. Betty came out looking lovely in a pair of black trousers and a sage colored twin set. "Good morning Mrs. Carter," she said with a smug smile. He opened the back door and she got in next to James. Robert introduced Betty to everyone.

"It's so nice to meet you. Janet talked about you and your daughter and new grandson, Ethan Nathaniel Dunbar. It's a lovely name. My name is Dunbar also."

"Hello, Margaret, Janet has spoken to me of you also and she did tell me that was your name. I'm very pleased to meet you." James and Betty greeted one another. Robert started up the car and looked out at Mrs. Carter. Turning around he said to Betty, "I wonder how many more scrubbings that doorstep can take before it disappears." They all laughed. Betty explained that it was Mrs. Carter's nosy way of trying to find out what's going on in the neighborhood.

"I'm so excited to be here. To see the beautiful landscape and to be going to such an exciting party," Margaret said.

"I'm quite excited also," James said. "I haven't been in Scotland for about fifteen years. Laura loved to travel so we went to different places every year."

"I want to thank you, Robert, and the Grants for inviting me," Betty said feeling more comfortable with them all than she thought she would.

"Well it's my pleasure to have you all here. Malcolm is beside himself waiting to see you, James."

"It'll be great to be with the two of you again. Are we going to do some fishing?"

"Of course. My daughter, Catherine, has a boat. We'll take it out." The ride up the Grampians was wonderful and Margaret enjoyed having Robert and James point things out to her and to educate her about the area.

Jonathan and Janet went to Frasers. It was the most unbelievable feeling being in this beautiful, elegant store and walking out with the different dresses that Christine, the couturiere, had picked out for her and modeling them for Jonathan. The look of appreciation on his face every time she walked out almost embarrassed her, but it made her feel more special than she had ever felt in her life. The dresses were beautiful, but she could tell that it was the way they looked on her that gave him that appreciative look. He was obviously enjoying looking at her. They both decided that they liked the silver-gray silk that came to mid-calf and flared out at the bottom. It had a slight plunging neckline.

Jonathan decided that it would be best for him to move into the big house and let the guests, Janet, Margaret and Aunt Betty, stay in his cottage. Robert knew that Nora would just make Janet miserable if she stayed with them and he didn't want to give her the opportunity to do that. Besides he knew that they would all want to be together. Isabel MacLean was so happy to have James stay with them. Robert drove them all, except Nora, over to the Grant's home. He wanted them to meet Janet before he introduced her to everyone else on the night of the party. They also were introduced to Margaret, whom Robert said was both his and Janet's friend. Isabel gave him a sly little look. Then he introduced Betty as his first wife's sister and Janet's aunt. They all had a wonderful time together. Catherine and Isabel had so many questions for Janet.

"Janet, did Robert tell you that I used to throw pots, also?" Isabel said feeling proud to share that with her.

"He did, grandma," she said which brought a beam to Isabel's face. "Do you still have some of your work?"

"Actually I do have one special piece that I would like for you to have. You come to my cottage and I will give it to you."

"That's wonderful. I'd love to have it. When dad told me that you were a potter, I decided to bring one of my pieces for you. We'll exchange tomorrow." They spent a couple of hours chatting then Isabel started to show fatigue.

"Time for us to go. I can see grandma is getting tired," said Robert helping grandma to her feet. After everyone was gone the ladies retired to the cottage. "What wonderful people. I loved your great grandma," Margaret told Janet.

"How old is she?" Aunt Betty asked.

"Jonathan told me she was ninety-five," Janet answered. "She is wonderful, isn't she?"

After talking for about an hour they decided to retire.

The next day Robert took Janet to his grandma's cottage. Nora had known she was coming and decided she would go into town. Robert enjoyed watching his daughter and grandma sharing their pottery with one another. Janet was delighted with the piece of pottery that Isabel had given her. It had a look of yesteryear and was so special to her. She let Isabel know that it was very dear to her. Janet had made a special piece for her great grandma and painted a scene from one of her pictures taken at the Biblical Garden.

"Oh this is absolutely beautiful, dear. I know this place. I've visited often. Did you paint this yourself?

"Yes! I hand paint on all of my pots. Margaret, my friend that you met last night, is a photographer and she takes wonderful nature pictures and I use them a lot in my work."

Robert was out of the room on his cell phone. Isabel leaned into Janet and whispered, "Is there something going on with Margaret and your dad?"

Janet laughed at the mischievous look on Isabel's face, and then she leaned into Isabel and whispered, "I think so, but I'm not absolutely one hundred percent sure. They do like one another."

"Good! She's a nice girl. I'm happy for him." Janet had fun gossiping with her grandma.

They laughed and then Robert came in. "What are you girls laughing at?" he said enjoying every moment of it. "I'm sorry I have to break up this girlie party, but I have an appointment."

"That's okay, Robert. It's about time for my nap." She turned to Janet and said, "At my age, I have to take about three naps a day." She had spent about an hour with Isabel. Isabel was still full of questions. She wanted to know about Alice, so Janet was happy to share her mother's humor, her giving heart and Isabel laughed when Janet told her about Alice's sayings, because Isabel knew of them and what they meant. It was a very enjoyable time for both women.

On the night of the party, Jonathan went over to the cottage to escort Janet to the house. He visited a while with Margaret and Betty until Robert and James came. James was going to escort Betty. Jonathan complimented the ladies on how lovely they looked. "In fact, you both look very elegant." All three women and Catherine had gone into Elgin and had their hair and makeup done. When Janet walked into the living room and joined them, Jonathan let out a whistle. "You look absolutely beautiful." He had never seen her so dressed up and having her makeup and hair done so fashionable. He loved the natural looking Janet, but to see how well she looked all made up and in the beautiful gown they both had chosen totally blew him away. He wasn't prepared for the fantastic looking beauty that stood before him. "You ladies are definitely going to be the belles of the ball."

At that moment there was a knock on the door. They knew it would be Robert and James. Robert was pleased with the way Margaret looked and she knew it by the way he looked at her and smiled. Jonathan asked them all to sit down for a moment. After they were all settled, Jonathan turned to Robert.

"Mr. MacLean, I would like to ask for your daughter's hand in marriage?" Only James, Betty and Robert were surprised. Finally Robert found his voice, "Of course you can."

Then Jonathan turned to Janet and took a ring from his pocket, "Janet will you marry me?"

Janet was trying hard not to ruin her makeup. She was flapping her hands across her face as though trying to air-dry the tears. "I've already said yes, but I'll say it again in front of family and friends, yes!"

He put the ring on her finger and they kissed. Margaret and Betty were trying to stop the tears also. Robert went over to his daughter and gave her a big hug. "I'm so glad you're going to be such a big part of my life." Then while James and Betty were hugging and congratulating Jonathan and Janet, he turned and smiled at Margaret. "Everything happened so fast I haven't had time to tell you how absolutely beautiful you look. You have impeccable taste."

"Thank you Robert. Thank you very much for everything." He kissed her hand.

Betty hugged Janet and said, "I wish my sister Alice were here tonight."

"I believe she is and her heart is full of joy."

"I think you're right, congratulations dear."

Everyone admired the huge diamond on her finger. "Try not to let people see it until I announce our engagement."

"It's going to be hard to hide it."

They walked over to the house together. There was a hush and every head turned as they walked through the door of a large room that made Janet think of a ballroom. Nora was glaring at them. First she glared at Janet. She knew who she was of course.

That little tramp's love child and who in the world is that young thing hanging on to Robert's arm; another little gold digger no doubt.

Her granddaughter Catherine interrupted her thoughts. "Look grandma! That's Janet with Jonathan. Isn't she beautiful? The lady with daddy is Janet's friend, Margaret. She's beautiful also. Behind daddy is his friend James from San Francisco and the lady is Janet's Aunt Betty."

Nora stared at Betty. *So that's probably what this Alice looked like.* She could see a slight similarity to Janet.

After a short while Robert asked Jonathan if he would mind if he introduced Janet to the guests. "Of course not. This is as good a time as any. I'll get everyone to quiet down."

He walked to where the musicians were and took the microphone in his hand and said, "Friends, could I have your attention please." When everyone quieted down he turned to Robert and said, "Robert has someone he wants to introduce to you."

Robert escorted Janet to where Jonathan was. He took the microphone. Nora was fuming. "He wouldn't do this to our family," she said in a whisper but Isabel heard her and said, "He wouldn't not do it to his daughter." Nora turned to her with a mean look on her face but Isabel was smiling.

"I would like to introduce you to my other daughter." Everyone looked at him in surprise. "Some of my friends here will remember, but most of you wouldn't know that when I was very young, I eloped with a girl I was in love with. My family disapproved of the marriage and had it annulled. My wife ended up moving to America to avoid all the negative publicity she was receiving from the media. However, Alice had a child by me over in California and I only found out this year. This is Janet."

Janet was nervous. She didn't know how these upscale people would take to her. She was afraid they would all be like Nora and look down their noses at her. Instead they smiled and clapped. Through the evening, in between all the gaiety and dancing, people came up to her and told her how happy they were that she and her dad were reunited. Most of them were curious as to how it happened. She was open with them all. They were sorry to hear of her mother's passing and fascinated with the journal although they said they knew that it had probably been hard for her to read it. Janet was so relieved that it was all out in the open and she was well received except by Nora MacLean.

Catherine and Isabel had come up and hugged her and told her how excited they were that she was there at the party with the rest of the family. Catherine spent quite a bit of time talking with her new sister and telling her that she would love to go to California and spend some time getting to know her better. Janet said she would look forward to having her.

After things quieted down a little and Nora noticed that Janet was alone, she went over and introduced herself as Catherine's grandmother. "It was quite a shock to our family, Robert having a child out there. We've never had a scandal before."

Janet didn't want to answer. She was afraid she would say something nasty. It was one thing to introduce herself as Catherine's grandmother and not hers, but it was something else to refer to her mother as a scandal. She finally took a deep breath, looked Nora straight in the eyes and said, "Well Mrs. MacLean," she wouldn't give her the satisfaction of calling her grandma, "my dad and I are very happy to have found each other."

With that Nora said, "If you'll excuse me I have some people to talk to." *People more important than you, you little nobody trying to get some of the inheritance,* she thought as she turned and walked away livid. Everyone Nora talked with congratulated her on having her other granddaughter with her.

She had had enough and was about ready to go home when Jonathan, once more hushed the crowd and said, "I have an announcement to make," and then reaching out his hand he motioned Janet to his side. "Janet and I would like to share with you our friends and family that we got engaged tonight and are getting married next spring. April 15th, to be exact." Everyone clapped, except some of the younger single women of course, who looked upon Janet with much envy. She had done in a few months what most them had tried to do in years. People went over to congratulate the couple and to view the ring. There were lots of "oohs and aahs".

Catherine rushed over to hug her. "Congratulations," she said hugging Janet and then Jonathan. "Will you live here when you get married," she said excitedly. "I hope so, then we can spend more time together and we can really get to know one another better." Catherine's smile was so wide and tears were coming down her face. She had a sister, something she always wished she had.

"We'll live in both places and we will spend a lot of time together, Catherine. You'll meet my other sister and two brothers and their families at the time of the wedding. "Where are you getting married?"

"Right here in Scotland and you will be one of my bridesmaids." Catherine was ecstatic. Janet motioned Margaret over. "Margaret will also be a bridesmaid."

By this time Isabel had also joined the small party of women. Isabel had never seen Catherine so excited. She was happy for both her great granddaughters. "You knew that they were planning on getting married, didn't you Margaret?" Isabel asked.

"Yes, I did Mrs. MacLean. I wanted to come over here at this time because I wanted to be with Janet when the engagement was announced."

"That was very nice of you, my dear. I haven't seen Bobby look so happy for a long time and I must say you look very lovely dear."

"Thank you!" was all Margaret could say. She thought the elder Mrs. MacLean was absolutely delightful and Catherine was such a sweet young woman but she was unable to take her eyes off Nora MacLean during the night. She noticed that as soon as Jonathan announced their engagement, she had made a beeline for the front door. She had left the party. She couldn't bring herself to offer congratulations to the newly engaged couple.

In the meanwhile, Jonathan's family and the relatives that came up from Aberdeen and other parts of Scotland were hugging Jonathan to death. Finally Malcolm and Helen came up to give Janet hugs. Helen had been crying and started up again. "My goodness, we thought our son would never get married. After all, he's thirty-two and he didn't show any interest in the other women that were in his life. I must say, we couldn't have asked for a much lovelier girl than you, Janet. Malcolm and I both said when we first met you that you fitted him like a glove."

Janet laughed.

"Helen's right; that's exactly what we said. We could tell there was great chemistry between the two of you," Malcolm said giving her hugs.

Then Stewart came over and hugged her. "Welcome to our family, Janet."

"Thank you, Stewart, even though I still have three and a half months until I'm officially a part of the Grant family," she said smiling.

Aunt Betty waited until everyone had finished congratulating her niece then she went to her, hugging and kissing her cheek. "Janet, I'm so happy to be a part of this. I can't wait to tell Alice. She'll be over the moon."

"What?" Janet asked.

"Oh, never mind dear. It's just that my daughter gets very excited over things like this."

The party and dancing went on and by around one o'clock, the people that were left started to go home. Once again they gave their congratulations and thanked the Grants for a wonderful party as usual. Catherine had left after the engagement announcement to take her great-grandmother home but she came back. There was no way she was going to stay away from all the excitement. Besides, she wanted to get back to Stewart. The only people left were the Grants, the MacLeans (minus Isabel and Nora) Janet, Margaret, James and Aunt Betty. They talked about the upcoming wedding. They all wanted to know where it would take place and where the married couple would live. Those seemed to be the two biggest questions. They were happy when they told them the wedding would be in Scotland. "Robbie, you and I have to start seeing to things. I assume you'll be giving her away?" Malcolm asked.

"Oh yes and I'll be so happy to do that. Do you know how many bridesmaids you'll be having, Janet?" her dad asked.

"My sister Maggie, who lives in Oregon, would be the maid of honor," she said to those who did not know of her sister, "and Catherine and Margaret will be bridesmaids."

"What about your other two friends that live in the Bay Area?"

"Well I thought that five would be quite a lot."

"I'll have to figure out my side of the party. Stewart of course will be my best man, but I'll have to figure out who among the cousins to choose."

"There are about five male cousins on your mother's side and four on my side," his dad said.

"I'll pick the younger ones. I don't think the older married with children cousins will care about being a groom's man," said Jonathan.

"There's Stewart and then you'll have to pick between Billy, Jeremy, John and Glenn," his mother said. "If you have two other friends you would like in the wedding," she said to Janet, "then Jonathan can have all four of his cousins and Stewart," Helen added raising her eyebrows to indicate she had just came up with the answer.

"Then it's settled," Robert agreed. Jonathan and Janet were happy with that solution.

The next day Jonathan and Janet drove her aunt to the train station. "I got lots of pictures to show Alice. I think I should wait until about two weeks before the wedding to tell her about it. Otherwise she'll be driving me crazy from now until then."

They both laughed, especially Janet because she was quite aware how excited Alice could get. "She's like my sister. They must both take after your side of the family, but I know you won't be able to keep it from her. Here comes your train. Goodbye auntie," she said affectionately, kissing her on the cheek.

Betty did tell Alice the next day. She definitely couldn't keep it back. "We're going up there to the wedding? You mean George and I are invited to it? It will be the biggest event in Scotland and George and I are going?" Alice almost screamed the words.

"You better head for the bathroom. I think you're about to have an accident," George told Alice.

Betty gave her as many details as she had then talked about the party itself.

"Look, I brought some pictures back," she said handing them to Alice. "Oh my gosh! Look at Jonathan and Janet," she said misty eyed. "Could they possibly look more beautiful?" She looked for a while at that picture. "Who is this handsome couple?" she said handing the picture to her mom.

"That's the man himself; Sir Robert MacLean and Janet's friend Margaret. A very nice girl she is."

"He's quite impressive looking. You know what I just thought of?" she said her eyes getting huge.

"What?" George asked.

"Robert MacLean is my uncle and your brother-in-law, mom."

"I never thought of that, but you're right." Alice looked at the next picture. She was about to ask who the distinguishing looking couple were, when she recognized her mother. "Oh mom, look at you. You look beautiful," she said letting the tears flow. She had never seen her mom in such an elegant setting and looking so lovely. "Who is the handsome man with you?"

"That is James. He was with Robert the night he met Aunt Alice. He lives in San Francisco and he was my escort that night. I felt so special being with this distinguished man in a lovely tuxedo and looking so important."

"Mom, this is all over our heads. Look at you sitting there like you belong with this aristocratic family."

"We do belong, Alice. They have made that a fact. You won't feel out of your element when you're there."

"Some of the pictures will be in the Society page in the papers. Wouldn't it be funny if your picture were there at the biggest event in Scotland? Mrs. Carter will be doing more than scrubbing her doorstep. She'll be all over the neighborhood showing everybody," Alice said laughing.

"There was someone taking pictures and asking who we were and how we were related. I told them I was Janet's Aunt Betty from Glasgow. You're right, Alice; it's a possibility. After all, I am related to the bride-to-be and everyone will be wanting to know who Janet is."

Sure enough, a few days later the engagement announcement was not only in the Society Section but it was front-page news with a notation saying pictures could be seen in the Society Section and sure enough the picture of Betty and James was in there. The neighborhood was abuzz. Mrs. Carter was in the middle of a group of the neighbors telling everyone that she had seen the big car come to pick Betty up and Robert MacLean himself had come to the door. "I just happened to be out scrubbing my doorstep," she told the neighbors. "I'm sure you were, Mrs. Carter," one of the men called out and everyone laughed.

By late afternoon the day after the party, the whole town of Charlestown was in a flurry. Mrs. Graham was in Nellie's Tearoom trying to find out what she could. "The Grants had their big Christmas party last night, Nellie, and I understand Janet was there and some other people that my friend Jennie said were strangers. Jennie did the catering for the affair but just as they were leaving she said Jonathan got up to make an announcement, however he waited until they had left so she didn't hear it."

"Doris, Jennie's helper, said it was so busy and they were running in and out but she said she could swear that she heard Mr. MacLean introducing Janet as his daughter," Nellie added.

"What? Jennie didn't tell me that. How can that be? I'll just call her up and ask right now." Mrs. Graham got out her cell phone and talked with Jennie. After she hung up she told Nellie, "Jennie said they weren't quite sure as they were just getting bits and pieces as they were going in and out but she said there were a lot of congratulations to Mr. MacLean and the American girl."

"Well I'll keep my ears open, Agnes, and let you know what I hear," Nellie promised Mrs. Graham.

Nellie and Mrs. Graham were not the only ones trying to find out what was going on. Catherine's friend, Joan, was doing some snooping of her own. Year after year she had been trying to get invited to the Grants Christmas party but no matter what she did, she couldn't get Jonathan Grant's attention. She knew she had made a terrible fool of herself at her parent's dinner party, but wasn't ready to give up. She wasn't getting very far with any of her other friends whose parents had been at the party. Either they didn't want to talk or their parents hadn't told them anything. Well Catherine was at the party so she decided she would go straight to the source. Catherine was not too happy to see her friend drive up. First of all, she knew why she had come and secondly, she was going over to the Grants to meet up with Janet and Margaret. They had asked her over so they could sit and talk with just the girls. "Hello, Joan."

"Hello, Catherine. How was the party last night? I hear that the American girl was there..."

"My sister, Janet," Catherine interrupted her.

"Oh yes, sure! I also heard there was another American girl. Another sister?" she said smiling facetiously.

"No, she's Janet's friend." Catherine was keeping her guard up. She felt she had let out too much information to Joan the other time she questioned her.

"What was her friend doing at the Grant's party?" she asked angrily.

"She simply wanted to come with Janet and the Grant's invited her along. Joan, I can't stay around to talk. I promised Janet and Margaret I would join them."

"Join them where? Am I not allowed to meet them?" .

"Right now we just have an intimate meeting between the three of us. We have things to talk about."

"You're being very secretive with me all of a sudden, Catherine. Ever since this sister came into your life you seem to be pushing me away."

"I don't mean to, Joan, but you're asking a lot of personal questions about my family that I'm not ready to share with you right now."

"Okay, if that's the way you want to leave it, goodbye."

Catherine was feeling different toward Joan lately. Maybe it was because she had accused Janet of being a fake when she told her Janet was her sister. Even before Janet came into the picture she was starting to get annoyed with Joan's obsession with Jonathan. Stewart didn't like her trying to use him and Catherine to try to get to his brother. She was just like her grandmother Nora, trying to twist everything around to suit her needs, not caring what other people wanted. She was glad her father had stepped in and taken some of the control away from her grandmother. *At least now that Jonathan is spoken for, maybe grandma will leave me alone.* She had been afraid she would find herself in a wedding where she was the bride marrying the wrong man.

Catherine got in her car and drove to meet with the other girls at Jonathan's cottage. She was thinking of the party and how Jonathan was so in love with Janet and was open about his feelings. She had hoped Stewart would have noticed her more last night because she looked as beautiful as she possibly could, yet he didn't make much of a comment. She still felt like his little buddy. She felt a little down about that. She wasn't sure how he felt about her.

As she drove up the driveway to the Grant's house, Stewart came out to meet her. "Hello Catherine," he said walking up to the car. She rolled down the window.

"Hello, Stewart. I'm going over to the cottage to chat with the girls."

Stewart smiled. He knew this was important to her to be with the other girls and to have an older sister. He leaned into the car. "I want to tell you that you looked gorgeous last night. To me you were the most beautiful woman there."

"Stewart, you surprise me. You've always treated me like your little buddy. I feel a little flustered."

"I know, Catherine. I'm the quiet brother. I wish I could be more like Jonathan but flattering words don't come easy to me. I'd like to have you be more than a little buddy to me."

"You don't have to flatter me, Stewart. I'd just like to know what you want me to be to you," she said opening the car door and getting out so she could stand and look into his face instead of bending her neck to look up at him. She knew this was a special moment and she wanted to be in the right position.

"Last night when I really looked at you, I thought, what am I doing? She's been my best friend for years and she has grown into an absolutely beautiful young woman. Where has my head been? I think we've been so used to being together that we've taken each other for granted. I didn't notice until last night how you've changed since our teen years. You are a beautiful woman. I would like to pursue a more serious relationship with you, Catherine."

"I have never taken you for granted, Stewart Grant. I've known for quite a while that I was in love with you and yes, I would like to pursue that relationship also," she said smiling at him.

She looked so tempting at that moment that he couldn't stop. He took her face between his hands and kissed her long and hard. Margaret just happened to look out the window to see if Catherine had come yet when she caught them in the embrace.

"Janet, quick!"

Janet ran over to her side and watched the young couple kissing and embracing. "Oh! How adorable! My little sister's in love with my soon-to-be brother-in-law."

After she left Stewart she went to the cottage to see the girls. They both met her with silly grins on their faces. "Were you two watching us?" she said turning a little flushed.

"Yes, I was looking out the window to see if you had arrived yet, and accidentally saw," Margaret said smiling.

"Congratulations Catherine. Is it serious?" Janet asked.

"We are about to embark on a serious relationship," she said smiling at them. "It took him this long to realize he loves me, but he was worth waiting for."

They had the greatest girl-time ever. At least it was for Catherine. She shared with them the relationship she and Stewart had since childhood and now it was about to change into something very special. Both Janet and Margaret were thrilled for her.

"You'll both be Mrs. Grant. You will have the same in-laws so that should keep you both very close. Your children will grow up together and have the same grandma and grandpas. It'll be a wonderful life for you," Margaret said.

They talked about the upcoming wedding. It was the first time Catherine had ever felt so close to girls in her life, and being that one of them was her sister made it that much more special.

When Catherine told her father about the girlie-hour he was very happy that his two girls felt so strong toward one another. She told her dad that she really liked Margaret also. That pleased him. He was especially happy when she told him that she and Stewart had professed their love for each other.

"That's my desire. To have you to be good friends and it looks like you're marrying into the same family, my friends' family. What could a father ask for?"

Ever since Janet came into their lives things had been wonderful. Everyone was happier, except Nora. She went down south to visit her relatives, until Janet and Margaret went back to California. That suited everyone fine.

"I really do like Margaret, daddy. What does she mean to you?" She had a feeling something special was going on and she wanted him to know that she was okay with it.

"I'm glad you like her, Catherine. We're just friends. I met her when I visited Janet and we found so much to talk about. I haven't talked so much to anyone than I did to her."

"I found out that you paid her ticket over here?"

"She wanted to come and was going to buy her own ticket but I think first-class would have been a little expensive for her and that's how I was bringing Janet over. I didn't want to think of Margaret in the cheaper seats by herself. I wanted them to travel together."

"I think that was sweet of you, but I think you like her and wanted to escort her to the party."

"You're right, Catherine. I do like her very much, but you know I'm fifteen years older than her."

"I don't think she cares about that," said Catherine smiling.

"Well, we'll just have to wait and see."

A few days after Christmas they said their goodbyes once again. Catherine and Janet both cried as they hugged each other. They had bonded real well. *After all,* Janet thought, *we have the same wonderful father.* Jonathan drove Janet, Margaret and James to the Glasgow airport. Jonathan took Janet's hand and said, "Excuse us," to James and Margaret then led Janet away so they could be alone. "These goodbyes are getting to be way too much, but you'll be back at the beginning of March and then we'll be together always."

"That sounds beautiful. Always!"

"I can't tell you how empty I feel when you are not with me and how thrilled I feel when you are with me. There's no doubt in my mind that you're the special girl for me."

"Here we are, both thirty-two years old and never had a serious relationship. It's as though we've been looking for each other and what a strange string of events that brought us together. I never thought I would take a journey from the beautiful wine country of California to the mystical highlands of Scotland to find the man who was looking for me."

"It makes me believe even more in Divine intervention. We are definitely meant for each other, darling, and I know it will be forever." He kissed her and they walked back to Margaret and James.

CHAPTER EIGHTEEN

The people in Charlestown had found out the same way Betty's neighbors did; that Jonathan Grant and Janet Stevens were engaged. The people were quite shocked because they still were not sure who this girl was and what she was doing up in the highlands that first day she arrived and didn't seem to know anyone. Nellie took it upon herself to make sure that everyone who talked about the engagement was aware that she introduced the couple. "She was sitting right there at that table," she would say, "and in walked young Jonathan. When he told me he had been in America, I said 'isn't that a coincidence this young woman here is from America' and then I introduced them."

"Aw Nellie! Why don't ye carve their initials on that table, like the characters in 'Sleepless in Seattle'? Their initials are carved at the Empire State Building. Ye can claim it as a tourist spot," said Jimmy Ramsey who loved to tease Nellie. Everybody laughed.

"Ye can all laugh, but I could tell it was love at first sight."

"But that doesn't tell us why she was here in the first place. I mean, she walks into town, a complete stranger, and a few months later gets engaged to Jonathan Grant," said a local woman reporter. The townspeople were baffled, but they loved a good gossip so right now Janet and Jonathan were fodder for them.

A couple of weeks after Janet and Margaret left, a few feet of snow fell on the Scottish highlands. It looked beautiful, but it was bitter cold and one had to be careful driving. Jonathan had a 4-wheel drive truck with snow tires. He drove into town to pick up some groceries for his mom and to get a newspaper. There were fewer people in town than usual due to the cold and the snow. He couldn't help thinking of Janet out in California in the warm weather. She would still be asleep at this time. *It would only be two o'clock in the morning over there,* he thought. He picked up the groceries and put them in the truck, then walked over to get the Glasgow newspaper. He liked to keep up with the big city news and also to read the business section. As he was about to put his money in the slot for the newspaper, his eye caught the headlines, Who Is She? Right under the heading was a picture of Janet. Then below the picture it said, Are the Powerful MacLeans and Grants Being Scammed by this American Beauty? Is She a Phony? Andy Bell, the same reporter that Jonathan had threatened, wrote the article. He started to read it but noticed some townspeople watching. He folded his paper and got in his truck and drove away. The tongues were wagging in town. "Why has she been kept such a secret?" some asked.

"She's a very nice girl," Mrs. Graham said and Nellie agreed. The Newspaper Shop was next door to Nellie's Tearoom.

"What I want tae know, is how did the Glasgow paper get the story when none of us right here could find anything out?" asked Nellie.

"Somebody must have told them," said Mrs. Graham then whispering, "dae ye think it was Nora?"

"Well she was determined that her granddaughter marry Jonathan, although not *this* one," Nellie said pointing at Janet's picture, "but I don't know how vindictive she is. We'll soon find out now that the story has broke into the media."

Jonathan was furious. *Surely Nora wouldn't do this. She'd have to know that Robert would kill her or at least kick her out of the house.* His thoughts were running wild. He couldn't think of anyone else it could be.

Malcolm noticed Jonathan driving rather fast over to his cottage, and then watched him get out of his truck and go inside. He didn't even take time to drop off his mother's groceries.

Malcolm walked over to the cottage and knocked. "Come in!" Jonathan called. He was on the phone and Malcolm could tell it was to Robert. Robert had just finished reading the newspaper article when Jonathan called.

"They went all the way back to my marriage to Alice and found the newspaper articles about her."

"Somebody had to have given them the information. Robert, you don't think Nora would have done it, do you?"

"I really think she would be afraid to do anything like this but I'll talk to her. In fact I'm going to call all of my family together and see if someone could have leaked something out."

"You did introduce her to everyone at the party."

"That's true, but they're our family and friends and you know what a tight group we are. We're all subject to the media. I can't think of anyone who would benefit by doing this."

"I feel so bad for Janet. Can you believe how much her life is mirroring her mother's life? Maybe we should have introduced Janet publicly so it would've been out in the open way before our engagement."

"You're right, Jonathan. That was my mistake. Maybe you and I should schedule an interview and tell the public the whole story."

"First, I want to find out who leaked the information," Jonathan said. Malcolm had picked up the paper and read the article.

"We need to show this to your mom and Stewart."

"Okay! Robert is gathering his family together to see if someone could possibly have leaked information. Maybe we should do the same."

Robert called his family together and showed them the news article. They were shocked, even Nora was surprised. "I know you're probably suspicious of me, but I swear I didn't talk to any reporters, nor have I given any information to anyone about Janet."

Robert was surprised to hear Nora mention Janet's name. Usually she called her "that girl."

"In spite of your dislike for her, I really don't think you would do it to this family or the Grant family, but how did it get out. I want you all to be thinking of anyone you may have talked to about Janet."

Robert and Jonathan knew they would be hearing from the media and they were trying to decide which medium to use, certainly not the Glasgow Herald, the paper that printed the story. They made it sound like Janet had made up this big story and sold it to Robert MacLean and Jonathan Grant. They called her a crafty con artist since she was able to fool the two biggest families up in the highlands. The phone rang and Robert answered.

"Robert, Sandy here. I'd like to interview you and Jonathan about this story that is in the Glasgow newspaper." Sandy was with the local news. "The media down in Glasgow and Edinburgh are having a field day with a big scandal not only involving the MacLeans but the Grants also. This is the kind of stuff they love getting their hands on."

"Jonathan is here with me. We were just discussing it. When and where do you want to do the interview?"

"It would be nice to shoot out at your estate. How about three o'clock?"

"Okay, we're looking forward to clearing up Janet's name." After hanging up the phone it rang again.

"Probably the Glasgow reporters," he said picking it up again. "Hello!"

"Daddy, I just got a call from a reporter in Glasgow asking me all kinds of questions about mom," she said almost crying. "What's happening?"

"My gosh! What time is it there?"

"Five o'clock in the morning."

"They got you out of bed to ask you questions?" he said enraged that they were imposing on her in such a way. "Someone gave information to a reporter in Glasgow and he went back, probably by microfiche, to find the old stories about your mom and me. Listen darling, Jonathan and I are going to be interviewed by my friend Sandy who's the anchor for the local evening news here. He'll be here in a little while and will give us a good interview."

"How did the information get out?"

"We don't know yet, but we'll find out. Here's Jonathan."

"Hello sweetheart! I'm terribly sorry about all this. It was a shock to us too. We'll get things straightened out and get back to you."

Sandy came over and asked the appropriate questions, "Who was Alice Douglas?"

"She was a wonderful girl that I fell in love with and married when I was very young. My mother annulled the marriage, and then the media blasted Alice so bad, destroying her reputation and her parents felt it would be better for her to move away until it all blew over. She went over to America to spend some time with her sister and while over there, she found out she was pregnant with my baby. Remember Sandy, we were married."

"Why didn't she come back?"

"She didn't come back because she was told to stay away from me. I didn't know about this. I thought Alice had walked out on me."

"How did you find out and why just recently?"

"Alice didn't tell our daughter, Janet. She was afraid it would make Janet feel like she wasn't part of their family. However, when she passed away early last year she left a journal behind. Janet found it, read it and that's how she found out about me. When she came up here she was trying to find out about me to decide whether or not she should tell me that she was my daughter. She met Jonathan and he assured her it would be a good thing to tell me that her mother, my Alice, had passed away and that she had written some things in a journal that perhaps I would want to read."

"For the sake of some of the viewers, I have to ask, how do you know your ex-wife left the journal and that Janet didn't write it herself?"

"There are things in there that only Alice and I knew and things that only Alice, her parents and my parents knew. Some of those things I just found out a few months ago. I didn't know that my mother had paid Alice's parents off to keep their daughter out of my life. Janet is my daughter. There is no doubt in my mind."

"How did you meet Janet, Jonathan?"

"I met her at Nellie's Tearoom. Nellie introduced us."

"You seem to have fallen in love awfully fast."

"Actually, I believe we fell in love right there in Nellie's Tearoom. When you know it's right, you go for it, especially if your sweetheart is living on a different continent. I didn't want to take the chance that someone else might sweep her off her feet. These newspapers said I was engaged to a gold digger and that I was being taken. I'm marrying the daughter of Sir Robert MacLean, probably the richest man in Scotland." The interview went on. It was very positive and Robert and Jonathan were pleased. Before they left the interview, Sandy said in front of the camera, "I would like to congratulate both of you. You, Robert, for being united with a daughter you didn't

know you had and you Jonathan on your engagement to the beautiful daughter of Sir Robert MacLean."

"Thank you, Sandy, and thank you for giving us this opportunity
to clear things up," Robert said.

"Thank you," Jonathan said shaking Sandy's hand. The interview
ended.

The big news networks in Glasgow and Edinburgh aired the
piece that Sandy did on the two men. It wasn't long after the interview was aired that the tongue wagging stopped. Jonathan had
asked Sandy if he could find out anything about the person that
gave Allen Bell the information.

Everyone in the area was glued to his or her television. Many
of Nellie's customers came in to watch it in the tearoom. She was
beaming when Jonathan mentioned her but when he said he felt
that they fell in love right there in her shop, she yelled to everyone,
"What've I been telling ye all."

Joan MacDonald also had been watching. She was furious with
the way everything turned out. Not only did she lose Jonathan but
she was losing her best friend, Catherine.

The people in town were happy with the interview and were glad
that they finally got the information they had been looking for all
along. When any of the Grant family or the MacLean family came
into town they were met by many congratulations, but the towns
people were still gossiping about who could have leaked the story.

Robert had called Janet after the interview. "Hello darling, I just
wanted to tell you that the interview went very well. The people
in town are happy and most of them, especially Nellie and Mrs.
Graham, have come up to me and said 'we never thought she was
scamming you. We thought she was a lovely girl right from the
beginning.' Then of course Nellie always has to add that she was the
one who introduced you both. I think she's looking for an invite to
the wedding."

"I'm glad everything seems to be turning out well. I would hate
to have my wedding day ruined by gossip and people believing lies
about me. I love Jonathan and that is the only reason I'm marrying
him," Janet said feeling relief.

"We all know that dear, the Grants and MacLeans, and that's
what matters."

"I know but I'm glad the town is kind and open enough to hear the truth and accept it. I'm sure they would accept it as gospel coming from the mouth of you and Jonathan. By the way, I *would* like Nellie and Mrs. Graham to be invited to the wedding. They've become very special to me."

"They'll be truly honored. I think you should not let them know until they receive the invitation," he said laughing mischievously.

"That's a great idea. I wish I could be back there when they get them. By the way, any clues as to who gave the Glasgow newspapers the story?"

"No, it could have been a number of people. After all, we gave the story at the Christmas party."

"You're right."

"Although, like I told Jonathan, they were family and friends and people who keep things to themselves. Jonathan has asked Sandy to see what he can find out from the Glasgow reporter. Bye dear. I'll call you in a couple of days."

CHAPTER NINETEEN

Jonathan was over visiting Robert. "It's kind of hard to put a wedding together when your bride-to-be is so far away. There are so many things to decide on," Jonathan said.

"I can see you're getting a little overwhelmed. Have you arranged for a wedding planner?" Robert asked.

"Yes mom has done that and she is working with her. She's getting all the ideas together and keeping them in a big folder, with each item filed separately. After she has finished going over all the things with Mary, the wedding planner, she thinks I should bring Janet back, so she can go through everything and make her own decisions."

"When Janet is going over things with you and your mom, I think you should have Mary there also, in case Janet has some questions or thoughts of her own that she would like to throw around."

"That's a good idea. I wish we could find out who leaked the story, because if it was malicious the person might continue."

"Me too, I was thinking the same..."

"Dad, I have to talk to you," Catherine said running into the room with a sense of urgency.

"What is it dear?" Both men looked at her with concern.

"I just left Joan and she was gloating over the story in the paper about Janet. Then I remembered that I had told her."

"You told her about Janet? How much did you tell her Catherine?" her father asked.

"When you came home from your trip to California and shared

with us who Janet was, Joan pestered me for information," she was nervous. "She wanted to know why you went over there to see 'that American girl' as she called her."

"What did you tell her?" he asked.

"I was angry with her for calling her 'that American girl' so to spite her I told her Janet was my sister and also that you had been married to her mother for a short while. I also told her that Janet's mother was from Glasgow. That is all I told her; I swear dad, honest Jonathan."

"Okay, dear. I think you have to ask Joan over to the house," then turning to Jonathan, "we have to confront her and make sure she stops all this nonsense. At least it's only a silly young jealous woman and not some malicious trouble maker."

Catherine invited Joan over to her home. When Joan saw that Jonathan and Robert were also there, she got very tense.

"Joan, Catherine told us that she had shared with you who Janet was. Are you responsible for giving the information to the Glasgow newspapers?"

"Mr. MacLean I can honestly say that I didn't have anything to do with it and I have no idea who did."

"We're not trying to accuse you, dear; we have gone through the same thing with both of our families. We just want to question people that had the information that might have given it to someone else."

"Well if you're finished with me, I would like to go about my business," she said.

"Of course dear. Please forgive us if we have imposed upon you but like I said, we have done the same to all of our family members." She left without looking at Jonathan. She almost felt betrayed by him. Shortly after she left, Sandy called and told Robert the person that gave the story to Alan Bell was a man. "He went to the reporter in person. When Bell asked who he should make the check to, the person told him to leave that area blank. When the reporter said he needed it for his records, he was told, 'Adam Jones, that's for your records, I still want the check blank.'"

"So obviously that's not his real name," Robert suggested.

"Probably not. Bell said he sounded like he might have come

from up here. He said the man definitely didn't sound like a Glaswegian."

"Do you think you can ask Bell if he can check with the bank and see if that check has been cashed and if so, who endorsed it?"

"Yes! He's going to keep on it and let me know when that has been done. I'll get back to you, Robert."

CHAPTER TWENTY

Sitting at the kitchen table in Helen Grant's house, Janet went over high-end designer wedding dresses with Helen and Mary. It was now the end of February (at Jonathan's request she came a week sooner), and the wedding was to be in the middle of April. She came back to help Helen with all the arrangements. They knew Nora would want nothing to do with it. Janet saw quite a few dresses that she really loved and finally chose an ivory silk with dropped waist A-line and a French lace bodice. Every one was in agreement. It was very elegant. Mary helped her pick out shoes and accessories that went well with the dress. They already knew that they would be married at the church the Grant family had attended for many, many years. In fact the MacLean family also attended the same church. It was an old sandstone structure that had been built in the eighteenth century.

Mary had recommended a caterer. "They do a wonderful wedding sit down dinner. I've used them many times for upscale weddings," Mary said.

"Janet, here are the wedding cars we have picked out. Jonathan got involved with this part of the planning," said Helen.

"Oh, they're beautiful old cars. Is that a Rolls Royce?" Janet asked.

At that moment Jonathan walked in. "Yes, it's the Phantom V State Limousine. I've always thought that's what I would want my bride to ride in to our wedding."

"It's beautiful, Jonathan. I also love the silver color," Janet said.

She was feeling a little overwhelmed by the elegance of this wedding. Robert MacLean was sparing no change for it. It wasn't overwhelming for him or the Grants but Janet was from a middle-class home, and this wedding was costing more money than she would ever have thought her wedding would cost. They broke up and Mary took her information and went back to her office to get to work on ordering the dress, and everything else she was responsible for. Janet had asked Jonathan if they could travel around Scotland for their honeymoon. He was pleased that she wanted to do that. He could have taken her anywhere but she wanted to get to know her new home. He made a reservation at Skibo Castle for their wedding night.

They were finally through with counseling and everything was in place. Janet had decided to stay at Mrs. Graham's the whole time before the wedding. One morning, about a month before the wedding, Mrs. Graham let out a scream. Janet ran downstairs to see what was happening. Mrs. Graham was standing staring at the invitation. Janet broke out in laughter. "Janet, I never expected this," she said holding out the invitation toward Janet.

"I wouldn't think of not inviting you. You have been a good friend to me. "Do you think Nellie has picked up her mail yet?"

"No, she gets hers a little later than me. Why? Did she get an invitation also?" she asked excitedly.

"Yes! How much later does she get hers?"

"Not very long, probably she'll get it in about a half-hour."

"Let's go have a cup of tea," Janet said laughing. Nellie was surprised to see them both walking in together. She knew Janet was busy trying to get ready for her big wedding and she had never seen her come in with Agnes before. "What can I dae fer the pair of ye?"

"We'll have a pot of tea between us," Agnes said. "By the way, Nellie, have you picked up your mail yet?"

"Yes I have. Why?"

"You might have a look at it," Agnes said smiling. Nellie went to get them a pot of tea wondering what Agnes was going on about. She brought back the tea and looked at Agnes suspiciously. "What can be in my mail that you're interested in?" Agnes just kept smiling. Nellie went to get her mail. She was so curious. They were sitting sipping their tea when Nellie let out a big yell. She came running out from the kitchen and ran over and hugged Janet. "Thank ye, oh thank ye, Janet."

"Well, after all, Nellie, you're the one who introduced us," she said laughing. At that Agnes Graham joined in the laughter and the two of them were having a good time at Nellie's expense. Nellie couldn't care less. She was going to Jonathan Grant's wedding to her new friend Janet.

Two weeks before the big day, Janet got a call. Mrs. Graham picked up the phone and handed it to Janet. "Hello! Oh hi Catherine. Yes of course I can meet you. At Nellie's? Sure! I'll be there in five minutes." She hung up the phone. Mrs. Graham was looking curiously at her. "Catherine seems upset. I'll be back in a little while." It was about six o'clock in the evening. By eight o'clock Mrs. Graham called Nellie's.

"None of them came in here tonight, Agnes," Nellie told her. "Is something wrong?"

"I'm not sure, Nellie, but I'm going to call Jonathan. I'll get back to ye." Mrs. Graham was feeling terribly uneasy when she called Jonathan. He had given her his phone number in case she needed to call him for anything concerning Janet. She told him that Janet had gone to meet Catherine at Nellie's. "She's been gone fer a couple of hours and Nellie said neither she nor Catherine had come in tae the tearoom tonight. I'm a bit worried, Jonathan."

"Thanks Mrs. Graham. I'll call over to the MacLean's to see if Catherine called Janet. I'll get back to you and thanks again." Jonathan immediately called Robert. He was anxious and he knew Robert would be too. "Robert, is Catherine home. If so, can I talk to her?"

"Jonathan, you sound disturbed. What's wrong?"

"Janet got a phone call, supposedly from Catherine to meet her at Nellie's. It's been two hours and she hasn't got back to Mrs. Graham's and Nellie said neither one of them were in her restaurant."

"Catherine hasn't been out of the house tonight. Hold on! 'Catherine'" Jonathan heard him yell. Then he heard the conversation between Robert and his daughter. "Jonathan, Catherine didn't call Janet. I'll drive over to your house and pick you up, in the meanwhile call the police and tell them to meet us over at Mrs. Graham's."

"You said you picked the phone up when it rang," Inspector Geordie Gordon said to Mrs. Graham. "Did the voice sound like Catherine's to you?"

"Actually it didn't. She only said 'Janet please' so I thought I might just not have recognized her voice," Mrs. Graham replied. "Besides, Janet said Catherine was upset."

"Did you ever find out who gave the story to the Glasgow paper," Geordie turned his attention to Robert and Jonathan.

"We've been so busy preparing for our wedding that we dropped the ball and I think Sandy has also," Jonathan said apologetically. He told Geordie that they were supposed to find out, through Sandy, who cashed the check. "He did tell us it was a man."

"Can you call Sandy and see if he can get a hold of the reporter down in the city and find out if the check has come in yet?" he asked Robert. Robert took out his cell phone and called Sandy. Sandy said he would get back to him but when he did he said he was unable to get in touch with Bell. He would call his office in the morning. "In the meanwhile, we're going to knock on every door between here and Nellie's."

"Geordie, Jonathan and I would like to help. We'll take one side of the street and you and your partner can take the other." Geordie gave them a briefing of what to look for.

"Write down any clues on a pad and be very, very inquisitive." Mrs. Graham came out of her office and gave both Jonathan and Robert a pad and pen. The search had been worthless. The only thing they got was that outside of one of the homes the owners heard a car take off so fast the tires squealed but by the time they looked out they couldn't even tell what kind of car it was.

"Well Jonathan, let's go back home and break this terrible news to our families," the older man suggested. They both looked haggard. "We've got to find her, Robert."

"I know, Jonathan," he said patting his back. "Maybe Sandy will find something out in the morning. He promised me he would call first thing. I'm sure Alan Bell will be happy to accommodate us when he hears what has happened."

"It was a woman that called. Let's call Joan MacDonald," Jonathan suggested.

"Call Catherine and tell her to call Joan."

"I already called her," Catherine said. "I thought of her immediately but she denies calling Janet."

"Thanks Catherine. We haven't found her yet. Your dad is coming to my house, maybe you would like to come over too." She agreed that she would. She gave the information to Nora and Isabel. Isabel was quite shaken and even Nora showed some concern. From the information they got about a car pealing out from the sidewalk close to the bed and breakfast just about the time Janet would be there indicated to them that she had been abducted. Jonathan and Robert stayed up all night hoping to hear from someone. They would even appreciate hearing from the abductor asking for a ransom. Both Robert and Jonathan agreed they would be happy to pay up but they knew Inspector Geordie would not want that.

Robert was in his office when the phone rang at 8:10 in the morning. "Hello Sandy! What have you found out?"

"Alan Bell called in to his office saying that he had a family emergency. He hoped to be in tomorrow."

"I'll call Geordie and see if he can have someone in command at the news agency work with the bank to see if they can find out the name. Thanks for your help, Sandy."

"Let me know if you need me to call back tomorrow and try and get a hold of Alan Bell."

She never saw the person that threw her into the back seat of the car. Both he and the driver were wearing ski masks. She was terrified. She had never concerned herself with the fact she was marrying a man of wealth and her father was a man of wealth so she didn't think about protecting herself better. She shouldn't have been walking out alone in the dark. She should have asked Catherine to drive to Mrs. Graham's. Of course by now she knew it wasn't Catherine that called. There was a woman sitting in the front seat next to the driver. The man in the back tied her hands and put a blindfold on her. She only got a glimpse of the back of the woman's head. She didn't recognize her. She was quite small. Probably she was the one that called. She listened to them to try and get any clues, hoping someone would drop a name. They drove for quite a while when they stopped and took her into a building, it seemed to be a house, and made her sit down. She knew her father and fiancée had a lot of pull and the police would put this at the top of their list.

After what seemed like ten or fifteen minutes they came back and took her back out to the car. Not long into the journey Janet realized they were pulling something; a trailer or perhaps a boat. She wasn't sure just how long they had been on the road when they came to a stop, perhaps thirty minutes. She heard only two men's voices. Either the woman was no longer with them or she was completely silent. Janet was sure it was the former. They were backing the car up to something. *It must be a boat they're trailing and now they are backing up to water,* Janet surmised. *It must be the Moray Firth.* The car was now being driven forward. *The boat must be in the water now. Where in the world are they taking me?*

The one who seemed to be the leader told the other one, "Get her on tae the boat." The follower opened her door and led her outside and onto the boat. She had been trying to loosen the rope around her wrists the whole time since they were tied. It was very cold out there in the water. There was a wind blowing and she naturally was not dressed to be there. She was freezing but they couldn't care less. *They probably have their sweaters and down jackets on.* Mrs. Graham did loan her a heavy jacket and she had a scarf that she could put on her head and cover her ears, if her hands were free. By the time they landed she felt stiff from the cold.

The follower helped her out of the boat and held her arm, guiding her while they walked. They entered a building. She had a feeling it was an abandoned building because it was cold inside and she could still feel the wind.

"Tie her tae that chair," the leader told the follower. After making sure she was secure, someone threw a blanket over her then she heard both men walk towards the door and shut it. She was sure they had both left but she sat still for about five minutes to make sure. It was all very quiet. After a short while she could hear the boat's motor start up. They hadn't searched her and she did have her cell phone in her jacket pocket. All she had to do was to get her hands free so she could use it. She tried to stretch the fingers of her right hand up to her left wrist. It seemed like the rope had been tied around her wrists three times. She could touch the bottom rope but she thought the knot was on top. She got her digit finger under the rope and tried to pull it down. She wasn't sure if this would tighten the knot more but she had to try something. Stretching her right arm, she managed to get her finger up into the second rope and her thumb on the top. Her arm was aching but she kept trying to turn the rope around so that she could possibly get her thumb and digit finger to untie the knot. She couldn't get it to budge.

About three o'clock in the afternoon, the day after Janet was abducted, Robert got a call. "Mr. MacLean?"

"Yes, who is this?"

"Never mind. We have yer daughter. Is she worth a hundred thousand pounds to ye?" Kenneth MacDonald asked.

"Yes!" He didn't recognize this young man's voice but it certainly didn't sound like a person with a very high education. "You better not have hurt her."

"Are ye threatening me, Mr. MacLean? I think it's time ye spread the wealth." If only he knew, Robert MacLean would have and could have paid much, much more than one hundred thousand pounds and he would for his daughter.

Joan MacDonald was concerned about what happened; especially since there had been suspicion that she was the one that called Janet. She started to worry that her brother might be involved. She did share with him what she knew about Janet. *Could he have been the one that gave the information to the paper?* she thought. She knew she shouldn't have shared with him but he was the only one she could go to and let go of her frustrations. She knew also that, after he missed out on his luck with Catherine, he was hoping that she would be able to make Jonathan fall for her. *He's greedy!* She called him and he told her to mind her own business. She knew she should call Catherine but she was a bit afraid of her brother.

Two days had passed and they hadn't heard any more. Jonathan hadn't had much sleep since Janet was abducted. Early on the third morning, there was a knock on the door. When he opened it there stood his dad, Inspector Gordon and a stranger.

"Jonathan this is Inspector Ryan from Glasgow. He would like to talk with you," Inspector Gordon said.

Malcolm had a worried look on his face. He had no idea what this was all about. First Janet had been abducted and now a detective from Glasgow drove all the way up to the highlands to talk with his son.

"Come in. Have a seat." Everyone sat down.

"Jonathan we found the body..." Jonathan froze. His throat closed and his stomach felt like he was going to be sick. "Of reporter Alan Bell," Inspector Ryan continued. "He was murdered."

Jonathan relaxed a little, but not much. "What does that have to do with me?"

"The receptionist at the Glasgow Herald said you threatened him."

"He went over to California and stalked my fiancé trying to get a story. I told him that I had given his name to the police over there and was going to send a picture. I only warned him that if he went over there and stalked her again, he would be arrested."

"You didn't threaten him with bodily harm?"

"No! He was alive yesterday morning because Sandy said he had called into his office and said he had a family emergency. I have plenty of proof that I was up here."

"Aye! I can vouch for him," Inspector Gordon said. "We probably should be looking at the guy who gave Bell the story about Janet. Maybe he didn't want Bell to finger him. We think he's from up here. I'm waiting to hear from one of the managers from the Herald to call me and hopefully have his name."

"Okay, maybe I'll stay around for a day or two," Inspector Ryan suggested. The policemen left.

"You look awful, Jonathan. What a mess. First Janet disappears then you almost get accused of murder. What in the world is happening?" Malcolm asked.

"I better call Robert and let him know that Alan Bell is dead."

"Don't bother. He's here," said Malcolm looking out of the window.

When Malcolm told Robert the story of Alan Bell, he was very concerned. "If the person who gave Bell the story is the murderer, then he's probably also the one who has Janet."

"The only thing I got from the conversation with him was that there is more than one of them. He kept referring to 'we'."

"He did promise that she was not hurt?" Jonathan asked concerned.

"Yes and I told him they better not hurt her."

The phone rang. It was Inspector Geordie. "Jonathan, when I got back to my office there was a fax waiting for me. I have some information. I tried calling Robert and his daughter told me he was with you. Is that right?"

"Yes, he's right here as well as my dad."

Jonathan put the phone on the speaker. Robert told Geordie about the phone call.

"You didn't recognize the voice?"

"No, I'm quite positive I've never spoken to the man. He sounded quite young. Maybe around late twenties."

"Okay! I'll check that out. However, we do have a fax of the front and back of the check. The writing is pretty bad but I'm sure I know who it is."

"Who?" was all Jonathan asked.

"Jonathan, you and Robert must promise not to do anything and mess things up for us?"

"We promise! We don't want to do that."

"We're sure it's Kenneth MacDonald. We can make out some of the name and I called the local banks and found out that he banks in Elgin. I drove over there and talked with the bank manager. I asked if MacDonald had deposited two thousand pounds, the amount that was paid by the news agency, and after checking they said he had banked fifteen hundred and took five hundred in cash. The date coincides with the newspaper article."

"That's great, Geordie. What's your next move?" Robert asked.

"We're on our way to his house to arrest him and search the house for Janet."

"Call us immediately." Robert and Jonathan both let out a sigh of relief as Jonathan hung up the phone.

"But I won't be happy until we see her and see her healthy," Jonathan said.

"But it does give us hope, Jonathan."

Joan MacDonald froze when she opened the door to Inspector Geordie Gordon and his partner John Maxwell. She thought they had come for her. "What do you want, inspector?"

"We came to talk with your brother. Is he home?"

"No inspector, I haven't seen him for a few days."

"May we come in?"

She opened the door wider and let them in. They asked many questions. She lied about not having his cell phone number because she didn't want to be responsible for getting her brother arrested. She told them who his friends were and gave the name of his closest friend and of his girlfriend. "I don't want you to give him any warning that we are looking for him. We'll know who tipped him off and you would be interfering with the law. Also the Grants and the MacLeans won't be happy."

She knew she wasn't going to do that either. She had done no wrong and didn't want to get in the middle of this thing.

"I would appreciate if you would call me if he gets in touch with you."

"I will inspector and would you let Catherine know that I'm cooperating with you?"

She woke up with a sore neck. It was still dark out but at this time of the year the sun doesn't come out in the highlands until quite late, after nine o'clock, so she couldn't tell what time it was. The only reason she was concerned about the time was because she wanted to get loose before they came back. She tried again to untie the rope around her wrists. Her neck was sore from the position she had slept in and her right arm was sore from trying to stretch it up to her left wrist. She had to keep trying. *If they come back today, they might search me and find the cell phone.* She tried and tried until she was so worn out she dozed off. She woke up with the sound of a motor. The sun was now out. *I must have slept at least an hour,* she thought.

She heard the motorboat getting closer. She panicked and tried again. "I've got to move my arm up a little more. Even if I break it, it will be better than what these people have in mind for me" she said aloud. She forced her arm up more. She thought she felt the rope move a little. She stretched her arm and fingers some more and could actually feel the knot. She tried to stick her finger into the knot. She felt it loosening. In the distance she could hear the motorboat getting quite close by now. She had to get away from where she was. If they came back and checked her they would be sure and tighten the rope again. She stuck her finger further into the rope and felt relief as the knot began to unravel. She was free. She undid the blindfold and ran out of the house. She saw some woods a little in the distance. Janet ran as fast as she could for fear that the motorboat was theirs. She was quite sure it was. She had to hold her right arm with her left hand as it was in a lot of pain. She was glad for all the walks and hikes that she and Margaret had done. At least her legs were strong.

When she reached the woods she got as far in as she could yet still be able to see the abandoned house so that she could watch them. She immediately tried to call Jonathan. She didn't get through. *I'll move to different parts of the island and maybe at some point I'll get through,* she thought.

The motorboat went on past the house. *It was probably fishermen.* She looked around to find a spot that would keep her hidden when they did come. She had some time to look around and found a grove of trees with some thick brush around them. She got in the center of the trees and found it a little warmer. She would be more sheltered there and when they did come she would force herself under the thick brush. She didn't care if she got all scratched up. They didn't come back that day but she still felt safer in the grove of trees, but she did go back and get the blanket and the couple of bottles of water and crackers she had seen on the table. That night she wrapped herself in the blanket and put her coat over the top and wrapped the woolen scarf around as much of her head as she could and buried her head into her coat. She was thankful for her thick socks and fleece-lined boots. She slept rather well, wakening up only three or four times, but only for a short while. A motorboat was approaching the island. It was them. She tried calling Jonathan from a different spot.

"Hello," she could hear Jonathan's voice but it wasn't too clear. She hoped he could hear her.

"Jonathan," she was yelling but not loud enough that her abductors could hear. "I think I'm on an island. They took me across water on a boat. I think it might be the Moray Firth. There's an abandoned house. They are looking for me. I have to hide. Can you hear me, Jonathan?" She heard him say the word "barely" so she hoped that meant he got some of what she said. "I'll try and call you later."

"Maybe somebody found her," Andrew Johnson said.

"We have tae look around. She might still be here," MacDonald said.

"How could she have untied herself? Naw, somebody must have found her. Maybe some fishermen."

"Why would they stop at this auld place?" MacDonald asked. "We better take a look around. We have tae catch her. At least she disnae know who we are." Janet watched them from the woods. They were coming her way. She had to get back to the grove and get under the brush. She had dug a hole for the blanket and covered it with dirt and grass. She got under the brush and covered the area as best she could with some leaves.

Jonathan immediately called Robert after she had hung up. "Robert, Janet called me."

"What? Where is she?" Robert asked.

"It was a very bad reception but she mentioned a boat. I also heard the word Moray. Do you think they've taken her across the Moray Firth?"

"I'm coming right over."

Malcolm saw Robert's car pass the house on its way to the cottage. He was going pretty fast. He walked over to the cottage to find out what was happening. Robert and Jonathan were looking at a map. They were trying to figure out where they possibly could have taken her.

"What's happening?" Malcolm asked.

"Janet called and I could barely hear her but we think she was taken by boat across the Moray Firth." Jonathan told his dad.

"It's not enough information. With so many islands, it could be any one of them," Robert said.

"It also sounded like she may have escaped because it sounded like she said they were looking for her, then I heard the word 'hide'."

"I hope she calls soon, because I don't know how long she can bear the cold weather. She's already been out there two nights, if they took her out right away," Robert said terribly concerned.

Janet tried to keep her head up from the ground. She was afraid the dirt and grass would make her sneeze. She could hear their voices so they were not too far away from where she was. She was still favoring her right arm so her left arm was bearing most of her weight and it was starting to hurt. They were getting a little closer and she could make out most of what they were saying. The leader was telling the follower that she had to be found immediately so they could get the money and get out of Scotland. She heard him say something about the reporter in Glasgow got murdered but it wasn't supposed to happen that way. As they got closer she heard him say, "He was only supposed to be hidden where naebody could find him and tell that I was the person who gave the story tae him."

"I dinna want tae be involved in any murder, Kenneth," follower said.

"I told ye no tae use names. You go that way and I'll go the other way."

At first she was not sure which one was coming towards her but pretty soon he started chanting, "Come oot, come oot, wherever ye are," then she knew it was the follower. The sun was going down and it was getting cold. Follower walked away in the direction Kenneth went. She could hear him shout to him, "I'm goin' hame, Kenneth. I'm no liking this anymore."

She heard Kenneth yell at him but she didn't know what he was saying. Only that he was angry. Finally as he got closer to follower he said, "Okay but tomorrow we'll come oot early."

"I dinna think she's here, but I'll come wi' ye in the morn." She heard the boat leave. She thought she would try Jonathan again, but this time she didn't even connect. It was very windy and she wasn't sure if that would affect the signal. "I'll try again in the morning at a different spot. I'll just walk around until I find the best place." She wrapped herself once again in the blanket just as she did the night before and once again slept fairly well. The grove of trees protected her from the wind.

She waited until the sun came up before trying different places to call Jonathan. She was starting to feel weak from lack of food. The crackers were not enough. She was thankful she had them and most of all she was thankful for the water but now both were gone. If she didn't get off this island she was not sure she could last very many more days. She was desperate to get a hold of him. She walked quite a ways and up a hill. At the top of the hill she could see the mainland in the distance. It didn't seem so far away. She dialed his number and waited with anticipation.

"Hello," he said and she heard the hope in his voice.

"Jonathan, can you hear me?" she yelled into her phone.

"Yes, darling. I can hear you very well. Just tell me everything you can. I won't speak unless I have to."

"It's so good to hear your voice. There is an abandoned house here. That is where they had me tied up. The leader's name is Kenneth. They are coming back to look for me this morning. I walked for a while up a hill and that's where I am now. I can see the mainland. It looks like the motorway over there. That's about all the information I can give you. It took approximately twenty to thirty minutes drive before crossing the water. They're here. I have to get back to my hiding spot before they see me. I hope this will give you enough information."

"How do you feel?" he said feeling very concerned.

"I'm getting weak from lack of food. I just finished the water I had and my right arm is terribly sore. Other than that I'm okay."

"If you have to get back to me, call me on my cell phone. Hopefully we'll be on our way to get you."

Jonathan called Robert and his dad and they met at his cottage to try and figure out once more where she could be. He told them the information she gave him.

"Well that could be the old house not very far from Cromarty. I couldn't tell you exactly where it is because I haven't been out there for a while, but I might be able to find it," Malcolm offered.

"I suppose we should tell Geordie," Robert said.

"We should tell him, but I'm not going to sit around here doing nothing. I want to go out and look for her," was Jonathan's response.

"I'll get Catherine's boat and I'll get my gun," Robert said.

Malcolm gave him a strange look. "What are you two about to do?" he asked.

"If he is in anyway intending to hurt Janet, I'll shoot him."

"Wait for me. I'll get my rifle," Malcolm said running out the door toward his house. Jonathan grabbed some blankets and towels.

They had split up. The leader was going off in the wrong direction but the follower seemed like he was heading right to her. She looked around for another place to hide but she was afraid any movement might get his attention. Suddenly he turned to the right and walked in a different direction. She was shivering so badly. If

Jonathan couldn't get to her soon, she didn't know how long she could survive the cold.

The follower was coming back. He was yelling at the leader. "Kenneth, she's no here. I'm freezing."

"We can't stop looking. Ye've nae idea how much trouble I'm in. I need the money tae get away frae here."

They were glad they brought their sou'westers because it started to rain. The water was a little choppy. They saw a boat docked near where Malcolm thought the abandoned house was. "Don't park too close to it," Jonathan said. "Let me go up and check around the house."

"Be careful, Jonathan," warned his dad.

"I will. You two keep your eyes open for any activity. I'm leaving this slicker here. It's too bright," he said taking of the raincoat. He was wearing a dark sweater and jeans that wouldn't stand out.

He climbed up to the back end of the house. There didn't seem to be anyone around. He saw the rope and the blindfold on the floor. He knew she had been there. *They're probably out there hunting her down.* He went back down to the boat to inform Robert and his dad. "She's out there somewhere with MacDonald and his friend looking for her. Did you see anything?"

"No we didn't, wait... hush!" Malcolm said.

They were quiet for a moment then they heard him. He was yelling at someone.

"The voice is coming from over there," Jonathan said. "I'm going to sneak around the side here and see if I can get behind them."

It was raining quite heavily now. He snuck quietly around the side of the house trying to listen to find out where the sound of their voices was coming from.

"Please don't pull on my arm. You're hurting me," Janet said.

He finally saw them. Kenneth MacDonald had Janet by the arm and was pulling her. He had to be careful since he didn't see Mac-Donald's friend with them. He could tell Janet was in pain. He was yelling threats at her. "You're hurting my arm," she said again, trying to pull his hand off her right arm. He slapped her face hard, causing her to fall to her knees. She yelled out in pain when he held on to her right arm as she was falling and yanked her back up.

He heard the hammer click on Jonathan's two-barrel shotgun.

He turned and saw Jonathan with the gun pointing at his head. "Let her go, MacDonald."

Janet's heart leapt when she saw Jonathan, but MacDonald pulled her in front of him like a shield against the rifle.

"I'm not alone and Police Chief Gordon is on his way along with Inspector Ryan from Glasgow."

There was a rustling to the left of him and he shot towards it. Robert and Malcolm jumped out of the boat and went in different directions. Andrew Johnson came out yelling "dinna shoot!"

Kenneth MacDonald started backing away from Jonathan with Janet still in front of him. He didn't get too far when he felt a rifle in his back.

"Get your hands off of her," Robert said with a fierce voice. Then gently, "Janet, walk toward Jonathan." Jonathan knew she was very weak so he threw down his rifle and grabbed her in his arms. Turning to MacDonald he said, "You don't know how close you were to having a bullet in your head. You ever try to hurt this girl again, you might just not be so lucky."

Janet had never heard or seen Jonathan or her father that angry. She was sure both of them could have shot MacDonald at that moment without flinching. She was impressed at how bold these usually elegant men could be.

He noticed that she was shivering really badly.

Malcolm had Andrew Johnson covered. They could hear the boat coming. "Gordon's going to get on our case," Malcolm said smiling. He felt pretty good. They had saved his future daughter-in-law and had the bad guys at the end of their rifles.

Jonathan carried Janet down to the boat. He took off her wet coat and sweater. It hurt her to try and get her right arm out of her sleeve.

"I think I almost broke it trying to untie the ropes," she told him.

Her blouse was quite dry. He wrapped two blankets around her and dried her hair with the towels and wrapped one around her head then put a fur hat on top of the towel. She felt very safe wrapped in his arms.

Robert and Malcolm turned the two men over to the inspectors and once back in the boat they headed home.

Shortly after the incident, Kenneth MacDonald and Andrew Johnson were found guilty of abduction. Johnson was put away for a few years. Later, it was found out that Kenneth MacDonald had someone in Glasgow kill Bell, although he insisted he had only asked the Glasgow thug to abduct Bell until he got his money. They both got a life sentence. Joan MacDonald moved to Inverness near her parents and her dad sold the house in Elgin.

CHAPTER TWENTY-ONE

Six days before the wedding, Janet's family and friends arrived. Everyone decided it was easier to ride the train. Aunt Moira, her husband Jack, Aunt Betty and her family rode the train together. Maggie and her family, Tom and his family and Ian all flew from Portland together and when they arrived in Glasgow, they rode the train up to Elgin. Even Margaret, Linda and Kathy took the train. Actually Janet had suggested it. Everyone talked about how much they enjoyed the ride up.

Janet had asked the MacLeans and Grants not to mention the abduction. "From this point on it's fun and happiness."

"I agree. No use getting everyone upset," Jonathan said. "But from now on, you're not out of my sight."

"Oh daddy, he's getting bossy with me already," she laughed winking at her dad and trying to talk with a Scottish accent. Robert loved his daughter's humor. It reminded him of Alice. She was spunky.

Linda, Kathy and Margaret shared Jonathan's cottage with Janet. The family stayed at Mrs. Graham's. Aunt Moira was happy to see Alice's kids and their families again. Betty and Alice were hugging everyone. It was the first time they had seen any of them. Betty had only seen Tom when he was a baby. Everyone was laughing and crying and Mrs. Graham was right in the middle of it introducing herself and getting her share of the hugs. She was so excited to have them all at her bed and breakfast.

Later they all went over to Nellie's and had a tea party. It had been arranged so that Nellie closed the Tearoom that night. She was bustling around as proud as a peacock to have them at her tearoom. She let them know that she was invited to the wedding, "Because I introduced them."

"You did a great thing, Nellie. Those two were destined to be with each other and you were the one that was used to make sure that happened," said Tom winking at Nellie.

Jonathan rented a bus big enough to hold all of them. The first trip was to St. Andrews the day after they arrived. Once there, everyone had their own agenda. The Botanic Gardens caught the attention of Moira, Janet, Margaret, Catherine and Helen. Tom's wife, Kim, and their children went to Craigtown Country Park along with Maggie and her husband and children. The children enjoyed the miniature golf and the model train-ride. Then the adults went with the children out in the boating lake that had a Dutch Village in the middle of it.

Of course Tom and Ian were excited to get on the "Old Course" which the Grants had applied for a while back. Jonathan and Stewart joined them.

"Wow! All of our golf heroes have played on this course," Ian said excitedly to Stewart and Jonathan. "This has been our dream for ages. I can't believe I'm standing here."

"I remember you mentioned that to me when I met you in California," Jonathan said to Tom. He was so happy he could do this for them.

They were having so much fun. On the way home on the bus Ian couldn't stop talking about playing golf on the "Old Course" at St. Andrews.

The next day they did local things. The Grants and MacLeans didn't always go with the group. On this day they visited the Elgin Cathedral and the Biblical Gardens. Helen Grant and Catherine with the help of Stewart and Malcolm prepared a large buffet for them when they got home around five o'clock that night. There were a mixture of lovely salads, smoked salmon, trout and sliced Angus beef with wonderful breads that they had baked that day. They were being treated royally and it excited them.

"Can you imagine, mom," Alice whispered, "Mrs. Grant and

Catherine MacLean cooking for us?" Betty smiled at her daughter, happy to see her and George having such a good time.

They shared their outings with Mrs. Graham who excitedly took everything in. She looked forward to hearing about their adventures. "I don't know what I'm going tae dae when the weddin' is over and ye all go back home. I'll be bored and lonely."

"With Janet going to be spending much of her time here, you'll get to see us once in a while. Maybe not all at the same time, but maybe at special events," said Betty.

"Like Mrs. Grant's Christmas parties," Mrs. Graham said. "You were at the last one, Betty."

"She came home and told me about it and I was so jealous, but now I'm here and I feel like royalty," Alice said.

"That's what I keep calling these families," Maggie said. "I told my sister she was marrying a Scottish prince."

They sat chatting until around eleven o'clock at night catching up with some and getting to know others."

The next day most of them took a trip to Edinburgh. Ian and Stewart elected to stay up north as they had plans to climb at Glenmore or Aviemore and to fish with Catherine in the River Spey. They left early in the morning. It was quite a rigorous hike but by the afternoon when they met up with Catherine, they got to relax and fish from the boat.

Ian was amazed at his catch. "I want to light up a barbecue and grill these babies. They're gorgeous."

"Ian, I can't tell you how delighted I am to be your sister, even if we are not blood relatives. Janet and I are and you and she are."

"I'm happy about it too, Catherine, and the fact that you love to fish makes it all so cool."

"After being an only child for twenty-five years, it's terrific to have two sisters and two brothers. You and Stewart are about the same age and you like the same things. You'll have to come back here often."

"I will! I'll make Scotland my holiday place. Heck, you have the things I like here, good climbs, great fishing and golfing. What more can a man ask for?"

Meanwhile the group in Edinburgh was having a great time visiting Edinburgh Castle. They climbed up to the highest point of the structure to take in the amazing views. They were told that on a very clear day you could look north and see the Kingdom of Fife.

"That's where we were when we were at St. Andrews," Robert told Margaret.

Betty and Alice were giving each other eye signals that something definitely was going on between Robert and Margaret.

The children couldn't believe they were actually in a castle. Maggie's youngest girl wanted to know who lived in it. She mentioned many animated characters like Cinderella. She kept looking around like she was expecting to see her at any moment.

"Mommy, this is better than that castle at Disneyland. This is much bigger."

They walked the Royal Mile stopping at various shops looking at the Cashmere sweaters and such as they headed towards the Palace at Holyrood. After a busy day of sightseeing Robert took the group to a lovely restaurant on Princess Street and bought them all a great meal.

CHAPTER TWENTY-TWO

The day finally arrived. Janet was in the elegant Rolls Royce with her father. It was a true highland wedding and all the men in the wedding party wore full highland dress. Her dad wore his MacLean dress tartan. *How absolutely sophisticated he looks,* Janet thought smiling at her father.

"I am so proud of you today. You look beautiful," he said to her.

"I was thinking the same about you."

"Be careful, Janet. You never call a highland man beautiful."

She giggled. "Okay, very handsome."

He smiled. He was so proud of her. "I can hear your mother laughing at us. She is having such a good time."

"I can hear her too, dad, and I can hear what she is saying."

"What would that be?" he asked.

"Happy is the bride that the sun shines on." It was a beautiful clear day.

Inside the church, everything became so real. In just a few minutes she would be standing side by side with her soon-to-be-husband while the minister pronounced them husband and wife. "I'm feeling a little nervous all of a sudden. I hope I don't get wobbly legs," she said to her dad.

"Just hold on tight to my arm," he said as they walked to the doors at the top of the aisle.

She looked down and saw Jonathan in his full highland dress of the Grant Clan. *He looks absolutely magnificent,* she thought. The church organist, who had been playing softly as the people were ushered to their pews, began to play resonantly Mendelssohn's classical Wedding March. Everyone stood and turned toward the bride and her father as they walked elegantly down the aisle. *Mom, I hope you can see this magnificent spectacle.*

Jonathan Grant was mesmerized as he watched the couple walk toward him. Tall, distinguished Robert MacLean, looking as proud as a peacock in the lovely dress tartan of his clan, and Janet looking more beautiful than any bride he had ever seen, in reality or in magazines with her long veil trailing behind her. She looked very happy to be holding on to her father. Her sisters Maggie and Catherine had tears rolling down their faces.

Like Jonathan, the impressive sight mesmerized Margaret. When the couple reached the front pews where their family was, Janet smiled at Tom and noticed he, too, had tears in his eyes. She wasn't sure they would get through all this without everyone crying.

Robert, very proudly, handed his daughter over to Jonathan and said to him, "I couldn't have asked for a better man to give my daughter to." Jonathan smiled and took Janet's arm in his.

Isabel, who sat in the front pew, smiled. She thought how lucky she was to be given such a moment like this as she was nearing the end of her life. It was a special, special moment to see her beloved grandson walking his daughter down the aisle. Even Nora was quite impressed and almost felt teary.

"Who gives this woman to this man in marriage?" the minister asked.

"I, her father and I know I can speak for her deceased mother, give Janet to Jonathan in marriage," Robert said adding his own words.

Maggie's tears were flowing once again. Janet looked up at her and thought *if I didn't feel so emotional myself right now, I would crack up laughing at Maggie.*

After the minister read from First Corinthians, chapter 13 from verse 4 to the end, they gave their vows to on another, placed rings on their fingers, then the minister said, "I now pronounce you husband and wife. Friends and family, may I introduce to you Mr. and Mrs. Jonathan Grant?"

Everyone stood up and clapped and cheered. They were both beaming. Janet looked around at all the faces smiling at her. Her dad was at the end of the pew in the first row and Isabel was sitting next to him. Behind her family sat Nellie and Mrs. Graham. They were all dressed up with fancy hats on. *This is probably the most magical time they and my family and friends have ever had.*

As they started back down the aisle, to the organist playing Beethoven's "Ode to Joy", she stopped to kiss her dad and to thank him. Then she leaned over and kissed Isabel on the cheek. She just smiled at Nora and to her amazement she actually smiled back. Catherine saw it. *Maybe grandma is softening towards Janet. After all, everyone else loves Janet,* she thought.

They had chosen an elegant hotel in Elgin to have their reception. Mary, the wedding planner, was there making sure everything was going well. After they had their delicious sit down dinner, the toasts started with Robert. "This has been a very emotional time for me, but a good emotional time. First, being united with my daughter that I didn't know I had. Then having my family being united with my best friend's family, the Grants. I could never have wanted anyone better for Janet. I know Jonathan will take very good care of her. Welcome to the family, Jonathan."

Next, the best man Stewart stood up. "I feel so lucky to have such a beautiful and wonderful sister-in-law. Janet gave me her permission to tell this little story. She didn't want you all to know this at first, but we had a scare for a while. She was abducted and was gone from us for a couple of days."

Everyone gave a gasp of horror.

"We knew about it," Nellie said to those at her table pointing to herself and Mrs. Graham, "but we were told not to spoil everyone's holiday, so naturally we kept quiet," she said quite proud and speaking as carefully as she could to make sure the Americans could understand her.

"My dad, Mr. MacLean and my brother got a clue as to where she was being held and went out across the Moray Firth and saved her," Stewart continued. "I want you to get a picture of all three of them, soaked to the bone, rifles pointing at the criminals, like the three musketeers. Janet told me that Robert De Niro, Al Pacino and Andy Garcia could not have looked any tougher than this trio. We had a good laugh at that. Welcome to the family, Janet."

Everyone was laughing now. There were more toasts then came

the dancing. It was such a celebration. "You Scots know how to have a good time," Janet said when she was up dancing with Jonathan. "We've never danced together. You're good."

"Your not bad yourself, girl," he said.

It wouldn't take them long to get over to the A9 motorway and drive up to Skibo Castle, he had told her, and since they were having such a good time they decided to stay quite a bit longer at the reception than they thought they would.

"Jonathan, this is beautiful," she said as they drove in to Skibo Castle. "It's like a fairyland. Maggie's girls would be in awe of this place. In fact I am."

"The Scottish Gaelic name is Schytherbolle which means 'a place of peace.'"

After they checked in they were taken up to their room. Janet was silently taking everything in. She was dumbstruck by the décor of the place. There was no sparing of luxury. She would look forward to touring around it in the morning. Right now she was walking with her husband to their romantic honeymoon suite.

"Oh, this is luxurious," she said as they entered the sitting room, then she checked out the bedroom and bathroom. "Jonathan, this is so beautiful it takes my breath away."

"I hope I take your breath away," he said reaching out to her. He pulled her to him and kissed her gently.

"You do, darling. You do."

That night his lovemaking was so magical that he took her to a much higher level. She knew he was right there with her. They didn't talk. In fact she knew they were communicating in the spirit. She had never been in such a high place before. She knew it was the energy of his love that took her to this heavenly place. He held her with her face on his chest. Eventually her eyes welled up and the tears flowed down her cheeks onto his chest. He still didn't move but just held her closer. She felt herself falling into a very deep peaceful sleep. She heard Margaret's words in her head. "Janet he loves you as a person not as an object. He's building up the love he feels for you and not looking for instant gratification. You're going to have a phenomenal love life because he is a man that really knows how to love."

"Yes! You do," she said very sleepily.

"What?" he asked, but she was sound asleep.